An Italian Affair

Caroline Montague

ORION

An Orion Paperback

First published in Great Britain in 2018 by Orion,
This paperback edition publishing in 2019 by Orion,
an imprint of The Orion Publishing Group Ltd
Carmelite House, 50 Victoria Embankment
London EC4Y 0DZ

An Hachette UK Company

3 5 7 9 10 8 6 4

Copyright © Caroline Montague 2018

The moral right of Caroline Montague to be identified as
the author of this work has been asserted in accordance with
the Copyright, Designs and Patents Act of 1988.

All rights reserved. No part of this publication may be
reproduced, stored in a retrieval system, or transmitted
in any form or by any means, electronic, mechanical,
photocopying, recording, or otherwise, without the prior
permission of both the copyright owner and the
above publisher of this book.

All the characters in this book are fictitious,
and any resemblance to actual persons, living
or dead, is purely coincidental.

A CIP catalogue record for this book is
available from the British Library.

ISBN 978 1 4091 8078 4

Typeset at The Spartan Press Ltd,
Lymington, Hants

Printed in Great Britain by Clays Ltd,
Elocograf S.p.A.

MIX
Paper from
responsible sources
FSC® C104740

www.orionbooks.co.uk

This book is dedicated to
the late Group Captain Iain Panton
and the late Gerry Tyack.

Acknowledgements

I owe so much to the late Group Captain Iain Panton and the late Gerry Tyack MBE, of the Wellington Aviation Museum, Moreton-in Marsh. They gave me their time and their immense knowledge and without these two remarkable men, this book would not have been possible. They tutored me on the Battle of Britain, they described how to fly and escape from a burning Spitfire, and helped to create the authentic atmosphere of these extraordinary times. I am only sad that these two wonderful friends are not here to see the published result.

My deepest gratitude to so many who have given up their time to listen or indeed to advise me. Chris Yeates, an engineer, who taught me how to cause an avalanche, blow up a bridge and endless other activities that were part of life as an agent in Special Operations Executive. Jo Frank, who with her professional skill and diligence helped me edit the very first draft before I had even shown it to my agent. My thanks also go to the following who have been so important during the process of writing this book: Gina Blomefield, Pink Harrison, Robert Coleman who as a dental surgeon was able to confirm the accuracy of my torture scene, similarly Dr Giles Bointon who taught me how to save the fictional dog, Nico.

Nicola Finlay who has been a constant support as I edited

and re-edited. John Steele, Chairman of the Air League, who checked all the final details of the RAF scenes, Lynn Bointon, Alex Gardiner, James Parker, Ben Wood, John Playfair. Captain Marcus Russel, Jenness Hobart, John Espedal, Louise Harwood, Squadron Leader Ian Smith, Corporal Adam Walster, Colonel Charles Radford. Each one of you has played such an important role.

Special thanks go to my wonderful agent Matilda Forbes Watson and her assistant Alina Flint at WME, who have been a constant inspiration and have given me so much of their valuable time. Also, to my amazing publisher Clare Hey at Orion and all her fabulous team.

I owe everything to my husband, Conroy, who has sourced locations with me, listened to my endless geographical queries with patience and kindness, and who has encouraged me every step of the way. Finally, huge appreciation has to go to my seven children and stepchildren who have endured this novel for the last four years. Emily Ryder, Henry and Eddie Coram James have been especially helpful with their valuable and at times extremely honest criticism! Extra thanks must go to Clemmie Coram James for reading this book in every incarnation without complaint.

Prologue

The boy lay in bed, in that strange half world where he was neither asleep nor fully awake. Shadows flitted across the net curtains, and the light from the street lamps cast a yellow glow on the ceiling. Outside a van circled Grosvenor Square and drove east towards the docks, but Robert didn't know these things as he emerged from the dark tunnel of sleep. In the years to come he would look back on that morning. He would sigh and wish that he could have changed it from the very beginning.

Robert climbed out of bed and padded barefoot to the window. Rain drummed on the glass, stippling the scene below. A road sweeper directed the rubbish towards his galvanised cart, and the occasional motor car crawled through the gloom, splashing up the rain. Robert let the curtain fall and dressed slowly. There was no school, the boarders had been sent home early.

'Breakfast, Robs, come and join me!' Anthony Marston called to his thirteen-year-old son. Robert picked up the unfinished aeroplane from his bedside table, placed it on the shelf beside the others, and went down two flights of stairs to the dining room, situated in the lower ground floor of the spacious Georgian house.

'Morning, Papa.' He helped himself to cereal and milk from the sideboard. He could feel his father's eyes on him.

'My, you've grown. You've only been away three weeks and I could swear you are two inches taller.'

'Do you really think so?'

Anthony Marston nodded. 'I certainly do, and soon your voice will break and in a couple of years I'll be teaching you to shave!' Robert laughed and settled down in the chair next to him.

'Shame about the boys with chickenpox,' Anthony said, looking sympathetic, 'but lucky break for you.'

'It is rather.' Robert grinned. 'But I'll probably get it next time. Selby had a spot on the end of his nose.'

Anthony grimaced. 'Poor old thing.'

He tapped Robert's stamp book that lay on the table between them. 'You've got this, I see. We'll go through it in a minute.' He pointed to two large paintings that filled the wall above the sideboard. 'What do you think of your mother's latest acquisitions? Your grandmother had something to say, I can tell you.'

Robert studied the paintings thoughtfully. How he loved this time with his father, just the two of them. It was true the splashes of paint seemed thrown onto the canvas, but they were vibrant and original, just like his mother.

'I think they're great – don't you?'

'I'm not sure what they are,' Anthony replied, 'but yes, I certainly like them.'

'So what was Grandmama's comment?'

'If I remember rightly, she called them meaningless daubs and alluded to the fact that your mother is half Italian. Your mother, of course, had some pithy reply, something about Raphael being Italian.' Robert giggled. His mother always had the last word.

*

It seemed to Wilfred Archer as he walked towards his van on a cold November morning in 1934 that the Great War hadn't changed anything for the working man. He kicked at an overflowing dustbin and cursed beneath his breath. The unofficial strike at Smithfield Market meant he had three times as much work for the same money. The big hotels wanted their meat in the kitchens by eight, and he'd been up since four and still hadn't finished. One more trip east to the docks, collect the order, make the drop, and then home. He knew it was risky, his boss getting round the strike like this, but the hotels needed the delivery to feed their guests, and hell, he needed the work. In the long years of depression since the Wall Street crash of '29 he was lucky to have a job at all.

Half an hour later, the meat was in the van and Wilfred was heading west. He glanced up at the starless sky; dawn would soon break: he would have to put his foot down. He yawned. The baby had kept him up, and when he was desperate for just two hours sleep, his wife had thrust a bottle in his hand.

'Sorry, love,' she had said. 'I've got one of my heads.'

On Piccadilly, a workman dragged his pneumatic drill out into the middle of the road, halting the traffic. Ignoring the queue that was forming, he began to hammer the tarmac. Wilfred wound down his window and stuck his head out. 'Give us a break, mate,' he yelled. The man looked at him with an easy grin, 'For you, pal, anything. Can't do much in this blasted weather.' He put down his drill on the side of the road and sauntered off in the direction of a workman's café. Wilfred swore. His wipers were drawing greasy, brown arcs across his windscreen; he made a mental note to clean them. He had only ten minutes to get there.

*

Anthony picked up his newspaper. 'I'll get the usual taxi on the other side of the square. Busy day ahead – jaw fracture this morning and an appointment in Whitehall this afternoon. I'll try to get back early and we can finish that plane. I have a scalpel perfect for the job.' He looked at Robert over his spectacles, his blue eyes crinkling at the corners.

'Terrific,' Robert replied, pushing his cereal bowl aside and piling his plate with toast. 'I'm having a problem cutting the balsa wood for the rudder.'

'Six o'clock then, after I've called in on your grandparents.' Anthony was about to read the headlines when he remembered the stamps.

'Shall we look at these now?' He picked up the book, flipping through the pages with his elegant surgeon's hands. 'You still have a gap here. Ah, the Penny Red. The dealer in Camden has a mint one. You will have to save up for it.'

'That would be grand.'

Anthony smiled, remembering his trip to the dealer the day before and his purchase of the stamp. He couldn't wait to see Robert's face when he gave it to him. He folded the newspaper, put his napkin into the silver ring and stood up. 'I'll go up and say goodbye to your mother. See you in a minute.' At the doorway he turned.

'You'll come up and see me off?'

'Of course, Papa.'

Robert's heart lurched. His father was like an actor from the motion pictures, his jaw square, his dark hair neatly cut, his suits immaculately tailored, but he was also the kindest and the best.

He took a mouthful of toast. There was no hurry, his father would be upstairs for a while chatting to his mother. She had the notion that breakfast in the dining room was a tradition that should definitely be ignored.

4

He could hear footsteps on the pavement outside, and a car hooting in the distance, but inside it was silent.

*

Wilfred started to panic. He wouldn't make it, and he was already on a warning. He couldn't lose his job, what with a sick wife and a baby not three months old. Turning off Piccadilly, he sped down Maddox Street and along Grosvenor Street in the direction of Grosvenor Square, his palms sweating.

*

The dining room had always been Robert's favourite room. He had been with his mother at Heals when she had picked out the bleached oak table and the high-backed chairs with the burgundy velvet upholstery.

'What do you think, Robs?' she had asked, sinking into a deep cushion. 'Sit down beside me.' And he had sat down and said that he liked them.

'Well then, these are the ones we shall have,' she had replied, laughing.

He finished the last square of toast and went into the hall to wait for his father. He was looking at the portrait when Anthony came down the stairs. 'Prettiest mother at school, I bet,' he said, coming to stand beside him. 'I like her hair like that, don't you?'

In the portrait, his mother's dark hair was pleated into a fashionable chignon, showing her long neck. Her grey-green eyes were directed towards them, with the hint of a smile. Robert nodded in agreement. 'She's someone you would want to know, isn't she, Papa?'

Anthony laughed. 'You are a funny chap, Robert, but yes, she certainly is.'

He glanced at the clock on the mantelpiece. 'Better be off, it's five to eight. Work on your science project and if you get a good grade I'll book tickets for the spring air show in Shoreham.' He put his hand on his son's shoulder. 'The next two years are crucial, Robert. You are at one of the finest schools in the country: study hard now and you will have a great future ahead of you.'

*

Wilfred sighed with concern. The doctor had told them to wait for the test results, but they both knew that she wasn't just ordinary sick. What would happen to the baby? He tried not to think of it, he mustn't think of it. He strained to look through the windscreen, focusing on the red light of the car ahead of him.

*

Anthony stopped by the hall cupboard and put on his coat, exposing the crisp, white cuffs of his shirt, and Robert was glad that his father was wearing the green enamel cufflinks he had given him for his birthday. It had taken him six months to save up for them. Anthony took the umbrella from the stand and gathered his medical bag from the hall table. He was at the door when he drew a small packet from his coat pocket.

'Nearly forgot to give you this.'

Robert opened the tiny slip of greaseproof paper. Inside was a mint-condition Penny Red. He looked up at his father, his eyes shining. 'Thank you so much.' He hugged him, inhaling the scent of citrus and cedar wood.

Anthony ruffled his hair. 'I wanted to surprise you, though now I'll have to spoil your sister Diana too. Thought I'd get her the crystal pendant we saw together at Selfridges. You liked it, didn't you?'

'I loved it, and De would love it too.'

'Well then, I shall buy it tomorrow. 'Bye Robs, my precious boy, look after that stamp.'

*

Wilfred glanced at his watch. It was three minutes to eight. In the corner of his eye a black car pulled out of a side street; it was coming fast. It was going to overtake him. He wouldn't let the bastard overtake him. Wilfred thrust his foot hard down on the accelerator.

*

When the front door closed, Robert crossed to the window. Traffic moved slowly round Grosvenor Square, but Upper Brook Street was empty. Anthony put up the umbrella and stepped from the kerb. He was halfway across the road when his medical bag fell open. Robert knocked on the window to warn him and Anthony looked up at his son. A gust of wind tugged at his umbrella.

*

Wilfred sped round the middle of the square avoiding the road sweeper and his cart and entered Upper Brook Street. The black car peeled away.

*

Robert and his father saw the van at the same moment and they both knew it would keep on going; it was their last sharing of conscious thought. Robert could see the rain settling on his father's coat in clear drops, further off a child with red boots, stomping through the puddles. He could hear the clock ticking in the hall. But he was helpless as time stretched towards the inevitable.

Wilfred's foot was on the accelerator when he saw the man in the road. He slammed on the brakes, working the clutch until the gears screamed in protest, but the van skidded out of control.

Wilfred could hear himself yelling as the body was flung upwards onto the bonnet and came hurtling towards him. The man's eyes were wide with shock and his fingers were splayed as he tried to protect himself, but flesh and bone were no match for unforgiving metal. As the man's face flattened against the windscreen, the scrunching, shattering of a thousand pieces of frosting glass exploded, until the face faded from him and only the blood remained.

Wilfred opened the door and vomited the contents of his stomach into the road, wiping his mouth on his brown overalls. He collapsed against the steering wheel, burying his face in his hands. The man was clearly dead and he had robbed some poor child of a father, and a woman of a husband. The police would have him and he already knew the outcome. He was going too fast. They'd get him for manslaughter, he'd do time. His wife was dying; he was broke and broken.

*

Alessandra Marston was lying propped against the pillows, reading *Wuthering Heights* for the third time, when she heard the screech of brakes in the street outside. She put down her book. There were voices; traffic was drawing to a halt, a man was shouting. Dread built in her stomach. It was nothing, she told herself as she put on the dressing gown her husband had given her, tying the satin belt. Absolutely nothing. She crossed the room, pulled back the curtains and then the scream came.

'No, not Anthony, please God not Anthony.' But it was her husband lying sprawled in the wet road. It was his bloodied face that stared up at the sky. As her son Robert threw himself down beside him, she knew with certainty that her life had changed for ever.

I

Peace

Chapter One

Two and a half years later

It was seven o'clock in the morning in the spring of 1937 when Alessandra Marston closed the door on the flat for the last time, put the keys through the letterbox and went to join her daughter Diana in the waiting taxi. As the London streets flashed past the window she remembered another spring morning when the light had the same luminous quality, and the trees were laden with white blossom. 'Now this,' her husband Anthony had said, putting his arm around her shoulders, 'is my religion, Alessandra. It's as if the world is reborn, and right here in England.' Now her husband was dead and she was leaving England with her daughter. She was leaving her friends, her father-in-law, but more importantly, her son.

In the last two years her life had been turned upside down and, in what was probably the irrational escapade of a grieving widow, she was going to Italy at a time when questions were beginning to arise about the prospect of another war.

Within half an hour of arriving at Victoria Station, Alessandra had everything, including her daughter, loaded onto the boat train. Diana was hunched on the seat by the window, her nose pressed against the glass. Leo, her threadbare lion, was clasped in her arms.

On any other occasion her appearance would have brought a comment from Alessandra. Some children were automatically tidy and others were not. Diana fell into the latter category. At this moment a mass of dark curls had escaped her hairband and her blue coat, only cleaned the week before, had mud on the hem. Her socks sagged in crumpled folds around her ankles.

Today however, Alessandra only longed to hug her. 'This doesn't have to be for ever,' she said.

'Nothing is for ever,' Diana replied, looking up at her, with eyes so like her own, and a knife turned in Alessandra's heart. At fourteen years old, Diana should be happy at her old school in the country. The lion would have remained on the cupboard shelf where it had been abandoned years before, and she should have the future she had planned with Anthony. But of course nothing was as they had planned.

When Diana was asleep, her hand pressed against her flushed cheek, Alessandra picked Leo up from the floor and placed him back in her lap.

She rubbed her temples. The last two years had played havoc with her emotions. Anthony had protected her, loved her, and then he was dead. She had found out that her brilliant surgeon husband, who was famous for his skill on the operating table, was less capable with his finances. She remembered the conversation with her father-in-law, Peter Marston, shortly after the funeral.

'I'm so sorry, my dearest Alessandra,' he had said, his hands unsteady as he sipped his glass of whisky. 'I'm not sure my son told you everything. You see, the crash of twenty-nine affected us all significantly. Our stocks, shares and most of our savings have gone. Anthony made a few bad investments; so did I.'

'What are you saying, Peter?'

'I am saying that we were ill-advised and both of us took risks. Before Anthony's death, these risks were manageable because of his large income, but now, it seems there is very little left. I fear I have let you down.'

'No, of course you haven't,' she assured him. But her husband had. How could he not have told her? How could the man she loved so dearly have left them with nothing?

As Alessandra's beautiful house in Upper Brook Street went, so did the housekeeper, the cook and the maid. Alessandra had rented a damp and depressing flat in Marylebone and had secured a job in Selfridges, selling the dresses she had once bought. Diana had been moved to a day school in London, while Robert was able to stay at Marchants thanks to the generosity and kindness of Douglas Gordon, Anthony's colleague and best friend from his schooldays.

'My dear Alessandra,' he had said. 'When Anthony asked me to be godfather to Robert, I was honoured. It is a commitment I take seriously. I would be delighted to help financially and otherwise.' Douglas hadn't faltered and Alessandra had smiled at him in relief. Anthony had been right about Douglas; he was a good man, one of the best.

Two years later, their lives had changed again. Alessandra had been hanging the decorations on the Christmas tree when the doorbell rang. Diana had taken off the chain to find an old woman on the doorstep, with a tapestry handbag wedged beneath her arm, who introduced herself as Mrs Browne. Alessandra remembered asking her into the sitting room and apologising for the uncomfortable sofa and the drab furnishings.

'Oh, goodness me, whatever for?' Mrs Browne had replied, patting her hand. 'In any event, it is quite probable that you won't have to put up with them for long. Has the solicitor not informed you of my arrival?'

Filled with curiosity, they learnt that Mrs Browne had

recently returned from Italy. 'I lived in Florence, you see. I helped your grandmother when she stayed at her apartment in the Brunelleschi Hotel during the winter months. I dealt with her correspondence, paid her bills, that sort of thing, until she passed away.'

'I wasn't aware that she had died,' Alessandra declared, feeling strangely emotional.

'You should have been notified,' the old woman tutted. 'I'm sorry.'

'I never met my grandmother, so there is no need to apologise.'

'That is something she always regretted, I promise you. Which brings me to the point of my visit. I have returned to England at her behest, but it was also the right moment for me. Though I have lived in Italy for the last twenty-five years, British condemnation of Mussolini's invasion of Abyssinia changed everything. Our little community was singled out by his fascist thugs—' She stopped mid-sentence, her face flushing. 'Of course, it is different away from the city,' she assured them, bending her head to rummage in her bag. Alessandra and Diana shared a glance, eyebrows raised. Mrs Browne finished with the bag at last and pulled a battered folder from the cavernous depths. Inside was a document tied in pink tape, a book of poetry and an envelope. 'I suggest you open the letter first,' she said, her eyes bright with excitement. 'I think, my dear, you may be in for a big surprise.'

Alessandra was intrigued. What could her grandmother possibly have to say after all these years? As she opened the letter, a photograph fluttered to the floor. It was taken outside the Catholic Church in Farm Street after her wedding to Anthony. Her face had been radiant, filled with hope for the future with her husband, before he had been snatched away. She remembered her mother sending the photograph to Italy. 'I don't know why I bother,' she had said, her lips pursed. 'What has my mother ever done for me?' But she had sent it anyway and here it was after all these years. Alessandra smoothed the thick paper and with Diana leaning over her shoulder, she started to read.

Villa Durante

My Dearest Alessandra,

It is sad that we have never met. I think of you often but I realise the damage has been done. When I wrote to your mother, begging her forgiveness, I learnt of her death.

Do you still have the book of watercolours? I painted them with the wish that one day you would visit us. Sadly not in my lifetime, because I am dying, Alessandra, but I can end my days in the knowledge that my beautiful house on the borders of Tuscany and Umbria, will be yours. I hope you will love the Villa Durante, as we have done, and that it will heal family wounds. You should know that my punishment has been severe; I lost not only a daughter but a beautiful granddaughter.

I entrust my friend Angela Browne to give you my will, this letter and a book of poetry by Leopardi. Read the poetry well for it will help you to understand this country and your ancestors. You have had your own tragic loss; so come home, Alessandra. Hitler and Mussolini bark at the heels of Europe, but their influence will not last for ever.

Con affetto, *your grandmother Durante, who has thought about you every day of your life.*

'So you see, dear,' Mrs Browne had said, after Alessandra finished reading the letter and the will. 'Unbeknown to you, your grandmother took great interest in your life and followed it carefully. She was satisfied that you would take the estate forward into the future. There is a small caveat. If you chose to accept your inheritance, you must return to Italy within a year and take the family name of Durante. If these conditions are not acceptable, the estate will go to the church.'

Alessandra remembered her shock. The woman who had disowned her own daughter, and had been indifferent to her plight, had now left her granddaughter the Villa Durante. There was the caveat of course, the sting in the tail: a peremptory demand that Alessandra should give up the surname of the man she loved, in favour of the woman who had brought her family nothing but pain. Her grandmother was manipulating her from the grave.

That night Alessandra had paced the small, dingy sitting room. Her grandmother had offered her a lifeline: the house from the book of watercolours would be hers and their financial worries would be over. Diana would have a new start, but what about Robert? He was happy at his school, a boy on the brink of manhood. Exhausted, she had slumped down on the sofa, remembering the morning of her sixteenth birthday, running down the stairs of their small house in Balham.

'A present from your grandmother,' her mother had said, her face expressing her disapproval. Alessandra had ripped open the paper to find the sketchbook inside. Each page, meticulously painted by her grandmother, showed a different aspect of a large stone house surrounded by woods and hills. There were interiors, exteriors, and landscapes set beneath a cloudless sky.

'When can we go to Italy?' The words rushed out and though her mother's lips held their thin line, Alessandra would not give up. 'Tell me, please, why do you never talk about my grand-parents? I want to meet them.'

'You may go to Italy if you wish, but it will not be with me.' Then her mother's expression softened and she had stroked her daughter's cheek. 'I am sorry, Alessandra, of course you should know. I was eighteen, not much older than you are today, when my bicycle had a puncture. As luck would have it, an Englishman, your father, came to my rescue. You may remember his manners, Alessandra, and his charming accent; even his name, Charles St John, was romantic. By the time my tyre was fixed, *allora*, I was in love. My parents wouldn't countenance our marriage,' she continued. 'Not only was your father socially inferior, he was a Protestant. We married anyway, and when his contract with the Italian railways ended we returned to England. And the rest you know. When your father died I wrote to my mother. You were small, and I was alone here. I wanted to take you back to Italy, but she never replied.'

Alessandra had returned upstairs. The book of watercolours was never mentioned again; but occasionally when her mother was at work, she would take it out, and dream of a world where the sun shone, the garden was brimming with flowers, and the house in the book was her house. She did write a short letter of thanks to her grandmother. It was the only letter she sent.

Now, as the London suburbs gave way to green fields, Alessandra tipped the contents of the folder onto the seat beside her and read the letter again. Though it was an apology of sorts, it could never make up for the years of misery her grandmother had inflicted upon her mother, when Valentina Durante's only crime had been to marry her father. She sighed. It was three months since Mrs Browne's revelations and they had been filled with every possible emotion.

*

Their journey took them from London to Dover, then a ferry to Calais and onward by train. Diana slept, wrote copious letters to her brother, or leafed through magazines, giving Alessandra hours to go through her grandmother's inventories and lists. The more she read, the more she was overwhelmed. She was embarking on a new life in a country she had never even visited. She was taking on a large estate that may or may not be run down, in a language that she had not spoken for years. When her head was buzzing with facts and figures and she could hardly breathe, she distracted herself by composing cards to Robert, bought in each destination on the way. She had finished the last card, a black and white photograph of the Eiffel tower, when an idea came to her. She pulled her diary from the suitcase in the rack above her. She hadn't written in it since that terrible day. Now she would start again. Her entries would be to Anthony. It would keep her strong, positive and, more importantly, it would keep her beloved husband alive.

'I'm sitting on the train, my darling,' she wrote, *'and Diana and I are on our way to a new life in Italy. To my amazement, after all these years of silence, my Grandmother Durante has left me her house and her entire estate! I find myself dumbfounded by a legacy from someone whom I had never met and, if I am honest, never really wanted to. On the one hand it is timely, since Selfridges and I have recently parted company. However, with civil war in Spain and an unsettled Europe, it has been a difficult decision. After months of deliberation and tussles with the Italian Embassy to obtain dual nationality, I have finally taken the plunge. Robert has chosen to stay at Marchants which has been difficult for everyone, not least his Mama! I know in my heart it is the right choice, but it is hard to leave him behind. You would have been proud of his resolve, and it is this that makes it easier to bear. Diana has vacillated between excitement one moment, and misery at leaving her brother the next. Fortunately, exams, packing up the flat, and Italian lessons from your delightful old patient, Signora D'Abramo, have left her little time to brood.*

Since you left us, England has seen a lot of change. King George has passed away, and his son Edward, whom you always believed to be a playboy, has abdicated the throne. He has recently married an American divorcee. Where for heaven's sake is his sense of duty?

You must wonder why your wife, who was once ashamed of being half Italian, would choose to move to Italy at such a time as this.

After your dear Mama died, I told your father that time is the greatest healer, but it was nonsense. I miss you so much. I am hoping this will be a new beginning.

You will remember I was a little rude about your friend Douglas Gordon – not about his stammer of course, but his annoying habit of knocking his pipe out on my spotless furniture. I have discovered he is the dearest of men. Perhaps we have given him a purpose after the tragic loss of his own wife Magdelene; perhaps his devotion to our son is his way of thanking you for your friendship. Whatever the reason, I am confident that I am leaving Robert in safe hands.

Now to the estate. Signor Innocenti, the manager, is apparently beyond middle age, but according to the numerous cryptic messages my grandmother has written in the inventory margins, he is honest.

The estate is still structured on the ancient system of mezzadria. *This means the welfare of the tenants, their livestock and their land are my responsibility. In return, half the income from their crops goes back into the estate coffers. Your wife will now have to learn about the olive yield, the vineyards, the crop output. Though the task is daunting, when the old insecurities surface, I will hear your calm voice telling me that I am up to this challenge. So, Anthony, I will try to be a good* 'possidente' *– a proprietor that you would approve of.*

With my love and devotion always, and until the next time,

Your loving wife, Alessandra

Chapter Two

After stops in Paris, Turin and Milan, Alessandra and Diana arrived in Florence at Mussolini's brand-new showcase station, Santa Maria Novella, at seven o'clock in the evening. They had never seen anything like it before. Gleaming high-speed trains stood beside steam engines and people thronged everywhere. Men with briefcases hurried beneath the vast steel and glass ceiling, while brightly dressed women gossiped in the cafés, their children running freely through the crowds. There were reunions and departures. Among the chaos, colour and noise, vendors of every description were selling their wares. Newsboys shouted the headlines and coal fumes mingled with the scent of flowers. As Alessandra paid for two almond pastries, she felt a stirring of excitement. The language her mother had taught her many moons ago returned like a forgotten memory. She was no longer ashamed of her heritage; Italy was beautiful, the energy different, more vibrant. It seemed her decision to leave England was right after all.

They spent the night in Florence at a *pensione* on Via Luigi Alamanni, and returned to the station in time for the three o' clock train. As they entered the building, a hush descended on the concourse. Children ran to their mothers, flower girls packed up their flowers. Even the newsboys were silent as a column of Fascist militia marched across the marble floor.

Diana moved closer to her mother. 'Who are they?' she whispered.

'They are just policemen working for Mussolini,' Alessandra replied, keeping her voice light, but she was unable to pull her eyes away from the Blackshirts, unable to stop the fear clawing at her chest. She remembered Mrs Browne's words before she left.

'Mussolini's influence does not impact significantly on country life. You will be safe at the Villa Durante.'

Now as the Blackshirts marched into the distance, Alessandra hoped Mrs Brown's assertions were true. She looked at her daughter's white face and squeezed her arm. 'They have left, so you see, there is nothing to worry about,' she said, trying to sound optimistic. 'Let's go and talk to the stationmaster, we need to find our train.'

The train took them through the Tuscan countryside, past hilltop villages and low-lying plains. Farms scattered the landscape, but the further they travelled from Florence, the more isolated it felt. Two hours after leaving Santa Maria Novella station, and four days after leaving London, they arrived at Camucia, at the base of the hilltop village of Cortona. It was pouring with rain. It would be another hour before a bus jolted to a halt outside the waiting-room door. Exhausted and disgruntled, they dragged their cases to the bus stop.

'*Buona sera, Signora e Signorina.*' The driver, who looked like a boy, jumped down and pulled off his cap, to reveal a mop of dark, unruly hair. He removed his cigarette and spat into the ground. Diana wrinkled her nose and looked away.

'Agh, the weather! But it's God's weather, you know how it

is,' he said, his mouth curved in laughter. Alessandra at that moment didn't know anything, and Diana didn't want to.

When he had stowed their luggage in the boot, he climbed back on.

'Are you old enough to drive a bus?' Alessandra queried, more than a little concerned.

There was a pause. 'I'm twenty-one,' he grinned. Scrambling the gears, the youth drove off at great speed, negotiating the mountain roads with complete disregard for the safety of his passengers or indeed his bus. He finally slammed on the brakes and the bus lurched to a halt in the village of Mercatale, some eleven miles from the station.

'This is as far as we go.'

'A taxi?' Alessandra swivelled her head but the street was deserted.

'To Sant'Andrea di Sorbello, at this time of night? You should have got here sooner.' He dumped the cases on the side of the road. '*Buona notte* my friends, and if you ever need me, my name is Pipo.'

'You can't just leave us,' Alessandra begged.

'I suppose *mio nonno* could give you a lift, but he is expensive. *Molto costoso.*'

Pipo ambled towards a small house on the other side of the road. Minutes later he returned with his grandfather.

Alessandra smiled hopefully.

Pipo rubbed his fingers together. 'Many lire,' he laughed. The old man scratched his head as if he were considering the option. He then returned to the house, to reappear a short while later with a donkey and cart.

Alessandra stared at the ancient cart. 'This is our transport?'

'Is it not good enough for the Signora? I'll tell my grandpa.' Pipo turned towards the old man but Alessandra grabbed his arm.

'No. Don't let him go, it's fine, I assure you.' She scrambled onto the cart, pulling Diana up beside her.

'Money first.' The old man held out his hand.

With their debt settled and their cases tied on the back, they moved slowly off.

'*Buona notte*,' Pipo jumped into the bus and winked at Diana. Despite herself she smiled.

At just before eight the donkey cart stopped at the end of a driveway. '*Non è possibile*,' the old man said, taking his hat from his head, and shaking off the raindrops. Alessandra could now see his face, lined from too many years in the sun, but his eyes remained a startling blue. He wiped his hands on his leather jacket.

'The road is too wet and my donkey too old. We can go no further.' He kicked at the water with his thick boot. Alessandra looked from the cart to the deeply rutted track ahead. Water gushed down the runnels and even if they walked, the ancient donkey would never manage the slippery incline. She climbed from beneath the cart's makeshift awning and found herself at the end of a small piazza. Narrow houses with faded green shutters lined one side of a square and, at the other end, a simple church with a portico and bell tower stood against another row of houses. Sandwiched in the middle, a bar with a wooden sign announced its status as one of the top destinations in Europe. How Italian, Alessandra thought: you could drink yourself to oblivion in one door, and pray for absolution in the next. A slumbering Diana stirred and peered from beneath the canopy.

'Where are we?' she asked.

'I think we are here,' Alessandra replied.

The old man untied their cases from the cart, and with a heavy sigh he picked them up and trudged to the church porch. 'I have put them in the dry, *è un po' bagnato* – it is a little wet.'

He climbed back onto his cart, '*Buona notte,*' he called. 'I hope you find somewhere to sleep.' Raising his hand in farewell, the old man and his donkey trundled into the gloom.

Alessandra looked around the deserted piazza and put on a smile. 'You stay here with the cases, I'll try the bar.'

In the dimly lit bar a few tables and chairs were scattered. A half-filled ashtray and an empty beer glass were relics of a recent customer, but for now only a small dog eyed her warily from a kennel in the corner. Alessandra called half-heartedly. She knocked on the wooden counter; a hollow echo was the only reply.

Outside, the silent, shuttered houses looked equally abandoned. She chose a house at the end of the row and knocked. A lace curtain twitched above her but no one came. It was the same at the next house.

It was getting dark, the church was locked, and she didn't have the keys to the villa. Even if they walked up the drive, they couldn't get in. She pounded on the door of the third house and stepped back in surprise when a woman's face appeared from the shadows.

'*Si?*'

'Will you help us?' The door drew back a little further and a woman, whom Alessandra judged to be in her mid-sixties, was observing her keenly.

'Why are you out in this weather? What are you doing?' The woman took off her apron and came outside.

'We are looking for the Villa Durante.'

'What do you want with the villa? Who are you?'

'*Sono Signora Durante.*'

A frown crossed the old woman's face. 'Don't jest. Signora Durante is dead and her family live in England.'

Alessandra thought quickly. She needed proof. The letter from her grandmother was in English, but she did have the photograph. She looked in her bag. She couldn't find it. Tears were stinging at her eyes – she had lost it on the train! Then she saw it in the side compartment. She held it out, her hands shaking. The woman reached in her pocket for her glasses. Squinting in the half-light, she turned the photograph over and read the names on the back.

'Signora – Alessandra! I have seen this many times. Is it really you? And with your handsome husband in the photograph, is it possible? *Ahh, Dio!*' She raised her head to peer at Alessandra. 'Your grandmother talked so much about you; she wanted you to come here, and at last you have.'

Alessandra felt a sob rise in her throat as the tension of the last months threatened to overwhelm her.

'Come,' the woman said grabbing their hands. 'Come inside. There is no need to cry, Signora, I will look after you, and your daughter, yes, Signora Carducci will look after you.'

And ten minutes later she set an assortment of cured meats and cheese on a table in front of them. 'In Italy, we know how to eat, and we know how to sleep. Tonight you will stay in the little attic bedroom, but you will sleep like kings.'

When they had finished eating, they followed Signora Carducci up the narrow stairs to the very top of the house. The lantern was scarcely out, and the shutters closed, when they had fallen into a deep sleep.

Chapter Three

The following morning Alessandra opened her eyes. She could hear a dog barking in the distance and church bells ringing. Somewhere nearby a cock crowed vociferously, announcing the new day. Alessandra stretched, letting the sounds wash over her and, for the first time in months, she felt at peace.

Climbing over her sleeping daughter's bed she leant from the window. Below her, the village square was filled to capacity and a few puddles were the only evidence of the previous night's rain. Children were playing hopscotch and the dog from the kennel was lying in a patch of sun. Women with muscled arms scrubbed their laundry in the village trough and hung it out to dry. The scene before her was a kaleidoscope of colour and vibrancy; even the cockerel strutted along the wall, ruffling its bedraggled feathers. Alessandra breathed deeply. Her family's happiness had been snatched away; but here in the Italian countryside they could start to rebuild their lives.

She remembered the night before their departure, Diana standing by their suitcases.

'We can't go,' she had said, clutching Leo. 'I won't be able to talk to Papa when I'm on the other side of the world.'

'Of course you can.' Alessandra gently tapped her daughter's forehead. 'He is in here always.'

'But he's not. He's going, fading like a dream, and I can't stop him.'

Alessandra wanted to hold her daughter and reassure her, she looked so young and defenceless.

'Your father would never leave you,' she had said gently. 'And besides, Italy isn't the other side of the world.'

While Diana continued to sleep, Alessandra followed the aroma of coffee downstairs. Signora Carducci was making pastry on a marble slab. She rolled it into a ball and turned to Alessandra.

'*Un caffè?*'

'Thank you.'

'You should eat.' She wagged a finger at her. 'You are too skinny.' She poured the brew into a small white cup, took an omelette that was warming on the stove, and placed it in front of her.

'Good Italian food; that is what you need.' She wiped her hands on a towel and collected a paraffin lamp that she put on the side.

Alessandra glanced at the lamp.

'For tonight, Signora, but don't worry, there is a generator up at the house. Flick a switch and *poof!* you have light. Apart from the Castello, it is the only house with electricity on this side of the mountain.' To Signora Carducci it was not only a miracle, but the subject of great pride. Alessandra looked suitably impressed.

'And your husband, he will come to Italy?' she asked.

Alessandra took a deep breath. 'I am a widow, my husband was killed in an accident; that is why we have come.'

'Ah,' Signora Carducci replied, and made the sign of the cross. She then returned to her chores.

*

29

Alessandra was drying her plate when there was a commotion at the door. She followed Signora Carducci into the narrow hallway where a short, thickset man stood at the head of a large gathering.

'I am your estate manager. *Il mio nome e Elio Innocenti.*'

A hush descended as Alessandra held out her hand. 'Signora Marston, *mi dispiace*, I mean Durante.' She smiled first at the man and then at her daughter who had tiptoed cautiously down the stairs to join her.

'And this is my daughter Diana.' Alessandra felt the tension ease from her shoulders, knowing instantly that her grandmother was right; here was a man she could trust. His faded trousers were held together with a wide belt and his blue shirt was frayed at the cuffs, but both were spotlessly clean. His canvas boots, layered with the dust of many summers, seemed as much part of the man as his smile, which started in his eyes and spread slowly, creasing his face into a thousand lines.

'We are glad you have come to us,' he said. 'For over a year now the house has been empty, the Villa Durante has been waiting for your return.'

They followed Signor Innocenti into the square where a donkey waited in the sunshine. Only the cases were piled onto the cart. As they walked up the hill, it seemed that the whole village had decided to join them. Every man had a word of advice for Alessandra.

'The olives need pruning and the grapes … there is always a lot of work, but truly, as God is my witness, Signor Innocenti he works hard for you, even when you are not here.' Apparently, everyone had a brother who worked on the estate, and everyone knew someone who would be able to help. Half a mile up the track Elio Innocenti came to a halt. The entire group followed his example.

'This is the land of your ancestors,' he said, spreading his arms wide. 'This all belongs to the estate.'

Alessandra followed his gaze. Below her, fields, meadows and forests were laid out in a rich tapestry of colour and shapes, and in the distance, a village clung to the hillside with a church at its centre. A lump formed in her throat. This was more than just a landscape, much more; not only was it achingly beautiful, it was also her future and her mother's past – a past she had left behind.

They turned the last bend in the drive. On a flat plateau, a curved wall enclosed a steep bank. In the centre of the bank, two stone posts supported a pair of rusting iron gates. Signor Innocenti leant against them and with a great show of strength he heaved them back against the wall. He continued up a short flight of steps, worn smooth from centuries of use and walked towards the house. At once the chattering stopped and everyone was silent. Alessandra lifted her eyes. It was the house buried in her childhood memories, the house in her book of water-colours. Shutters still hung at the windows, traces of the green paint still visible on the silver-grey wood. The loggia was there, wisteria twisting haphazardly through the arches; it was all as she remembered from the paintings. The fountain was dry now, chipped and tilting drunkenly, but it was the same cherub, and the same stone dog at the large front door. She walked towards it and was about to turn the handle when Signora Carducci came up the steps behind them

'I have the key. We always knew that someday a Durante would return.'

The key turned easily in the lock and everyone drew backwards. Signora Carducci pushed the door open and Alessandra stepped over the threshold. Before she could even see the interior, she could feel the coolness in the air and she could smell the damp of disuse.

Slowly her eyes adjusted, and she was aware of a long, rectangular room filled with furniture. Paintings and faded gilt mirrors hung from the walls. As Signora Carducci opened the shutters, the sunlight spilled inside, fracturing the dust into spinning particles, fading the terracotta floor tiles to a pale, rosy pink. A chandelier hung from the ceiling, the candles burnt to stubs, the clouded crystal spattered with wax. Alessandra pulled the dust covers off two sofas that stood either side of a stone fireplace; she ran her hand over an upright chair with a tapestry seat and she could see the room, not as it stood at this moment, but as it would be one day in the future.

'Thank you for taking care of the house,' she said.

'It is nothing,' the older woman replied. 'Now, the windows can be left open and Signor Innocenti will do as I tell him and mend the holes in the roof.' She stared at the estate manager accusingly, and he shrugged his shoulders and ambled into the hall.

'See,' she pointed to the buckets placed strategically on the floor and then at Signor Innocenti. 'Your job.'

Signor Innocenti spread his hands to show that he was aware of the problem.

'It is true,' he said. 'But the house will welcome you, just as we welcome you. We will mend the roof, and if the generator is not working, we will fix that before nightfall. The plumbing,' he smiled, 'that is also a little difficult, but there is a shed in the garden, a good shed, though a little overgrown. Dario is already cutting down the weeds.' When Alessandra's face looked anxious, he reassured her in his slow and musical voice.

'This is now your home. It is the only place you should ever be. I can see that you both have your health and that is the most important gift in life.' Alessandra liked the optimism of her estate manager. He was right; in time it could all be fixed.

While the men chopped wood for the fires, Diana ran up the

wide staircase. She had exchanged her winter coat for a light floral dress with a wide skirt, and her hair, liberated from the hairband, was a riot of dark curls. As her mother inspected the two armoires on the landing that were filled with linen, Diana ran from one room to another, pulling open windows, doors, laughing in excitement. When she came to a bedroom with cream-painted furniture, she felt a strange yearning. Perhaps it was the pale yellow walls that reminded her of her bedroom at Upper Brook Street. Perhaps it was some forgotten ancestor that drew her like a magnet. She sat down at a desk and opened the drawers. They were filled with drawings and letters as if some child from the past had left only moments before. She looked up as her mother entered.

'Can this be my room?' she asked

'Why ever not?' Alessandra agreed.

When she had gone, Diana continued to explore. In the cupboard, dresses from a different age hung in neat rows, and several pairs of shoes were in a rack on the floor. A small pouch filled with costume jewellery was hanging on the door. As she held the trinkets up to the light, she was reminded of the crystal pendant Robert had given her for Christmas.

'Papa was going to buy you this,' he had said, as she unwrapped the crystal heart suspended on a delicate chain, 'but he never had the chance, so I bought it for you instead.' Diana's mood changed immediately. She slid to the floor and let her tears fall. She missed Robert so much and she missed her father. She remembered being summoned to the headmistress's study at her school in Sussex, being told her father was injured. They had not said he was dead. And then in the hall in London, her mother, Robert, Grandpa Peter, all turning towards her as she came through the door. She had known immediately. Robert had followed when she had bolted upstairs.

33

'We'll get through this, De,' he had said, catching up with her, holding her sobbing face against his chest. 'We'll do this together.'

They were so close, and now she had left him.

She didn't hear Signora Carducci come in. She touched Diana's shoulder, and the young girl started.

'You are unhappy.' It was not a question.

Diana nodded. 'A little.'

'It looks like a lot to me. Come, I have something to show you,' she said, and Diana followed her into the garden.

High up in an oak tree, hidden among the foliage, was a small wooden house. 'You are fourteen years, no? This belonged to your grandmother. She was given it at about your age. It can be your own special place and I will tell no one.' By her gestures Diana understood that they were sharing a secret and Diana was good at keeping secrets.

Alessandra was on the balcony outside her new bedroom when she noticed Diana talking to Signora Carducci. They were standing beneath an oak tree and Diana was laughing. There was something reassuring about Signora Carducci. Diana obviously sensed this too.

As Alessandra returned inside, she caught sight of a painting on the wall beside the large wooden bed. The sitter was dressed in white with a black ribbon tied around her neck. The pose was serious, and yet the young girl's eyes were animated and alive. The family likeness was unmistakable. Beside it was a photograph of the same girl, older now, in a long dress covered in crystal beads. There was a feather in her hair and she was smiling into the camera. When Alessandra looked closely she realised that it was her mother, wearing the same dress she had given her for the medical school dance. She must have worked on it for weeks, altering it to make it fashionable. At once she felt a wave of longing and nostalgia for her dead mother. At some time during her life, that youthful optimism had gone, her spirit broken. Alessandra vowed she would never give up like her mother, and she wouldn't let the same thing happen to Diana.

She sat down on the stool in front of the dressing table and closed her eyes. For a brief moment she was young again, entering a ballroom in a beautiful gown. She could remember the laughter and the music, and the couples as they spun beneath the crystal chandeliers.

'Would you like to dance?' A sandy-haired student with pale blue eyes and a faint stutter had bowed in front of her, and they had joined in the whirling, elegant throng until another student cut in.

'Excuse me, Douglas, do you mind?' he had asked, tapping her partner on the shoulder. As she looked up into the handsome, smiling face of Anthony Marston, then a fifth-year medical student, she felt a lurch in her stomach that was entirely new.

She turned back, but her partner had released her, melting into the background and she was left with Anthony. For the entire evening he stayed at her side, charming her, until she was left in no doubt of her feelings. It seemed that the attraction was mutual, and as the days turned into weeks they became inseparable.

A month after Anthony qualified they were engaged. At Valentina Durante's request they were to be married at the Catholic church in Farm Street.

'My faith is still important to me, Alessandra,' she had said. 'Like you, I was an Italian married to an Englishman.'

'You are wrong, Mama, I may be Catholic but I am English like my father.' But inside, Alessandra believed she would always be different from her school friends; deep down she was still the little Italian girl.

Anthony had of course agreed to her request. 'I will assure

the priest that I will be a good Catholic,' he had laughed. 'As long as you understand that my fingers will be crossed behind my back.'

As she stood beside him at the altar, Alessandra knew that whatever his beliefs, Anthony would be honourable and true for as long as he lived. She hadn't guessed he would be taken so soon.

By dusk all the mattresses had been beaten and turned, and the floors swept. The increasing bonfire was stoked, and the donkey cart continued to travel back and forth, bringing food and other necessities. When the cooking range was hot and supper prepared, the children from the village arrived to join their parents. Everyone sat down around the large kitchen table. Alessandra found the pasta with beans and the skin of a pig salty and difficult to chew, but she washed it down with the local red wine. Diana ate heartily as if it was the best cuisine in the world.

When supper was finished, Diana ran outside, followed by a stream of children. Alessandra was about to caution her, when Signora Carducci stopped her.

'Leave her be, Signora. Give your daughter some freedom and Italy will heal her.'

Alessandra hesitated but then she smiled. Signora Carducci was like a rock, solid and dependable, her brown eyes calm in her square face. She was right, of course; she must squash this relentless anxiety; allow Diana to live without constantly warning her of the dangers.

Later they stood together on the terrace. They could hear bullfrogs croaking in the distance, and a dog barking in the valley below, but nearer at hand, high up in an oak tree came the sound of children's laughter.

*

Alessandra was unpacking her suitcase when she took out Robert's cloth rabbit. She had adopted it when he first went to boarding school, refusing to take the rabbit for fear of being teased. He was just eight years old and it was one of the only arguments she had with her husband. 'I don't care if you went to the same prep school, Anthony; Robert is too young,' but in the end Anthony had prevailed.

This time Robert was sixteen; no longer a child. She remembered the last night of the school holidays, a week before they had left for Italy. Douglas had taken them all out to supper. Diana had been very quiet, pushing her food around her plate, and Robert had put on a brave face but she could see that it was a façade. It was actually Douglas who had saved the day.

'I have thought of a new anagram, Robert: *decimal point*. I'll give you fifteen seconds,' and he had winked at his godson.

Robert's expression had altered immediately when faced with his favourite challenge. '*I'm a dot in place*,' he laughed. 'And I've got one for you, Douglas, but this time I'll give you the answer – *I'll make a wise phrase*. You have ten seconds because you're older!'

It took Douglas only five. '*William Shakespeare*. If I may say so, Robert, that's a good one. Congratulations, young man.'

Diana looked up at her brother. 'That's clever, Robs, where did you find it.'

'A boy at school told me,' he grinned.

Alessandra placed the rabbit on her pillow. How she missed her son, but she acknowledged, wiping a tear from her cheek, they were so lucky to have Douglas as a friend.

It was approaching midnight when her case was finally empty and her clothes and possessions were tidied away. She picked a record from the selection she had brought from England and went to the study downstairs. It was Anthony's favourite piece of music: 'The Lark Ascending'. It had become her agony and her solace. As the music reverberated around the room, she could feel Anthony's presence. He was telling her she could manage without him; she was strong and brave even if she didn't realise it yet. She could see him at the desk, bent over his work, his horn-rimmed spectacles balanced on his nose, his short, dark hair exposing the vulnerable white skin of his neck. Then he took off his spectacles, rubbed at an imaginary speck of dirt, and he was glancing across the room at her, his smile lighting up his eyes. She wanted to go to him, drape her arms around his neck and breathe in the smell of him, warm cashmere mixed with cedar wood and a hint of antiseptic. But he had gone and there was only an empty chair and the music. She wiped her eyes as the door opened.

'Couldn't you sleep?' she asked, as Diana stood on the threshold.

'I miss Papa and Robs.'

'Come and sit down and we can miss them together.' They curled together on the sofa. 'And Grandpa Peter too,' Diana murmured, her dark lashes flickering against her pale cheeks as she fell asleep in Alessandra's arms.

Chapter Four

Alessandra stopped chopping the onions, wiped her eyes with the back of her hand and turned to Signora Carducci.

'Signor Innocenti says there is enough money in the estate coffers to employ you on a full-time basis.'

'Are you are asking me to work for you, or telling me?'

'Forgive me, it is my Italian, Signora Carducci, I would never tell you. Never, but it would be a great honour if you would resume your position as housekeeper.'

Signora Carducci sniffed. She picked up a tea towel and passed it to Alessandra.

'I will consider it.'

Alessandra dabbed at her streaming eyes. 'Though Signor Innocenti is extremely efficient and he has managed on his own until now, I intend to become fully involved in the running of the estate. It would make it so much easier for me.'

'Efficient, Signor Innocenti, *eh?*' she sniffed. 'We had a good crop of olives last year, that is why there is money in the coffers.'

'Does that mean yes?'

'I was fifteen when I start to work for your family, so yes, I will resume my duties, but we need to employ a handyman. Is there enough money in the coffers for that too?'

As Signora Carducci walked down the hill, laughter bubbled

inside her. It was quite clear to her that this elegant slip of a woman from London had never done a day's physical work, but she now wanted to take on a man's world. It would be a hard task, but her grandmother had done it, and now the Signora would do it. She had something to prove to herself and to her family.

Three days after Signora Carducci accepted her position, Alessandra caught sight of herself in the drawing room mirror. Her skirt and her headscarf were spattered with white paint. She put the paintbrush in the tray and climbed down the ladder. She stopped in front of Dario, whose role now encompassed decorating, gardening and many of the household chores.

'I believe, Dario, there is more paint on my skirt than there is on the walls?'

'There is also paint on your nose, Signora, it has been there all morning.'

'Why didn't you tell me before?'

'Because I thought it would be impolite, but may I suggest that the Signora buys some more suitable clothes.'

'And where should I buy these clothes?' she enquired.

'They sell everything at the market in Umbertide,' he replied.

I am enjoying painting the house, she wrote to Robert. *Diana is helping, and Dario, the handyman. With every brushstroke the house seems to come alive. It's as if it has been sleeping, waiting for us to arrive. I can't wait for you to see it.*

On the first Wednesday in May, Alessandra waylaid Signora Carducci as she mopped the landing floor.

'Diana and I are going to the market.'

The older woman leant on her mop.

'So you will go on your own, eh? To the biggest market of the year?'

'It will be good for Diana's Italian.'

'They will see you coming,' she muttered, 'but if you think you will do it better than me...'

They parked their bicycles in the square and strolled through the stalls. There were cheese counters, tables laden with fruit and vegetables and stalls filled with household goods. Chickens and goats heading for slaughter clucked and bleated from their wooden cages. As they passed a cage containing a small kid goat, Diana clutched her mother's arm.

'Please can we buy it, Mama?' she begged.

'And who will look after it?'

'I will.'

Alessandra looked at her daughter's anguished face and relented.

'Only one goat,' she agreed.

While Diana negotiated with the stallholder to buy the goat, Alessandra brought painting overalls for herself and Diana, and sensible shoes. Next she purchased a length of cream linen and an assortment of vegetables, which she packed in a canvas bag. When she caught sight of Diana, walking towards her with a triumphant look on her face, pulling an unwilling goat, she remembered the wan child who had left London only a few weeks before.

When they reached the end of the drive, instead of going up the hill, they took a lane to the right of the piazza and arrived at the *fattoria*, the large stone farmhouse where Signor Innocenti lived. Diana lifted the goat out of the bicycle basket and led her through the yard, past the stables and the pigsties, to the oak front door. She knocked twice. 'This is Griselda and she is not for the pot,' she said, introducing the tiny animal to Signor Innocenti. 'I hope she will behave.'

'*Si* Signorina,' he had said, his eyes crinkling. '*Grizelda,* a most unusual name.'

Back at the Villa Durante, Signora Carducci was unpacking the canvas bag when she pounced on a mouldy tomato. 'I told you they would rob you, Signora,' she said holding it up, a wicked gleam in her eyes.

'But we have a very fine goat, I assure you,' Alessandra replied.

Alessandra made curtains for the drawing room from the cream linen. As the sewing machine whirred in the sunlit room, Signora Carducci watched her with growing respect. When Alessandra hung the curtains on the faded gilt poles she congratulated her.

'Signora, each day I marvel at your resolve. It is good that you have returned to us.'

By August, temperatures hovered in the mid-nineties and Alessandra's resolve was crumbling. The heat and the dust seemed endless. While Diana swam in the lake to cool down, Alessandra's consolation was her bath. One Sunday when she turned on the taps and the water spluttered and reduced to a brown trickle, she asked Diana to bicycle down the drive with a message for Signora Carducci.

'What's wrong?' the older woman asked, as she puffed into the house.

'I have no water. I am unable to have a bath.'

'Signora, I thought someone had died. Forgive me, but if you send for me on the Sabbath telling me to come immediately, please let the problem be of a serious nature. It didn't cross your mind to ask Dario, I suppose?'

'But he doesn't live here, Signora.'

'And I do, but a mile down the drive!'

'I am sorry,' Alessandra apologised, her face turning pink. 'I didn't think.'

'Perhaps, Signora, next time you will.'

When Signora Carducci had sufficiently regained her humour she tried the taps in the kitchen, then she adjusted the stopcock, both to no avail.

'A new well is necessary; you need the water diviner.'

'A water diviner?'

Her face softened. 'Don't look so concerned, Signora; it is how we do it in Italy.'

As the summer progressed, Alessandra worried about the coffers running dry as well as the water in the well, but with careful budgeting and hard work, the gardens returned to their former beauty. Under Alessandra's supervision, Dario relaid the parterre with box hedging and the kitchen garden was restored. White roses were planted in the beds and lavender and rosemary bordered the paths. In the loggia, among the trailing geraniums and the terracotta pots, an engraved stone relief was added to the other carvings. It was for Anthony. His only memorial.

One fine evening, as the sun dropped behind the hills, Alessandra stood on the terrace. Now was the time to remember her last moments with Anthony, her final parting in the cramped space of an ambulance. She could see his beautiful, battered face, his eyes closed as if asleep. It had been her last private moment with him, she would never again feel his skin beneath her fingers; his hair in her hands. As she had felt the warmth fading from his body, she had kissed his lips and told him how much she loved him. 'You are my life,' she had whispered, 'my reason.' She had lifted his hand to her face; let his fingers touch her mouth. 'Goodbye my love,' she had said.

Then the ambulance man had tapped on the door. 'It's time, ma'am, you need to let him go.'

As Alessandra looked towards the distant hills, she realised she would never let Anthony's memory go, but now was the time to release him to the sky.

Holding her daughter's hand, she read the words engraved on the relief: a quotation, chosen by Robert, from Khalil Gibran.

'For what is it to die but to stand in the sun and melt into the wind?'

Diana opened the small wooden casket her mother had brought from England, and together they scattered his ashes and watched them lift and disperse on the evening breeze.

That night Alessandra took out her diary.

My Darling Anthony, she wrote.

Today we said goodbye to you. It was just as you would have wished, no ceremony, only a line from Khalil Gibran. It was a fitting tribute to the man I love. But as I stood on the terrace celebrating our life together, I thought of the morning when it all ended. I remembered you leaning over me on the bed as you kissed me, and your parting words: 'There is something that is troubling me, Alessandra. I will tell you when I get home.'

What was it, my beloved? I am hoping the answer will become clear.

We are adjusting to life at the Villa Durante. The house and the estate are impossibly lovely. I find I have to pinch myself each morning when I look out of the window to the distant hills, breathing in the scent of jasmine and honeysuckle. Though Italy is ruled by a Fascist dictatorship, there are as yet no signs of aggression towards us.

You wouldn't believe the change in Diana, she is smiling again at last, even laughing. It is a joy to see her. I believe Signora Carducci, our new housekeeper, deserves much of the credit. She pretends to be stern but she is not, she is wise, kind and totally loyal with a wonderful sense of humour. Diana seems to flourish in her company and her Italian is improving daily. I have found her the perfect school – a convent in Cortona. It is eleven miles from the house, on the other side of the mountain, but she can come home every weekend. I do hope she will be happier than she was at her day school in London.

Robert tells me in his letters he is doing well at Marchants, and Douglas supports this, but I have a feeling that all is not as it seems. Before we left for Italy he had another migraine, but this time it lasted all day. Douglas, who has recently been appointed as professor of neurology at London University, assures me that it is hardly surprising under the circumstances. He says that in time they will pass. I pray he is right.

Every week I hear from your father. He is a brave, wonderful man, but with your mother gone, I can tell that he is lonely. I have asked him to come with Robert and Douglas for Christmas.

With my love and devotion always, and until the next time.

Your loving wife, Alessandra

Chapter Five

September had arrived and with it Diana's first day as a weekly boarder at the convent school in Cortona.

'Let me walk you to the bus stop,' Alessandra suggested, adjusting her daughter's rucksack.

'No ... not today.' Diana kissed her cheek. Her mother's anxiety would only increase her own.

There were nine hundred and eighty-nine paces to the bottom of the drive, and another nine hundred to the bus stop. If she hurried it should take her twenty-eight minutes precisely. She arrived within target and waited for Pipo. He didn't let her down.

'*Buongiorno,* Signorina,' he said, helping her up. 'You know the words of the Lord. *The first day is always the worst day.*'

Diana smiled and went to an empty seat at the back. Today even Pipo's humour couldn't calm her nerves.

She pulled open her rucksack and found Leo. Holding him to her chest, she remembered her eighth birthday.

'A lion for my Leo,' her father had said, and she had danced about the room, and he had lifted her up and held her close.

'I can hug him when I'm missing you.'

'But you will never have to miss me, because I will always be with you,' he had said; but it wasn't true and today the threadbare lion was all she had left of him. As the dry landscape sped past the window, she remembered the chapel of rest, her father's body raised on a slab and her mother's warning.

'I beg of you, Diana, don't go in, he is not the same at all.' She had ignored her, and as she had inched her way across the floor, one blue tile after another, she had prayed to Jesus and to Mary to make her strong, but they didn't make her strong enough. The man with the bruised face didn't look like her father and when she had touched his arm, picked up the cold, lifeless hand, he was a stranger.

'His fingernails are dirty. Papa hates dirty fingernails,' she had cried before she fled back through the heavy swing doors.

The bus stopped at the convent gates and Diana wiped her eyes. She touched the crystal heart at her neck and climbed down the steps.

'Be strong. The nuns, they will look after you,' Pipo called after her.

She lifted her hand to wave and made her way to the cloister beyond.

Three nuns were waiting for her. 'Ah, the Durante child,' they said, their faces beaming beneath their starched wimples.

'And you are to be in my class,' said Sister Maria, a nun with rosy cheeks, leading her away.

Each Monday, Diana said goodbye to her mother and Signora Carducci, and walked to the bus stop. She soon discovered that every journey to school was different. As the weather changed, so did the colours around her. One week the landscape would be ochre, burnt sienna, olive; and the next the world was shrouded in silver. Sometimes poppies would surprise her at the base of an olive tree, or an orchid emerging through the long grass. Everything was new; she was discovering the freedom of the

Italian countryside and of a different culture. If at first the pupils were wary of the 'English girl', they soon overcame their reserve. On Friday the same dilapidated bus would arrive at the convent gates and Pipo would return her to the bus stop near the bottom of the drive.

'*Buona sera*, Signorina,' he would call after her and she would wave back to him. '*Buona sera*, Pipo,' she would say with a shy smile.

In late September, Sofia entered their lives. Diana was sitting at the table beneath the loggia, labouring over her homework set by Sister Maria; her mother was buried in estate accounts. They both looked up as a girl swept along the terrace towards them.

'Who is she?' Diana asked.

'It must be Sofia,' her mother replied. 'She is Signor Innocenti's eighteen-year-old granddaughter. Apparently, we have to take her on because she is extremely capable.'

Sofia stopped in front of them and smiled, showing small, white teeth. '*Buon giorno*,' she said, appraising them. 'My grandfather says you need a cook.'

'Yes, yes we do. My daughter Diana also wishes to learn.'

'It would be my pleasure, Signora.' She turned now to Diana. 'And when you are good enough, you can share the cooking.'

'Well then,' Alessandra said, trying not to laugh, 'we shall start with a trial period.'

'Shall we say three months,' Sofia replied, 'and I shall let you know if I wish to stay.'

Diana and Alessandra exchanged a look. It seemed the interview was over. Halfway down the stairs Sofia turned and regarded them both.

'I will come tomorrow; God will forgive me for working on the Sabbath. Good day, Signora.'

As Sofia left, her brightly coloured skirt swaying around her legs, Diana began to giggle. 'It seems we have just been employed!'

Sofia's duties were varied, some set by Alessandra, some by Signora Carducci. While the housekeeper was able to concentrate on the laundry and the housework, Sofia was put in charge of the produce from the garden and estate. When she wasn't preserving fruit or curing meat, she gave cookery lessons to Diana. It wasn't long before Sofia allowed Diana unsupervised access to her recipes and 'her' kitchen.

Whether Sofia was singing or scolding Dario for an offence committed in the vegetable garden, the atmosphere was vibrant. Her singing voice, like her personality, was rich and varied. Sometimes she would sing cheerful ballads, at others, melancholy love songs. With her help, Diana learnt the Italian ways. Sofia explained to her how the produce of each season, whether wild or cultivated, was important. She learnt how garlic was essential to Italian cuisine, but its medicinal properties were equally significant. Before long, she knew which mushrooms were edible and which were to be avoided.

'This is called the death cap, and it will kill you,' Sofia said, pointing to an innocuous-looking mushroom with a pale green cap and a bulbous end at the foot of the stalk. 'It has a long Latin name that you won't understand.'

'It doesn't look sinister.'

'You will take my word, it is.' Sofia raised her eyebrows, and Diana laughed.

'Good,' Sofia said, surveying her. 'You are no longer the gloomy, pale-skinned girl from London my grandfather told me about. See, you have freckles on your nose, and your arms are as brown as a workman's.'

Diana looked at her arms and smiled. She linked one through Sofia's. 'After my father died, I didn't see a way out of my misery.'

'We have to take happiness in both hands,' Sofia replied. 'Life is never easy, but my mama taught me, you have to embrace the good moments and never take them for granted.'

'Your mother is wise.'

'My mother is dead.'

Diana looked at her, ashamed. 'I'm sorry, I didn't know.'

'Why should you? But we have much in common, you and I.'

Diana looked forward to Fridays – when she had tea with her mother, followed by a cookery lesson with Sofia. Diana soon learnt that while she had an aptitude for cooking, Grizelda had an aptitude for stealing the remains. After the cookery lesson was over, and the kitchen cleaned to her mother's exacting standards, the two girls would take the goat for a walk, where secrets were shared and a close friendship forged.

'I love my brother more than you can imagine,' Diana confided to Sofia, as they sheltered from the rain beneath an oak tree. 'I miss him every single day. To start with, I longed to return to England, but now I'm happy here. Is that disloyal?'

The older girl had looked at her and laughed. 'Do you think your brother would want you to be sad? No, Diana, he would want you to enjoy Italy. Miss him, yes, but get on with your life.'

One morning Sofia and Diana were going shopping in Arezzo. There was a flurry of excitement and activity in the house before their departure.

When Diana came downstairs in a dress of Sofia's and presented herself to her mother, Alessandra's heart sank. The dress may have looked fine on Sofia but it was too short on Diana, too tight, and in her opinion highly unsuitable. Her feelings must have shown in her face.

'You don't like it on me, do you?'

'I'm not sure darling? It's just that...' Her voice trailed off.

'You think it doesn't fit me, that I'm too fat.'

'No, not at all, but Sofia is about six inches shorter than you and she is an entirely different shape.'

'So that does make me fat!'

Alessandra was not going to win either way. 'Diana, you are beautiful, but the dress may give the wrong impression to people you meet.'

As Diana stormed from the house with an unusually apologetic Sofia following her, Alessandra sat down at the kitchen table, exhausted. What was it about young girls, she wondered. One minute Diana was an angel, the next completely impossible. But of course it must be difficult; she was changing into a woman and growing into her new body. A smile crossed Alessandra's face as she remembered incidents with her own mother. She couldn't blame Diana; they were exactly the same.

When Sofia and Diana returned that evening, Diana was wearing a long cardigan over the dress.

Alessandra drew Sofia aside. 'The cardigan?'

Sofia rolled her dark eyes. 'A boy in the piazza pinched her bottom, Signora, and she didn't like it at all.'

Alessandra kept a straight face. She hugged her daughter. 'I hope you have had a wonderful day.'

Chapter Six

As the weather changed, Alessandra's optimism faded. The rain started, the rain continued. Instead of shoes, she needed wellingtons, and as she tried them on among the trowels and seed drills in the tightly packed hardware store, she grieved for Anthony. Despondent and lonely, she wedged the boots into the basket on the front of her bicycle and started the journey home.

'The worst weather we've had in years,' Signor Innocenti grumbled, as the stream became a torrent, the lake burst its banks and mud flowed down the hill. Alessandra slipped on her way to inspect the barn in the upper meadow and sat despairing among the sodden leaves. She was cold and filthy; this was not the Italy she had imagined.

Signor Innocenti found her. 'Ah, Signora, you take a tumble. Let me help you up and I will bring you home. In a few months the summer will come and you will be content. There is nothing on God's earth that can't wait until tomorrow.'

Autumn turned to winter and Alessandra eventually got used to the rain and the cold. The farmers worked hard in an unforgiving climate to eke out a meagre living, so how could she complain?

With renewed determination, she immersed herself into the

running of the estate. Each day she met with Signor Innocenti. 'I wish to learn everything,' she told him. 'Together we will visit every farmer. We will discuss drainage, irrigation, fertilisation … yes, Signor Innocenti, I will earn their respect.'

On a late November afternoon when she was faced with stony indifference from one impoverished farmer, it was clear that she would struggle to gain his respect. Signor Avorio was a widower with three young children, looked after by their grandmother. To him, Alessandra was as redundant as the system of *mezzadria* she represented. It was a feudal system and it was outdated. What did the woman from England know of poverty and hardship? He wanted to move forward to a new and modern system.

When Alessandra arrived home, she took off her woollen hat knitted by Signora Carducci, and her boots, and sank down into her favourite armchair.

It is winter now, she wrote in her diary, *and while I relax in a warm house, with a glass of wine, I know that life for the tenant farmers is a constant struggle. This afternoon a grandmother gave me her last drop of brandy as an offering of friendship. These people have nothing and yet they will share the little they have with their neighbour. In the past I put false value on possessions: the glorious fur coat I persuaded you to buy was extravagant and unnecessary, and for that I am sorry. Tomorrow I am going to Rome. I intend to sell it, for though our revenue has increased there is little surplus for other pressing needs. I am praying I have your support.*

With my love and devotion always, and until the next time.

Your loving wife, Alessandra

Alessandra took the train to Rome and as she handed the sable to the furrier, she felt bereft. She was selling her last present from Anthony.

'*Un buon pelliccia*, Signora,' the man said, looking up at her with kind eyes. 'I will give you a good price.'

With the money Alessandra was able to buy a new generator and grain for the following season. More vines were ordered and the poorest farmers were given a sum for improvements. A particularly good amount was set aside for the widower, Signor Avorio. Nothing was asked for in return.

'How can we take half of nothing?' she said to Signor Innocenti as he tried to balance the books. 'Next year, perhaps, but not now.'

*

Alessandra was dressed and ready for her day with Signor Innocenti when she went into the kitchen.

Diana had somehow managed to use every single saucepan, bowl and spoon, notwithstanding that she had only produced scrambled eggs.

'Diana, please clear up this mess.'

Diana glared at her mother. 'Arturo Agazzi will never play at the Colosseum again.' She stabbed her finger at the programme. 'It's a once in a lifetime opportunity, Mama. Sofia has asked me to go with her. You wanted us to be friends, so why are you stopping me? Don't you trust her?'

'Of course I do, but she is three years older than you. It is not about Sofia, but her friends – some of them are twenty, Diana. They are too old. Whatever you say, the answer is still no.'

She glanced at her daughter. A bandana was tied around Diana's forehead and Alessandra couldn't help thinking how exotic she looked, her curls tumbling around her face, her eyes flashing.

'You never let me do anything,' she retorted, and flounced from the room banging the door behind her.

As Alessandra walked up the windswept hill to meet Signor Innocenti, she reflected that even the most obdurate farmers were easier to deal with than her hormonal, adolescent daughter.

Diana was standing in the kitchen later that day, her back resting against the stone sink. The room was immaculate and Alessandra could see from her face that she was sorry, even if she wasn't able to say the words.

'You should know that I'm not stopping you going to the concert in Rome to make your life miserable, but because I'm concerned. So I have decided to take you myself.'

Diana's face fell. 'I'd prefer to go with Sofia.'

'Well, it's either your mother or no concert, I'm afraid.'

A fortnight later Alessandra and Diana left their cases in the *pensione* opposite the Trevi Fountain. Wearing hats and thick winter coats they set off for the Colosseum. As the jazz reverberated around the torchlit amphitheatre, Diana leant forward with rapt attention. Watching her face, Alessandra was filled with emotion. She had always been aware that Diana was closer to her father, but now, in the aftermath of grief, they were beginning to build a different relationship, one that she hoped would pull them together through the times ahead.

As she lay in bed that night, she thought of the gladiators who had fought for their lives in the amphitheatre two thousand years before. Tonight the musicians had played in the same arena, but in an atmosphere of peace. Soon that peace might be shattered again. They were facing a world of uncertainty and if war was declared some time in the future, her son would be on the other side.

His recent letter had upset her.

'Dearest Mama,' he had written. 'Forgive me, but Douglas has enrolled me in a course of boxing training at the beginning of the school holidays, and he has suggested a trip to Paris afterwards. I hope you won't mind if I don't come for Christmas.'

Alessandra minded terribly. Douglas knew how she longed to see her son. She closed her eyes; she wouldn't be resentful, she was so grateful to Douglas for everything he had done. Now, of course, she would have to find the best way of telling Diana.

They had just arrived home when Diana opened a letter from her grandfather. She read it to her mother.

> *My dearest Diana,*
>
> *As I drink my morning cup of tea, I imagine you in the cloisters of your school, chatting with your new friends; I assume you now speak Italian fluently! Thank you for your letters, they are the highlight of my week.*
>
> *Robert came to tea last week with Mr Gordon. Your brother looked taller and quite splendid. He has filled out a little, probably the boxing. They told me their plans for Christmas have now changed. Sadly I don't think my old bones will be up to travelling alone. I will miss being with you this year and I send you all my love.*
>
> *Grandpa Peter*

'Why didn't you tell me Robert wasn't coming for Christmas?' Diana demanded.

Alessandra looked at her daughter's flushed face. Her eyes were wet with unshed tears and she was biting her lip, as she had done as a small child.

Alessandra cursed silently; if only she had told her first.

'We must be happy for Robert,' she said slowly. 'He loves boxing and the fact that he is eligible for trials means he will be in the team. Come on, we'll have a great Christmas.' She moved towards Diana, but she backed away.

'I hate Douglas, Mama.'

'Of course you don't. I am just as disappointed as you, but we shall go to London very soon, I promise.'

Chapter Seven

In December 1937 the convent employed a young man called Davide Angelini as the school carpenter. As far as anyone could remember there had never been one before, but it was apparent from the nineteen-year-old's work that he was no ordinary carpenter. Soon new carvings appeared in the chapel and picture frames were regilded and restored.

'The countryside is good for my father's health,' he told Diana, as he sanded a desk in the classroom. He bent his head to his work, stopping any further questions, but he chose to sit next to her on the bus journey home. As it wound down the hill from Cortona, Diana noticed his eyes, the colour of cornflowers, and his even, white teeth. By the time they had reached his stop, she had noticed his hands, long and elegant with rounded tips to the fingers. They were not a workman's hands.

It was another week before she had the courage to enquire about his father's health. They were standing at the convent gates. Davide's eyes were tight against the afternoon sun and she could no longer see the blueness. He paused before he answered and for a moment Diana thought he would ignore the question. 'He is a goldsmith from a long line of goldsmiths,' he said at last, 'but for now he needs the country air. We have temporarily closed our house in Arezzo, and have leased a farm in Mengaccini.' He paused, seemingly unwilling to reveal any more. 'Time to get on the bus, you know how Pipo likes to stick to his schedule.' He smiled at his joke, his face softening, and when half an hour later the bus screeched to a halt at the bottom of the drive to the Villa Durante, he jumped down after her. 'I shall accompany you home, it is good for me to walk further.'

'But you have missed your stop, this is out of your way ...'

'My mother says I spend too much time inside and I should take more exercise.'

Diana believed the extra mile he had to walk each way would exceed even his mother's expectations.

As the weeks drew on, Davide offered to help Diana with her work.

'It can be difficult to think in two languages,' he said with a smile. 'It would be an honour to help you.'

Soon Diana found problems with her work where perhaps they did not exist. Italian translations that had been easy the week before were difficult, and issues with mathematical equations were insurmountable. Whether they were on the bus or walking down the dusty lane, she would glance sideways, storing everything for later. After she had gone to bed she would recall the sound of his deep voice, and the way he said her name, his voice lifting when he reached the 'a'. She would remember the intense concentration in his blue eyes as he leant towards her, and the way he walked, as if he needed to release some of his pent-up energy. Sometimes he would stride ahead of her and turn back towards her laughing; at other times he was silent, his face shadowed with sadness. On these occasions, she realised, it was better not to ask.

When Davide gave her a book on the great sculptors of the world, she was profoundly affected. It was as if by offering her this gift, he was opening a door into his own dreams and aspirations.

'Look,' she said, turning the page to an image of the Venus de Milo. 'Isn't she exquisite?'

'Ah,' he said leaning over her, 'she is also known as Aphrodite of Milos, the Greek goddess of love.' As he said the word love, Diana lowered her eyes, confused by the new sensations she was feeling.

Davide taught Diana to fish in the lake and before long, under his tutelage, she became skilful. He showed her how to cast the line from the small wooden jetty, and to kill the squirming fish quickly and painlessly.

'The lakes in Bolzano where my grandfather taught me had the best carp in the world,' he said, standing behind her. And Diana overcame her fear, and the quicker the death, the easier it became.

One evening as the sun started to set and they stood at the side of the lake, Davide's arm slipped around her waist. She turned towards him, unable to breathe.

He was smiling down at her. 'Now you swing your arm like this,' he said, but Diana was no longer interested in fishing.

That night, unable to sleep, she padded across the floor to the pier glass in the corner. Lifting her nightdress she could see, faintly outlined in the mirror, a slimmer version of herself. Her legs were now lean and tanned from cycling and her full breasts were no longer a cause for embarrassment. Even her face looked delicate in the moonlight. She let the nightdress fall and as the heat rose within her she returned to her bed where she tossed and turned till morning.

Chapter Eight

Diana was at the kitchen table, hunched over a newspaper, when her mother came in. She looked up, her face pale.

'Mama, it's happened. Germany has annexed Austria.'

Alessandra leant over her shoulder and scanned the headline. '*On this day 12 March 1938 at 8 a.m. Germany crossed the border into Austria. Any potential opponents of the Nazis have been arrested.*'

Alessandra sank down on a chair. She had been so busy on the estate she hadn't listened to the news. Robert was right, war would come and soon, but she mustn't panic, not in front of Diana.

'Will there be war?' Diana cut into her thoughts.

'Britain is dead against it. Prime Minister Chamberlain wants peace.'

'But we're in Italy, Mama, Mussolini is Hitler's ally.'

'I know. But Hitler doesn't want to go to war either,' she lied. 'Instead of worrying, think of our holiday in London. This time we are flying, it's a special treat because we can't miss a moment of Robert's Easter holidays.'

Though Diana was temporarily reassured, Alessandra was not. That night as she lay in bed, faces of young men she had known before the Great War haunted her. Many of them had never come home and of those who had, there were few without mental or physical scars, including her husband. Now it seemed it would happen all over again.

Two weeks later, Alessandra and Diana landed at Croydon Airport. It had been over a year since they last saw Robert. They had been counting the days, crossing them off each morning on the big calendar in the kitchen.

As the plane touched down on the runway, Alessandra remembered the moment she had said goodbye to her son.

'I'm fine,' Robert had said, but from his trembling lip, Alessandra could see he was not.

It had been so difficult to leave him but to her relief, as the previous spring turned to summer, Robert's letters contained reassuring anecdotes of school life and his friends. A boy from his preparatory school had invited him to Cornwall for the first part of the summer holidays. Afterwards, Douglas had offered to take him to Berlin.

'I simply can't bear the thought of missing Italy,' Robert had written. 'But with Douglas paying the school fees, I believe I ought to go with him.' Then there was his new passion, boxing, involving competitions, trials, and the regional finals. There was always something that prevented him coming to Italy.

Now at last she could see him through the glass doors. He was almost a man. A steward let him through and he was bounding across the tarmac, lessening the distance between them. He was in her arms and she was trying not to cry. He went next to his sister.

'Oh, Robs!' Diana hugged him. 'I've been so miserable without you. You've grown and your voice is just like Papa's. I feel like I have missed half of your life.'

'A lot has happened, De,' he said, embracing her tightly, 'but we have a whole fortnight together and I will tell you everything.

He held her away from him. 'You look positively glowing, doesn't she, Mama?'

'She most certainly does,' she replied.

Shortly afterwards Douglas Gordon strolled across to join them. He was wearing his habitual tweed jacket and his sandy hair was parted on the side.

'I didn't wish to interrupt,' he apologised, 'but the driver is waiting in the car.'

Alessandra kissed his cheek and together they walked into the arrivals lounge.

'I've arranged a service apartment in Kensington using the draft you sent me,' he said, as their driver turned onto the London road. 'It's near to your father-in-law's so I hope you like it, and though small, I'm told it is well run. After you have settled in, I'd like to take you all out to dinner. I've taken the liberty of booking a table at the Savoy.'

He proceeded to light his pipe and Alessandra withdrew into the corner of the car.

'Thank you, Douglas, that is incredibly kind,' she uttered, trying not to cough. 'You think of everything.'

Douglas took the pipe from his mouth. 'In the case of your family, I certainly try.'

Later that evening, Douglas was waiting for them outside the Savoy, as promised. He took Alessandra's arm and led them through to the dining room, where a table was waiting for them.

After they were seated, and the wine had arrived, Douglas picked up his glass.

'Forgive me,' he said. 'We all know the recent news, and the impact it may have on our lives, but I want to say one thing. I am sure we will all come through this very difficult time and if I can be of any help at all, know that I will be here for you.' He raised his glass. Tonight his stutter was imperceptible. 'Now let us forget politics and enjoy the evening.'

There was a murmur around the table and Robert squeezed his mother's hand.

'Sometimes,' Alessandra replied, trying to contain her emotion, 'we feel quite isolated in Italy and it is easy to question my decision to go there. All I can say is that thanks to you, Douglas, I feel secure in the knowledge that my son is safe in your care.'

'Being part of your family has meant so much to me, particularly after the loss of my Magdelene, so I should be the one thanking you,' Douglas assured her.

After the first course, Diana put down her fork. 'Sofia says that the way to a man's heart is through his stomach. Is that true, Mr Gordon?

'Only partially,' he smiled. 'Personally I believe there are other more important attributes.'

'If love were judged on the ability to cook, Diana, your father would never have married me,' Alessandra confirmed, happily.

Robert looked at Diana. 'So you now have the answer, little sister, but I think it would be wise to wait until you are older before putting it to the test.'

Diana punched him. 'Don't be pompous,' she laughed. 'You are not that much older than me.'

As the wine flowed, so did the conversation, and the normally reserved Douglas seemed to sparkle.

'Tell me, Diana,' he asked. 'How do you get around in Italy, do you have a car?'

Diana spluttered into her glass. 'A car? Mummy can't drive and I'm not yet sixteen, but we're fine, we bicycle everywhere and of course we take the bus.'

'Well, I suggest your mother learns, and you, young lady, need to persuade her.'

Alessandra laughed. 'I admit it would make life easier, but we have a bus driver called Pipo and we can't possibly desert him. However, if we have a good harvest we'll consider it next year.'

'So,' Douglas said. 'To Alessandra's car and her wonderful children.'

Glasses were raised and while Douglas engaged Robert and Diana in conversation, Alessandra compared the joyful reunion with the dreadful days of indecision before leaving England, and the scene in the tearoom near Marchants.

'Sell the house in Italy,' Robert had yelled. 'Contest the will. If another war comes, Italy will be on the wrong side.'

'I won't leave you Robs,' Diana had sobbed, and the customers in the teashop had stared at Alessandra, their faces expressing their disapproval. And then in the weeks afterwards Robert had pushed her to go. 'I've been selfish, it's a new start for Diana. Douglas will look after me. Go, Mama, you can't miss this opportunity.' Now, a year later they were together again, the bond between her children seemed as strong as it had ever been, and Robert was growing into a man. Douglas had been as good as his word. He had looked after her son.

When dinner was over, Douglas took them in a taxi back to the apartment.

Alessandra stayed behind at the door. 'You have a way with young people, Douglas. One day you should marry again, have children of your own,' she urged.

Douglas flushed.

'I'm so sorry, that was thoughtless. I didn't mean to embarrass you.'

'You have not,' Douglas replied. 'It's just that... Forgive me, it's late. I'll take you back to the airport on Monday next, and afterwards I will drop Robert back at Marchants. That is, of course, if you wish.'

'I would like that very much. Anthony was so lucky to have you as a friend.'

'I would be happy to be…' Douglas coughed, and took his pipe from the inside pocket of his jacket.

'G-goodnight Alessandra,' he stammered. 'I had better be on my way.'

The week was filled with excursions to the Odeon cinema, to museums and art galleries. At Diana's request, they bought tickets to the Rodin exhibition and, as she wandered through the spacious rooms, it was Davide's broad chest and strong arms she saw in the *The Thinker*, his chiselled face. When she came to *The Kiss*, a bronze study of Paolo and Francesca, two lovers, joined together in fatal embrace, she felt the colour rise in her cheeks, but she couldn't get it out of her mind.

In the British Museum, they went first to the department of Egyptology where Diana was captivated by three terracotta panels taken from the tomb chapel of Nebamun.

'Three thousand years old, and still perfect,' she sighed.

They were leaving the museum when she came across the sculpture. It was displayed in a glass cabinet in a small room on its own. The walls were lined with black silk and a single light shone down on the cabinet. The subject was a bird in flight, its elliptical wings caught in movement. Diana was unable to pull herself away.

She remembered Davide bringing a small lump of clay to the house, sitting down on the wall overlooking the rose garden, moulding the material with his hands until it was recognisable and beautiful, a small bird in flight. All the while she had watched his fingers, tactile and supple as he shaped the clay, and the concentration in his eyes.

'You have so much talent,' she had said.

'But what use is talent when you are not allowed to use it?' Davide had replied.

*

On the last afternoon, they took Peter to a matinee showing of *Swing Time* with Fred Astaire and Ginger Rogers. Following the performance, while Robert went out to dinner with Alessandra, Diana spent the night with her grandfather. They ate supper in the kitchen, the news on in the background.

'Hope you don't mind, De,' he said. 'We don't go in for formalities now your grandmother has gone.'

'Of course I don't mind,' she answered, sitting down at the small table. 'We always eat in the kitchen at home.' But she did mind about her grandfather being lonely, with only the Bakelite wireless and the housekeeper who came in daily for company.

'Do you listen to the news in Italy?' Peter asked.

'It's not Outer Mongolia, Grandpa. I know what is going on, but will there really be another war?'

Peter patted her shoulder. 'I think it might come to that, but let's not talk of war. I want to hear about you. Do you like it in Italy, I mean really and truly, not just letter-writing like it?'

Diana nodded. 'Yes, at first everything was strange, the language, the Italians, the countryside, but now I find London strange. There are too many people and too much traffic, but I miss you and Robert and of course I miss Papa. Please will you tell me about him? Not when he was an adult, but when he was a child?'

Half an hour and several anecdotes later, Diana got up from the table.

'Sometimes I dream about him, and my dreams are so vivid when I wake up, I believe he is still alive.'

Peter smiled. 'You're a good girl, Diana.'

But it wasn't about being good. Grandpa Peter was an extension of her father. 'Why can't you come and live with us in Italy?' she asked.

'De, I've lived here all of my life, and I am too old for change.

67

But you are blossoming into a beautiful young woman, and as long as you write to me I will know of your adventures.'

'And you'll keep on writing to me?' she asked.

'Try and stop me,' he smiled.

The same chauffeur picked them up for the drive back to the airport.

They were in traffic on the embankment when the demonstration came towards them. Students were holding placards with the words 'Germans go home' written in red paint on one side and 'Nazis' on the other. They were chanting at the top of their voices, thrusting the placards skywards. Alessandra was shocked. She hadn't expected this level of intolerance in England, particularly when many of the Germans in London were Jews escaping persecution in their own country.

She turned her face away, but she couldn't block out the noise and hostility of the oncoming crowd.

Suddenly they all looked at Douglas. His hands were shaking as he wound down the window.

'Have you nothing better to do?' he yelled. 'You are stupid idiots, all of you.' He drew in his head and collapsed onto the seat.

'Can't stand this nonsense,' he muttered, wiping the beads of perspiration from his brow. He managed a rueful grin. 'Sorry, don't know what came over me.'

Alessandra put her hand over his. 'You look shaken.'

'I'm fine, thank you Alessandra.'

When they arrived at Croydon, Douglas professed his need to work on his papers in the airport lounge, while Robert went with Alessandra and Diana to collect their tickets. Pushing aside all thoughts of the demonstration, they had a drink in the cocktail bar and then wandered beneath the colonnaded foyer of London's first international airport terminal building.

'Those clocks tell the times in different parts of the world,' Robert said, pointing to the time zone tower, and though Alessandra tried to feign interest she was defeated. She listened only to his voice, the new deep tones, the way it lifted in amusement just like his father's. She observed only the way he had grown and how it had happened in such a short time. When their flight was called she held her son in her arms.

He finally pulled away. 'Douglas is giving a lecture in Paris during half-term. He has offered to take me. Will you meet us in Paris, Mama?'

'Of course I will,' she replied, the pain of separation as bad as it had ever been. 'You look pale.' She brushed her hand against the side of his face. 'Not a migraine?'

He shook his head. 'Not this time, Mama.' He looked at her for a moment. 'Goodbye,' he said at last. 'Please take De and go.'

Alessandra was almost at the departure gates, when she ran back to Douglas. 'Thank you for looking after him,' she said, gripping his arm, kissing his cheek. 'I will never be able to repay your kindness.'

'Alessandra, I …' He put an envelope into the side pocket of her coat. 'I was going to post this, so don't read it until you are on the plane.' He got no further because Alessandra had gone.

'I'll write,' she called back to him. Then she gathered a sobbing Diana and walked across the tarmac.

Robert and Douglas remained on the tarmac while the Imperial Airways aeroplane taxied along the runway. As the plane lifted into the sky and disappeared into the clouds, Douglas put his arm around the young man's shoulders. When nothing remained but a trail of white vapour, they walked back to the terminal building. It wasn't only Robert who had a lump in his throat.

Alessandra was in her bedroom at the Villa Durante three days later, unpacking her clothes, when she remembered the letter from Douglas. She took it from her coat pocket. Inside the envelope was a draft for five hundred pounds.

> *Dearest Alessandra,*
> *Your wonderful husband was kind enough to lend me some money when I needed it. Think of this as a repayment of that loan. It has nothing to do with the school fees, that is my welcome duty as a godfather. So please use it to buy a car. I can't bear to think of you without any form of transport save a bicycle, or indeed a bus driven by Pipo, however pleasant he is.*
>
> > *With fondest love*
> > *Douglas*

Alessandra looked at the letter for a long time, then she took out her diary.

My darling husband, she wrote. *We have finally arrived back at Villa Durante after our trip to England. While aviation is opening up the world, it still takes three days to get to Italy! It was a great success, though difficult to leave. It is strange for you to imagine, but your son is nearly a man. He is so like you and with many of your opinions. He is convinced that if we are once again forced into war, Churchill is the man to lead our country.*

Your father was in great form though a little frail, and Douglas was generous and kind as always. He took us for dinner at the Savoy and had exchanged his tweed jacket for a suit. Now that, you would say, is a miracle!

With my love and devotion always, and until the next time.
Your loving wife, Alessandra

Chapter Nine

The women from the village had come to prepare the house for the priest's blessing. Though they were paid for this task, the spring cleaning was as important to them as the harvest for the men. Rugs were dragged into the sunshine, floors were mopped and polished until they shone, linen washed and mattresses re-stuffed.

This year, as they fulfilled the Easter tradition, there were some at the Villa Durante who thought not of the preparation for the summer months ahead, but of the darkness of a coming war.

The priest sat at the head of the table for the customary leg of lamb, with rosemary roasted potatoes, served by Sofia and Signora Carducci. Having drunk enough to bestow ten blessings, he fulfilled his duty in the small chapel below the house.

When the priest had left, Alessandra and Signora Carducci stood together on the terrace and watched as the women ambled down the hill. Not for the first time Alessandra wondered when they shunned their coloured clothes in favour of black. She asked Signora Carducci.

'Black dyes are cheaper,' she replied. 'It is also the colour of mourning and represents the severity of loss and pain. I think,

Signora, you wear black in your heart, but perhaps it is time to shed your grief and come into the light again.

'You know everything, don't you, Signora Carducci?' Alessandra replied, amazed at the insight of the housekeeper.

'I am an old woman,' she replied. 'It is right that I have learnt some wisdom on the way.'

'Would you know where to find a dog?' Alessandra asked as she helped Signora Carducci clear away the last of the lunch.

Signora Carducci smiled. 'I believe so, Signora.'

'Yesterday, complete strangers approached Diana when she was shopping in Umbertide. She was obviously a little scared.'

'Fascist strangers?' Signora Carducci enquired

Alessandra nodded, her face anxious. 'Diana tells me they were. I believed it would be different so far from Florence, but it seems I was wrong. I try to remain calm, but I would be much happier if she had a dog. It should be big enough to protect her, but not too big.'

'I shall start looking,' the older woman replied.

Diana was in the house when Signora Carducci arrived with a dog. Alessandra called her outside.

Diana looked at the dog and the dog at Diana.

'He is a Pastore Abruzzese,' Signora Carducci said, passing her the string. 'He's only nine months old and a little ungainly, his tail is broken, but don't worry, he will grow into himself.' The dog shuffled forward as if frightened of his own shadow, but he continued to look at Diana.

Alessandra was doubtful. 'We need a dog, not a scared lion.'

'I know he may be larger than you hoped, Signora, but he has a gentle nature. We use them to guard the sheep from the wolves. Give him a little time and he will be part of the family. Diana, he will protect you.'

'I'm sorry, but I don't want a dog!' Diana dropped the string and ran towards the house, leaving Signora Carducci and Alessandra staring after her.

'It's a pity,' Signora Carducci said at last. 'In time this dog would give his life for Diana. Perhaps, before I take him, you should give him time to make her love him. He comes from a village on the far side of the valley. The children beat him with sticks and broke his tail. I thought they would help each other.'

Alessandra raised her hands in frustration. 'It seems she has made up her mind, I apologise, Signora.'

'I believe Diana has a fear of loss, but she must learn to welcome life and all its tragedies.' She took the string and was halfway down the steps, dragging the reluctant dog, when Alessandra called her back.'

'He obviously wants to stay, let us give him a chance.'

Diana tried to ignore the dog, but he would not ignore Diana. When she shut him outside, he would sink to the floor, his eyes fixed on the door until it opened again, and if she went for a walk he followed behind, weaving round her heels.

'Go away, you gangly mutt,' she said, as he trailed after her, but the faster she walked, the faster he followed. She wouldn't allow herself to love him, not when her father's last promise had been to buy her a dog.

'This will be our secret, Diana,' he had said. 'First, I will have to persuade your mother,' but there was no longer any secret, and no dog from her father.

One night Diana woke to find the dog lying across the door to her bedroom. She took him downstairs and into the loggia. 'Stay,' she said, wagging her finger and he sank to the floor and lowered his head as if he had all the pain of the world on his furry shoulders. A flicker of a smile crossed Diana's face. 'No, you will not get into my heart,' she said firmly, but the dog could tell she was not firm and his broken tail began to swish from side to side.

When Davide did not appear at the bus stop after the Easter holidays, Diana stood with her foot on the step, willing him to come. She had been longing to see him, and her disappointment was like a physical blow. She looked at her watch and then down the long white road. There was no sign of him.

'There's no rush,' Pipo said, watching her. 'We'll wait for your young man.'

While the other occupants of the bus muttered their disapproval, Pipo pulled a dented tin from the pocket of his trousers and levered it open. Lighting a yellowing stub he leant against the bus and exhaled smoke rings into the sky.

Diana kicked at the dust. How easy to be Pipo, she thought, able to accept life with all its consequences, while her life was a series of turbulent emotions.

'Let's go Pipo, he's not coming.'

'There will be a reason, and a good one I'm sure.' Pipo shrugged his shoulders and flicked the stub into the dirt. He climbed back on after her.

Sister Maria was at her desk in the classroom when Diana ran in. As always, her habit was in slight disarray and the white coif of her wimple was loose around her forehead.

'Where is Davide?' Diana blurted, stopping in front of her. 'He wasn't on the bus, he is not at school. Something is wrong, I am sure of it.'

Sister Maria barely looked up.

'I know he is your friend, but I have to tell you: he is no longer at the school.' She closed one of the exercise books and went on to the next.

'No longer here?' Diana gripped onto the desk, remembering

another schoolroom, being told of another tragedy. 'He is not dead?'

'He is not dead, Diana.'

The nun put the last book on the pile and tapped them together in order. The sunlight slanted across her face, showing the wrinkles she had gathered in the convent gardens.

'My dear,' she said at last, 'I don't want you to think that he would go away without telling you. His family are Jews and it is not safe to be Jewish in Europe today.'

The chalked numbers on the blackboard spun before her eyes. 'Jewish? He can't be,' she whispered. 'He makes carvings for the church, he is Catholic.'

'His family's real name is Levi. They changed it when they left Bolzano.

'But they lived in Arezzo before they came here.'

'They had to leave there, too.'

A knife turned in Diana's chest. She was used to people from all nationalities and she didn't understand this madness.

'In Italy being Jewish has become dangerous,' Sister Maria said, interrupting her thoughts. 'You must have heard the whisperings, even here in Cortona. The Fascist police went to his father's house in Arezzo and ordered him to leave. Since the *Manifesto della razza* – the new race laws – Jews, they can no longer own property or hold professional positions, they have been stripped of their Italian citizenship. But Davide's family were victimised before the race laws even came into place. It's disgraceful.' She adjusted her wimple and cleared her throat. 'I don't understand either. To persecute someone because they are of a different faith is not God's way.'

'His family has been in Italy for generations, they are Italian.'

'Child, I would of course agree with you, but Mussolini wants to keep on the right side of Hitler and I am afraid it is not for us to get in the way of that.'

Sister Maria stood up. She put the books under her arm, dislodging her wimple even more.

'This is a private conversation and not to be repeated,' she said firmly. 'You must be discreet for the safety of Davide and his family. I know you are very fond of this young man but don't get too close. There will be no safety for the Jews, even in Italy.'

'But he is my friend. I would never desert him.'

'I know, Diana, but it is my duty to warn you. You will find him at his house in Mengaccini. At least in the countryside he is safe for a while.'

Sister Maria was halfway through the door when she turned. 'He had to leave the school, Diana, for his sake and for ours.'

The school bell rang, and Diana could hear footsteps running along the corridor outside, but in the classroom it was silent. She bit her lip, trying to remain calm, but her stomach was churning. Davide's family had lost everything and she hadn't even known. Religion was a subject they had never discussed and the fact that he didn't go to Mass at the convent was of no significance. There were twenty churches in Cortona alone; he could have gone to any of them.

She was waiting at the bus stop when she overheard a group of boys gossiping. The ringleader was Guido Tremonti, a pupil from the boys' school nearby.

'My father says the filthy Jew was sacked from the convent for thieving.'

Another boy piped up. 'Jews are like rats, they get everywhere.'

Diana was shaking with fury as she turned to face them. 'Davide had to leave because of people like you. You are ignorant, mean and despicable. You should be ashamed of yourselves.'

Some of the boys shuffled their feet and looked away. Guido Tremonti laughed.

'So the little English girl likes the Jew.'

'He is my friend,' she confirmed. 'In the same way that you are not!' With burning cheeks she moved to the end of the queue.

Chapter Ten

Diana climbed from the bus to find the white dog waiting for her. 'Shoo,' she said, but the dog trotted after her. At the bottom of the drive she hid her bag in the ditch. She had to see Davide.

She called to the dog and together they ran back down the lane. As she approached Davide's farmhouse she felt unsure. Would she be welcome? She had never been there before. She opened the garden gate. Davide was turning the soil in the vegetable garden, his back to her. She touched his arm and he whipped around.

'There's no place for you here, go away.'

She stepped back, shocked by his coldness.

'I thought we were friends.'

'Open your eyes, Diana. I'm a Jew I'm not allowed to have friends.' He rubbed his cheek, leaving a muddy streak and Diana took out her handkerchief and gently wiped it away. She put her arms around him.

'Davide, I don't care about any of that,' she assured him.

From her kitchen window Signora Angelini watched her son move into the arms of the English girl. She could see from the rise and fall of his shoulders that he was crying, and though her heart went out to him, she was also afraid. Outside the gate, she could see a large white dog panting in the heat, its eyes fixed on the girl. She picked up the polenta pan and scrubbed so hard that she brought a silvery shine to the inside not seen since she'd received it as a wedding present. *No good can come of this, Davide,* she thought. *Go home, Diana.* She brushed her hand across her eyes and hung the pan with her collection of pans she had imagined she would pass on to her daughter-in-law. But that was the least of her worries. Davide should be going to art school, the *Accademia delle Arte del Disegno.* How could a civilised nation ban the right to education? Why, when they had lived side by side with the Italians for centuries would they now turn against the Jews? But her Davide didn't look Jewish with his blond hair and a scattering of freckles across his nose. She remembered the comments in the synagogue, the whispered asides.

She stared at the English girl; she was pretty, with dark, curly hair and glowing skin. Of course her son only had eyes for her.

She sighed, recalling the little boy who had produced his first carving all those years ago.

'Go and play in the garden,' she had said impatiently. 'Look at the mess you've made. The kitchen is not a workshop, and don't use my best knives. That's another blade you've ruined. It takes your father days to earn just one of these knives.' Pushing the boy outside, she'd returned to clear up the table, only to find a small carving hidden among the shavings. Picking it up, she marvelled at the craftsmanship.

'He's got talent that boy, big talent,' she said to anyone who would listen.

By the time Davide was sixteen his carvings were exceptional.

'Well, who would have thought it?' her husband had commented on entering the church of San Domenico and seeing his son's first commission. 'His angels look just as an angel should look, and his saints look just like him.' That year she had given

Davide the roll of woodcarving tools she had been promising him. Back then, she had assumed that in another year he would begin his training as a sculptor at the top school in Florence. She wanted the best for him.

She recalled the moment eleven years earlier when her husband told her he wanted to leave their village in Northern Italy. He had arrived home early from work. This was not in itself a surprise; it was their anniversary and they were going to the little restaurant in the piazza to celebrate. But when he drew her into the small sitting room, she knew something was wrong.

'Rachel, my dear, I have something important to say. The growing unrest in Germany worries me.' He had sat down beside her on the long wooden settle, his eyes blinking behind his spectacles. He took them off and rubbed at the lenses. 'It seems that out of the dust of the Great War a new evil has emerged. Have you heard of this?' He took a book out of his pocket and tapped his slim fingers against the title: '*Mein Kampf*. Cousin Frank sent it to me.' She shook her head, but the tension in her stomach told her that this was something bigger than the book in her husband's hand.

'It's a memoir by Adolf Hitler. It blames the Jews for all of Europe's misfortunes. Hitler is using every possible means to turn the country against us. Trouble is coming.'

'It will pass, it always does. Everything will settle down. Frank is now manager at the bank in Berlin – nothing is going to happen to him.'

'I fear this man will become the voice of the people. They are fed up with poverty; they want a hero. I know it's asking a great deal, but for the sake of our children, for Lotti, Jaco and Davide we'll be safer away from here. Let's go south, a long way from Bolzano. Most of the people in this region speak in German;

they will also think in German. No, Rachel, I want my family as far from Germany as possible.'

'What about Mama?' she had cried, panic rising. 'We can't leave, Lotti is just a baby.'

'Rachel, I have never asked much of you. I have accepted certain things, but I'm asking this now. Listen to me, my dear. This Hitler will not go away.'

Looking into her husband's face, she had believed him, for he was wise and kind. It was true, he had never asked anything of her.

'We'll go,' she said, entering her husband's workshop a few days later. He was standing with his back to her, a visor protecting his eyes as he softened a small strip of gold on the burner. 'I'll ask Mama to come with us, but she'll never leave Bolzano.'

Turning off the burner he straightened and lifted his visor. 'Thank you, Rachel, it is the right decision and it is a chance for a new start. As a precaution, we should change our name. Angelini is a good name, after our son's beautiful carvings.'

On their arrival in Arezzo, they had walked up the steep hill that rose from the flood plains of the River Arno into the Piazza Grande and believed they had found their home. The medieval houses and palazzos had an air of affluence. As Signor Angelini looked from the sloping brick pavement beneath the Palazzo del Tribunale to the gracious loggia extending one side of the square, he felt sure the inhabitants would appreciate the work of a master goldsmith. The town would provide a good living and plenty of opportunities for his children.

'I think this will suit us, don't you agree?' he said, turning to his wife.

Rachel did agree: though different from Bolzano, where the peaks of the Southern Tyrol rose majestically above the towns and villages, and the mountain air was fresh and clean, Arezzo appeared to be the sort of town where she could raise her children in peace and prosperity.

They bought a house with money left to her by her father and with a small loan they made up the balance. In a short time Signor Angelini had an order book filled with commissions. His pieces were always finished on time, even if he had to work through the night to complete them. His name quickly spread among aristocrats and burghers alike who admired his Medici-influenced designs. There were rings set with cabochon rubies, fine golden crosses with delicate ornamentation, chalices set with precious stones, and silverware with heavily embossed crests. Before long three assistants found employment in his workshop and business was thriving.

When the first wave of anti-Semitism came to Arezzo, and their house was daubed with paint, Rachel went to her room and locked the door. They had left their family, their friends, her mother had died without the support of her daughter, and it was all for nothing. What would she tell her children? Lotti was six and too young for such things.

If her husband was frightened he didn't at first show it. 'It's just wayward boys, Rachel. They are letting off steam. Don't be concerned.'

But inside he knew better. He had felt the depths of the hate that was spreading across Europe and he had seen the hesitation in some of his clients' eyes. As his commissions dwindled, he was forced to face the truth. He had taken his wife and family away from everything familiar, but the place they had settled had not been the sanctuary he had promised.

After replacing the broken glass in the *salotto* window for the fifth time, his confidence in the citizens of Arezzo had gone. His wife was frightened and his children were confused.

When only a short while later a loud rap on the door disturbed his sleep, he got out of bed and gathered his clothes. He dressed on the landing, all the time aware of the voices outside. The rap came again. Two Fascist police were standing on the doorstep.

'Your house is required,' they told him.

'Signore, my workshop is part of my house. I can't let my patrons down.'

'Your patrons will have to look for another goldsmith, one that's not a Jew. You need to be out of here tomorrow.'

As he closed the door behind them he could hear their laughter ringing down the street.

When the first light broke through the curtains, he went to his workshop and gathered up his tools. He sank onto his stool and gazed around the empty workbenches. *I shall remember this day*, he thought.

'Was it our door they were knocking at?' Rachel demanded, coming into the workshop later that day. 'And where are your tools?'

Signor Angelini spread his hands. 'I'm sorry, my dear, but we have to leave Arezzo.'

She started to cry. 'Not again, please not again.'

Signor Angelini put his arm around his wife's shoulders.

'One of my customers has offered us his empty house in a hamlet not far from Cortona. We'll be safe there, my dear, and we'll be back before you know it.'

At the sound of footsteps Signora Angelini was drawn out of her memories of the past. She could hear the girl's voice.

'Would you introduce me to your mother, I would like to meet her.'

She opened the door. 'Come inside, you must be hot.' She took the lemonade from the larder, removed the muslin from the jug, and poured them each a glass.

Davide spoke first. 'This is Diana.'

'I had guessed.'

'How lovely to meet you, Signora. Davide has told me all about your family.'

'Davide should be in art school now.' Signora Angelini's shoulders sagged. 'And as for my poor husband...'

'I've heard his work is exceptional. Are those candlesticks made by him?'

Signora Angelini followed Diana's gaze to the seven-branched candlesticks on the sideboard. 'They are,' she agreed. 'But they are simple in comparison to many of his designs. Would you like to see them?'

'I'd like that very much,' Diana replied.

Signora Angelini returned to the room carrying a large folder.

'This one he made for a duke,' she said, showing Diana a drawing of a silver stag with a full set of antlers. 'And this was for a merchant.' As Signora Angelini turned the pages, the knot in her stomach eased. The girl was clearly a nice girl and though not Jewish, she obviously had a special place in her son's heart.

'One day, Signora, his work will be known again,' Diana murmured when Signora Angelini had closed the final page.

Diana was walking down the path when Davide ran after her.

'Thank you for being kind to Mama.' He put his hand on her arm and she could feel the warmth of his fingers through her thin blouse.

'You don't need to thank me,' she whispered.

'*Veramente*, I do.'

She pulled her eyes from his face, and with the dog at her heels she ran through the gate.

She was halfway up the drive when she stopped to catch her breath. No one had ever been scared of her before and yet Signora Angelini's hands were shaking as she leafed through her husband's drawings. She picked up a fallen branch and hurled it into the ditch. Davide was better than anyone she had met, and his mother seemed gentle and intelligent. How could the authorities take away a man's dignity? How could such bigotry exist in a modern world?

Much later Diana was lying in bed. The scent of jasmine wafted through the open window and 'The Lark Ascending' was playing on the gramophone downstairs. The atmosphere was tranquil, peaceful, and yet in a house nearby, the man she now knew that she was in love with was being hounded because of his religion. She closed her eyes and turned her face to the wall.

'Please God,' she prayed, as tears slipped down her face. 'Protect Davide and his family and end this hatred. Make people realise that Hitler's words are poison. Stop this before it is too late.'

She opened her eyes as her door creaked open. First a black nose appeared, followed by a large white head. The dog padded towards her and held out his paw. When he was not rejected, he climbed up and rested his head on her arm, his brown eyes watching her. Diana put out her hand and buried it in the deep fur of his neck.

The dog gained two things that week, a name and a bath.

'I will not have that smelly mutt in my house,' Alessandra exclaimed the following morning. 'It either has a bath or it stays outside.'

Diana pulled down an old tin bath from the attic and put it into the loggia, and with Sofia's help, they bathed him.

'Nico,' Diana announced, when the dog was covered in a frothy white lather. 'He looks like a Nico.'

'He is ridiculous,' Sofia replied. 'But yes, Nico is a good name.'

The dog looked at them indignantly. With a leap he dived

from the bath, and shook his great white body. The girls were showered with water and soap, and before they had time to stop him, Nico sloped into the garden and rolled in the dust.

Chapter Eleven

In early summer of 1938 Alessandra was changing the chapel flowers when she heard Signora Carducci cry out.

She ran back to the house to find the older woman clutching her arm.

'It's a wretched hornet, it has stung me, Signora.'

Alessandra could see her arm had already started to swell and there was a sheen of sweat on Signora Carducci's brow.

'Come, do sit down,' she said. 'And I'll get some ice.'

She took some ice from the refrigerator tray and hurried back to Signora Carducci. 'I told you the refrigerator would be useful,' she said, wrapping a tea towel filled with ice around the older woman's arm. 'All that fuss when I bought it.'

'Pah,' Signora Carducci grimaced. 'Since the beginning of time we have lived without one, so why would we need it now?'

'For just this reason!'

When Signora Carducci went grey and the jesting stopped, Alessandra was concerned.

'I'm going to call for the doctor just in case. Better still, I will take you to Cortona in the car. I'll ask Dario to fetch it.'

'But you have only just bought the car. Can you drive?'

Alessandra was not sure whether Signora Carducci found the prospect of her driving, or the hornet's sting more vexing.

'Of course I can,' she lied.

With Dario's help, she bundled her into the new car and they set off down the drive. Alessandra found the gears particularly troublesome.

'I think you have been fibbing to me,' Signora Carducci panted when they stalled for the third time.

'All right,' Alessandra finally admitted. 'I can sort of drive, don't you remember I had a lesson in Cortona?'

'But it was one lesson, and months ago.'

'It's like riding a bike, you never forget!'

'Merciful heaven, you will kill us, Signora,' the older woman replied.

They arrived at the doctor's house in Cortona to find their doctor was away.

'Don't worry,' the old woman behind the desk reassured them, 'Doctor Biochetti from Arezzo is covering today.'

In less than a moment a doctor came towards them. He was tall, with thick hair that was greying at the temples.

'*Buona sera,*' he said. 'Please come in to the surgery.'

He took a magnifying glass from the desk and examined the sting, and Alessandra couldn't help noticing his hands. They were wider than Anthony's but they were nice hands none the less.

'The worst is already over.' He raised his eyes, and she noticed they were brown, unlike her husband's. 'Give her one of these pills tonight and one in the morning, and your mother will be fine.

'The Signora is not my daughter.' Signora Carducci glared at the Doctor. 'This is the Signora *Inglese* from the Villa Durante.'

'*Mi dispiace,*' he apologised to Alessandra and handed her a small bottle. When their hands touched, she blushed.

'It is no problem at all, Dottore. Thank you.' When Alessandra helped a grumbling Signora Carducci back into the car, she was smiling.

That night, Alessandra thought of the doctor. He was charming, definitely, and his voice was reassuring. It was a good voice. Alessandra bit her lip and turned out the light. The doctor was efficient, certainly, but nothing more.

Later she got out of bed and went to the window. The moon was a silver crescent in the sky and she remembered Anthony holding her in his arms on a night just like this in Paris.

'One day a man will go to the moon,' he had said, and she had laughed.

'Why?'

'Humankind testing its limits, but it won't happen in our lifetime.'

'Thank goodness for that,' she had replied, and they had returned to the hotel and he had made love to her with the moon shining through the curtains.

She closed the window. How she missed a man in her life; her reaction to the doctor was merely that of a lonely woman.

*

A cool breeze blew into the loggia from the meadow, slightly breaking the heat of the August day. Alessandra could hear the clatter of the cicadas and smell the baked earth. It struck her as a dichotomy, that extraordinary beauty and staggering cruelty could coexist in one place.

She picked up her daughter's half-finished plate and stacked it with her own.

'You should eat.'

Diana looked up. There were dark shadows beneath her eyes. 'Davide can't get a job because of the race laws. He's hard-working and talented, first school, and now this. He wouldn't even come on my birthday, he's so angry, Mama.'

Alessandra worried for her daughter, and for Davide. But the persecution wasn't confined to the Jews. The Roma, homosexuals, communists, all were now hounded by the Fascist regime. Any country where Hitler had influence was affected.

Carefully worded letters from Robert told her the news from home. England was ill-prepared for war, and worse for invasion. Her chest tightened as she returned to the loggia with a bowl of fruit. She pushed the bowl towards her daughter. 'Perhaps I can help. Ask him to come and see me next week. I'll offer him a job here.' Diana scraped her chair backwards and ran to her mother.

'Don't get excited, De, he may not want our help. He seems a proud young man.'

'He'll take it. His brother and sister fight all day. His father shuts himself away in his workshop, but I know he's not working.'

'I will try to convince Davide that my offer is not out of charity but because we need him.'

Diana threw her arms around her mother's neck and hugged her. 'Are you sure we can afford it?'

'No, but we shall find the money from somewhere.'

'You are the best.'

'Really?' Alessandra raised her eyebrows.

'Truly, Mama, thank you. You know how much this means to me.'

Alessandra smiled. 'Of course I do,' she replied.

Alessandra was looking through a sheaf of invoices when Davide walked across the terrace towards her.

'Come and sit down,' she said, gesturing towards a chair.

Davide took off his hat, twisting the brim between his fingers. 'Forgive me Signora, but I am not sure why I am here.'

'Diana has told me of your family situation,' she said. 'I'm sorry. I know you were going to study art, and this will be very different, but could you work for us here? I will pay you what I can.' As she looked at him she thought of another young man, her son.

'No, Signora.' He looked at her, the pain making his eyes darker. 'You don't need to offer me work.'

'This isn't out of charity, Davide. We really could do with more help. Signor Innocenti isn't getting any younger, and though he would never admit it, the milking at four o'clock in the morning is too much for him. If you take the position, you can live in the small flat above the barn. It requires a little fixing, but you will manage, I'm sure.'

'If it is true that you need me, then I welcome the opportunity.'

'We are hoping to plant another six hectares with vines. There is more work than we can cope with. Are you interested in wine, Davide?'

'I know only a little, Signora, but I am happy to learn.'

'Well then, you will find a good teacher in Signor Innocenti'.

Observing the attractive and thoughtful young man in front of her, Alessandra could understand why Diana was determined to help him. She stood up. '*Arrivederci*,' she said, holding out her hand, 'and thank you for coming. Shall we say you start next Monday?'

That night Alessandra took the diary from the drawer in the sitting room. The pages were filling fast.

'Today, my beloved, I have probably been foolish, but I believe you would have done the same. I have taken on an assistant for Signor Innocenti. The young man is educated and handsome, and our daughter is in love with him, but I am filled with conflicting emotions. I will be throwing them together and she is not seventeen, surely too

young to be thinking in terms of children and marriage. There is another reason I have employed him. I feel powerless in the face of Hitler and in some small way, by helping one Jew, I am showing my own hatred and defiance of the prejudice threatening to engulf us all.

With my love and devotion always, and until the next time.

Your loving wife, Alessandra

Chapter Twelve

On his first day at the Villa Durante, Davide had a lesson on vine management from Signor Innocenti.

'You will treat them like children,' the old man said. 'Nourish them and they will flourish, neglect them and they will fail. These shoots we cut, and these we leave behind. Now, take up your hoe and clean between the vines.'

Diana watched Davide in the vineyard learning his new tasks.

'So it seems I am teaching you too,' Signor Innocenti said with a smile.

Signor Innocenti quickly observed Davide's affinity with animals, and it was not long before the Villa's cow, Rosa, along with the two oxen, were added to his responsibilities. The work was hard but Davide found an inner peace working in the quiet of the barn and a sense of achievement as he mastered the art of milking. He welcomed the distraction of work and being close to Diana.

One evening the milking was interrupted when he felt her presence.

'You startled me,' he said, jumping to his feet, nearly tipping over the pail of frothy milk.

'I didn't mean to,' she replied. 'Sofia suggested I should learn to milk Rosa, in case...'

'In case of what, Diana?' Davide was looking at her intently.

'In case you left us.'

'I have no intention of leaving you. Unless of course the world changes and I can go to art school, become a man you would be proud of.'

'It doesn't matter what you do, Davide, I would always be proud of you.'

'It matters to me.'

Diana could feel his frustration. She put her hand on his arm. 'One day you will go to art school, but for now you are safe here.'

'I am not sure that I am safe anywhere.' His words were bleak and Diana wished she could protect him.

She sat down on the small stool. 'Teach me,' she said.

Davide wedged himself behind her. He took her hands and placed them on Rosa's warm udder, rhythmically drawing the milk. Diana was conscious of Davide's breath on her neck, his body moulded against her, and his voice in her ear.

'There is no more,' he said, when the last drop was squeezed into the bucket. 'So now you know how to milk Rosa, and my job is done.'

Diana smiled shyly. 'But you may have to teach me again.'

The weeks flew past and Diana longed for the summer holidays when she would leave school for ever.

She was chopping tomatoes in the kitchen with Sofia when the older girl put down her knife and gazed outside.

'Look.' She elbowed Diana. 'Davide is scything the grass.'

Diana looked through the window to see Davide in the meadow, his shirt discarded nearby.

'I'm looking,' she breathed.

'He is handsome, no?'

'Oh yes, he is, Sofia.' She started to giggle and Sofia laughed with her. Alessandra came in to see what the commotion was about.

'Oh, I see,' she said, trying to keep a straight face. 'Have neither of you seen a young man without his shirt before?'

'Not one that looks like that,' Sofia replied.

Soon after starting at the Villa Durante, Davide's new quarters above the barn were ready. The two rooms smelt of hay and beeswax and the lavender bags Sofia had given him. He fell back on the mattress his mother had made and felt comforted by its softness. He remembered teasing her as she had stuffed it, the feathers flying around their kitchen in Mengaccini. 'Mama, you put more feathers in the air than you do in my mattress.'

'I will not have my son sleep on a hard bed wherever you are,' she had said, and though she had laughed, he had known how difficult it was for her to watch her son doing agricultural work instead of fulfilling his dreams. He reflected on the new life he was having. In a few months the sun would go and he wondered how it would be in the winter ahead and where his future lay? Would Diana be part of it? Though everything else had been taken from him, he was still allowed to dream.

Diana was composing a letter to her brother when she heard Davide's voice beneath her window.

'Come for a walk?' he called. 'It's a beautiful evening.'

'Yes, I'd love to.' Diana pulled on her favourite shawl, grabbed her hat and ran downstairs and into the sunshine, Nico following at her heels.

'Nico,' Diana called, as he charged towards the lake.

'You love that dog,' Davide observed.

'Of course.' She looked up at him. 'Though I didn't mean to.'

'Well then he is clever to find a way to your affections.'

'He is devoted to me, it would be impossible not to love him.'

'Does that apply to humans as well as dogs?' Davide was teasing her now and Diana felt herself blush.

'Come on,' he said. 'I'll race you to the top of the meadow.'

Diana took the challenge and ran like the wind. She crossed the dry streambed, scrambled through the coppice, racing through the rough grass, on and on, up through the meadow, every muscle in her body taut with exertion. Her lungs were bursting, but she kept on going. When they reached the top, they both fell together in the long grass.

'I definitely won,' she laughed.

'You like to win, Diana?'

'I do,' she replied laughing, her eyes teasing, 'doesn't any girl?'

Davide raised himself on his elbow and looked down on her. She was lying beneath him, her chest rising and falling, her mouth open with laughter. He longed to kiss her flushed face, bury his lips in her neck; the thought of it kept him awake at night. He wanted her love as he had never wanted anything before. He leant towards her and was about to kiss her when he drew back. It was too soon, he mustn't rush her. He sat up and Diana pulled herself up beside him. The sun was setting behind the distant hills and the sky had turned from pink to a deep purple.

'Do you see those vines?' He pointed to the distant hill where the young vines had been planted. 'They are the future. They will bring prosperity, and with good fortune, a label that your mother will be proud of.'

Diana turned towards him and suddenly nothing mattered but the beating of his heart and the longing he felt. He pulled her to her feet. His lips brushed her hair and he put his hands around her waist. He couldn't wait any longer; he had to kiss her. He had to know if she loved him. He could feel the warmth of her body against him, and as she lifted her face, her lips slightly parted, he knew it was the moment he had been waiting for.

'Diana, where are you?' Her mother's voice echoed through the meadow.

Davide pulled away; he could see the disappointment in her eyes and he could feel his own blood pounding. 'Your mother is calling.'

'She is,' Diana replied.

'Well then,' he said lifting a strand of hair from her face, kissing her forehead. 'I had better take you home.'

Chapter Thirteen

The summer of 1938 was drawing to a close when the winds came. They started in the trees, the leaves rustling gently, and swelled like waves breaking on the beach. Alessandra stood on the terrace. She watched her vines with their plump grapes stirring. For the first time in months, she felt helpless. If the crop wasn't ready and the rains came it would ruin in a matter of hours.

Below her, Signor Innocenti pushed his hat to the back of his head and reached for a grape. The farm workers were silent, the women and children were silent. Everything rested on his opinion. Lifting the grape to his mouth, he looked at his audience. It was his moment, as it had been his father's before him. With a flourish he swept the grape into his mouth. Millimetre by millimetre a smile spread across his face, deepening the lines around his eyes. 'We are ready to harvest,' he announced. 'This will be our finest year.'

Now the Vendemmia truly began. The grape harvest was the most important event of the year. Men and woman armed with secateurs toiled in the sun. There was an easterly wind to cool them and they worked quickly and efficiently.

When the first tub was filled to overflowing, Davide heaved it onto his shoulders and returned it to the wagon. As the sun moved round, he brought the oxen into the shade. Diana filled her basket, conscious of him working beside her, of his long fingers as he cut the grapes, his strong back as he turned away. How she longed to put her arms around his waist, lean against him as she had done in the barn... When he came towards her with a flagon of water, her stomach fluttered and she could hardly breathe. She tried to keep her gaze steady. 'How is my girl from the city?' he teased.

'I can't imagine going back. This is my life now.' It was true, it had become her life; she loved the rolling hills, the baked earth, the very smell of it, and of course she loved Davide.

It was late afternoon when they finished the first day's picking. Men and women collected their belongings as they moved away from the lines.

'Even Mussolini would be glad of such a crop,' Diana laughed, as she picked up her basket.

Davide stopped in front of her, blocking out the sun. 'How can you mention Mussolini after my hard day's work for your mother? He has turned us out of our home, taken everything.'

'I didn't mean it, Davide. I'm sorry. Is that better?'

'Better? Are you serious? Nothing can make it better, Diana, unless of course you can tell your friend Mussolini to stand up to Hitler and stop tormenting the Jews.'

Diana looked away, but not before he had seen the tears in her eyes.

'I'm sorry.' He lifted her chin and brushed a tear away with his finger. 'That was mean of me. I have no right to take my anger out on you.'

'And I was stupid and insensitive. I hope you will forgive me.'

'I could never be cross with you for long.'

*

99

Davide was releasing the oxen into the meadow when Diana ran towards him. Her hair curled in sweaty tendrils at her neck and her face was flushed from the sun.

'Davide, I have an idea, please will you take me to Florence? I want to see the sculptures from the book you gave me, and I want to see them with you.'

'How can I, Diana? The word *Jew* is stamped on my papers. I am like these oxen, branded!'

'Don't say that. Besides, look at your blond hair, they would never check your papers.'

'Your mother would never let us. No, it is impossible, Diana.'

'Nothing is impossible if you want it badly enough. My father taught me that.' Diana's hand was on his arm and she was looking up at him. 'I want to spend the day with you. Please?'

Davide laughed. Of course it was foolish, mad even, but he couldn't resist the chance to spend the day with her.

'I suppose there is no harm in asking.'

Diana was jubilant. A day in Florence with Davide – she would make it happen; she would make her mother see the sense of it. She skipped away before he could change his mind.

'Don't tell my father,' he called after her.

Preparations for the festa that marked the end of the Vendemmia began. All day Diana toiled in the kitchen with Sofia. They made omelettes with black truffles; tortellini with spinach and ricotta, stuffed peppers and zucchini. When the last pepper was filled, she found a space on the larder shelf and went upstairs. Leaning out of the bathroom window she breathed deeply. Now she would dress for Davide.

Diana got out of the bath and pulled a towel around her shoulders. Opening her mother's cupboard she searched for one dress in particular – pale blue organza with small pearl buttons that ran down the front. It had been a gift from her father to her mother on their honeymoon. Tonight she was allowed to wear it.

She laid it on the bed and touched the soft fabric. She would look pretty and sophisticated, and she would impress Davide. She stepped into the dress and did up the buttons one by one, but they strained across her chest. Her disappointment was overwhelming.

Why couldn't she have her mother's figure? Why did her mother have everything? She undid the top two buttons and though not a perfect fit, the effect was pleasing and perhaps a little seductive. She turned this way and that, and the fabric floated around her. She chastised herself. Of course her mother didn't have everything, the man she loved more than anything in the world had been taken from her.

Davide was putting a match to the bonfire when Diana emerged from the house half an hour later. He was wearing dark trousers and a crisp white shirt. The sky was darkening, and light from the lanterns cast shadows across his cheeks.

'You look pretty,' he said softly.

'Thank you,' she replied. 'I hoped you would notice,' she added with a blush.

'I always notice,' Davide replied.

Alessandra was welcoming the guests when Diana approached. She turned around. 'Diana . . .' she breathed, her words hanging in the air. Her younger self was standing there in the dress Anthony had bought her in Paris. But Diana was curvaceous, seductive, more womanly.

She remembered the shop – a tiny boutique in the Latin Quarter. Anthony had pulled her inside.

'This is the dress,' he had said, finding it among the rails. 'Try it on,' and he had followed her into the cubicle.

'You shouldn't be here,' she scolded him.

'Why not?' he had laughed, kissing her lips, drawing her close, closing the curtain behind her.'

When they emerged from the cubicle, flushed and breathless a short while later, the young girl at the till had taken their money, commented on the weather, and wished them all the fortune in the world.

Alessandra held her hands out to her daughter. 'You look wonderful,' she said.

Over Diana's shoulder, she could see Davide waiting at the top of the drive. 'I think you need to go to your young man,' she murmured, releasing her daughter. 'It appears his parents haven't arrived.'

And Diana was gone, running through the grass to his side.

'They aren't here?' she asked touching his sleeve.

'They have obviously changed their minds.' His eyes clouded as he watched the children playing. 'It would have been fun for Lotti and Jaco. It's my father, of course. He's a shy man, not good in crowds.'

'Well then,' she said. 'We'll ask your family another time.'

Barely an inch of the tablecloths was visible. Bottles of wine wrapped in raffia were squeezed between the dishes – wines from previous years that had been saved for this special occasion. Dario had shot a wild boar and was roasting it on the spit.

When everyone was seated Alessandra toasted Signor Innocenti, Signor Innocenti toasted the Signora and the celebrations began. The feasting was barely finished when he reached beneath the table for his accordion. 'My favourite ballad!' he announced. 'And then, the moment you wait for, the dance!'

He ran his fingers over the keys, and at once the air was filled with his rich, baritone voice. Dario joined in on the fiddle, with his two small boys jumping around him.

Diana had finished her plate of tortellini and was on her

second glass of wine when she leant over to her mother. 'Will you forgive me?' she asked.

'What for?'

'For being difficult. I can see how hard it was for you to leave Robert, but you were right to bring us. Everything has changed, and though I still miss him dreadfully, and Grandpa Peter, I love it here, Mama.'

'Is Davide part of this everything?'

'Sort of.' Diana smiled.

'There is nothing to forgive. Well … Perhaps there is a little.' Alessandra reached for her daughter's hand. Inside she was elated and relieved but these feelings were mixed with concern. It seemed Diana was growing up and she was finding her own happiness.

Soon the estate workers, the children and even Alessandra were dancing inside the circle of lanterns. Nico took the opportunity to steal an entire omelette, and while the children chased the dog, Davide and Diana moved into the circle. With the bonfire flickering behind them, Diana laid her head on Davide's shoulder. As the music got faster her body grew languid. It was a dream, she thought, leaning against him, that she didn't want to end.

'I didn't think I could feel joy again,' Davide whispered into her hair. 'But when I'm with you, everything is different.'

'When I am with you, I am different,' she replied.

Alessandra was on her way to the kitchen, her hands full of plates, when she saw her daughter in the arms of Davide. She stopped. It was not just their proximity that troubled her, but the look on her daughter's face. Each day the plight of the Jews grew more desperate. She could see only trouble ahead.

*

The following afternoon Alessandra had returned to the house after inspecting a new plantation with Signor Innocenti, when a small boy approached. He had wide brown eyes in an elfin face. She recognised him immediately as one of the Avorio boys.

'Hello, young man,' she said. 'Have you come to see me?'

The boy inched his way towards her, embracing a terracotta pot containing an olive tree. Though the tree was in fact quite small, it seemed huge in his arms. With a big sigh, he put it on the floor.

'My Grandma asked me to bring this, to thank you for last night. She says you are always good to us, even though you are a little strange.'

Alessandra wanted to laugh but she kept a straight face. 'Well thank you. It's Carlo, isn't it? Shall I plant your tree beneath my window, so that every time I look at it I will be reminded of you?'

The boy nodded and smiled, showing the gaps in his teeth. 'Thank you, Signora. I am very proud.'

Alessandra watched him as he skipped back down the drive and she felt like skipping herself. A gesture like this meant everything to her. She may seem strange to these hard-working, impoverished farmers, but she must be doing something right.

Sofia was singing as Diana entered the hall. Nico sank to his haunches.

'He likes your voice,' Diana laughed.

'I sing a Puccini aria and you interrupt me to talk about your dog. *Dio*, have you learnt nothing? And please take that filthy blanket from his mouth before I burn it. I'll not have it in my kitchen.'

'You know he loves it,' Diana laughed.

'And take him away too.' Sofia wiped her face with her forearm. 'I have a letter for you, it's in my pocket but my hands are covered in flour.'

Diana retrieved the letter from the pocket of Sofia's skirt.

'From your handsome brother?' she asked.

'You haven't even met him.'

'He looks good in the photograph,' she replied.

Diana threw herself onto the grass outside and tore open the envelope.

'*My Dearest De, I have something to tell you.*' She sat up again, her heart quickening.

*After Christmas I have an interview with the Royal Air
Force. I am hoping to become a fighter pilot, but please don't
worry, the chances of my being accepted are small. If Papa
were alive today he would support my decision. I hope you
will too. Please don't tell Mother just yet; this must be our
secret. Remember, you and I have always shared secrets.*

    Your loving brother always.

    Robert.

Diana buried her face in her hands. She couldn't bear it. She had lost her father and now she would lose Robert. How could he do this to them? It was selfish and stupid. Millions had died in the last war, but it hadn't ended anything and Robert was asking her to support his decision before war had even been declared. He would be one of the first to go, one of the first to die. Well she wouldn't accept it. She would write to him immediately. She read the letter again and screwed the paper into a ball, hurling it into the meadow. Nico ran after it and brought it back to her. That night she wrote to her brother.

Darling Robs,

*If you die I shall die, so just remember that when you are
playing aeroplanes. And how am I meant to keep this from
Mama? What a ridiculous request, she'll only have to look at*

me to realise something is wrong. I beg of you to reconsider and think of your family. We already know that you are brave so you have nothing to prove to us. When the war comes there will be plenty of time to fight, but it has not come yet.

Your sister Diana
One kiss only.

Chapter Fourteen

It was five o'clock, and the morning of her trip to Florence with Davide. Diana threw off the bedclothes and went to the window. Mist shrouded the valley, muffling the sounds of dawn. A small light glowed in the barn nearby.

Had Davide slept, she wondered, or like her had he tossed and turned all night with a mixture of apprehension and excitement?

She dressed quickly, put a disgruntled Nico in with her mother and went downstairs.

She had eaten breakfast and was tying her hair in a velvet ribbon, when she turned to see Davide standing in the doorway, his broad shoulders filling the frame.

'*Buongiorno*, Diana,' he said, his voice soft. 'And are you ready for Firenze?'

Diana's heart turned over and she could only nod in reply.

They climbed onto the bus to Camucia, for their onward journey by train. After Diana had greeted Pipo, Davide followed her down the aisle to find a seat at the back. She was wearing a blouse printed with forget-me-nots, and a white cotton skirt. He longed to reach out his hand, pull the ribbon from her hair, stroke the soft skin untouched by the sun. He wanted to tell her of his love but he couldn't find the words. Outside a buzzard floated on the thermals, feathers dazzling in the bright morning light, but today even this didn't absorb him; he could only think of the pressure of her body against him, the smell of jasmine on her skin.

When the bus reached its destination, he jumped down and took Diana's hand, for though the expedition to Florence was a mad idea, he had a whole day with Diana in one of the most romantic cities in the world.

After Davide had bought the tickets, they boarded the train and pushed their way through the corridor. It was heaving. Priests in brown robes jostled with noisy children on a school outing. There were farmers, businessmen and soldiers. It seemed to Diana the whole world was converging on Florence. At last they found a place in one of the closed carriages. Diana sat beside an old woman with her head bent to her sewing. Davide sat opposite, next to her husband. When she ran out of thread, Diana offered to get her some more from the suitcase in the rack above her.

'No, it is not necessary.' The old woman glanced at the bulging suitcase, her eyes darting in fear. 'Besides, I have some in my bag.' She produced some white cotton and tried to thread the needle. When she failed, Diana intervened.

'Your work is beautiful,' she observed, handing back the needle.

'Ah,' the old woman sighed. 'It was a tablecloth for the Sabbath, but what use is it now?' She glanced at Diana, her eyes filled with despair, the same look that Diana had seen in Davide's eyes.

They were nearing Florence when a guard from the railway militia came into the carriage. 'Papers please,' he demanded, stopping in front of Diana.

She fumbled in her bag, fear blooming in her stomach. Her mother had warned her. She was right, of course; Davide may well be in danger. He could be taken away. She squared her shoulders. 'I think you will find them in order.' She smiled flirtatiously, encouraging him to look at her.

'You are in order,' he replied, his eyes lingering on her breasts. When he moved on to the elderly woman, his smile had gone. 'Are these yours?' He pointed to the suitcases in the rack above.

'No, they are mine.' Diana stood up. The guard's face was inches from her own – so close that she reeled from the sour smell of him, but she couldn't back away.

'And what are you doing in Florence?'

'It is my cousin's wedding on the second,' she replied.

The only sound in the carriage was the guard tapping his baton against his black boot. The seconds ticked by.

'So your cousin is getting married on a Sunday?'

'I mean the first. As you can see from my luggage, I am staying a few days.'

The guard looked up at the suitcases, and back at Diana. She held her breath.

'Have a good wedding,' he said, handing back the old woman's papers. He left without a glance at Davide.

When he had gone, Diana's legs gave way and she started to tremble. She sank into the seat and the old woman squeezed her hand.

'*Grazie mille*, thank you a thousand times.'

'You are crazy,' Davide leant towards her, 'but you have done a good thing today, Diana.'

'She certainly has,' the old woman's husband replied.

When the train arrived in Florence, Davide lifted their cases from the rack above, and carried them down the steps. He shook the old man's hand. 'Good luck,' he said. 'And good fortune.'

The old woman turned to Diana.

'Again I thank you and God bless.' She pressed the tablecloth into her hands. 'I want you to have this. It is for you and your young man, so you can remember this day.'

'I can't take it, it is too much.'

'Where I am going, I will not need it. You shall have it, my dear.' She then signalled to her husband. 'Come quickly,' and they were gone, dragging their bags along the platform. Diana called after them, but the old woman and her husband were hurrying away.

After examining the exquisitely embroidered tablecloth, Diana folded it carefully and put it in her bag. She turned to Davide. 'Where will they go?'

'I have no idea but I hope they have a plan.' He stroked her cheek with his finger. 'My dear little Diana, you mustn't be sad, for today is our special day and I will not let anything get in the way.' He grabbed her hand and together they ran along the Via Panzani and into Via de Cerretini. By the time they reached the Piazza Duomo and the Baptistry, they were hot and breathless.

He pulled her through the bronze doors and into the dimly lit interior. 'Forget the Fascists, forget Mussolini. Today it is just you and me.'

They stopped in front of a wooden sculpture. Diana recognised it immediately. 'Mary Magdalene by Donatello, one of the most important treasures in Florence,' she breathed.

'So my Diana has remembered. She is beautiful, no?' Davide was silent, waiting for her reaction, but for that moment Diana was aware only of his proximity, of his lips almost brushing her shoulder, his low voice.

'She certainly moves me,' she said at last, trying to concentrate. 'But I would not say she is beautiful.'

'That attribute, little Diana, is in the eye of the beholder.' Diana could feel the warmth of his breath on her cheek.

They crossed the short distance from the Baptistry to the Duomo. Diana sat down on the steps beside Davide.

He pointed at a group of tourists, his expression changing.

'They take photographs as if everything is normal. Don't they know what is coming?'

'We are no different, Davide. We are all trying to enjoy ourselves. We have to, don't you see?'

Davide laughed. 'I don't know how you put up with me.'

'Put up with you? I …' The colour rose in her cheeks and she jumped to her feet. 'Come on, let's go inside.'

Davide steered her to a life-size statue of Mary and Jesus, with Nicodemus and Mary Magdalene. 'Michelangelo's Florentine Pietà,' he said, his fingers brushing the marble. 'His first Pietà was commissioned for St Peter's in Rome, but this was meant to decorate his tomb. Can you imagine, he worked on it for eight years, then he discovered an impurity in the marble, and tried to destroy it.'

Diana touched the scars left by Michaelangelo. 'You see this in terms of the marble,' she said softly, turning to Davide, her eyes not leaving his face. 'I see only Christ lying dead in his mother's arms.'

'I understand his passion for sculpting, it is the artist in me.'

'And I see only loss, and that is the woman in me.'

He lifted her hand to his lips. 'I thought everything was finished, but you have given me hope, Diana, I can take anything if you are beside me.'

She looked up at him, her expression changing. 'I'll remember that,' she said.

After buying her mother a silk scarf in the Mercato Nuovo, they found a *trattoria* off the Piazza della Signoria. As they sat in the shade, eating linguini and drinking red wine, the hours slipped away. Diana had finished her second glass when she leant forward.

'I shouldn't be telling you,' she whispered a little too loudly, 'but Robert is joining the Air Force. I begged him not to. I'm so afraid.'

'He's a man now, Diana, you have to let him go.' Davide was looking at her intently.

Diana twisted the stem of her glass, 'I've lost my father and now I could lose my brother.'

'Don't try to hold him back because of your father's death.'

She looked up at Davide. 'Every day I want to tell him what I'm doing. I feel this awful pain and I can't believe it's still here after all this time.' She rested her hand on his arm, liberated by the wine and the sunshine and the warm feeling that ran through her. 'And I am sad that he never met you.'

'But he may not have approved.'

'Papa? Of course he would,' she replied.

Davide paid the bill and took her hand. 'Come on,' he said. 'There is something I want to show you.' Diana followed unsteadily; everything had become a little blurred and her head was spinning. At the end of the Piazza he stopped in front of the nude statue of David.

'How can any man compare?' he whispered, and Diana gazed upwards, taking in each contour of the marble. Davide was letting her know that he wanted her and she was conscious of the tension between them.

'Let's go,' he said at last. 'It is time to take you home, we must remember your mother's instructions.' But Diana's heart sank because the day was nearly over. He stopped in front of the church of Santa Maria Novella. 'Is that not a beautiful name?' he laughed softly. 'They have even named the station after it. There is no time today, but I will take you there.' He hugged her close and almost breathed the words into her hair.

They were nearly at the station when Diana froze. The star of David had been daubed on the front of a house, the red paint bleeding down the wall. She grabbed Davide's hand and tried to pull him down the street, but he sensed her distress and turned around. For a moment he stared at the wall and then at Diana.

'So you really want to be with me?' he asked, his blue eyes boring into her.

'More than ever,' she stated simply. But she wanted to weep. She remembered the demonstration in London on their way back to the airport, Douglas hunched by the window. It seemed that bigotry and hatred was everywhere. But she wouldn't let it spoil everything, couldn't let it.

She stood on tiptoe, her face so close to his and kissed him on the mouth. 'So now do you believe me?' she asked.

They boarded the train with only minutes to spare. The carriage was empty and Diana settled herself in the seat opposite Davide. As she pressed her face against the window, her dark brows drawn together in concentration, the ugly scene near the station had been pushed to the back of her mind. Her thoughts had taken a different direction and she was no longer ashamed of them. They weren't sinful; she wanted to spend the rest of her life with this man. If the fear of impending war had thrown them together, it didn't matter.

They were on the bus when Davide took her hand.

'You're not speaking to me?' He turned her hand over, kissed the soft flesh of her wrist.

Diana shivered. 'I don't want the day to end,' she whispered, staring at the floor.

'It doesn't have to.'

Davide was looking at her, his eyes were questioning. Diana's stomach tilted, every sense in her body magnified.

'Well then,' she said, unable to think of a better reply.

As Diana climbed from the bus, she wondered if she had detected a look of appraisal in Pipo's eyes and a new tone to his customary '*Buona sera, bella* Signorina.'

Now as they walked down the dusty white road to the drive she was at last alone with Davide.

'We could always swim in the lake before going home. No one ever goes there.' Her words were out, inappropriate words. 'I'm sorry, I…'

'I would like that very much.' Davide was smiling down at her.

Diana found a towel where she had left it to dry on the small wooden jetty. 'There's only one, I'm afraid.' She turned her face away so he wouldn't see her embarrassment.

'Then we'll have to share.' Davide's voice was sensuous, teasing.

He stood on the jetty with his back to her and took off his shirt, pulling it in a sweep over his head, exposing his broad shoulders, his slim waist. Though she had seen him working in the fields, this was different. She could almost smell the sweet saltiness of his skin. When he stepped from his trousers she wanted to reach out and touch the small strip of white at the waistband that had never seen the sun. Lifting his arms, he dived into the still water.

'Come in, it's perfect,' he called.

'I'm coming,' she replied, emerging from the trees, the towel wrapped around her. At the end of the jetty she dithered on the edge. She wanted Davide to take control, to show her how much he wanted her, but she was afraid. Taking a deep breath she dropped the towel and jumped into the water.

She swam towards him and with each stroke the fear she had felt on the jetty dissipated. This was what she wanted and she was strong enough to accept the consequences. She started to shiver. 'Are you cold?' he asked, swimming towards the jetty. She nodded, her teeth chattering.

They climbed out and she was aware that her breasts were visible through the cotton of her bra. She reached for the towel and pulled it around her. Davide lowered his head to kiss her, softly at first but when she tangled her arms around his neck, he drew her close, ran his hands through her wet hair, brushing his lips along her neck. He unclipped her bra and stroked the top of her breasts. 'I want to see you,' he said, holding her away from him. 'Don't hide yourself from me, you are beautiful,' he murmured, inching his fingers slowly up the inside of her thigh, fondling her through the thin material of her pants.

She pushed herself towards him, and felt his hardness, straining against her.

'I must stop this now,' he said at last, his breathing ragged.

'No, don't, I'm staying here with you.' She saw his brief flicker of surprise, felt her own determination. Today she wouldn't let common sense get in the way. Life with all its losses and upheavals had brought her to this moment.

'You know what this means?' he asked, his eyes never leaving her face.

'I know that I want to be with you always,' Diana responded.

'I won't be able to marry you. The law forbids it.'

'Do you love me?' she asked.

'I have loved you from the first moment I saw you.'

'Well then, one day these new laws will be swept aside and you will marry me.'

As they walked into the long grass Davide took her hands.

'This will not be my first time, Diana. Do you mind?'

She shook her head.

'I promise I will never do anything to hurt you.' He laid the towel on the ground and pulled her down beside him, kissing her gently at first and then more deeply. He caressed her skin, trailing his fingers down her back, taking her nipples in his mouth, teasing her until she arched her body towards him and cried out, powerless to stop this strange new passion. Slowly he peeled down her pants and removed his own. Diana opened her eyes and for a moment they stared at each other.

'You are perfect,' he whispered, running his hands over her

stomach and lower still until Diana groaned and parted her legs, silently begging him to assuage the powerful longing. When he touched her, every nerve in her body responded. He stroked her slowly at first and then faster and when she was ready for him, he moved on top of her.

'I will be gentle,' he whispered as he entered her. For a moment Diana was startled as a tearing pain shot through her, but then it was gone and her body rose to meet him, and she felt the wave of their two bodies joining together as if they were one.

Then, without warning, he rolled away from her and shuddered as the tension left his body.

'I'm sorry, but I promised not to put you at risk.' He looked into her face and gave a half-smile, 'but I can still give you pleasure.' Slowly at first, and then urgently, she followed the rhythm of his fingers until with a force she didn't understand, she cried out, her body shuddering. As her breathing subsided, she let her head rest on his chest, inhaling the smell of him. He put his arm around her and she relaxed into it, all the tension of the last hours gone. She looked up at the darkening sky, wanting to remember all the details of this moment, their bodies so close together. Even as she lay there, she believed that what had happened existed almost as a dream.

She raised herself on her elbow and looked down at her lover. She marvelled at his beauty, a young god, David in the flesh. 'I love you,' she said for the first time. The words sounded wonderful and she said them again and laughed. 'I love you, Davide,' she called, her voice echoing around the lake until he put his hand over her mouth and kissed her again. 'Hush, you are too loud, someone will hear us.'

Diana giggled. 'No one will hear us, not even Nico. She stroked her finger across his taut stomach, marvelling at his body. 'Whatever happens,' she said, looking at him, 'this time, this place will always belong to us. Now tell me again that you love me.'

Davide started to laugh. 'OK, I love you, Diana Marston Durante, but not just because you are beautiful, but because you are funny and brave.' He paused. 'You are also stubborn and at times pig-headed, but I love you for your flaws as well as your perfection. It is your idiosyncrasies that make you who you are. Is that enough for you?'

'Umm,' she said, tickling him. 'You may have to try a bit harder.'

Reluctantly they dressed and sat with their backs against a tree. Davide lit up a cigarette. He smoked it slowly; stopping to look at Diana as if each time he saw her was the first time.

He picked up a coil of her hair and twisted it in his fingers. How could anyone feel so much love, it was almost too much for any man. He let the strand go, watched it fall against her cheek. He traced the outline of her nose with his finger, her full lips, her chin, stopping at the soft hollow in her neck. Somehow he felt safe with Diana. He couldn't explain it even to himself but when he was with her, the panic that often threatened to overwhelm him subsided.

'What you did today in the train was incredible, but why?' he asked, breathing in the smell of damp grass, the air and Diana.

'Because I could see her fear, and she was Jewish like you, and she was escaping Italy.'

'But her papers?'

'You can get false papers. You should take your family from Italy, go to England while there is still time. My mother would help you.' Diana was serious now, her face filled with love.

He smiled. 'So now you have had your way with me, you want me to leave?'

Diana opened her mouth to complain but he kissed her again.

'My beautiful Diana, I wish it were so simple. My father is a proud Italian. He refuses to hide from his own countrymen. No, little one, we shall see it out, and I shall protect my family.'

It was just before eight and Alessandra was in the kitchen making supper when her daughter came in. Diana looked radiant.

'Did you have a lovely day?' Alessandra asked her. 'You weren't stopped by any officials?'

Diana shook her head.

'What did you see?'

'Everything.' Diana floated past and dropped a small package on the table. 'I bought this for you.'

'Thank you, darling,' she replied, but Diana had gone drifting up the stairs without hearing her.

Alessandra shook her head and smiled. She had obviously had a wonderful time, but there was no use asking her tonight, better leave it until morning.

She collected a glass of wine and went into the study, at once lonely and missing Anthony. She put a record on the gramophone, but tonight it was a piano piece she had brought for her husband: Erik Satie's 'Once Upon a time in Paris.'

As her head filled with memories, she opened the drawer of her desk, her hand closing around a lavender bag. *Claridges* was embroidered on the muslin in scrolling purple letters. She held it to her nose. A hint of scent remained, reminding her of the bridal suite at Claridges, her first evening as a married woman, holding her husband's hand as they swept through the lobby, past bellboys with trolleys piled high with luggage, and maids with starched uniforms who nodded as they passed. When they had reached their suite, she had paused on the threshold, dazzled by the confection of satin and thick-pile carpet, and Anthony had swept her up into his arms and laid her on the bed.

Giggling, she had finally pulled herself away. Opening a wardrobe door, she had twirled in front of the mirror, her cream suit dishevelled, her hair undone, and she had seen the lavender bag.

'I am going to keep it,' she had said, plucking it from the shelf. 'For ever.' Then she had run past Anthony into the bathroom. 'Come and look,' she had called, opening the crystal bottles, smelling the contents. As Anthony leant against the door frame, his eyebrows lifting in amusement, she picked up the soap dish and the bottles of shampoo. She turned on the bronzed taps and laughed in delight as the water gushed forth into the Art Deco bath; hot, hot water.

'I think you approve,' Anthony smiled.

'Oh, yes,' she had replied. She had just stepped into a book and she didn't want to turn the page.

Much later the liveried waiter wheeled a trolley to the table by the window, and as Alessandra sat on the gilded chair, her stockinged feet tucked on the rail, he uncorked the champagne in the ice bucket, and removed the lid from a silver platter. 'Your supper, madam,' he had said, slicing the delicate beef, placing the potatoes and green beans onto a piping hot plate. When the waiter had gone, Alessandra got down from the table and went to her new husband. He pulled her towards him and unbuttoned the front of her ivory silk blouse, pushing his face against her neck. 'You smell so good,' he said, breathing deeply.

'You have spoilt me with Chanel,' she replied.

He had laughed and pulled her closer still, twisting a strand of her hair, so that his fingers brushed against her skin. 'It would seem, Mrs Marston, I have lost my appetite for food.'

Alessandra pressed the lavender bag to her face then returned it to the drawer. She opened her diary and, as the exquisite notes filled the air, the profound sense of longing and melancholy matched her own. She took out the black Parker pen that was Anthony's. A large tear slipped onto the page.

Our daughter is in love, she wrote, *and I am jealous of her love. Why did you leave me?*

Chapter Fifteen

The leaves were turning when Alessandra met Robert and Douglas in Paris. It was only a short trip, while Douglas attended some lectures. Diana, despite her protestations, was doing a secretarial course in Perugia.

As Alessandra stood beneath the Arc de Triomphe with her son, she was reminded of her honeymoon twenty years before.

'Your father brought me here,' she said. 'It was not long after the Great War ended and we stood in this same spot over the tomb of the Unknown Warrior. He was very quiet. I could tell that he was remembering unimaginable horrors. I will always remember his words: *Let us hope that lessons have been learnt from this carnage.* But I am scared, Robert; I don't think they have.'

'I'm very much afraid,' he said, walking beside her down the Champs Elysees, 'that the slaughter will begin sooner than expected.'

That night Douglas took them to dinner. Before coffee, Robert stood up.

'Do you mind if I go back to my room? I have my exams next week and I have brought some revision.'

'Good night, old chap.'

Robert kissed his mother 'See you in the morning, Mama.'

They were sipping cognac when Douglas put his hand over Alessandra's. She froze, the colour draining from her face.

'There is something I need to say, Alessandra.'

'You are not ill?'

'No, I am quite well, thank you. In fact, more than well, I am here with you and Robert, and I...' Alessandra drew back her hand, wondering where the conversation was going.

'I would be so happy if you would consider me more than just a friend. You must know that I have deeper feelings for you.'

Alessandra had a sinking feeling in her stomach. 'I had no idea,' she replied; but as she said the words it all started to make sense.

Douglas shifted in his chair, his face turning crimson and Alessandra was embarrassed. Deep inside she had known that he was fond of her, but had hoped it was part of his loyalty to Anthony.

'I h-h...' He paused and started again, the words coming out in a rush. 'I have been in love with you for a very long time. Is there any way you could see yourself sharing my life?'

Alessandra swallowed. 'I am so sorry, you are my dearest friend; I'm truly honoured that you think of me in this way but I am still in love with Anthony. He was and still is the love of my life.'

Douglas wiped his brow with a handkerchief. 'Of course, how stupid of me.'

'Please don't let this change anything. You mean so much to me.'

'Forgive me for presuming anything, Alessandra, I wish I hadn't mentioned it.'

'It is entirely my fault. I have always turned to you and this must have given you hope. Please forgive me. You have been a marvellous godfather to Robert and a friend to us all.'

*

Alessandra turned the key in the lock and pushed open the door. There was something about a single bed in a hotel bedroom that heightened your sense of oneness. This person is on their own, it said, this person is lonely. But she wasn't lonely; she was always busy with work and the estate. There weren't enough hours in the day. But there was the nub; it was only the day. At night she didn't have that wonderful, comforting sense of togetherness, the warmth of a human being next to her, touching her, holding her.

How easy it would have been to have encouraged Douglas. He would have given her a good life, but not the life she wanted. Poor Douglas; she had suspected he held a torch for her, but being in love with her was entirely different.

'It's you he comes to see,' Anthony had teased after yet another lunch at Upper Brook Street all those years before.

'What utter nonsense,' she had laughed.

She remembered dancing with him at the Guy's Hospital medical school dance, until Anthony had loped over, a grin on his handsome face. 'Do you mind if I cut in and dance with this beautiful girl?' he had asked his friend, and Alessandra had smiled at the young man with the laughing eyes. Now she could see how insensitive she had been. With the carelessness of youth, she hadn't given Douglas a second thought, and now she had rebuffed him again.

She sat on the edge of the bed and twisted her wedding ring. How she missed Anthony and the life she'd once had.

*

Alessandra was in Arezzo market buying sheets when it happened. They were not just ordinary sheets but heavy linen, exquisitely monogrammed sheets. They were second-hand and the initials were not her own, but you could usually find at least one initial that matched. She was loading up the car, putting the packages in the boot when her eyes widened. She dropped her handbag.

'Signora, are you all right?' A young man rushed to her side,

'No, no I'm not.' Couldn't he see that she couldn't move? Her back was agony.

'The doctor, I'll fetch the doctor.'

When Alessandra thought about it later, she must have been an unusual sight. A woman groaning over the boot of her car, but at that moment she could only think of the pain.

She turned her head a fraction to see a man with long legs – she could see only his legs from this angle – carrying a medical bag approaching her at pace.

'We have a problem, your back is out?'

'It's more than out, it must be broken.'

'I don't think so, Signora.' Then his hands were on her spine – she screamed.

'What have you been doing, Signora?'

'What do you mean, what have I been doing?'

'Have you been lifting?'

'Of course, I live on a farm.'

'Lifting is man's work.'

'And what, may I ask, is women's work?' She felt a sudden jolt in her back and something clicked into place.

'All better now, I think.'

Somehow the intense pain had gone. She straightened gingerly and looked into the face of Doctor Biochetti.

'It's you.'

'Ahh, Signora Durante. I can see you better from this angle.' Now the doctor was talking in English, terrible English for that matter, and he was definitely making fun of her.

Alessandra blushed. 'What do I owe you, Dottore?' she asked, stiffly.

'For the pleasure? Nothing.' Alessandra did not find it

amusing, in fact at this moment she did not find the doctor amusing, even though he was still extremely attractive.

'Thank you, Dottore.'

'If you insist on lifting, may I suggest you carry lighter loads.'

Later, as Alessandra struggled out of her clothes and climbed into a very hot bath, she could still feel the impression of the doctor's hands on her back.

Chapter Sixteen

It was late December when Robert left London for his first visit to the Villa Durante. As he walked down Victoria Station's platform two, he turned to his godfather.

'Are you sure you can't join us for Christmas?' he asked. 'Mama would love to have you.'

'I've a deadline on my research project. No, this is your adventure.' Douglas handed Robert a cheque. 'And here is your present, don't spend it all at once. Got your passport and tickets?'

'Yes, sir.' Robert looked at the cheque and his eyes widened in surprise.

'You are always too generous.'

Douglas smiled. 'For my godson, only the best.'

'You really won't come?'

Douglas patted Robert's back. 'I'd better not,' he said.

They were nearing the train when Douglas removed his pipe. 'One bit of advice from an old man: your mother and Diana have lived under a Fascist regime for over two years now, and they may not find their politics as distasteful as you do. Try to be tactful and not voice your opinions too strongly.'

'Yes, sir!'

'I shouldn't be lecturing you. Get on with you before I get emotional; and please give them my love.'

He smiled again and Robert had the impulse to hug him, but he held back. He was a young man now, travelling through Europe in unsettled times, but the pull of seeing his mother and sister was stronger than any qualms about the Fascists.

He climbed onto the train. ''Bye Douglas,' he said. 'See you on the seventh.'

The train was pulling away when Douglas called after him.

'What's an anagram for *Evangelist?*'

Robert thought for a moment. '*Evil's Agent,*' he called through the open window.

Douglas gave him the thumbs up and Robert grinned. After all these years playing the anagram game, they were still trying to outwit each other. This one was no exception. As the short, balding professor receded into the distance, Robert felt a tug in his heart.

Only two months had passed since Alessandra had seen her son in Paris, but as he emerged from the steam on that cold winter's day just before Christmas, her heart turned over. He had grown even more like his father.

'You are here,' she said. 'At last.'

'I am.' He kissed his mother, and then Diana was in his arms, hugging him tightly.

'Oh, De,' he said, kissing the top of her head, 'it's so good to see you.'

Diana hung on to him. 'You are so handsome, like Cary Grant. And your voice, it's so terribly English. Please become an actor, Robs, instead of—' She stopped mid-sentence.

Robert held her away from him. 'And you, my little sister, when did you get so thoroughly grown up and glamorous?'

Diana punched him. 'Now you are teasing. Come on, let's get out of here.' And they all linked arms and walked out through the concourse. When a street seller approached, Robert selected a wreath of holly with bright red berries as he chatted easily with the vendor.

'You speak Italian,' Alessandra cried. 'You didn't tell me.'

'It's my surprise, I thought you'd be pleased.'

Alessandra was more than pleased; her heart was bursting with happiness. She had been waiting so long for this moment.

'When did you learn?' she asked, hanging onto his arm, feeling the muscles beneath his coat.

'Douglas employed a tutor. Did you know he speaks five languages?'

Alessandra shook her head. 'I had no idea.'

When Diana opened the door of a burgundy Fiat saloon, Robert ran his hand over the paintwork. 'She's beautiful,' he said. 'Good old Douglas, he has no need to be so extraordinarily generous.'

'It was the repayment of a loan from Papa,' Diana interjected, 'so it's him we have to thank.'

'I think we should be grateful to both of them,' Alessandra said firmly. She climbed into the front and turned on the engine. 'But if we have a good harvest I'm going to start paying him back.'

'You are?' Diana asked.

'I am,' she replied, realising at once it was the right thing to do. Before Diana could say any more, she let out the clutch and the car rattled over the cobbles and into the streets of Florence.

As various landmarks approached, Diana pointed them out. 'Do you see the Baptistry?' She leant over the seat, shouting in Robert's ear. 'And the Duomo with Giotto's bell tower?'

'You mean the *campanile*.'

Diana punched his arm, 'I forgot you speak Italian.' Then she was off, chattering in excitement again.

She was about to launch into a recitation on her favourite

renaissance statues, when a column of Fascist militia marched towards them. The streets emptied.

'Bloody Fascists,' Robert muttered.

'It's because we're in Florence,' Alessandra reassured him. 'In the countryside they don't bother us at all. In fact, the farmers approach Mussolini for subsidies. Our estate has benefited from his agricultural reforms.'

Robert's expression had changed. 'What?'

'Farmers and landowners can apply for grants. We were lucky enough to qualify and have reclaimed thirty hectares at the bottom of the hill.'

'You would never be a Fascist sympathiser, Mother?'

'Of course not!' she retorted, glancing sideways at her son. It was one thing to accept their subsidies and quite another to be a sympathiser. Did he think she would collude with them? She bit her lip and stared through the windscreen.

'Have I offended you, Mama?' he asked.

'Well, I'm not about to jump into bed with Mussolini,' she retorted.

By mid-afternoon, as the first flurry of snowflakes settled on the ground, they turned into the drive of the Villa Durante. The car crept reluctantly up the winding hill and Robert opened the window. For two years he had thought of this moment, dreamt of it, imagined it, and now it was here. 'Your photographs don't do it justice,' he murmured, trying not to let his feelings overwhelm him.

Alessandra stopped the car at the top and parked under the trees. In the distance, the turrets and battlements of the ancient Castello di Sorbello were bathed in yellow light, and the wooded hillsides were frosted with snow. She watched her son's face.

'The land, all this,' he spread his arms wide, his voice cracking with emotion. 'It is even more beautiful than your description. I am not surprised that you love it.'

Alessandra put her arm though her son's. 'How I have longed to hear those words. Come on, let's go inside.

At the front door Robert was greeted by a large white dog. 'And you must be Nico,' he said. Nico wagged his tail happily in reply.

It was twilight when Robert and Diana ambled through the avenue of umbrella pines towards the lake. The snow was settling and was soft beneath their feet. Robert could hear rustling in the undergrowth.

'Wild boar,' Diana announced, showing him the muddy hollows where the animals bathed. 'But they won't come near us.'

Robert looked at his sister, appraising her.

'What are you looking at?' she asked, smiling.

'You.'

'I can see that.'

'It seems,' he said tilting his head onto one side, 'that the London schoolgirl has grown into a young woman.'

'I'm not a child any longer.'

'And does the young woman fish also?' he asked, seeing two wooden rods lying on the jetty.

'Yes, she was taught by Davide.'

'Davide?' Robert enquired. His sister had said the name in the car, but her letters contained no mention of him.

'He works for us and he is my friend.' Diana offered no other explanation. As they walked slowly back to the house, Robert wondered about the man named Davide, but he wouldn't ask her now.

They were about to go inside when he caught her arm. 'I received your reply to my letter. Sorry, De.'

'It was a shock.'

'It was wrong of me to ask you to keep it a secret, and it must have been so difficult not telling Mama.'

'It still is; impossible, actually. You have to tell her soon, Robert. You realise it will break her heart?'

'Of course I realise. But war is coming, and then I'll be called up anyway.'

'But it hasn't come yet. You are so young, only eighteen. You could wait.'

'Look at me, Diana. If I join up now, they will have time to give me the best possible training.'

'Oh, Robs.' Diana leant against his shoulder. 'I'm so scared I will lose you too.'

When Robert had unpacked he returned downstairs and handed the holly wreath to his mother. 'My offering is rather small in comparison,' he laughed, glancing at the hall decorated with garlands of holly, mistletoe and a sturdy six-foot tree.

Alessandra kissed her son. 'Nonsense, it is the best gift of all.' She uncorked a bottle of red wine and passed each of them a glass.

'Let's drink to the family being together in Italy for Christmas, and to your father who is with us in spirit.'

After the toast they sat down to a feast cooked by Diana and prepared by Sofia before she went home for Christmas.

Later, when Robert had finished the last mouthful of *Torta al Limone*, he put down his spoon. A fire flickered in the grate and above the murmur of voices, he could hear wind tearing at the trees, but in the kitchen, all was calm and still. He glanced at his mother; her hair was shorter and no longer pulled back in a chignon. She looked more youthful somehow. He cleared his throat.

'Forgive me, Mama, but I wish to speak to you.'

'You look serious.'

'I am.'

He drew in his breath. He couldn't bear to see the laughter die in her eyes and witness the same sorrow he had seen after his father's death, because this time, he knew he would put the sorrow there. He took his mother's hands. He had to tell her.

'I'm going to join the RAF,' he said.

There was silence in the room.

'Please don't look like that, I'll be fine.'

Alessandra pushed him away. She scraped back her chair, collected the plates and glasses and thumped them down on the sideboard, her hands shaking.

Robert caught his sister's eye.

'It's all right, Robs,' Diana whispered. 'I understand.'

Alessandra whipped round. 'No, it's not all right,' she yelled. 'You don't understand. Neither of you understand. How can you when you haven't had children?' Robert could see she was fighting back the tears. He went over to her and put his arms around her.

'I'll be safe, I promise you.'

'You can't promise that. No one can. Look at what happened to your father. He was only crossing the road.'

'If you can die crossing the street, you're never safe anywhere, so I might as well do something noble. I have a real chance to serve our country; believe me, war is inevitable. I am English and though it will be hard to fight, with you living in Italy, England is still my country.'

'When war comes Douglas can get you a desk job,' she begged. 'We read the papers, Robert. Every day young men are killed, brave, strong young men, and that's only in training.'

'I don't want a desk job. Don't you see, I want to fly. Papa fought in the Great War, he would never want me to shirk my duty. He would have encouraged me, Mama, and I want to make him proud.'

Alessandra put the coffee on the table and collapsed into her chair. In her heart she had always known this would happen. Though her son was sensitive, he had always been brave. Now he would join the Air Force and nothing she could do or say would stop him. His father would have given Robert this freedom just as she had to.

'I can tell your mind is set on this,' she said.

'It is, but I will only be able to give the RAF my full commitment if I know you are safe. I want you to promise me that if and when the war comes to Italy, you will be prepared to leave if you are in any kind of danger.'

Alessandra looked at her son. Though she was at risk of crying, he deserved a reply.

'I give you my word,' she confirmed, struggling to keep control. 'But please come back to us, Robert.'

When they had sat down after dinner by the drawing room fire, Diana gave Robert her present, a Maltese cross on a silver chain.

'I commissioned Davide's father to make it. The eight points symbolise the aspirations of the knights of Malta. One of them is justice. That's appropriate, don't you think?'

Robert put the cross around his neck. 'I'll never take it off,' he said.

Alessandra gave him a photograph in a silver frame of Diana and Nico running through the meadow. Diana was laughing and the dog was jumping up at her.

'This will come with me always,' he said, swallowing hard, and then he brought out his own presents. 'De, this is for you, and this one is yours, Mama.'

After Diana had fastened the jewelled hair clip into her hair and his mother had tried on the blue kid gloves, he got to his feet.

'Goodnight, Mama, De – will you forgive me for ruining Christmas?'

Alessandra longed to take her son in her arms, but it was true he had nearly ruined Christmas.

'I'm sorry.' He smiled endearingly.

'So you should be.' She allowed him to kiss her and Diana flung her arms around him.

Robert walked up the wide stone staircase, relieved his decision was out in the open at last. His mother was frightened but she had to understand that he was not her little boy any more. He was a man and he had to lead his own life, he couldn't do everything to please her. He stopped at the mirror on the half landing. His father's face stared back at him, and yet it was not his father's. The high forehead and long straight nose were testament to his Italian ancestry. He touched the chain around his neck. He would come back to them; he wanted more than anything to come back to them.

He opened his bedroom window and looked across the frozen meadow. Generations of his family had lived on this land, and now it was home to Diana and his mother. As he fell asleep he held on to the thought that, for the time being at any rate, they would be safe.

Alessandra didn't go to bed: not immediately – instead she scrubbed the kitchen surfaces and cleaned the stove until her hands were raw. She rearranged the cupboards, and washed out the cloths; then she went up to her bedroom, dragged herself onto the bed and curled into a tight ball.

She knew what it was like to live through war. She had seen streets in her neighbourhood torn apart by death. She had watched for the telegram boy, prayed with her neighbours that it wasn't their door he was coming to, and when it was their door, she had been glad that her father had died before it had begun, so she didn't have to suffer as they were suffering. She remembered walking to school with her best friend, Katherine Long. It was the beginning of July 1916 and the sun had been shining on a perfect summer's day, but her normally ebullient friend was despondent.

'My father has been sent to somewhere in France,' she had said. 'Near the River Somme. Apparently the battle will hasten a victory and he will be able to come home.' She had stopped in her tracks and turned to Alessandra. 'But I'm frightened. Our men are going to be killed, I'm sure of it. All this talk of dying for our country; I don't want my father to die.'

The following day Katherine did not come into school, and when she had returned a week later, she'd been a different girl.

'He's dead,' she had said, her face bleak. 'And he is never coming back. I was right, Alessandra.'

Though Anthony had been one of the survivors, Alessandra found that the war had never left him; not really. They never talked about it, never mentioned the nightmares when he would wake up screaming. They never talked of the times she held him in her arms until the shaking subsided. But that is what war did to you, and now her precious son was going to fight for his country. He would know the same danger as his father.

Chapter Seventeen

Robert looked up from his newspaper as a blast of cold air blew through the kitchen. A man was standing in the doorway wearing a thick coat and a red knitted scarf. He was holding a metal can. Robert guessed it was Davide.

'*Buongiorno*, come in, you must be freezing.'

'I've brought your milk.' The man pulled off his boots and his woollen hat and emptied the milk into two large jugs.

'Coffee?' Robert held up the pot.

'No, *grazie*, I have work to finish.'

Davide fiddled with his hat and the two men stared at each other. Was it Davide's diffidence that unnerved him, Robert wondered as he racked his brains for something to say, or his appearance? He looked more German than Italian.

'*Mi scusi.*' Davide pulled on his hat, and was gone in a blast of cold air, closing the door behind him.

Robert jumped up and called after him, but Davide was gone, trudging across the snow. Diana came into the kitchen. She poured herself a coffee.

'Have you met Davide?'

'Briefly.'

'You *were* nice to him, I hope?'

Robert put down his coffee, 'It was a little awkward, actually. But of course I tried.'

'Perhaps you should have tried harder. He's Jewish, and his family home in Arezzo was confiscated; he's been excluded from art school. That's why he works for us.'

'But his blond hair?'

'Not every Jew has dark hair,' she snapped.

'I didn't mean that, it's just unusual.'

'I can assure you it's true, and by the way, I like him...' She paused for breath. 'Very much.' Diana marched from the room with Nico trotting at her heals like a small lion.

So Davide was a Jew. Robert hated intolerance, but his sister's reaction concerned him. She was protecting Davide. Was he jealous, he wondered. Did he hate the fact that there was someone else in his sister's life, a man she turned to instead of him? But Davide must be a good man; their mother obviously liked him. He deserved his kindness not rudeness; he would make it up to him.

He found his sister sprawled across her bed, reading a book. The dog was lying beside her.

'Why did your letters never mention Davide?'

Diana put down her book. 'Because I love him, and I wanted to tell you in person. And because I'm frightened for him, for his family.'

'De, I'm sorry.'

'So am I.'

Robert put his arm around her shoulders. Now he understood her reluctance to tell him and she was right to be afraid. He had seen the park bench in Berlin and the sign saying 'Juden Verboten'.

'Typical, isn't it?' she laughed. 'I could have done something simple, found a nice Catholic boy, been married in the church in Cortona. Instead I have fallen for a Jew.'

'But you have never been ordinary, De,' Robert said with a smile. 'You have always been yourself.'

'What is that supposed to mean?' she laughed.

'You have always been impulsive and passionate, and...' he paused '...obstinate and infuriating.'

Diana picked up the pillow and threw it at him. He threw it back, bursting a seam. Soon feathers were flying everywhere with Nico jumping among them adding to the mess.

Diana was holding her sides, tears streaming down her face.

'You are positively wonderful, De. Look at you, feathers in your hair, up your nose. I am dull in comparison.'

'Don't say that,' she said fiercely. 'You are the best person in the world and you have never been dull.'

Chapter Eighteen

At the end of December 1938 an invitation arrived at the Villa Durante to celebrate the New Year with the Tremonti family from Spedalicchio.

Diana studied the card. 'Guido Tremonti was at the school next door to the convent. I never liked him, but he may have changed.'

'We can introduce Robert to some of the locals, and we shall dress up for a change.' Alessandra put the card on the mantelpiece where it remained in splendid isolation.

'But I don't have anything to wear.'

Alessandra laughed at her daughter. 'I have no doubt that you'll borrow something of mine.'

Alessandra winced as Diana skimmed through the dresses in her cupboard, sliding them along the rails, pulling one out, putting it back again in the wrong place. Diana plucked an emerald satin dress from the rail and held it to her body.

'What do you think?'

'You'd better try it on.'

She undid her skirt and her blouse and slipped into the dress. She twirled in front of her mother.

'When did you get so utterly gorgeous?' Alessandra laughed.

'Are you saying I was ugly before?'

139

'No, no of course not.'

'I was only joking, Mama.'

Alessandra watched as Diana danced from the room. Since Davide had entered her life her daughter had become a breath of fresh air. She lit up the room with a wonderful, vibrant glow. Alessandra had possessed that energy once, but it had died with Anthony.

She remembered getting ready for the dance on the night she had first met him, putting on the dress, her mother's shoes, the long silk gloves, and her mother's words as she left: 'I was like you once, but then your father died and I had no time to look pretty, just work, work to look after you.' Alessandra had been angry and hurt by her mother. It had taken her husband's love to set her free. Now Diana was beautiful and her own beauty was fading, but she refused to be a martyr like her mother, she would never take it out on Diana. On her dressing table was a photograph taken at her twenty-fifth birthday party. The hall at Upper Brook Street had been cleared of furniture and the room was full of elegantly dressed people.

'A quarter of a century,' Anthony had teased, clasping her waist and twirling her around. 'Let's hope you will live to be a hundred.'

'I don't want to be a hundred unless you are with me, but by then we will be in bed by six and I'll have false teeth and you won't want me anyway.'

'I will always want you,' he had said, and she had believed him. Now she was nearing forty and she minded getting old, because one day soon her children would have their own lives, and she would be entirely on her own. She held the photograph to her chest and felt the ache of loneliness. Anthony would never come home.

She put down the frame and put on the pearl drops he had given her; powdered her face pale, dabbing at the smudges beneath her eyes, and put some salve upon her lips. She would enjoy herself tonight, she would enjoy every day she had left with her son, and perhaps one day in the future she would allow herself to love again.

'It's strange.' Diana leant over the front seat of the car as they drove to Spedalicchio. 'Only a short while ago the Tremontis were peasant farmers; now they are rich. Last year it was a new house, and three months ago a tractor. No one has any idea where the money is coming from.'

Alessandra lowered her voice. 'It is possible that Signor Tremonti found an Etruscan hoard on his land. It would account for his change in fortunes, but there might be another reason. According to Sofia, he has made several trips to Rome.'

They each made their own speculations until Alessandra stopped the car outside a high wall. 'Whatever you think of the Tremonti family, we have to get on with them.' She held on to her son's arm. 'Please be careful.'

'So why do you mix with them?'

'We don't, not usually, but they have strong links with the Fascist party and it's good to keep in with them.'

'Then we certainly shouldn't be here,' Robert snapped in reply.

A maid opened the door and ushered them into the hallway. Alessandra drifted into the crowd and left Robert and Diana standing by an ornately carved fireplace.

'It's unlike you to be short with Mama.'

'I mustn't be hard on her, it can't be easy, but I wouldn't have come to this party if I'd known.' He caught his mother's eye and waved. He then selected two glasses of champagne from a silver tray and passed one to his sister. 'To the Royal Air Force, to your future, and to mine.'

He drained his glass and helped himself to another.

'Tell me about school, Robs,' Diana asked. 'I mean, what it was really like.'

Robert looked at her for a moment and came to a decision. He had been withholding the truth for so long, it was time to tell her.

'It was difficult when you left,' he admitted. 'I didn't tell you because I knew you would worry.'

'I worried anyway.'

'I let my friends drop me. I was punishing myself for Papa's death. It was my fault. I distracted him when he was crossing the road.'

'Your fault? Of course it wasn't, you were trying to warn him.'

'So you knew?' Robert looked at his sister, amazed.

She nodded. 'I have known for ages, the housekeeper told me. This nonsense must stop now, Robs, do you promise me? It was never your fault!'

They were silent for a minute, reflective, then Robert hugged her. 'You know what this means to me?'

'I do,' she replied.

They found a small alcove where they could talk in relative privacy.

'Did you know Mama wrote to my housemaster every month until recently?' Robert ran his finger round the rim of his glass. 'He tried to be kind but he didn't have a clue. It meant a lot to me that she recognised what I was going through.'

'I think I gave her a hard time,' Diana said. 'I blamed her for everything. It must have been so difficult when Papa had always looked after her.' Diana reached out her hand and touched the scar above his eyebrow. 'Do you want to tell me about that?'

'Boxing.'

'I thought as much. It didn't affect your migraines?'

'I haven't had one in ages.'

'Thank goodness for that.' She scrutinised him for a second, her head on one side. 'It's funny, but you seem so much more confident, more...' She paused, trying to find the word and a smile crossed her face. 'More worldly! Do you have a girlfriend?'

Robert grinned and shook his head. 'Not yet. Too much time spent boxing.'

'So,' Diana said, her fingers digging into his arm, 'if you apply the same focus to your flying, you will come back to us. And no more secrets, OK?'

They looked up as a young man came towards them. He bowed and held out his hand.

'Guido Tremonti, and you would be Diana's brother?'

Robert nodded, taking an instant dislike to the sleek Italian. Guido's dark eyes flicked over Diana. 'She is beautiful, no?'

Robert's fist curled at his side.

'I will take you for a dance.' Guido took Diana by the elbow and manoeuvred her onto the dance floor. He put his hand in the small of her back, and it took all of Robert's resolve not to break them up. When Diana grimaced, her eyes begging to be rescued, Robert crossed the floor towards them.

'I would like to dance with my sister, do you mind?'

'I'm sorry Guido, but my brother is only with us for a short time.' Guido let her go and Diana followed her brother. 'He's so vile,' she whispered when Guido was out of earshot.

'We shouldn't be here,' he replied.

They found Alessandra talking to an elegant woman with grey hair holding a cigarette holder in her slim fingers.

'The Contessa Ranieri di Sorbello,' Alessandra said, introducing her to Robert. 'She lives in the Castello.'

Robert shook her hand.

'I was admiring your beautiful home from our terrace,' he said. 'It looks magnificent.'

The Contessa smiled. 'Alessandra, you must bring your

enchanting family for a drink before your son returns to England. I can introduce them to my own son, Giovanni, and his new wife, as they are soon arriving from Rome.'

'We would like that very much,' she replied.

Robert was helping himself to some food from the extravagant display on the sideboard, when Guido appeared at his side.

'Diana is a fine woman,' he stated, leaning towards him, his mouth close to his ear. 'I like her. And quite soon your little *English* sister may need someone to protect her.'

'I believe she's already spoken for.'

'Who is the lucky man?'

Robert moved away but Guido followed.

'I can't think of anyone, unless you mean the Jew dismissed from her school?'

'I don't know what you are talking about.'

'It is foolish of your mother to give him work on the estate.'

Robert could hardly contain his anger. 'My mother can employ whom she pleases.'

'You can't allow your sister to bed a Jew.'

'My sister isn't bedding anyone, and she will never be with you. Now if you'll excuse me, I find this conversation highly offensive.' Robert walked away. It was only his concern for his family's welfare that prevented him from putting his fist through Guido Tremonti's perfect white teeth.

He found his mother with Diana.

'It's time to go.'

Alessandra, who had been watching the exchange, stood up. 'Something tells me this was not a good idea.'

'It wasn't,' Robert said, handing his mother her coat. 'Next time, Mama, you need to be more careful whom you mix with.' He put one arm through Diana's and the other through his mother's and wheeled them both towards the door.

The following morning Robert remembered the conversation with Guido. He hoped it would be quickly forgotten, but in his heart he feared that Guido was not the forgetful kind.

On Robert's penultimate day, the priest came to bless the Villa Durante. The rite, usually reserved for Easter, was being performed several months early, but unlike the Easter celebrations of new life, the priest would ask God to protect one of his faithful subjects. As Robert knelt at the altar in the small chapel, the priest called upon Saint Michael the Archangel to defend a servant in battle. Alessandra also said her prayers. But these were not for the coming war, not for victory or gain.

'Dear God, please bring him home safely to me,' she whispered, her eyes fixed on her son.

Diana sat on the edge of the bed as Robert folded his clothes and put them into his suitcase. He was eighteen, old enough to die for his country, but he was also her brother. She bit her nail, the anxiety building in her chest, threatening to explode. It was Robert she had run to after their father had died, and it was Robert who had rescued her toy lion Leo when she had dropped him into the freezing Serpentine. On her tenth birthday he had grabbed the wasps from her hair knowing he would take the stings, and he had held her as she cried. Now he was going away, and it was quite possible that he wouldn't return.

She threw herself into his arms. 'I love you, Robs,' she sobbed, clinging on to him. 'But I can't come to the station, it's too hard to say goodbye.'

Robert picked up his suitcase. The dog followed him to the door. He glanced around his bedroom at the books and pictures, at the mahogany barometer hanging on the wall. Everything chosen by his mother, the woman he loved and admired most in the world. He might never see her again; never see his beloved little sister. It was the hardest decision he had ever made and yet it was the right one. He was now a man with a duty to his country, as well as a burning ambition to fly.

He was sitting at the kitchen table writing a quick note for Diana when the door opened. Davide was standing there.

'I've come to say goodbye,' Davide spoke first.

'I wanted to apologise,' Robert replied. 'Last time we met I was rude. I didn't know what to say.'

'We were both unsure, but it is of no matter. Here, I have made this for you.'

Davide drew a small package from the pocket of his sheepskin coat. 'Diana tells me you are going to be a pilot; it is what we call in Italy a *talismano*. It is for luck and to keep you safe.' Robert pulled the tissue paper apart to reveal a carving of the Virgin Mary. Her face, though tiny, was exquisitely carved, and the folds of her dress revealed the talent of the sculptor.

'Thank you, it's beautiful.'

'The Virgin Mary made by a Jew!' The corners of Davide's mouth lifted, and Robert smiled with him. It was easy to see why his sister was in love. One day, God willing, he would get to know him better.

'I am sorry for your family's troubles; the world has gone mad.'

'I hope we will survive the madness.' Davide looked up and their eyes met.

'My sister is lucky to have found you. You have my blessing.'

Davide's voice shook. 'That means everything. Thank you.'

They walked outside. At the top of the stone stairs Robert clasped Davide's hand.

'Please look after Diana and my mother.'

'*Ovviamente*, of course. With my life,' he replied.

Alessandra had the car ready in the drive.

'Let's go,' Robert gripped onto the dashboard. He gritted his teeth; he mustn't cry, not now, not when the last of his resolve was crumbling. When the car had negotiated the first bend, he turned to look back. Diana had joined Davide. They were standing at the top of the steps, their hands raised. Robert waved in return. He watched until they were just small figures in the landscape with a white dog by their side.

They were nearing Florence when Alessandra drew into the side of the road, and turned off the engine. She turned to look at Robert, with tears in her eyes. 'I can't change your mind?'

'I'm sorry, Mama. I have to do this, don't you see?'

'I do,' she said, 'but I had to try, you understand.' Her face was turned towards him and Robert wanted to comfort her but he couldn't.

'You must let me go,' he whispered. 'You must let me be a man.'

She nodded and blew into her handkerchief. 'Forgive me,' she said, starting the car and staring blindly through the windscreen. 'I'll be better in a moment.'

They were on the platform when he stepped into her arms. He could smell her Chanel perfume, feel the veil on her hat prickle his nose. 'Dearest Mama, you have to be strong and you have to believe that I will come back to you.'

Alessandra held on to him.

He undid her fingers. 'I must go or I'll miss my train.' He dragged himself away and climbed up the steps and onto the train.

'I'll come back.' He pulled down the window and leant out so that he could see her, touch her hand. 'I promise I'll come back soon.'

Alessandra took his outstretched hand with her own, held it as if she would never let it go. This was not a boy returning to school, but her son training for war. Very soon he would know unimaginable dangers and she wouldn't be there to protect him.

'Goodbye, my darling boy.' Alessandra dropped his hand and walked away down the platform. She stopped by the barrier and waved. She was wearing her favourite red coat and small red hat, knowing her son would take this image of her away with him, acknowledging it might be his last.

Chapter Nineteen

It would be over two months before Alessandra picked up her pen to Anthony.

On the fifteenth of this month, she wrote, *German troops marched into Czechoslovakia. It is the end of appeasement. There will be war. Our beloved son who is training to be a fighter pilot will be in the thick of it.*

I try to be brave but I am so tired, and each night when I go to bed I cannot sleep. How I need your strength at this moment.

Diana has thrown herself into being an adult with spectacular enthusiasm. The secretarial course was a dismal failure and she has decided that teaching is a much worthier profession. I am completely behind her decision, for though Mussolini encourages education, in the countryside many of the children are illiterate. Diana is doing a course in Perugia. Next month she starts as an assistant at the Scuola Elementare. I admit to being hugely proud of her.

With my love and devotion always, and until the next time.

Your loving wife, Alessandra

Robert had been gone six months when Alessandra collapsed. Perhaps it was the strain, she thought, as she gasped for breath, coughing until her lungs hurt. In any event Signora Carducci finally overruled her objections to seeing a doctor.

'I will send for him now,' she said, helping Alessandra to the sofa. 'And if it is any consolation we will find that nice doctor from Arezzo.'

'I don't know what you mean.'

'I saw the way you looked when he smiled at you, it is impossible to fool Signora Carducci.'

'What utter nonsense,' Alessandra replied, spots of colour appearing on her pale cheeks.

Sofia and Signora Carducci put Alessandra to bed, while Signor Innocenti was dispatched on his bicycle to the telephone in Mercatale. Within an hour the doctor was on his way.

Doctor Biochetti leant over the bed where Alessandra was sleeping. He put his hand on her forehead and she opened her eyes.

'I'm sorry to be any trouble, there's nothing wrong with me that a good night's sleep won't cure,' she mumbled, her eyelids drooping.

'I think I am the judge of that.' The doctor smiled at her. The Signora was not in grave danger, he was sure of it. She was pale and her breathing rapid, but her symptoms were hopefully temporary.

He put the stethoscope on her chest and listened. 'You have pneumonia,' he said.

'I thought only the weak and the old got pneumonia?'

'I can see that you are neither, so perhaps you are in contact with someone?'

'I was visiting one of the farms. I had tea with Signora Avorio and her three grandchildren. She didn't seem well. Could you check on her before you return to Arezzo?'

'Of course,' he replied, wondering why he had agreed. He had a full list ahead of him, more than enough patients for one day. It seemed the Signora had an effect on him and though he hadn't seen her since the day in Arezzo, he had certainly thought about her. She was beautiful, of course, and spirited, with a steely determination. He smiled at his foolishness. How could he have known these things when she had spent much of their previous conversation in pain and more than a little cross. But today, with her dark hair spread over the pillow and her green eyes looking up at him, he had sensed her vulnerability.

'And your back, it is better?'

'Much better, thank you,' she replied.

This time the Signora had seemed pleased to see him. The doctor went down the stairs with a spring in his step.

'The Signora has pneumonia, but she will recover with this prescription and a lot of rest,' he informed the assembled company who had gathered on the loggia.

'*Grazie a Dio.*' Signor Innocenti took off his cap. 'When she collapsed, we were worried, I can tell you.

'And with Signorina Diana teaching in Perugia,' Signora Carducci added.

'You did the right thing to telephone me, Elio.'

'On my instructions,' interjected Signora Carducci.

'Please reassure the Signorina her mother will be fine.' He smiled at Signora Carducci, smoothing her ruffled feathers.

He picked up his bag. 'If you will forgive me I must visit one of the tenants now. I will be back to see Signora Durante in a few days. In the meantime, give her lots to drink and keep her warm.'

It was only three days before Alessandra saw the doctor again. On this visit she had exchanged her pyjamas for something more delicate.

'Good morning, Signora.' The doctor was smiling down at her and Alessandra felt shy, exposed. She pulled the sheets up to her chin.

'Forgive me, but again I need to listen to your breasts.'

'You do?' Alessandra was trying not to laugh, and then she was trying not to cough. 'I think you mean my chest,' she wheezed.

'The Signora makes fun of me.'

'No Dottore, I would never do that.'

'Umm,' he said, his brown eyes amused. 'I am not entirely sure.' He put the stethoscope to her chest and as the cold instrument lay on Alessandra's white skin, she wondered if her heart rate had quickened.

When the doctor had gone, Alessandra lay back on the pillow. Despite their inauspicious second meeting in Arezzo, she had thought about him many times. Today she had noticed something in his eyes; could it have been tenderness? No, she was imagining it, he was a doctor simply concerned for his patient. He probably had a wife and at least ten children. But for a fleeting moment when he had looked at her she felt as if she was the only person in the world.

She smiled when she thought of the doctor's English. It was ridiculous but there was something endearing in the fact that he tried so hard. She was still spluttering with laughter when her daughter came bounding up the stairs. She hastily put on her woollen bed jacket and composed her face.

'Are you feeling better?' Diana threw herself down on the bed. 'Poor Mama, it's boiling in here. Do you want me to open the window?'

'That might be a good idea,' she replied.

Chapter Twenty

Diana had just finished her third week as teaching assistant at a school in Perugia, and her first week in a class of her own.

She put down the book she was reading to her young pupils and smiled at their rapt faces.

'That is the end for today,' she announced.

As the children packed away their textbooks, Diana was drawn back to her own childhood, when at bedtime, dressed in her brushed cotton pyjamas, she would curl in the crook of her father's arm, while Robert nestled in the other. She could still see her father's face as he read to them; hear his voice, warm and full of life. He had given her the gift of storytelling. Sister Maria had continued his legacy, encouraging her and pushing her, never giving up on her.

One day she would pass on her father's gift. She would start her own school.

She was on her way home when the solution came to her. The school at the end of the valley had long since closed and few local families could afford to send their children to the convent in Cortona. The church in Sorbello would make the perfect schoolroom. The pews would serve as benches and when the time came she would ask Davide to make her some desks. Her mother would lend her the money for books and chalks;

education, or the lack of it, was one of the causes she championed. On Fridays the church would become a church again, but during the week the children would be occupied, distracted from the anxieties of a coming war.

As the bus trundled through the Niccone Valley, she thought of her mother working hard to make the estate flourish, exhausting herself to improve the lives of her tenants. She had left everything familiar to give her daughter a new life in Italy, even though it meant leaving Robert behind. Starting a school in Sorbello would support her mother's work and it would be doing something worthwhile.

They were nearing the village when a tightening in her chest pushed away any thoughts of the school. It was the same breathy excitement she always felt when she was about to see Davide. She imagined him walking towards her. Lifting her in the air.

'My little Diana.' How she loved the word *little*. She could see his blue eyes light up and a smile curve around his mouth. She felt the familiar longing. She had heard there was talk in the village about them, but she really didn't care. They couldn't know what it was like to be this much in love.

The bus stopped and she could see Davide at the foot of the drive waiting for her.

'*Ciao, bella Diana.*' Pipo winked at her. 'Go to your young man.' She blew him a kiss and was off the bus, running past the square, past the women gathering in their washing: she could see them whispering together by the village pump.

'*Buona sera,*' she called. They glanced at her, smiled and returned to their whispering, but Diana kept on running until she reached Davide.

2

The War at Home

Chapter Twenty-one

It was July 1940 and Robert was sitting in a deckchair outside the dispersal hut. The grass airfield sparkled with dew and above stretched a vivid blue canopy of sky. A warm breeze stirred gently and the patches of early morning mist were fast disappearing. It was going to be a perfect summer's day. He looked upwards and squinted into the bright sunlight, a knot of apprehension turning in his stomach. It was his first day on an operational squadron. He shut his eyes, letting his mind wander back to his interview at the Air Ministry. It was only twelve months ago, just two months before the war started, but it seemed a lifetime away. The naïve boy who had hesitantly paced the red linoleum had gone for ever.

He remembered sitting in front of the three RAF officers on the selection board. 'Your ambition to become a fighter pilot is no guarantee of success.' An officer was addressing him but Robert couldn't keep his gaze steady. The man's glass eye was fixed ahead of him, while the other moved naturally. 'It is our task to decide which of our young candidates not only possess the aptitude to fly, but also the qualities of resilience and leadership to meet the challenging demands ahead of you.'

'Are you Anthony Marston's son?' Robert's head swivelled to the officer at the end of the row. He was thin with an aquiline nose and light brown hair.

'Yes, sir.'

'Thought you must be. Bloody good doctor and a decent chap. Awful business.' He looked at his watch. 'So, Marston, what makes you think you are good enough to join the most elite flying force in the world?'

After half an hour of hard grilling, deflated and exhausted, he was dismissed.

'Go for your medical now, Marston; the MO is in room thirteen, second on the left.'

'Robert Marston?' A medical officer looked up from a long table.

'Yes, sir.'

'Unbutton your shirt, I need to listen to your chest; and take off your trousers. You can hang them over the chair.'

'Is there any medical condition I need to know about?' the officer asked, after a thorough examination. 'Anything at all that could affect your flying should you get in?'

There was a small pause as Robert thought back to the agony of his migraines. I am convinced there is nothing sinister to report, the specialist had told him.

He looked at the officer. 'No, sir,' he said.

Robert recalled the days after the interview as he waited for the post, and the overwhelming sense of relief when he received the formal letter of acceptance by the Air Ministry. He visited his grandfather before he left.

'Well done, Robert,' he had said. 'Look at you, all togged out in your uniform, you really are the spit of your father.'

Robert could see that his eyes were watering.

'Listen well to everything they have to teach you.'

'I'll be fine, Grandpa,' he replied.

'You'd better be.'

He was at the end of the road when he turned to look back. His grandfather was still standing in the doorway.

Robert opened his eyes and looked at his watch. It was seven thirty. A fellow pilot in the next chair smiled at him reassuringly.

'Don't worry, it's the waiting that's worst. The bastards are late today, possibly a bit of fog over the French airfield. But they'll be here sooner or later.' Robert tried to look confident. He leant back; this was what he had always wanted. He thought of his childhood letter to Diana: '*Went to air display at Hendon with Papa. Saw the Hawker Harts, they were spectacular, like silver birds, you should have heard the sound of the Rolls Royce engines.*'

His first experience of flying had been a few weeks later.

'Come on, Robs, you need another layer, it'll be freezing up there.' His father had helped him into his coat before paying ten bob, five shillings for each of them, at the small kiosk. To Robert, the next few moments in the Avro biplane would define his future.

His father had been dead four months when the school bully had made him his target. Small things at first, then an insidious campaign against him, led by Lawson. He realised the level of harassment had changed when he found his aeroplane removed from his shelf and crushed on the floor. It was the last thing he had shown his father.

His black school shoes came next, taken in the middle of the night. By the time he found them he was late for chapel and the door was closed. They were singing 'Jerusalem', but to Robert it didn't feel like England's green and pleasant land. Then his tailcoat and starched white shirt went missing. He had to go to science in his sports jacket and trousers, where the 'Welshman', as they called him, summoned him to the front.

'Now, boy, why are you in half change? It's Monday, not the bloomin' weekend.' Robert explained he'd lost them.

Though he longed to be taken away, he said nothing in his weekly letter to his mother.

A few days later he was on his way to the maths block when he remembered he hadn't locked his tuck box. He swore and looked at his watch; he would be late for class but he had to go back. When he reached the end of the corridor, his door was ajar. He had left it closed. He started to run. The smell hit him immediately. Someone had pissed in his room, and at the centre of the vile pool lay the stamp book his father had given him. The pages were sodden, the stamps destroyed. The only consolation was they didn't get his Penny Red. He always carried it on him.

The Matron appeared in the doorway. She was Swiss and severe but had a soft spot for Robert. '*Gott in Himmel,*' she said, staring at the mess on the floor, taking it all in. 'Who has done this?'

Robert bit his lip. 'I don't know,' he said, trying not to cry. But he did know.

'I believe it is that Lawson boy,' she had said, passing him a handkerchief. 'He is a coward. Only cowards behave like this.'

After lessons had finished, when Robert was alone in his study, he took his father's jersey from the cupboard and lay on his bed. Holding it to his face, he breathed in deeply. The smell of citrus and cedar wood had gone as his father had gone. His mind went back to that awful day.

'I didn't see him,' the driver in the green overalls gasped to a bystander. 'He weren't looking. I'm sorry, it weren't my fault.'

Robert had stared at his father's pounded face. Somewhere behind him his mother was screaming. He put his hands over his ears to block out the noise.

The ambulance screeched to a halt in the wet road. Three men jumped out. Two attended to Anthony, while the last put a blanket over his shoulders. 'Come away, lad,' he said. 'Don't look.'

Robert clung to his father's hand. 'You can't die,' he whispered to him.

'We need to get him into the ambulance.'

'I'm not leaving him, you can't make me.'

'The sooner he's at the hospital the better his chances.'

Robert pulled a small sliver of glass from his father's hand and struggled to his feet.

It was quiet in the hall, the clock went on ticking, the stamp remained on the hall table. His father had given him a gift he longed for and in return he had killed him.

He was in Whitstable on a weekend break with Douglas when he finally admitted to the bullying. They were paddling in the sea and Douglas's tweed trousers were rolled up to his knees.

'You're a natural sportsman, Robert. I saw it last week in your rugby match. You were brave in the tackle and aggressive in the attack, so here's my suggestion. Boxing. It will refine the brain and revive the spirit. It will also get rid of the bullies. A quick punch, that will put them off, I assure you. Hit them where it hurts. Trust me, I know.'

'I'll take your word for it,' Robert replied, and as they walked back across the pebbles, he realised that it was time to make a stand.

He had taken to boxing like a duck to water. His reflexes were quick and in the ring he concentrated only on his opponent. His problems remained outside. Ducking and diving, jabbing, he escaped into a glorious dance of artistic aggression. What was more he was good at it. As Robert's technique improved, so did his confidence.

When Archie Lawson cornered him in the hall, his friends circling around him, Robert was no longer afraid.

'So,' Lawson said, thrusting his face towards him, 'is your mother sleeping with the Fascists?' Robert was filled with an instant, blinding rage. Lawson could torment him, but he would never insult his mother. He curled his fist into a tight ball and flattened the other boy. As Archie Lawson moaned on the floor, Robert put his foot on his chest.

'If you ever speak of my mother again,' he said. 'I will kill you.' To Robert's surprise word sped round the school and his new status was confirmed. He wrote to his mother, and this time the contents of his letter were true.

Robert walked back into the dispersal hut and glanced at the clock: seven forty-five. He sat down in one of the battered leather armchairs and tried to read the newspaper. He put it back on the table and closed his eyes, thinking instead of the months of training that had brought him this far. How his flying instructor had pressed him: 'Come on, Marston, your technique is passable but it could be better if you put your mind to it', and so he had. He had been determined to get his Pilot's Wings and to complete his course. When his colleagues were suspended for failing their tests, Robert kept his head down and worked harder. When two of his contemporaries were killed in flying accidents, though overwhelmed with the loss, he went to his instructor. 'I need to know, what went wrong and why?'

'I'm sorry, Marston,' the instructor replied. 'Pearson and Greene were confronted by circumstances beyond their experience.' Robert understood that it was how you coped with the death of a friend that defined those who had the resilience to continue. But it didn't stop him going to the mess.

He was on his second whisky when a pilot officer came into the bar. He was tall, with an easy grin and brown hair which flopped over his forehead. Robert had seen him the day before. He was supposedly Canadian, but it was immediately apparent that he was, in fact, American and had defied the neutrality laws. 'I risked going to prison to help you,' he had joked with the boys.

He sauntered across to Robert.

'Hey, buddy, I could sure do with a drink.'

Robert looked confused. 'It's Robert, actually.'

The man looked amused. 'In America, everyone is "buddy".' His voice was smooth and rich like double cream, and the vowels were long and rolling.

'Mind if I join you?'

'Go ahead, I'm not going anywhere.'

'You OK?'

'No, not really. Pearson and Greene died today. You won't know them but they were decent chaps, both of them.'

The man put his hand out. 'Harvey Lorch. Let's drink to them; and you can tell me about yourself.'

Robert smiled a lopsided, slightly drunken smile.

'It's OK to talk, buddy, we have a lotta time.'

Robert finally told Harvey about his family, and about his father. After the fifth whisky he looked up at his new acquaintance with glazed eyes. 'It seems you have my life story!'

'Well, buddy, that sure makes us friends.'

Robert grinned foolishly. The American was everything he aspired to be. After that night they were inseparable, and as the fatalities increased, Robert depended on Harvey's friendship.

'You look after yourself,' Robert said to him, punching his shoulder.

'There's Irish blood on my daddy's side, so I'll be just fine. Anyway, I've told the folks back home you're coming to visit as soon as this is over.'

They were together in the mess on the first day of September, 1939 when they heard that German troops had swarmed over the border into Poland – the Blitzkrieg had begun.

'Hitler won't withdraw and it will be war,' Harvey had stated, his normally cheerful face grave. He was correct, and two days later the commanding officer came in to the mess and turned on the wireless. The young pilots put down their pints. There was silence in the room as Neville Chamberlain's voice came over the airwaves, declaring that a state of war existed between Britain and Germany.

Months passed and, as the course progressed, Robert perfected his judgement with low-level flying, and he mastered the skill of flying on instruments. He kept his head in simulated emergencies and suppressed the inner fear he experienced on his first spinning exercise. He worked on the Morse code at midnight when his eyes ached with fatigue and, with Harvey's help, he crammed passages from the *Manual of Air Force Law* from cover to cover for his test the following day.

'Come on, buddy,' Harvey said, leaning over the desk where his friend was working.

'I can't remember any of it, Harvey; I'm going to fail.'

'Jeez, stop taking yourself so seriously, of course you can do it,' and Robert got up and boxed his ears and they had both laughed. The effort paid off. Robert passed his elementary flying training course on the basic Tiger Moth biplane. But any complacency was eliminated when he started the second stage of flying training, and a mishandled recovery from his first solo spin nearly brought disaster.

On the ground, a lapse in his attitude towards the physical training and ceremonial drills brought him to the attention of his instructor. 'These drills are part of your transformation into young officers and proficient pilots,' he told him sternly. It was a sobering lesson.

With hard work, Robert came to terms with the daunting aircraft, learning to master its tricky landing technique and improve his aerobatic skills. Once he had passed his intermediate navigation exams, he was presented with the greatest test of his courage yet: night flying. After only two night-time dual flights with the instructor, he was sent on his first solo night flight.

It was a moonless sky with no clear horizon and no lights from the blacked-out towns and villages below. He was totally dependent on his flight instruments. It was like finding your way through a darkened room. Aloft, sitting in the cockpit with only the fluorescent glow of the instrument panel and with a cloak of blackness around him, he could feel the apprehension building in his chest, almost smothering him. To survive, Robert knew he must rely upon his training. As he fought to control his breathing, he forced himself to concentrate on his flight instruments in order to fly straight and level. Slowly his panic subsided and his breathing returned to normal. When he landed and climbed from the cockpit, his legs gave way beneath him. His instructor caught hold of him.

'Marston, you are not the only one to feel a little shaky the first time; you'll get used to it.'

After more night dual-instruction he was once again sent out on his own. His confidence had returned. The stubby, brutish Harvard training aircraft became part of him. Before long he found delight in launching into a starlit world, sweeping in to land between the comforting flares, and afterwards going for a drink with Harvey and the boys.

When Robert was judged ready to take his final handling test and his final theory exams he was filled with doubt. If all went well he would be awarded the coveted pilot's wings. If he failed . . . it was a prospect he couldn't even contemplate.

With little more than half of the original intake remaining, and eleven months after joining up, with one hundred and twenty hours dual flying in his logbook plus forty hours solo flying, Robert completed his exams. To his immense relief he graduated successfully. After the Commission ceremony, his flying instructor congratulated him.

'Well done, Marston, you'll be delighted to know you've been recommended for fighters, and I've heard on the grapevine that your friend Harvey Lorch will be joining you.' Robert was doubly thrilled as he shook his instructor's hand. As Acting Pilot Officer Robert Marston, he was now entitled to wear the thin blue ring on his sleeve and the elegant Wings on his chest. He looked in the mirror. 'I've passed, Papa, so first bit accomplished. And I can't wait for the next.'

The pace of the war had quickened drastically, and Robert and his classmates had qualified at a critical moment. The heavy losses suffered by the squadrons of the RAF's Advance Air Striking Force had created a grave shortage of pilots.

In June 1940, a few days after his graduation leave, Robert and Harvey were posted to an Operational Conversion Unit to learn to fly the Spitfire MK1. Each time Robert climbed into the cockpit, curling his long legs into the confined space, he was amazed that at barely nineteen years of age he was flying the beautiful, sensitive but deadly fighter plane. His dream had finally come true. But the pressure was mounting relentlessly to complete his training. He needed to learn to use his aircraft as a weapon. Firing his guns for the first time in practice proved a startling experience; he was unprepared for the shattering cacophony of sound produced by the eight Browning machine guns in the wings of his plane, and the shuddering of the entire aircraft at the recoil. It was only a two-second burst but enough to emphasise the terrifying, lethal force at his fingertips.

One week after the evacuation of the remnants of the British Expeditionary Force from Dunkirk, Robert and Harvey were posted to an operational squadron. They travelled south with two other young pilot officers. As the train rattled through the tunnels, Harvey slept like a baby but Robert – fired with adrenaline – could only think of the days ahead.

He took a newspaper cutting from his pocket. The evacuation

of Dunkirk had been a triumph salvaged from disaster, but the photos of the destroyers, merchant ships, yachts and fishing boats that had made their way across the Channel to rescue the stranded troops showed the cost of the evacuation. Fires blazed from the burning ships while guns blazed overhead. A sea of humanity struggled through the water or waited in the sand dunes and piers under continuous German attack.

He folded the newspaper and for a brief moment he allowed himself to think of his mother and Diana at home in Italy. God willing, he would survive to see them again. He was only too aware his chance of survival was slim, for though the battle to save France was lost, the battle to save Britain had only just begun.

The train pulled up at the station and the four men took a taxi to Kingsley Down Airfield. Standing in front of his commanding officer a short time later, Robert noticed his worn and crumpled uniform, the bright purple and white ribbon of the Distinguished Flying Cross newly sewn on below his wings. Though he conveyed a compelling sense of authority, the man was only three or four years older than he was himself. Those tired eyes, Robert thought as he looked into them, had already seen more than a lifetime of death.

'Good to have you with us,' he greeted Robert, surveying him. 'You have joined a very famous fighter squadron, you have a lot to live up to. How many hours training?'

'Two hundred logged, sir.'

'Better than most,' he responded wearily. 'Get a room in the mess and report to "B" Flight Commander. He'll brief you and authorise you for a flight to familiarise yourself with the local area. After a couple of circuits he'll match you with an experienced number one. You will be operational tomorrow. Have you any questions?'

Robert's mouth was dry. He found it difficult to respond. 'No, sir,' he finally replied. The commanding officer smiled wryly. 'I expect you need a livener. See you in the bar.'

That night the livener turned into several and, as Robert drank with Harvey, it became easier to forget the following day.

'Here's a nice cuppa, sir,' his batman had said, waking him at dawn. 'You'll meet your room-mate, Pilot Officer Hendry, when he's back from leave this evening. He's a nice young man, you'll like him, I'm sure.' He had taken a clean shirt from Robert's cupboard and put it over the chair. 'I'll leave you to get dressed. I'll see you tonight, sir.'

'Yes, yes of course.' The door closed and Robert hoped there would be a tonight, that he would meet Hendry, and he would need his batman the following morning. He dressed quickly, wishing to be in good time for the weather briefing. He was halfway down the corridor when Pilot Officer Jackson, one of the new recruits he had travelled with, greeted him cheerfully. 'Breakfast?' he asked.

'No thanks,' Robert had muttered. 'Not sure I could keep it down.'

Now, while Harvey slept in the armchair next to him, Robert got up and paced around the dispersal hut. He needed to get on with the task at hand. He dropped his letters into the Adjutants' tray and glanced at the other men. To the uninitiated they looked calm, composed, but Robert knew each man in the hut was probably hiding his own fears. Many of them had trained together, fought in the air together; had drunk together in the mess or in the village pubs. They were all trying to cram as much as they could into their very young lives.

The Luftwaffe's tactics had now turned to attacking the fighter airfields, the bombers coming over in their droves to drop their deadly cargo, joined by the fighters at low level on strafing runs.

Robert stepped aside as Pilot Officer Jackson fled past him and retched on the doorstep.

'OK, old chap?' Robert asked.

'Not really,' Jackson answered shakily. 'Breakfast wasn't a good idea after all.'

Chapter Twenty-two

The Sector Operations telephone in the dispersal hut rang shrilly. Everyone was quiet as the young airman orderly grabbed the receiver and started jotting figures on a pad. The Squadron Leader entered. He waited until the orderly had finished, then he read the pad and gave his instructions.

'Sector Ops say there is a large enemy formation building up over the French coast. For once we have plenty of time, which will give us a height advantage. We will scramble as a squadron instead of individually to make angels three zero climbing on a vector zero nine zero. Formation will take off by sections in V formation; radio-telephone and oxygen checks will be on my call. Keep your eyes open and stick with me.'

There was a commotion inside the hut. The pilots were tightening their Mae West life vests, grabbing their leather helmets, and running outside to jump into the waiting truck. The young airwoman from the Women's Auxiliary Air Force drove fast but carefully as she tried to avoid the heavy tyre tracks criss-crossing the field, but Robert still had to grip onto the edge to prevent himself falling. She reached the squadron's dispersal area and stopped at his plane, calling its code letter. Robert was about to jump down when he looked over at Harvey.

'Good luck,' Harvey said cheerfully. 'See ya later.'

Robert pulled on his goggles. 'See you, my friend.'

His ground crew, whom he had met the previous evening, were waiting for him.

'The engine's already been warmed up and was running sweetly. It won't let you down,' his fitter Brian said. The rigger, Jock, had put his parachute on the tail plane. Robert put it on while Brian restarted the engine.

'Everyone is nervous the first time, sir,' he yelled.

Robert tried to smile but his lips were fixed in a grim line. He signed the serviceability log with an unsteady hand and climbed into the cockpit. He put on his helmet and his gloves and strapped himself in, connecting his radio-telephone lead and oxygen tube. He breathed deeply, trying to calm himself. At once the still air was shattered by the sound of a dozen Merlin engines exploding into life with a staccato clatter, then settling into a smooth, rhythmic rumble. He swiftly ran through his pre-take-off checks, confirming that both his oxygen and petrol tank gauges were indicating full, quickly registering the readings of his engine instruments and finally checking the operation of his flying controls. Everything was in order.

'Good luck, sir,' Brian mouthed, his voice drowned out by the sound of the Merlin engine. Robert waved the chocks away, released his brakes and started taxiing along the perimeter track behind John, his section leader. They turned into wind and lined up in formation waiting for the squadron leader to give the hand signal for take-off. Suddenly they were off, four sections each in Vic formation, surging together; twelve Spitfires leaping forward at full throttle. Robert could feel the controls becoming effective as he gained speed, keeping straight with the rudder. Once airborne he raised the undercarriage and with his teeth gritted in concentration, he held his position a wingspan's width from his leader as the entire formation turned onto the climbing heading. The squadron opened up into loose battle formation and continued the climb, the houses diminishing quickly until they were merely specks below, and the fields and woods a patchwork of colours.

Robert relaxed a little, maintaining a safe distance from John on his left. He caught his eye, and when John gave him the thumbs up, Robert felt a surge of elation. Flying wingman to an experienced fighter pilot gave him confidence; he could fly with the best of them.

A few tufts of cumulus clouds were forming and as they passed through ten thousand feet Robert checked his oxygen flow. He looked around him, his eyes scanning the deep blue sky above for traces of condensation trails, which would highlight an enemy presence. Though he could see nothing, he could hear over the crackle and static on his radio-telephone that the expected raid was coming towards them at twenty thousand feet. It was still a significant distance away and on the squadron leader's instructions they continued the climb to achieve a tactical height advantage. Robert checked his instruments again. Everything was still as it should be, engine oil pressure and temperature normal. He turned the safety catch on his gun button to fire, switched on his gunsight and turned his oxygen to maximum flow. The cockpit was becoming very cold; Robert shivered.

His muscles were tight in his chest, his breathing shallow. 'Just hold your battle formation position and don't let them spot you before you spot them,' he recited. At twenty-five thousand feet they levelled out, carefully keeping just below the contrail height, to avoid their vapour trail being seen. Robert scanned the sky, every nerve in his body tense. Suddenly the squadron leader's calm voice broke though the RT static.

'Red Leader, bandits at your ten o'clock low, range ten!'

John acknowledged him. 'I can see about a dozen 109s at three thousand feet below.' The squadron leader then led them all into a steep descending turn to attack the 109s from behind. Robert followed John as they curved down fast to the rear of the enemy. The sun was behind them, blinding their presence to the Hun.

John the Red Leader straightened out of the diving turn and called, 'Steady, spread out and take your pick.' Robert was now ready for the fight, his head was clear and his apprehension was replaced by a fierce concentration. They were closing fast on the unsuspecting Messerschmitt fighters, almost within firing range; when suddenly they were spotted. 'Watch yourself, boys' came over the RT from Red Leader, as the enemy formation broke upwards into a tight climbing turn, too tight for the attackers to bring their guns to bear. The squadron opened out and descended upon a group of Heinkel bombers, which the Messerschmitt fighters had been escorting. That part of the sky exploded into a melee of individual fights.

Robert had succeeded in pursuing the last tail-end 109, which was lagging slightly behind the others. He turned his craft on its wing tip, opened his throttle to maximum boost and hauled round inside his enemy's steeply banked turn. The blood drained from his head and he was on the verge of blacking out when for a brief second the 109 swam across his gun sight; it was a perfect target. He fired a short burst. The 109 rolled into a dive. Robert followed, turning tightly, trying for another shot. He fired again. He felt sure he had hit him and this time saw smoke streaming from the engine. He felt the surge of adrenaline flowing through his veins; he had a hit on his first operational sortie. Leaving nothing to chance, he gave it a last burst. Flames now licked the underside of the fuselage. Overhauling his target, Robert could see the pilot trying to open the cockpit hood. He could see his desperate struggle as he tried to get out. At once he was no longer the adversary, just a young man like himself. 'Get out,' he yelled. 'For Christ's sake get out.' But the pilot couldn't release the hood and the flames engulfed him. Slowly the aircraft rolled on its back and dived vertically to the water far below. Making a bright splash it sank without trace, the ripples spreading on the calm sea.

Soaked in perspiration, Robert felt physically and mentally exhausted. In a few wild seconds he had run the scale of emotions, but now the adrenaline had gone and with it the desire to kill. A strange melancholy came over him as he looked around the sky. There was not an aircraft in sight and, apart from the crackle and static on his radio-telephone, he felt completely alone. Looking behind him, just a handful of fluffy white cumulus cloud was set against an azure sky: all was clear, it was a peaceful summer's day.

The carnage and brutality of seconds before seemed part of a different world. He knew he was fortunate, his first kill, but at this moment he didn't feel fortunate. 'Hell, I'm tired.' He wiped the sweat from his eyes. He looked at his fuel gauge: it registered only a quarter full, he needed to get home. He was over the land now. The cliffs were receding behind him and the seaside towns to his left. The nearer he got to his base, the more the weight fell from his shoulders. For now his squadron was his home, his temporary family was the group of men he flew with and served with. These men would be his constant companions in everything. Their extraordinary way of life would be his life. The battle had been a fight to the death: today his opponent was dead; tomorrow it could be him.

When the squadron intelligence officer debriefed him, his score was established. A vigilant coastguard had confirmed the time and position of the kill. Robert's first victory had been witnessed.

Later, as he sat in the mess with his squadron, he felt a momentary sense of pride. He was being accepted as a member of this elite fraternity. But should he be proud? Did he truly believe it commendable to be celebrating a man's death? He got up and ordered two glasses of Scotch, one for himself and one for Harvey. He checked his thoughts, they were inappropriate; it was a fight to the end. If they didn't rid the skies of the enemy, Britain would be lost. He downed the Scotch and looked up to find Harvey watching him.

'I know what you are thinking, but death is part of war, there's no way round it buddy.'

'It was awful watching the pilot trying to bale out, bloody awful.'

''Course it was. But you can't dwell on it. Come on, a fleecing at cards will cheer you up.' Harvey pulled a new pack of cards from his pocket. 'A little poker, guys?' he asked.

Mike, a large Canadian, who looked as if he wouldn't fit into a submarine let alone the cockpit of a Spitfire, ambled over. 'Sure thing,' he replied. Soon five of them were playing.

'Why aren't the rest of you bloody Yanks in the war with us?' Mike asked cheerfully.

'Back home they think it ain't our war, but I sure fear they're wrong. It's only a matter of time,' Harvey drawled. When the conversation moved on to Italy and Fascism, Robert was silent.

'Sorry, Robert, your family live in Italy,' John apologised.

'Why should you be sorry?' he replied, but when the card game resumed he couldn't concentrate. He was grateful when a young man entered the mess and threw his bag onto a leather armchair beside them.

'You must be Robert Marston,' he said. 'Crispin Hendry. I'm your room-mate, glad to share with you, old chap. Hope you're moderately civilised but according to rumours you were quite rowdy last night.' Hendry was of medium height and stocky with a twinkle in his brown eyes. Robert liked the look of him immediately. 'A one-off only, I assure you,' he said, laughing. 'But you may wish to join us for a drink.'

Chapter Twenty-three

Two days later, on 2 July, they were relaxing in the mess. Harvey was reading a letter, looking unusually solemn.

'From your family?' Robert asked.

'Yeah, my Grandpa. He's sick, dying actually and it's my birthday next week. I'd sure like to be with them.' He coughed and took a large slug of whisky.

'It's OK, old chap; my grandfather means an awful lot to me. I tell you what, will you come with me to see him in London on a day off?'

'I'd like that, and then you can show me the town.'

Robert laughed in amazement. 'You've never been to London?'

'You ever been to Mobile, Alabama?'

'I hope to, but first it's London for you, my friend.'

The following Saturday at noon, the two young men emerged from Kensington High Street station and picked their way through the busy streets. Adding to the throng were hundreds of other men and women in uniform.

'Come on, we'll be late for Grandpa and he's a real stickler for time.' Robert pulled Harvey by the arm. 'And stop gawping at every girl that passes.'

'Shame to cover those legs,' Harvey grumbled, looking at a

pretty WAAF in thick, regulation stockings. 'Boy, what I'd give to see her in a pair of nylons!'

The jesting stopped once they arrived at Peter Marston's terraced house in Derry Street, to be let in by the daily help.

'Grandfather, this is my friend Harvey Lorch,' Robert said, ushering Harvey into the sitting room.

Peter peered into the young man's face and shook his hand. 'Good to meet you, Lorch.'

'Good to meet you too, sir, your grandson has told me all about you.'

'Nothing to tell, I'm an old man but you, you're an American,' Peter said with no small amount of awe.

'I hope you won't hold that against me.'

'Quite the opposite, you've come a long way to help us.'

'Your grandson is going to show me around your grand old city.'

'I hope it will remain so, but I have my doubts. The Hun have it in their sights, unfortunately.' He walked over to a mahogany cabinet. 'Drink, boys?'

'Yes please, sir.'

Half an hour later Robert hugged his grandfather goodbye.

'Take care, Robbie,' the old man said. 'I worry about you.'

'Well, you mustn't, it's a picnic up there.' But Robert held on to him for a moment because Grandpa Peter was an extension of his father.

'I may be geriatric, but I can read through the propaganda. And you, Lorch, keep an eye on my grandson.'

'I sure will, sir.'

'Where are you going now?'

'The Tower of London, sir, then I believe a famous bookshop; Robert is in charge.'

'Make sure you don't disturb the ravens; if they leave the

Tower, the Kingdom will fall,' Peter chuckled, his humour restored.

'To think the war could be lost for a few old black birds,' Harvey quipped.

'I like this boy.' The old man looked at Robert. 'Do all Yanks have a sense of humour?'

'This one certainly does. Goodbye, Grandpa.'

'One day you'll see London without the sandbags.' Robert commented as they went outside.

'Yeah, it is a bit of a shock,' Harvey agreed. 'But it's better to have a few sandbags and taped-up windows than having a heap of glass shattering over you in a bomb blast... There are, of course, compensations.' He was now grinning at an entire group of WAAFs who were gazing into a shop window filled with women's apparel. 'I'd like my girlfriend to have a figure like that!'

'But you haven't got a girlfriend, oaf!'

'Well I'm out to get me a nice English gal!'

'And you think they'd want a loud American like you?'

''Course, buddy, they won't be able to resist me!'

After a visit to the Tower of London followed by Foyles bookshop, their last destination was the Café Royal for a well-earned drink.

'I want the biggest cocktail they have on offer,' Robert instructed Harvey as he went to the bar. 'Something diabolically sweet and fantastically strong, next round is on me.'

Harvey came back with two long glasses decorated with pink paper umbrellas.

'Pink?' Robert queried.

'I told this pretty little gal it was my favourite colour! Get it down, old man.'

They did get it down, and several more. An hour and a half

later the two young men were grinning at everything, funny and otherwise.

'What does your father do for a living?' Robert asked, trying to be serious.

'Airplanes.'

'Is he a mechanic?'

'No, not really, but he's a good man with a wrench.' Harvey started to giggle. 'He's actually a designer for an airplane factory.'

'Come on, Harvey, you're being evasive.'

'Well, he sort of owns an airplane factory.'

Robert looked at him, one eyebrow raised. 'Anything I have heard of?'

'Possibly – Hammonds Aircraft Corporation, only small but it's quite significant.'

Robert whistled. 'It's one of the best aircraft manufacturers in the world. No wonder you like flying.'

'My dad first let me fly solo at thirteen. I'm here to save y'all.' He was serious for a moment. 'Actually it is sort of true. I have a skill and I want to put it to some good. You see, I don't like bullies, Robert, and Hitler is a bully. I think your little country needs all the help it can get.' He polished off his cocktail. 'I'm expected to take over one day, you could always run it with me.'

Robert draped an arm around his shoulder. 'I'd love that. If you weren't a bloke I'd probably kiss you.'

'Well I am, so don't even think about it.'

From there they swayed to a taxi and instructed the driver to take them to a jazz club in Soho. At three o'clock in the morning Harvey got on the stage, having bribed one of the musicians to give up his trumpet. His Louis Armstrong was passable; that is, until he fell into the audience.

Somehow they got back to the base and staggered to their rooms.

The following morning when Robert's batman arrived with

the customary cup of tea, he was surprised to find Robert still dressed in his uniform, face down on his bed. Crispin Hendry left him a note:

'Hope you had a good time. Remind me, who was the chap who said he didn't snore?'

During a very late breakfast with Harvey, Robert pulled a package from his pocket.

'Happy birthday. Hope you like it, I bought it in Foyles yesterday.'

'So that's what you were doing sneaking round the bookstore.'

Harvey tore open the paper. Inside was a small book of poetic prose: *The Prophet*, by Kahlil Gibran. He opened the book and read the inscription. He looked up, his eyes serious. 'Hey, this means a lot, old buddy.'

'It was my father's favourite poem. Words from *The Prophet* are engraved on his memorial stone. I'm pretty sure you'll enjoy reading it.'

'I know I will.'

Robert took the book from Harvey. 'Look at this line. *'You talk when you cease to be at peace with your thoughts.'* Sometimes I say it to myself when I'm flying. I find it pretty lonely up there. Anyway, enough of my sentimentality, how do you feel?'

'Like some critter is knocking inside my head.'

'We could always go for a walk, that'll clear it,' Robert suggested.

'A walk? Harvey put down his toast. 'Y'all crazy.'

Their walk in the Kent woods was curtailed when Harvey sank onto a felled log. 'Enough torture,' he groaned. 'Sit down.'

Robert laughed. 'Where's your stamina? You're only one year older than I am.'

Harvey punched his arm. 'Actually, I have a proposition,'

he said, laughing. 'And I mean a serious one. The only thing I remember from last night is asking you to join me in the family business. I meant it, why don't you come back to the States with me when all of this is over? Aviation is your life, we could train to become aeronautical engineers, and when my dad retires we can run the business together. What do you say?'

'Harvey, I'm honoured and it's a great idea, but I can't plan so far ahead. Neither of us have any idea if we will survive this madness.'

'You can't think like that,' Harvey remonstrated. 'If we don't make plans we have nothing to dream about. I need to believe in a future, otherwise I couldn't climb into the cockpit every day.'

'But you never seem frightened. How do you always seem so positive? Only last week when your plane took a hit, you were laughing when you came in. "It's only a few little ole bullets", you said.'

Harvey turned to him. 'Yup, I'm scared. I want to see my momma and my sister again. The only way I get through this is to believe I will return home to them.'

'Well then, I will come to Alabama; we will have the dream, my friend. Now, back to the mess, the boys will have returned.'

As they opened the door to the mess, their squadron, having finished for the day, were waiting for them. A banner saying *Happy 21st Birthday Harvey* was strung across the bar.

'You're a long way from home,' John said, thrusting a present at him. 'We thought you might need a bit of cheering.'

'This is from me.' Toby, a new recruit with a mop of red hair, handed Harvey a box of chocolates, and Crispin pulled a copy of *Health and Efficiency* from beneath his jacket. When everyone had given Harvey a present or a card, he opened the magazine.

Soon the entire squadron was leaning over his shoulder, arguing over the attributes of the naked women. When the cook entered with an enormous pink cake and placed it in front of him, he shut the magazine quickly.

'This is very moving,' Harvey said, a little tearfully. 'But why pink?'

'Because it is your favourite colour.'

'It is?' Harvey looked incredulous.

'Your friend here,' the cook interrupted, pointing at Robert, 'said it had to be pink. Something about cocktails and parasols.' She picked up the magazine. 'And if you think you're the first lad in the mess to own a sexy magazine, I can tell you, you're wrong.'

When Harvey plunged the knife into the pink cake everyone cheered. Robert brought out the cards from Harvey's family and Harvey stood on the table.

'I want to thank y'all,' he drawled, 'for welcoming an all-American boy into your hearts. It sure is appreciated. So may I suggest a toast. To each and every one of us... and now folks, let the party begin.'

Chapter Twenty-four

A big raid came on 27 July. The Germans were on their way to Dover to bomb the shipping at anchor in the harbour. Robert had to abandon his lunch; he swore lightly, knowing he should learn to eat faster. He waved to the girl at the wheel of the truck as he jumped to the ground. She was new and pretty, another member of the WAAF. He wondered if he had the courage to ask her for a drink.

The checks on the plane came to him automatically now, and sometimes he thought he could fly in his sleep. As the section climbed, leaving the airfield behind, Robert looked out of the cockpit. Below him, a haze had settled over the fields. It looked so peaceful, untouched by the war that raged in the skies, a war he would be part of in less than half an hour. How beautiful it was, England basking in the summer sun. He imagined the fields of Tuscany, now golden as the harvest approached. A lump formed in his throat; he missed his mother and Diana but at least they were safe, away from all this. '*The war continues to elude us,*' his mother had written only the week before. '*It's as if we are in a small bubble, protected from the outside world. We hear about it of course, mainly from our friends in Rome, but the talk is more about the plight of the Jews in Germany and Poland than the war itself. Thankfully D's family are fine. Keep safe, my darling boy.'*

Thank God for her letters; the last was in his pocket, sent care of Douglas, via Spain.

The squadron had just passed Dover harbour and were over the Channel at eighteen thousand feet when Robert's radio transmitter sprang into life. 'Ten o'clock, below you at ten o'clock. Bandits, fifty of them at twelve thousand feet.' His mind was at once on the job in hand.

With his senses alert, he set his sights and turned the gun button to fire. He remembered his instructor's advice: 'In the combat zone never fly straight and level for more than a couple of minutes, and if you have a bandit on your tail, go into a steep turn, dive and get the hell out of there.'

At thirteen thousand feet they spotted them below, Junkers 88 bombers with their escort of Messerschmitt 109s weaving above them. He glanced at John flying next to him.

'Red Section going down.' John pointed to the first of a group of five bombers who flew in tight formation. 'Guard my tail and watch the flak.'

Flashes from the British anti-aircraft guns were coming up at them from all sides. 'Can't they see we're on their bloody side?' Robert muttered as seconds later he was in the thick of it. Harvey as number three had selected his target, and Robert had chosen his own. He was in range. He could see the gunner of the Junkers 88 in his turret facing rearward.

Robert pressed the firing button and, as the eight guns pumped bullets into the upper fuselage, the gunner slumped forward, his own weapon silenced for ever. Robert glanced quickly back: there were no telltale black crosses, no Messerschmitt 109s lurking behind him. He manoeuvred his plane to place the 88 in his gun sight for a deflective shot and held down the firing button once more. Now it was time to finish off the plane. As the lead from his guns ripped into the stricken bomber, black oily smoke poured from both of the engines. Their battle was over and their end inevitable. As the bomber banked into a spiral descent, Robert broke away. When only two parachutes opened below him he thought of the gunner and the other crewman who remained inside. 'Poor bastards,' he groaned, as the plane entered its terminal dive. His sympathy was short-lived when shells hammered into his own plane and it lurched sideways. *Christ, I've been hit*, he thought.

As he slammed into a hard break to outturn his attacker, he felt a stab of fear. He had been caught unawares. Craning his neck he could see a Messerschmitt now clearly on his tail. Why hadn't he seen it before? He tightened his steep turn, juddering on the threshold of a high-speed stall. He had to get away; he had to get rid of the sod. As he dived away, multicoloured zigzags moved across his line of vision and blinding pain grew above his right eye. His neck was aching and at once his stomach started to cramp. Panic built in his chest; he couldn't have a migraine, not after all these years. For the next few seconds he fought for his life, avoiding the hail of explosive shells. The pain in his head was building to a crescendo. He peered through the windscreen. His vision was blurred, he felt the bile rise in his throat, he was going to be sick. He mustn't be sick. Somehow he managed to keep control, but every time he thought he had lost him, the Messerschmitt was there. He yanked his rudder and hauled the stick back to tighten the turn even more. He was sweating profusely and on the point of blacking out, when suddenly it was over. The Messerschmitt dived away and was gone. At that moment Robert spotted Harvey closing on the enemy plane. *Thank God for Harvey.*

He limped home, his plane riddled with holes, his head throbbing like a hammer. The cliffs were ahead of him when

Harvey joined him and flew protectively at his side. Harvey had saved his life and in doing so had risked his own. Robert gave him the thumbs up to reassure him that he was unhurt, but he felt far from well.

'Just a few more minutes … keep going, Robert, you can make it,' he muttered to himself.

His concentration was broken by a voice on the RT.

'First one to get laid gets a fiver,' Harvey quipped over the airwaves. Robert grinned weakly. Only Harvey could wager on their manhood so publicly and at a time like this.

'You're on,' he said, trying to ignore the pain that had tightened like a vice around his head.

Though his landing was not achieved with the customary elegance, he managed to get the plane down and jolt back across the airfield to the dispersal point where Brian and Jock waited anxiously.

'Glad you're back, sir. Watching you come in gave everyone here a few bad moments. Looks like the plane has had a bit of a bashing.'

As Robert climbed out of the plane he was violently sick.

'Sorry, Jock,' he said wiping his face on his handkerchief. 'Bloody Hun bounced me.'

'You OK, sir?'

'I will be.'

Harvey, who arrived at his side, grinned at Jock. 'Your pilot was dreaming of beating me at poker.' He glanced at Robert and his smile faded. 'You need a trip to the doc.'

Robert was surprised to see blood soaking through his trouser leg. He hadn't noticed it before.

Overwhelmed with exhaustion, he grabbed on to Harvey's arm.

'That might be a good idea.' He tried to smile but his legs

gave way beneath him. Harvey held him up and supported him to the waiting truck.

'You can tell me what this is all about,' he said to Robert as the truck drove to the hospital.

Robert nodded. 'Later, my friend.'

The damage to his leg was fortunately only a flesh wound and after it was dressed, Harvey helped him to his room. 'Thank you, Harvey,' Robert said, and without waiting for a reply he fell onto the bed and sank into oblivion.

It was dark when Robert awoke several hours later. He sat up and put his head in his hands. The migraine could have resulted in his death, but of more concern to him was that it could have caused the death of others in his squadron.

When he returned to the mess, John looked up from his newspaper and smiled. 'Glad to see you're OK. Had me worried.' There was a general mumble of approval from the other pilots.

Crispin Hendry came over and clapped him on the back. 'Couldn't do without my room-mate, but of course I might actually get a good night's sleep.'

Laughter followed, then John spoke again. 'HMS *Codrington* was hit, and *Sandhurst*, but many of the ships were saved. Your Junkers was confirmed, by the way. Seriously, Marston, you are a great pilot and invaluable to the squadron.' There was a murmur of assent and glasses were raised.

Harvey was writing a letter in the corner of the mess, when Robert sank into the chair beside him. He looked up, his slow, easy grin lighting up his face.

'Nothing like a bit of appreciation. How ya doing?'

'Not great.' Robert winced.

'Cigarette?'

Robert made a face. 'No thanks, but I could do with a brandy. Will you put it on my tab and one for yourself?'

Harvey came back with two large brandies.

'So now you are gonna tell me?' Harvey asked, sitting down in the chair beside him.

'I don't know how to begin, it's truly awful.'

'What can be that bad?'

'This can.' Robert sighed and his body sagged forward. 'I'm a fraud, Harvey. I didn't tell the selection committee. I could have got you killed.'

'What the hell are you talking about?'

Robert looked up at him and took a deep breath. 'I used to have migraines. The specialist said I would probably grow out of them. I thought I had, but I was wrong.' He put his head in his hands. 'I'll have to resign.'

'But you didn't.'

'Didn't what?'

'You didn't get us killed.'

'But I could have. Harvey, what the hell am I going to do?'

'You're gonna do nothing.'

'What?'

'You heard what I said. This was the first one in years, right?' Robert nodded.

'I'll bet it won't happen again. You're needed. You're a damn fine pilot; so don't even think about it.'

Robert lifted his head, their eyes met, and Harvey knew what he was thinking.

'I have no intention of dying, buddy.'

'Please don't. I can't lose another person I care about, not after my father.'

'So, I'm a father figure, am I?' Harvey laughed.

'No. But you are my friend and in times like these, friendship is the most important thing we have.'

It was two days before Robert was cleared for flying. He was with Harvey in the mess and the bar was closing when he put his glass on the counter. 'Two of the same, George,' he said.

'Are you flying tomorrow, sir?' asked George, the regular barman who had ample experience with drunken young pilots.

'Yes, but not for six hours.'

'Rules, sir, I'm afraid.'

'Not even a little snifter?

'Not even a little snifter, sir.'

'Come on, buddy,' Harvey took his friend by the arm. 'We can continue this tomorrow.'

After an exhausting and costly day over the Channel, Robert and Harvey were sitting in the local pub. The atmosphere was subdued, the young airmen refusing to think about Charlie Simpson, another member of their squadron who hadn't come home.

Robert ordered a pint for both of them.

'I had beer for the first time when I was fifteen at a cellar in Berlin,' he said, passing a glass to Harvey. 'It was Lowenbrau. I went with my godfather in the autumn of thirty-seven, he was giving a lecture on the central nervous system at Universitats-medizin Berlin. It doesn't seem possible now.'

'What was it like?' Harvey asked.

'Lowenbrau? It's my favourite.'

'Not the beer, Germany, you fool.'

Robert grinned, then his face became sober. 'It was strange. Horrible, actually. Douglas took me on a tour of the city. The streets were immaculate, wide boulevards, banners everywhere, monuments to the Nazi order, but there was an atmosphere of subjugation, and of fear. It was like another world: so orderly, and yet terrifying.

'We went for a walk in the park and there was a sign on a bench, *Juden ist verboten*. I remember saying to Douglas that every man was equal in God's eyes. He reminded me that Hitler didn't care about God. He would probably eradicate Christianity too if they won the war. Then he told me an anagram in the cellar to cheer me up.'

'What was it?' Harvey put down his pint.

'*Dormitory*.' Robert smiled. 'I didn't get it.'

Harvey looked into the long glass and then up at Robert.

'*Dirty room*.' He grinned.

'Bastard!' Robert punched him nearly spilling the beer. He took a draught of his own. 'Funny thing, Lowenbrau was also my father's favourite beer.'

They had finished supper and Robert had lit his first cigarette when he leant towards Harvey.

'Thank you for listening.' He made smoke rings on the ceiling. 'In the squadron, I feel I'm worth something. I'm not the cool guy like you, and I'm often scared, but in this place everything is different.'

Harvey leant back in the chair and crossed his long legs. 'But I wasn't always brave. At junior high I was this skinny kid that everyone teased. Perhaps that's why I'm the joker now. My dad, he's a big man, larger than life, and most weekends he'd go off in the truck with his friends. They'd shoot deer, hogs, turkeys, you name it; he expected me to go with him, take the dogs, be an all-American kid. But I hated it, I didn't want to take life in the name of sport. I don't like it now; but this is different, it's war. It was a big decision, leaving my home and family. Even getting here was quite an adventure, but I had to come. I was always afraid of being a disappointment to my father, but I reckon he'll be proud of me now.'

As they talked into the night they understood what had drawn them to each other during their training.

"Night, Harvey,' Robert said when they arrived back at the base and went to their separate rooms. "Night, y'all,' Harvey grinned.

As Robert fell asleep, the memories of the stark lonely years at school melted away and, despite the mayhem around him, for the first time since his father's death he felt content.

It was the beginning of August when Robert waylaid Harvey on his way to the mess. 'I have an idea.'

'Sure, what is it?'

'I thought we could go to the Allington village fete, it's on our day off, Bank Holiday Monday.'

'Now that's kinda tame, isn't it?'

Robert grinned. 'Firstly, it's time you witnessed a great English tradition, and secondly, we might meet some girls to show us around.'

Harvey started to smile. 'Do you think John might lend us his car?' he asked.

John did lend the car, a battered but serviceable Austin with a removable hood. Dressed in their newly pressed uniforms, Robert drove Harvey to Allington. They walked into a large field decked with bunting. There were darts, a tombola, skittles and several young women with children at foot, but as far as they could see, few single girls.

They were sitting on a hay bale surrounded by inquisitive children, when Robert nudged Harvey.

'Over there.'

Standing by the coconut shy were two girls in green jumpers.

'Land girls,' Robert sighed. 'And they're on their own!'

Harvey was on his feet and about to make a move when Robert grabbed his sleeve.

'Can I have a snifter?' he begged, and Harvey passed him a flask of brandy. 'You're not nervous, are you, buddy?' he teased.

'Nervous, me? Never.'

'Admit it, you're a virgin.'

'If I am, so are you!'

Harvey sauntered over to the girls. 'If I try my hand at the coconuts will you wish this poor old American boy luck?' he asked, his eyes twinkling. The girls giggled and in less than a minute he had landed two coconuts.

'For you, doll,' he handed them to the girl with large blue eyes and blonde hair tied back into a ponytail.

'My but you're pretty,' he breathed.

'And you're not so bad yourself,' she replied. 'I'm Joan and this is Nora.'

Harvey winked at Robert, who was now trying his luck at the coconuts. He landed one and ambled over to Nora. 'I'm Robert,' he said, putting out his hand.

The carefree afternoon was filled with flirtation and banter. Though Nora wasn't beautiful, she was attractive and she made him laugh. They learnt that the girls had come from London to work on a farm nearby and until recently they had never seen a cow, let alone milked one. When Robert won a bear with a tartan bow around its neck in a game of skittles, he gave it to Nora.

'This will remind you of me,' he said, his confidence buoyed by a considerable amount of brandy.

'Really?' she asked, and Robert decided she had a lovely mouth, and the more he drank the prettier she became.

Later that afternoon, amid furtive giggling and abandoned clothes, Harvey and Robert lost their virginity in a barn not far from Allington. Afterwards they took the girls back to their farm where Joan took a photograph of the two young men, their arms draped around each other, a look of carefree happiness on their faces.

'I'll get the film developed and give you the photograph when I next see you,' Joan said to Harvey, kissing him.

'You're on, doll,' Harvey quipped.

The girls waved them off and it was not until they were halfway down the road and the girls were out of sight that they took off their caps and whooped with delight. They had fought in the Battle of Britain, they had faced mortal danger many times in a day, but until now they had never slept with a woman.

'We've done it,' Robert cried out, overjoyed.

And Harvey clapped him on the back. 'I surmise,' he said trying his best English accent, 'we can call our wager a draw.' And they laughed together some more.

'I think I'm in love,' Harvey breathed as they neared the base. 'My, does Joan have the ...' He paused and winked at Robert. 'Bluest eyes. Can I ask her to marry me after the first date?'

'Was that your idea of a date?' Robert chuckled, and Harvey grinned foolishly. 'No, but it was sure as hell good. What a great English tradition.'

It was now raid after raid from first light at dawn until well after dusk, but August had brought about a change in German tactics. Robert's squadron were now trying to stop the Germans knocking out the RAF's airfields, communications centre and radar masts. Each time Robert touched down at the station, he was amazed that he was still alive. There had been many near misses, and too many times when he had limped home in a battle-damaged aircraft to Jock and to Brian. How he admired the Erks, the dedicated ground crew who maintained their planes. If the plane seemed beyond repair they fixed it, working through the night to make sure it was serviceable for the following morning. When their base was hit on 1 September, the Erks took it in their stride. 'You can be glad we're not at Biggin Hill, sir, forty killed there yesterday. What are a few planes compared to our lives?'

On and on it went, relentless, wave after wave of German aircraft. Robert no longer thought in weeks, but in days and in hours. Each sortie he knew could be his last. When the Luftwaffe changed its strategy and started targeting London and other major cities, the Blitz truly began. Dusk flying, getting up at dawn, more flying, there seemed no end to it. After he witnessed the devastation of the East End of London, with the docks ablaze, oil and petrol tanks burning, entire streets and warehouses lit up like a circus, he knew he just had to keep going.

Robert would always remember the afternoon of 7 September. He was playing cards with Harvey and Hendry, relaxing in the late summer sun. Many of the squadron were sleeping, regaining their strength after the past gruelling weeks.

At four o'clock the call to scramble came. The squadron were at an altitude of twenty thousand feet when then they saw them, an inexorable procession of German bombers and their escorts crossing the Channel below, an Armada of planes. At first they seemed motionless, Heinkels, Dorniers, Messerschmitts, glinting in the sun. Layer upon layer as far as the eye could see, all flying at the same speed. To Robert they looked like a swarm of locusts, ready to devour everything in their path. Nothing in his life had prepared him for this sight. For a second he was paralysed with shock, but as the bombers broke into smaller groups, Robert glanced at John flying beside him. He looked calm and focused. Robert knew that the only way to get through this was to treat the terrifying spectacle as any other day. John selected his target and pointed below. He flew down towards the Dornier: Robert followed.

All afternoon and evening the squadrons were battling to

survive in the mayhem, refuelling, rearming, out in the battle again. A few fighters pitched against an unending force, trying to prevent the bombers from dropping their lethal load on London.

Robert and John were successful with the Dornier bomber, and later, Robert shot down a Heinkel on its way back to Germany. This time he felt no remorse.

Harvey and Robert limped home that evening, traumatised and exhausted, but they had survived. Many had not. Hendry was shot to pieces as he hung from his parachute, after bailing out of his plane.

Robert was drinking at the mess bar when their squadron leader called them together. The twenty-six-year-old judged his words carefully. 'Hendry was a great pilot and a fine young man; Jackson, too. They will be sorely missed by the entire squadron. Today, London was put to the sword, but with your extraordinary courage and skill, we will regroup again. We all know Hitler is gearing up for invasion, but the only thing I can say is: he has to get past us first. We are the finest and the best and we will not allow the Luftwaffe to gain the upper hand.

Much later Harvey, accompanied by his batman, arrived at Robert's door. 'Brought my bags, thought you needed a bit of cheering up, so I'm moving in.' He dumped the suitcases on Hendry's bed and the batman proceeded to unpack them.

He produced a pack of cards, which he shuffled. 'Now let me fleece you again.'

That weekend, Nora was waiting for Robert in a room above a pub near Allington.

'Hello Robbie.' She jumped up from the chair and flung her arms around him.

'Would you like a drink?' he asked. 'I've brought a bottle of Scotch.'

'No, thank you.' Nora looked at him, and smiled, but Robert was nervous suddenly. In the barn he'd been drunk and now he was stone-cold sober.

'You may kiss me,' she said, and Robert started to kiss her, but when he fumbled with the buttons of her cream silk blouse, she backed away.

'Last time was your first time, wasn't it?'

Robert felt the heat rise in his face. He must have made a pretty bad job of last time. 'Was it obvious?'

'A little.' She smiled. 'It was fun, but this time we shall make it even better.' She took off her blouse, then unclipped her brassiere, but she wouldn't let him touch her. Then she took off her skirt, dropping it to the floor, so that her only remaining clothing was a pair of suspenders, stockings and white lace panties. She rolled her stockings down and kicked them away, then she slowly undid her suspenders.

'Now you may touch me, Robbie,' she said, taking his hands and placing them on her firm, young breasts, her voice low and husky. He stroked her creamy skin, and buried his face in her breasts, inhaling her scent, pulling her towards his arousal, until once again she stopped him. 'Slow down, Robbie, we have all night.' She undid his shirt first, then came his belt, and finally the buttons on his trousers. She started to kiss him and took his hand, placing it between her legs, guiding him. She closed her eyes and leant backwards, moving her hips, a small moan escaping from her mouth until there was no going back.

'Lesson over,' he grinned, pushing her onto the bed.

There were more times after that, many more hours of solace and comfort.

'Come to me and I will help you forget,' she promised. And while he was in her arms the danger and chaos seemed far away.

On his brief stand-down periods they walked together, long, healing walks where they made love in every possible location. 'So what are you going to do when all this is over?' she asked him. Robert thought of Harvey's suggestion; it seemed a great offer but he didn't want to share it with Nora.

'I'm not sure,' he replied. 'Retrain, get a job. I can't think that far ahead.'

'I'm going to be a veterinary assistant,' she informed him. 'When I lived in London, the only cow I'd seen was in my mother's china cabinet, but now I've discovered I have a gift with animals.' Robert raised his eyebrows and she boxed his ears.

'Don't you mock my ambitions, young man,' she said, and it took a significant amount of grovelling before he was allowed to touch her again.

Nora's laughter and her lack of demands was just the distraction Robert needed – that is, until the last night she spent with him at the pub.

Robert woke to find her looking down at him. She was leaning on her elbow, her soft brown hair falling forward. Without her make-up she looked prettier, more vulnerable.

'Good morning.' She leant forward and kissed his brow. 'What are we doing today?'

'I have to be back at the base, I promised Harvey.'

'I suppose I'll get used to having him around.'

'What do you mean?' Robert sat up, alarm bells ringing in his head.

'He's your best friend, he'll always be part of our lives.'

Robert was completely awake. Nora was talking about commitment. He swung his legs over the side of the bed. Had he led her on? He didn't think so, but she obviously believed there was a future. He didn't wish to hurt her but he had never loved her. His future was not with Nora.

'Sorry, old girl,' he ruffled her hair, 'but I have to go.' He could see the disappointment in her eyes. He kissed her on the mouth. 'You take care now,' he said, 'and I'll ring you later, I promise.'

Robert was having supper in the mess with Harvey when Mike, the large Canadian, stopped by their table.

'Thing is,' he began, looking first at Harvey. 'You are off ops tomorrow, both of you. Apparently you've done too many hours.'

'Off operations? That's strange it's not on the board,' Harvey replied.

Mike looked sheepish. 'It will be, I've only just been told. Sorry, old chap, I know how cosy you are with your Spit, but the bad news is, I am also detailed to fly her.'

For a moment Harvey looked frustrated. 'Well, you had better look after her,' he said at last. 'She's my gal and I want her back in one piece.'

'Upon my life,' Mike grinned and sauntered away.

The following morning when Mike failed to arrive back at the base, Robert and Harvey waited anxiously. By three o'clock when a blank space remained on the board, they knew Mike would never come home. They walked back to the mess in silence.

'It was my plane,' Harvey whispered at last, his legs straddled over the bar stool, his head in his hands. 'It should have been me.'

Robert couldn't answer, tears were stinging his eyes, but he wouldn't cry, he wasn't a child in the nursery. With a shaking voice he ordered another round.

'Look at me.' Harvey grabbed his wrist and held on to it. 'I'm always the guy who makes the jokes, the guy who's the funny man, but for once I'm serious. I have a feeling you'll get through this. *Please* get through it for me.'

Robert nodded, unable to speak and Harvey got down from the stool.

'Sorry, Rob, I'm tired and I'm going to bed. I'll be better in the morning.'

Robert followed Harvey to their room. He sensed his friend was crumbling under the strain. He knocked before going in.

'Give me a moment,' a voice replied, but Robert went in anyway. Harvey was sitting on the side of his bed. Robert could see he had been crying. Harvey wiped his eyes.

'Sorry Rob.'

Robert sat down beside him and he slung his arm over his shoulder.

'You shouldn't see me like this,' Harvey said, his shoulders shaking.

'For God's sake, Harvey, I'm your friend.'

'I can't do this any longer. I came over to help; I wanted to be the hero. But at least I saved you. I would die for you, buddy.'

'Likewise, my friend,' Robert responded, because he would do anything for Harvey, anything at all.

Harvey got up and went to the window. Outside, the Spitfires stood in neat rows on the mown grass, but Harvey was staring beyond them into the gathering darkness. He picked up a jam jar from his desk. 'Do you see, honeysuckle? I found it climbing up the wall of the dispersal hut. Can you imagine such a tender little flower growing among this madness? We have it around the porch back home, and in summer you can smell it all over the house. Momma puts it in vases and it looks right pretty. Such a sweet smell, she says. Oh, buddy, I want to go home.'

Harvey was miles away and Robert couldn't reach him. He was at his house in Mobile, Alabama, with his mother.

'I know what it's like to be homesick,' Robert said, trying

to draw him back, trying to help him, but he couldn't. The honeysuckle had opened the floodgates of Harvey's misery; he was twenty-one years old and he had faced too much danger for any sane man.

Chapter Twenty-five

It was the end of September. The day started as any other. The pilots on duty met at dawn and were given their orders. The Sector Operations telephone in the dispersal hut rang as it normally did, and even though a sortie was anticipated and all were ready for action, its metallic ring still came as a surprise. Grabbing their kit and orders the young men ran to their aircraft.

They climbed quickly after take-off and made for the sun. At ten thousand feet Robert noticed his fuel gauge was signalling less than a quarter full. If he didn't return to base immediately he would be out of fuel. He cursed loudly; he was sure he had checked it. He signalled to Harvey and turned to port. Harvey grinned at his friend and with a small salute he flew onwards into the fray.

Robert smiled in relief. Harvey's positivity had returned.

When he landed, he was greeted by Jock. 'A slight problem, I'm not sure if it's the gauge or the tank,' he said jumping down.

'I'll fix it, sir.' Jock wiped his hands with an oil-stained rag. 'Did you meet the Jerry over the Channel? Hundreds of the buggers, apparently.'

'No, Jock, I missed it.' Robert felt a lurch in his stomach. 'Suppose you couldn't get me up there again?'

'I'm afraid not, sir, but don't worry, I'll have it sorted by the morning.'

Robert was worried, very. He wandered around the airfield, watching, waiting. He was thinking of Harvey. *He'll come back*, he assured himself, lighting a cigarette, *of course he will*. Nothing would happen to Harvey.

Several cigarettes later the planes trickled in. He could see Harvey among them. 'Thank God,' he said, laughing with delirious relief, but as the plane drew nearer it wasn't Harvey at all.

As Robert paced the ground beside dispersals, staring into the sky, he started to pray. 'Come home, Harvey,' he begged. 'Please come home.' But God wasn't listening. And then Robert saw it. A plane coming down fast towards the airfield.

'Get the undercarriage down.' He was shouting now, tears pouring down his face. 'Please God, not Harvey,' but he knew instinctively that it was Harvey. He could see the smoke and flames pouring from the engine and he heard the thud of impact in the field adjacent to the perimeter track. Robert was running, his legs pumping across the ground, his heart churning. 'Get out,' he yelled, 'Harvey, get out,' but Harvey couldn't hear him. He was trapped in the burning wreckage of his plane. The ambulance and fire tender rattled past him through the rough pasture. 'Help him,' he screamed, his lungs bursting. 'Please get him out.' He kept on running. 'I'm here, Harvey,' but as he ran towards the plane the firemen caught hold of him. 'Come on, sir, you can't go there.' But he had to get to the plane, because Harvey was inside, he had to get to his friend.

That night when the customary farewell drink was put up on the bar, Robert drank one for Harvey, then another. As he stared through the window into the bleak landscape beyond, he remembered Harvey's words. 'I have a feeling you'll get through this. *Please* get through it for me,' but he no longer wanted to.

There was a dull ache in his soul. He knew that breaking point wasn't far away but he didn't ask for leave, it wouldn't help; it was too late.

'Please, sir, may I write to his parents?' he asked the squadron leader.

'Of course,' he replied. 'You can also pack up his personal belongings to ship home, that is if you would like to. I'll inform his batman of your intentions.'

The squadron leader watched Robert go with a heavy heart. How many times would he have to talk like this to his men, how many times would he watch the brightest and the best cut down in their prime? He closed the door, sat down at his desk and took up his pen. At least Marston would save him one letter; he had another three to write.

As Robert entered the room he had latterly shared with Harvey, the past crowded in on him. The photograph taken by Joan after the fete at Allington was on the bedside table. Harvey's arm was around his shoulder; they were laughing, happy, as if they hadn't a care in the world.

Robert sank to his knees and banged his fist on the floor. He was not sure how long he stayed there, but as the light faded he dragged himself to his feet. He brushed his hand over the surface of Harvey's suitcase. His name was written on the front. How was it possible that he would never see him again?

He took his birthday cards from the mantelpiece and read each of them in turn. Hendry was gone and poor red-haired Toby, eighteen years old and only two weeks in the squadron before he was killed. 'I saw him going down,' Harvey had told him. 'The poor kid panicked. He didn't fire a round.' And now Harvey was gone, his best friend was dead. 'I will look after your grandson,' Harvey had assured Grandpa Peter, but he hadn't done the same for him. He put the cards in the suitcase and picked up a silver frame. Harvey's mother and his little sister smiled in front of a large, colonial house with dogs milling at their feet. He would never meet them now; never go to Mobile, Alabama. The future that Harvey had planned was gone.

The Prophet was on Harvey's chair, the book he had given him. He opened it at the first page.

'To my dearest friend on your twenty-first birthday, may I know you for three times twenty more.' There would be no more birthdays. There would be no more Harvey. He was about to put the book in his pocket along with the photograph taken by Joan, when an envelope fell out of it.

Flying Officer Robert Marston, soon to be promoted! was written on it in bold writing. Robert sat down on the bed and opened the letter.

Hello Buddy, I am hoping you will be the person to clear out my stuff and find this letter. Probably right now you have your blue-spotted handkerchief at the ready.

So here goes.

If you are reading this I have gone to join the brave boys who have died before us. I can see you sitting on my bed, a perplexed look on that handsome face of yours, wondering how I know. I just do. I missed it by a whisper when Mike died, and I felt I would be next. I had this premonition; maybe it's my Irish blood.

It breaks my heart to leave you, but the point of this letter is not to cheer you up, but to make you go on. So put away the handkerchief and stop snivelling. The boys need you because you are not only a damn fine pilot; you are one of the best. I want you to promise me you will try to get through this and, God willing, make it to the end. Have a great life, and please live some of it for me.

The last few months have been the happiest in my life, and that is largely thanks to you. When you climb into the cockpit every day it is not for the adventure, it is a call of duty. You respect life, both friend and foe.

In the drawer by my bed you will find my signet ring and a note. Would you break the news to Joan and give her these with my love? There is one more thing I would ask of you, when all of this is over, some day in the future, will you go and see Momma? She knows all about you and though it won't be her son coming home, she would love to meet the best friend that I have ever had.

For you ole buddy,
Harvey.

Robert opened the drawer. Taped to the top of a small blue box was a letter for Joan. He opened the box and took out the signet ring. The last time he had seen it was on Harvey's finger, but he always took it off to fly.

'Just in case,' he had grinned.

Engraved on the yellow gold, a goat stood proudly on a rock, with the word 'Liberty' beneath. Harvey had died to bring liberty to a nation on the other side of the world.

Robert snapped the box shut. He had known unbearable pain when his father had died, now he knew it all over again.

He took his writing case from the drawer and stared at a blank piece of paper. How do you tell a family that their precious son has died, that his sacrifice was worth it, if you no longer believed it yourself?

*

After a weekend break with his godfather, Robert returned to his squadron. Despite Douglas's concern, Robert had refused any help.

'I'm fine,' was all he said.

Douglas put a hand on his shoulder. 'You know I'll always be here if you want to talk, day or night.'

But as Robert said goodbye, he realised that unless you had lived through the highs and the lows of a fighter squadron, you could never understand. Robert had seen friends die in one sortie, and he had flown again an hour later; he had been to hell and back again.

'Thank you, Douglas,' he said. 'I will call you, I promise.'

Robert had a feeling about Friday the thirteenth from the very start. It wasn't terror or dread, it was just a feeling. He had cleaned his teeth, shaved, combed his hair and wondered at the tired and lined face in the mirror. He was twenty, barely a man and yet he looked years older. He went through the mechanics of the morning; he smiled at his remaining friends, nodded at the new boys who were younger now, so very young that it was shocking, helped himself to a cup of coffee in the dispersal hut and waited for the bell.

The bell went, the sortie passed uneventfully and they all came home. Soon, he thought, looking at the boys in the dispersal hut, their fresh eager faces would be drained like his, or they wouldn't be there at all.

Only an hour later they were scrambled again.

So this is it, he reflected as Jock pulled away the chocks. This is what you feel when death awaits you. He thought of Nora as he taxied along the perimeter track. He had to tell her it was over, it was only fair. He didn't want to hurt her. No, it was more than that, he couldn't bear to hurt her, but he didn't love her, didn't want to spend his life with her. He would break the news on his return.

*

He was flying a patrol line at thirty thousand feet. There was no John; his flight commander had been shot down the week before, but at least he was alive. A new man was leading, posted in from another squadron. It was cripplingly cold and each time he cleared the windscreen it froze again. Coming down through a break in the cloud he saw them, dozens of German fighters, escorting the Dornier bombers below. The might of the Luftwaffe was coming to blow him out of the sky. He selected his target and opened fire but he was wide of his mark. He rubbed his hand across his eyes, trying to focus, trying to find the acute awareness that had kept him alert and alive, but it had blurred with exhaustion. He felt a huge jolt and a massive deceleration. A Messerschmitt had got him from behind. Immediately the engine seized and the propeller blades stopped rotating. Burning oil obscured his windscreen. He was now hideously awake. Tongues of orange flame licked through the cockpit floor. He had visions of Harvey; of the young German pilot he had shot down and his futile struggle to escape. He couldn't die like this; not like Harvey.

Black smoke was filling the cockpit, he couldn't breathe, his lungs were bursting; he had to get out. He was struggling to jettison the canopy when a fierce flash of flame seared his hand, disabling his fingers. Panic gripped him. 'Tug at the release knob...' He was talking out loud now, anything to stop the immobilising terror. 'Tug, Robert, tug.' Suddenly the canopy flew off and the fumes were whipped away, but the aircraft was now in a steep glide. He had to raise the nose before he plunged into the water below. Pulling back on the control column, the nose gradually lifted and the speed fell away. When the plane was level he released the RT lead and his cockpit safety harness and rolled the plane into the inverted. He pushed the control column sharply forward and he was pitched into the vast, unfriendly sky. He was falling fast, plummeting towards the sea. At last his fingers closed around the D-ring. He pulled, and the parachute opened with a sharp, painful tug, blossoming into a great white canopy. Beneath him he could see the winding plume of smoke trailing his aircraft as it plummeted into the sea. The water was coming towards him, dull grey and flecked with foam. It rose towards him like a brick wall.

Wrapped in silken shrouds, he plunged into the freezing depths. Struggling to the surface, he was dragged face down through the water, his lungs screaming, until at last he set himself free. As the final cords floated away from him, he turned onto his back. The water closed around his head and as he stared up into the grey emptiness, he imagined his sister and mother smiling at him from the warmth of a sunlit sky. Then they were holding a letter, their faces contorted with grief, and in that moment he knew he must fight for his life. He couldn't let himself die.

He started to count. If he counted he would remain conscious and awake. He must remain awake. He was cold now, so cold. He could feel the water in his boots, heavy water that tried to pull him down, his life jacket dragged at his neck. He started to shiver. By the time the shivering stopped his mind had become muddled, his calculations illogical; he knew he shouldn't sleep but he was so very tired. God would look after him. God would let him sleep. Engines rumbled in the distance. But they weren't engines; it was only the sea.

Chapter Twenty-six

Alessandra was in the post office when the official letter arrived.

'For you, Signora.' The postmistress took a letter from the pigeonhole behind her. 'From England.' Alessandra's hands trembled as she hurried past the small queue. She could see dark eyes filled with sympathy; she could hear the intake of breath. Her head was spinning as she fled through the door. She was propped against the wall outside when an old woman touched her arm.

'Can I do anything?' she asked. Alessandra shook her head, tears pricking at her eyes. 'It is kind, Signora, but no.' She clambered onto her bicycle and the old woman hobbled away. With each turn of the wheel Alessandra prayed more fervently.

Signora Carducci came out of the house towards her. 'The ham is finished and there are weevils in the flour and—'

Alessandra held up the envelope. 'This is about Robert. What should I do?'

'You need to open the letter, Signora.'

Alessandra held her breath and tore at the envelope. 'Robert has been shot down but he is alive,' she said, collapsing against the stone wall.

'Thanks be to God.' Signora Carducci crossed herself. 'Has he injuries?'

'He's in hospital with hypothermia and burns, but only to his hand. They say he will make a good recovery. Do you think this is true?'

'Signora, I would believe what it says in the letter.'

Alessandra finally accepted Signora Carducci's reassurances and as the old woman folded her arms around her, Alessandra relaxed into her embrace.

Alessandra shut the door to her bedroom. She needed to be alone.

'Mama...'

She could hear her daughter's voice coming down the corridor. 'Mama!' The voice was louder now, more insistent.

'Come in,' she said at last and Diana sat down on the bed next to her.

'I have to go to him,' Alessandra declared. 'I need to be there for him now.'

'You know that is impossible,' Diana replied. 'How would you get to England? We are at war! At least for the time being he is safe in hospital and he is hardly likely to be flying again for a while.'

Chapter Twenty-seven

It was several days before Robert was aware of a doctor in a white coat leaning over his bed.

'Hello, young man,' he said. 'You're back with us then?'

'Where have I been?'

'You were plucked from the sea just in time. Luckily there'll be minimal long-term damage. Let's have another look at your chest.' He undid the buttons on Robert's pyjamas and placed a cold instrument against his skin.

'Last night you were talking some bloody nonsense about getting back to your squadron. Forget that, old boy, for the time being anyway. You might need surgery on your hand but that can wait for a while.'

Through a veil of drugs Robert could see the bandages, smell the tannic acid on his skin, but even the morphine couldn't mask the excruciating pain.

When he was on his own once more, Harvey's face floated in front of him.

'Harvey,' he whispered. 'Hello, old friend,' but the face was replaced with another face, a woman with a starched white cap. She held a glass of water to his lips; he took a sip and sank back against the pillow. 'There's a young woman to see you.' A different face came into focus. 'Are you up to it, I can always tell her to go away?'

'No, I'll see her,' he said.

Nora came and stood by the bed. He lifted his damaged hand and dropped it back on the cover.

'Nora,' he whispered. 'How's Joan?'

'OK,' she said. 'Sort of. I thought you'd had it, Robs, I really did. Thank goodness you're safe.'

As Robert looked into her kind face, he knew it was time to tell her the truth.

'I'm sorry, Nora,' he said softly, 'but I can't be with you any longer. I'm so fond of you, truly I am, but I can't love you the way you deserve to be loved. I hope you'll forgive me.' Nora kissed him on the forehead. 'Oh Robbie, you old fool, you could have lied to me, most men would, but I sort of understand, and I'm sorry too.' She took his good hand and held it gently.

'You poor old thing, you've had a horrible time; Harvey and now this.' She bent down and kissed him again, and he could see the tears in her eyes.

'Now you know why I'm going to be a veterinary assistant – it's much easier to make an animal love you.' She disappeared through the curtain and Robert's heart broke because Nora was special. She was funny and loyal and he was sad that he couldn't love her. When she had gone, tears slipped unchecked down his face. He wanted his mother, his father, Diana, and his dear friend.

When Robert opened his eyes, Douglas was reading in the chair beside him. He put down his newspaper.

'You gave us a bit of a fright, but thank heavens you are safe.'

'How long have you been here?' Robert asked, smiling weakly.

'An hour or so. I brought your grandfather in yesterday but

though you mumbled a bit, you didn't wake up. He had to see for himself that you were alive.'

Robert touched Douglas's arm.

'You have no idea how much this means to me.'

'Well, my boy, if you had died...' Douglas coughed and turned away. 'I have written to your mother assuring her that you are going to mend. The official letters are all very well, but they don't tell you everything.'

'Thank you.'

'You don't need to thank me.' He leant forward and adjusted Robert's sheet. 'Better?'

Robert nodded. 'When is this going to end, Douglas?' he whispered, his voice breaking. 'So many of my friends gone, so many dead.'

'War has the unfortunate effect of destroying everything in its path. My wife's death was one of the consequences. We can only hope that it will end very soon.'

'I say yes to that, but while Hitler lives... who knows.' Robert's voice trailed off as he closed his eyes.

Chapter Twenty-eight

Alessandra had cleared away supper and was turning out the landing light when she noticed Diana's door was ajar but Diana wasn't there. Her first impulse was panic, but this quickly changed. Alessandra wasn't a fool; she had seen her daughter's face, the faraway look in her eyes. If she was honest she had speculated on her daughter's virginity many times.

When she reached the barn she wasn't surprised to see a lantern flickering in the upstairs window or to hear her daughter's voice floating on the night air. But she was angry. Why had Diana chosen tonight to behave like this? They had just heard about Robert; it was immoral, inconsiderate, but it obviously wasn't the first night! Her hand was on the barn door; the latch was open. How could her daughter break every rule of decency? It was against everything she had been taught and, at this moment, it was also against the law. She would confront Davide; tell him to leave immediately. He had taken advantage of her generosity, taken advantage of Diana. She was halfway through the door when she turned around. She was as much to blame as anyone. She had employed Davide, unwittingly enabled their love to blossom when it was obviously going to be doomed. They couldn't marry, have children, Davide's world had now shrunk to the confines of the estate. Even here he was in danger.

They were obviously reckless but they were in love. Diana was now eighteen and some of her friends had already married.

Panic built in her chest. What would happen if her daughter became pregnant and the father was Jewish?

She went back to the house and poured herself a large whisky. 'Tell me, Anthony,' she whispered. 'What would you do?' But she already knew. Anthony would want her to support them. He would tell her that the laws against the Jews were the worst kind of laws. 'Let Diana be with the man she loves,' he would have counselled. 'Don't forget both you and your mother fell in love with men from different backgrounds. She is simply repeating history.'

Less than a week later a slight man with stooped shoulders stood in the loggia.

'Can I help you?' Alessandra opened the door.

'*Scusi*, Signora,' he said. 'I am Davide's father and I would be grateful to talk.'

'Of course, Signor Angelini, do come in.'

Signor Angelini took off his glasses and cleared his throat. '*Mi dispiace, Signora*, we are strangers to this area, but we still hear rumours.'

'Forgive me, I don't know what you are referring to.'

'The young lovers up at the house, the Jew and the heiress, that sort of thing, it is not good, not good at all.'

Alessandra could feel herself blushing but she forced herself to look at him.

'I don't know what to say, Signor.'

'I'm convinced you do not condone this.'

'Are you sure you don't want a drink?'

'No, thank you.'

'Well, I would like one.' Alessandra poured herself a glass of wine. 'I have thought about this and, as I am sure you appreciate,

I have come to my own conclusion. Diana loves your son and it is only the Italian Racial Laws that forbids marriage between Jews and non-Jews. I'm afraid I cannot stop them, and actually I now realise I do not want to.'

'But Signora, do you not see...' He paused and started again. 'You need to understand that in the Jewish faith we are expected to marry within our religion.'

Alessandra smiled wryly. 'It is the same in the Catholic faith, but do you agree with that?'

Signor Angelini looked at her, his expression changing. 'I am not sure,' he replied. 'But it is the race laws that concern me more. In Germany the penalty for breaking them is either the concentration camps or death. It is my guess that Italy will follow suit. Though I am sure they try to be discreet, our children are putting themselves in grave danger.'

'I am not reckless, Signor, I worry too, dreadfully, but danger is everywhere. I believe they are a support to each other through these mad times.'

Signor Angelini ran his hand through his hair. 'I have no doubt of that, but the differences between them are irreconcilable. Davide isn't allowed to have a proper job. This is a good job, of course, and we are so grateful, but he could never support your daughter. She is from a different world.'

'You should know that if my grandmother's heir, my uncle, hadn't died of tuberculosis when he was forty, we would be living in a small flat in London. So you see, we are no different,' Alessandra smiled.

'But we are Jews!'

'And we are Catholics, also persecuted at different times. We are also English, not expedient in Italy today, so please, Signor, our children are in love, at least we can drink together. Sit down, I insist.'

While Alessandra fetched another glass from the cupboard,

Signor Angelini picked up a book that was open on the sofa beside him.

'So you like Leopardi's *Canti*? He is a great poet, no?'

'My grandmother left me the book and yes, I read a poem every day.'

'Well then, you will like this poem.' He leafed through the book until he found the page he was looking for.

'Will you read it to me?' Alessandra asked.

Signor Angelini blinked. 'Yes, yes if you would like.' He started to read and as Alessandra listened to his soft, Italian voice, the words became more beautiful still.

When he had finished, he handed her the book. 'Leopardi is a great philosopher as well as poet.' He relaxed against the cushions, the tension leaving his face. '*Death is not an evil, because it frees us from all evils, and while it takes away good things, it takes away also the desire for them . . .* One of my favourite quotes.' He smiled. 'He understood the human condition, did he not?'

Alessandra agreed, and the time flew by. It was dark when Signor Angelini climbed onto his bicycle. 'Signora,' he said, 'thank you. This has been a pleasure and I must assure you that though I would have once preferred my son to marry a Jewish girl, I would be honoured to welcome your daughter into my family. I only hope that one day they can have the future they deserve.'

After that evening the Angelini family often came to the Villa Durante. Davide taught Jaco to fish in the lake and Diana would disappear with Lotti to the tree house where they would stay for hours.

'It is a long time since I have heard her laughter,' Signora Angelini observed, as she stood on the terrace with Alessandra, enjoying the late summer sun.

Alessandra raised her glass. 'To living in the moment,' she said, and a warm look passed between them.

Alessandra would always remember when Lotti first brought her grandfather's violin and took it from the velvet-lined case.

'"Violin Sonata No.1" by Robert Schumann,' the child announced gravely, looking at Alessandra, then she lifted the bow and started to play.

When she had finished, she raised her grey eyes once more, and it was as if Alessandra could see a lifetime of sadness in front of her.

Alessandra stood up and clapped. 'One day the world will know of your talent,' she said, and Signor Angelini took off his glasses and rubbed the lenses until the mist had gone.

As the weeks passed Alessandra became concerned for Signor Angelini. They were sitting in the study when she pressed him.

'You look exhausted,' she said, filling his glass with water.

'Yes, I admit I am tired,' he replied. 'But not from working. It is the worry and not knowing what is happening with our people all over Europe. I watch, listen. The news we hear is not good. What are we to do?'

'My uncle in Bolzano has told me that four hundred thousand men, women and children have been rounded up and forced into a tiny ghetto in Warsaw. His cousin is one of them. The conditions are inhuman, and the inhabitants are dying of starvation and disease. Anyone trying to escape is shot.'

'No, it's impossible!' Alessandra's hand flew to her mouth.

'I'm very much afraid it is true, and so many children.' He shook his head in disbelief.

Rachel Angelini, who was sitting in the chair by the window, cleared her throat. 'Signora,' she said, and the room became silent as she gathered her composure. 'I want...' She stopped for a moment, her fingers pleating her white lace handkerchief.

'I want to thank you for your kindness to my son; without this job I don't know what he would do ... It means so much to him.'

'I should be thanking you.' Alessandra looked at Rachel's anguished face, the enormity of the unfolding tragedy hitting her. She wanted to reach out and comfort her, but Rachel was a proud woman and it would cause her embarrassment.

'Davide is an extraordinary young man,' Alessandra said, choosing her words carefully, 'and we feel privileged that he is here. Your family is gifted, Signora; look at Lotti.'

'It is Lotti I wanted to talk about.' Rachel paused again, her eyes searching for her husband's. 'This is so difficult but I must say it. If anything should happen to my husband, to me, would you encourage my daughter Lotti to follow her dreams?'

'You know I will,' Alessandra replied. 'But nothing is going to happen to you, nothing at all.'

3

War Abroad

Chapter Twenty-nine

Two and a half years later

It was a damp Friday evening in 1943 as Robert strolled along the front corridor of the RAF Uxbridge officers' mess to the bar; he could certainly welcome a drink. Through a haze of smoke, he could see that the room was packed to capacity. Singing erupted from a group of fighter pilots in the corner. Robert looked at them enviously. He downed his first drink and pushed it towards the barman.

'Another of the same.'

'Coming up, sir,' the man replied. 'Letting off steam with your friends?' He nodded his head in the direction of the young officers.

Robert stubbed out his cigarette. No, he was a 'Penguin'. He had wings but he couldn't fly.

He frowned. His own job, gathering intelligence on the Luftwaffe's future threat, was vitally important, but not a job he was trained for. He wanted to use his skills and experience in the sky. He thought of the times the doctors had listened to his chest: 'Sorry, old chap, still your lungs. We can't give you a clean bill of health, I'm afraid.' They would shake their heads, scribble in his file. If he had heard that once in the last two years, he had heard it a dozen times.

The faces of dear, dead friends swam in front of him, Toby, Crispin, Mike and, of course, Harvey. Of the eighteen young men in the original squadron, only five had survived. He had another drink.

The singing got louder. It seemed everyone in the bar was joining in, everyone except him. He was on the point of leaving when someone called his name. 'Come on, Marston, how about a song?' Robert shook his head and made for the door. At once the group of visiting officers started chanting, 'Sing, Marston, sing.' Why bloody not? He was out of tune but no one seemed to care. He began to enjoy himself and once again the pints began to flow. By the time he had downed a few more pints he had no inhibitions and no remaining songs.

'One more!' everyone chanted. Robert was now standing on a table. He peered around the room. Familiar and unfamiliar faces were holding their tankards, encouraging him. He thought for a moment, grasping the threads of a lullaby from his childhood. His grandmother had sung it to him, his *nonna* from Italy. He sang slowly at first, the words elusive, and then louder until each man and woman turned towards him. After several encores he bowed. With many hands helping him down he staggered from the bar and outside into the night air. He sat on the steps in front of the mess until several officers lifted him under his arms and took him to his room. When he awoke the following morning the words of the lullaby were still ringing in his ears. Little did he know it would change the course of his life.

*

Robert was about to leave the mess for the office he shared in Group Headquarters when the post came. He hadn't heard from his mother in weeks, and it was nearly four years since he had last seen her. She had wanted to meet him in Switzerland but he had dissuaded her. Though Switzerland was a neutral country, the journey through Italy would be dangerous. Now he felt the usual heavy disappointment that the only letter in his slot was official.

He was about to ignore it when he noticed the War Office stamp. He tore it open, scanning it quickly; a Major General Struthers wished him to present himself at Norgeby House, number eighty-three Baker Street at two p.m. on the fifteenth April. There was no explanation, only the usual formalities at the beginning and end of the letter. Robert put the envelope in his pocket. He was intrigued.

Wearing his No. 1 Service Dress uniform, Robert took the underground into London.

As he walked the streets he felt the usual anger. The Luftwaffe had reduced the city to a bizarre landscape where untouched streets were next to streets that no longer existed. Houses with shorn-off fronts displayed fireplaces, even furniture. A whole side of a wardrobe had gone but the dresses still hung there.

Fortunately, the apartment building in Baker Street remained unscathed. He took the lift to the fourth floor and rang the bell.

A secretary opened the door.

'Flight Lieutenant Marston? Do come in.'

He followed her down a long passageway.

'Please wait in there.' She indicated a room on her left. 'Major General Struthers will be with you shortly. There's a pot of coffee on the trolley, and I have managed to salvage some biscuits from rations.' He was about to take a second biscuit when a tall man with a receding hairline and clipped moustache entered the room. Robert jumped to his feet.

'Flight Lieutenant Marston, congratulations. I saw the announcement of your Distinguished Flying Cross in the *London Gazette* a couple of months ago. Well deserved. Do sit down.' Robert sat at once, aware of calm brown eyes surveying him.

'You may be wondering why we have called you here. I see you have applied six times to return to your squadron.'

'Yes sir, but—'

He was about to make excuses but the man waved his hand. 'There's no need to apologise, Marston, I assume you find your current position a little tedious after your experience in the Battle of Britain.'

Robert wondered if he had been called in for a reprimand.

'No sir, not at all.'

The man smiled and looked down at his papers. 'I see you have a penchant for Italian nursery rhymes.' Robert could feel the heat rise in his face. This was not going as he had imagined.

'More tea?' Struthers didn't wait for an answer. 'And you are an old hand at Latin translation; Pliny the Elder's *Natural History*? That was a thorny one to cut your teeth on.' Robert was confused. The translation was from his school days at Marchants, why on earth was he mentioning it now?

'Boxing, yes, that's always useful, and indeed your eight credited kills. We have studied your service record and think you are an ideal candidate for the Special Operations Executive, for our future operations in Italy.'

Robert leant forward in his chair, his heart pounding. He would be back in the action again.

'Don't answer yet; you need to think about this. Your commanding officer is aware of this meeting, and the Air Ministry is prepared to release you for duties with us. The average survival rate of an operative in the field is only about six months. Mull it over on your own. Come back and see us in a week's time.'

'I don't need a week, sir,' Robert replied. 'May I come back in a couple of hours?'

After leaving the apartment building, he walked to Hyde Park and sat down on a bench by the Serpentine. It was here that he had fed the ducks with Diana and his mother and sailed the small toy boat with his father. As his childhood memories flooded back, he knew his decision. Though it was not the one his mother would have wanted, it was the only one he could make. He had promised he'd do his best to stay safe, but the six months life expectancy was no worse than that of a fighter pilot. He had to fight for his country.

Two hours later he stood before Major General Struthers once more. 'The answer is definitely yes,' he stated.

'We would never coerce you. Ours is a voluntary organisation, and you can leave at any time during your training. If you stay, you must tell no one about the nature of your work.'

'I am sure, sir.' Robert's voice was firm. 'I have faced danger in the sky and if that avenue is now closed to me, I would be glad to be of service another way.'

Over the course of the next hour Robert's questions were answered. His role would be the training of a secret underground army, co-ordinating the activities of groups of partisans, sabotaging lines of communication, bridges, rail junctions, airfields and so on.

'This will be very different from a Spitfire squadron. What you did openly, you will now do covertly. The training will be tough and comprehensive, lasting several months. You will then be sent into the field to live among the Italian partisans. You are not there to lead the partisans, merely to advise and instruct. Your role will be vital in helping to build Italian resistance against the Axis powers. One more thing, Marston, I know it will be a comfort to be nearer to your family, but you must stay away from them for their safety. We have learnt to our cost in France and other occupied countries that there is always a risk of reprisals.

'I think that covers everything. Goodbye, Marston, my secretary will show you out.'

As the door closed on Robert, Major General Struthers picked up his notes. Robert Marston was everything the organisation needed. He had an unerring sense of duty and a record of exceptional bravery. They had a war to win, and sometimes young men had to sacrifice their lives. It was the huge cost of war.

Chapter Thirty

In early May 1943, Robert reported to Squadron Leader Hawkings in an intelligence department in the depths of the Air Ministry. The elderly officer, wearing the campaign ribbons of the First World War, glanced with admiration at Robert's DFC.

'Fighter Command, eh?'

'Yes sir.'

'This meeting,' he explained, 'is to tie up loose ends regarding your new posting. It shouldn't take long. Have you had any second thoughts?'

'There is no change, I wish to serve my country.'

'Thank you. I had to be sure.' He gathered up some forms from his desk and passed them to Robert. 'While you fill these in, I'll give you the lowdown on issues you won't find in the newspapers.'

The Squadron Leader leant back in his chair. 'The situation in Italy is hotting up. Last November, Galeazzo Ciano, Mussolini's son-in-law, approached Anthony Eden as his counterpart in the Foreign Office, to seek terms with the Allies. We understand Count Ciano continued to urge Mussolini to broker peace, but this resulted in his dismissal. I'd put money on it that Mussolini will be out by the end of the year. So, old chap, you will be entering the dragon's den.'

After Robert had put down his pen, and passed back the forms, the older man stood up. 'I wish you good luck, and remember what enabled you to survive as a fighter pilot: always watch your back.

'I must warn you,' he said as they walked to the door, 'the integrity of the fighter squadrons will not exist where you are going. If you are caught you will be tortured. Many break under duress and some agree to work for the other side. Watch everyone and keep your own counsel.'

As Robert trotted down the steps of the Air Ministry into Whitehall and through Horse Guards Parade he thought of Hawkings' words. He was entering a very different world with a very different set of rules. Sitting on a park bench he reflected that within a matter of days his uniform would be mothballed and he would become an anonymous figure in the shadows.

After a late lunch with Douglas, Robert went to visit his grandfather.

'After training, I am being posted abroad, Grandpa. I will try to see you again before I leave.'

'You take care, my dearest boy.' He shook his hand and Robert was overwhelmed by the obvious fragility of his grandfather's bones. Grandpa Peter was his link with his father and he loved him more than he could possibly believe.

'Nurse says you won't go down to the shelter.'

'The raids are infrequent now; I'll take my chance if you don't mind.'

'I do mind. The bombs come when you least expect them. Please, Grandpa, I couldn't bear it if anything happened to you.'

Robert clasped his grandfather's hand before letting himself out. He was halfway down the street when the air-raid sirens started to wail and the beams of the searchlights criss-crossed in the gathering darkness.

He turned around and went back to his grandfather.

'Sorry,' he said, fetching his coat. 'You are coming with me.'

He helped him down to the underground. It was not yet five o'clock. Families were taking up their positions. Robert waved at a small boy who was holding a bottle of Tizer and a packet of crisps. The boy grinned and held up the packet.

'Want one?' he asked.

'No thanks, young man,' Robert replied.

He took off his jacket and placed it on the floor for his grandfather. 'See, not so bad,' he teased.

'It may not be the Savoy,' Peter chuckled. 'But at least I'll have more time with you.'

They accepted a mug of tea from a woman who had claimed her space next to them. While she chatted to Peter, Robert thought of the Balham underground disaster of nearly three years before; the armour-piercing bomb that had fallen on the station, and the number 88 bus that had plunged into the crater during the blackout.

He imagined the terror as the tunnels collapsed and the gas and water mains fractured, the children's screams as a tide of water swept them from their mothers' arms.

Tonight the people in the tunnel were optimistic, refusing to believe a bomb would drop overhead. They had lived through the Blitz and, despite their personal suffering, they kept on going.

When the all-clear siren shrilled two hours later, the boy waved his now empty bottle of Tizer.

''Night, Mister,' he said, showing an expanse of gums where his milk teeth had been. Robert tossed him a sixpence.

Chapter Thirty-one

Alessandra stretched. It was the tenth of May, her birthday and another year without Anthony, another year of missing him.

'Happy Birthday, Mama.' Diana put her head around the door and advanced into the room. 'Look what I've got for you; real tea, black market of course, from Signor Innocenti.'

'It must have cost him a fortune.'

'It's your day to be spoilt. You needn't get up, not yet, I've made the bread and Sofia has done the hens.' She set down the cup and pulled a package from her pocket. 'And I've got this for you.'

Alessandra tore at the paper. 'Daphne du Maurier,' she cried, knowing the effort it would have taken. The English bookshops had closed well before the war started and the post was impossible. 'I've wanted to read this ever since it was published.'

The shift in her relationship with Diana hadn't happened overnight, but she had watched her daughter change from an insecure child into a confident young woman. Their quarrels were rare and though Diana was capable of powerful, often overwhelming emotions, she tried her best to control them. She wasn't always successful, of course, but Alessandra had seen evidence of a new thoughtfulness and today was another example. She opened the cover. '*To my mother on her 44th birthday.*' Alessandra grimaced.

Through the open door she could hear Sofia downstairs singing in the kitchen, and the new girl, Beatrice, grumbling as she scrubbed the floor. She had recently employed Beatrice at Signora Carducci's request. 'So many of our young men gone and more will be conscripted to fight for our country, pah, what country?' the old woman had protested. 'Beatrice is a strong girl, her mother taught her to work like a man. Sofia and I could do with the extra help.'

But Beatrice was sullen and resentful.

'Only two of you living in such a big house?' she had remarked.

'She's always watching us,' Diana complained to her mother. 'I'm not sure that I trust her.'

'I'm inclined to agree with you, but now that Dario has joined the partisans, we could do with another hand. Let's give her a little more time.'

Beatrice was scrubbing the hall floor when Alessandra came down. She greeted her, but the girl didn't reply. Alessandra was on the verge of rebuking her, but she changed her mind; she would save that for later, after she had written to her son.

She was writing to Robert when Davide knocked on the door.

'Sorry for disturbing you, Signora, but I have a present for your birthday.' He handed her a wooden stick with a ram's horn handle. 'This is to keep you safe.'

Alessandra ran her hands over the carving. 'It is beautiful, Davide, thank you, I shall treasure it.'

It was late afternoon and Alessandra had just finished the third chapter of *Rebecca* when Diana ran upstairs to her bedroom.

'Mama, the doctor is here to see you, is something wrong?'

'The doctor?' she asked. Alessandra's heart beat a little faster. She hadn't seen Doctor Biochetti since she had recovered from pneumonia. If she was honest, she had been disappointed, but what was he doing here now?

She went to the mirror, straightened her dress, and ran a brush through her hair.

'Why are you tidying yourself up? It's only the doctor,' Diana said, leaning against the door.

'You know I hate to be a mess,' she replied unconvincingly.

The doctor was standing in the hall when she came downstairs.

'*Scusi*, Signora.' With a flourish he produced a bunch of pink roses from behind his back. 'I have brought these for your birthday and I want to send you beautiful wishes, they are a little thirsty so I suggest you drink them.'

The doctor's English was as bad as it had ever been, but the sentiments were charming and she was more than happy to see him.

'How do you know it's my birthday?'

'Signor Innocenti says you hate birthdays and you love flowers, and forgive me, but I have your records.'

'So you know how old I am?'

'*Si*, I mean no. I think about thirty-five.' Alessandra laughed and thanked him. She asked him in for a drink and wondered what had taken him so long.

'Why do you always speak to me in English?' she asked when they were sitting on the sofa in the study.

For a moment he looked affronted. 'Because you are English,' he paused. 'Because I try to impress you.'

'I'm half Italian.'

'You are still English to me.'

Alessandra looked up and their eyes met. She could feel her cheeks burning but she wanted to stay in the warmth of his gaze.

'Your wife, does she mind you if you give me flowers?' she asked, when they were on their second glass of wine.

'Sadly, she is dead like your husband. Forgive me, but in these parts everyone they know about the Signora.'

'I'm sorry… about your wife, I mean.'

He paused for a moment. 'She died in childbirth. And me a doctor. I couldn't save her.' His face looked bleak and Alessandra wanted to hold him, take away the pain.

'That's awful.'

'It was a long time ago, Signora, and now, if it is not considered rude, may I fill my glass of wine?'

An hour flew by and Alessandra didn't want the doctor to leave. He was handsome, intelligent and compassionate and, even if his socks were odd, she was fed up with being lonely.

'Thank you for the flowers,' she said when he was leaving.

He kissed her hand. 'The pleasure was mine. I would have come last year, but I was a little afraid.'

'Of me?'

'Of myself, Signora.'

'Well, I am glad you are here now.'

'So,' Diana said, coming into her room while Alessandra undressed, 'why did he bring you flowers?'

'Because it's my birthday.'

'Because he likes you.'

'Is that so bad?'

'It's strange, but I expect I'll get used to it.'

'There will be nothing to get used to, Diana.' But as Alessandra said the words, she hoped she was wrong.

Diana went downstairs and put the kettle on the stove. Her mother liked a man and it wasn't her father, and it felt strange.

More than that, there was a lump of sadness in her chest that wouldn't go away.

But it would be selfish to mind: she had Davide and his love had healed the wounds of her father's death. There was so much good in her own life, she should be happy for her mother. And now there was the school. The church had been cleaned until it shone. Davide and Signor Innocenti had crafted the desks and a blackboard, immediately transforming it into a schoolroom. Sofia had sewn some pads for the pews: 'For the children's bottoms,' she had proclaimed with a grin as she produced the little striped seats.

Diana recalled the first morning. Five pupils sitting at their desks. Within days a trickle more, arriving shyly, until eleven expectant faces turned towards her. The first English lesson, and their charming attempts to master the language. She remembered the following days, the joy of teaching, and the rewards. Now she was doing something useful, which gave her a purpose as well as helping the children.

*

It was late May. A light breeze ruffled the bedclothes where Diana and Davide were sleeping. Diana stirred as Nico padded to the window. The dog jumped up, resting his two front paws on the sill.

'Nico is growling,' Diana murmured, nudging Davide.

'Let him growl.'

Diana smiled. She bent her head and kissed him, first his cheek and then his neck, until Davide was no longer tired.

He put his arms around her, pulling her on top of him.

Diana was dressed and returning from the henhouse, when she bumped into Beatrice coming the other way.

She jumped as they collided. 'I'm sorry,' she said. 'I didn't see you.'

'You could look,' Beatrice muttered, walking on by.

Diana stared after her. Why was the girl so rude?

She put the eggs in the larder, locked the door and put the

polenta on to boil. She was stirring vigorously when Sofia's singing distracted her. She found her in the linen cupboard.

'Help me with your Mama's bed.' Sofia passed the sheets to Diana. 'It is so much quicker with two.'

They were tucking in the sheets when Diana spoke. 'I don't like Beatrice. Am I being unreasonable?'

'If it weren't for her poor, sick brother, I would get your Mama to be rid of her. I sense trouble with Beatrice and your Davide has enough trouble of his own.'

Chapter Thirty-two

In June 1943, Robert travelled to the Arisaig Peninsula in the Scottish Highlands for the most physically demanding stage of his training as a member of the Special Operations Executive.

'It won't be easy,' Lieutenant Fairbairn warned him on his arrival. 'We are going to push you to your physical and emotional limits. You will no longer have a sleek and beautiful plane between you and your enemy, now you will kill with your hands, with knives, with anything you find at your disposal. I teach what is called *gutter fighting*. There's no fair play, no rules except one: kill or be killed. By the time you finish here, your squadron will seem soft in comparison.'

Robert remembered his first kill in the skies above Britain, and his emotional struggle afterwards, but he now accepted it was a necessary evil in the devil's own war.

At Arisaig, he handled a variety of guns that were new to him. By the end of six weeks, he had paddled a canoe silently and stealthily across a loch, learnt how to detonate a charge to destroy a model bridge using plastic explosives, and he had practised the most effective way of killing with a knife. A night exercise to lay a dummy charge on a train supplied to the SOE by the West Highland Line was to be his final test.

He devised a plan, hoping to fool the instructors by splitting the dummy explosive into three. One of the smaller pieces he would place in an obvious position – against the chimney. The second piece he would conceal adjacent to the piston. The largest piece he would strap to the inside of the piston cylinder casing. To find this would mean lying under the locomotive.

The first explosive was soon found. 'Here we are, sir,' the sergeant said to one instructor and turned to the others. 'Come on, there'll be another.'

'Nice try, sir,' the instructor acknowledged when they found the second explosive. 'No one's used that trick before but it's still a fail.'

Robert could no longer contain himself. 'I think you had better look underneath the train.'

The sergeant's face dropped.

The instructor grinned. 'That's a pass.'

Having completed the parachute course in Manchester, Robert was sent to Beaulieu in the New Forest. Here the rambling house was nicknamed 'the finishing school for spies'. The last and longest phase of his training began. He was briefed, together with another student heading for Italy, by an elderly Polish professor of political history.

'So,' the professor began in meticulous English, 'in order to understand your future tasks, you need to know about the strategy of SOE's operations in the Eastern Mediterranean. With the planned invasion of Italy by the Allies, and the imminent possibility of Italy suing for a separate armistice, it is certain that Germany will have no intention of withdrawing from the Italian mainland.'

The professor's blue eyes bored into those of his two students and, as his smooth voice continued, Robert learnt about the bands of partisans that were being formed to strike at both the Fascists and the Germans. 'It will be your job to train these

239

men, to arm them and plan their strategy with them. There will be several different groups, some communist, some anti-fascist, but they will have no cohesion or discipline. You will make new and secure contacts.'

In one of the several buildings located in the grounds, Robert was shown how to use a radio set, with the identification procedures for contacting the control centre and members of the local resistance. He refreshed his skill in using Morse code. He was taught how to act when the Gestapo or the Fascist militia were following him or had him under surveillance.

'No glancing behind, no change in routine, act normally.' He was given a temporary identity, with forty minutes to assimilate the background information of a lifetime before his interrogation began. The simulated cross-examinations went on for hours, and as the beams from the two powerful lamps shone relentlessly into his eyes, he focused on his mother and his sister in Italy.

Later, with the help of charts and slides he was taught the rank of every member of the German forces. 'Have it ingrained in your mind,' the instructor advised. 'Is the Fritz an officer? What is he wearing? A stupid error may cost you your life.'

The last stage of Robert's training was in Italian conversation, and when that was done, the senior administrator gave him the results of his final assessment. In less than twelve weeks, he had been turned from an officer and a gentleman to a sabotage expert, an undercover operative capable of killing in a very different way.

*

It was late August and the last destination before his journey to Italy was Baker Street. Here in the flat where they had first met, Major General Struthers took him through the final details.

'I know that Squadron Leader Hawkings filled you in before you left for your training, but you will appreciate the situation changes daily. With the arrest of Mussolini by the Italians, and the fall of Messina concluding a victorious campaign in Sicily, we believe the armistice is imminent. Everything you have learnt will now be put to the test.' He leant forward and put his hands on the table in front of him. 'When they surrender it will count as a victory for the Allies, but it doesn't mean that peace is coming to Italy. As you know, it will be precisely the opposite – the struggle will become bloodier. The Germans will pour onto Italian soil and that is why we have trained you.'

He smiled, his posture relaxing and looked down at his notes. 'Anyway, to the nitty-gritty. In the unfortunate event of capture and interrogation you will assume a new identity. From the moment you land in Italy you will be known as Roberto Gianelli, an antiquarian print dealer originally from Arezzo, now working in Florence. Because of your occupation you must think in terms of print strikes and restrikes, of colour tints and copper plates.' He picked up a folder and tapped it thoughtfully.

'You will of course need to memorise this, but we are hoping you will not get caught and the effort will have been for nothing. Everything has been checked and rechecked for authenticity, now it's up to you. It will tell you your school, your collar size, your best friend, your father's regiment, even the cigarettes you smoke... do you want one?'

Robert took the proffered cigarette and lit it.

'You will have to ditch the lighter, everything has to be Italian.'

Robert drew in more deeply and coughed.

'Better get used to it: Nazionale, it's your favourite brand. Your wife will be your radio operator and will act as your assistant.'

'My what?' Robert nearly choked on the cigarette.

'Sorry, didn't I tell you? You are married. Couples working together in German occupied territory are less conspicuous.' He passed him another folder containing a street map of Arezzo, his new passport, ration card, and identity card. 'Your wife's passport is in the leather wallet. If you wish to choose her call sign, I will need it today. Fingerprints please, there, just below the photograph.' Robert put out his cigarette, pressed his fingers into the inkpad and then firmly onto the card.

'When you have been issued with your clothes you have an appointment with the optician who will give you your glasses – you are long-sighted so you will only use them for reading. One more thing, we are only as good as our agents. Without you getting your information back to us we are nothing. Here is your itinerary; you'll leave for Newquay in the morning.'

Robert glanced at the itinerary and back at General Struthers. 'The call sign, sir.' He jotted it down on the back of an envelope and handed it to Struthers.

'*Brown Ale 8*,' General Struthers read. 'I assume this is a personal association?'

'It is known only to me, sir.'

The General raised his eyebrows.

'It's an anagram from Lowenbrau.'

'Any reason?' he asked.

'It was my father's favourite beer.'

A flicker of a smile crossed the General's face and was gone. 'You are sure it is unique? Nothing that could lead the enemy to us? I don't need to tell you how important it is.'

'I'm sure.'

'In future, it will be known only to you and your radio operator.'

Robert was sitting in the passage outside when a middle-aged female officer came towards him.

'I'm Lieutenant Swan. It's time for wardrobe.' She led him into a nearby room where she picked up a pile of clothes and handed them to him.

'Anything that's not Italian will give you away. Shop labels, fabrics, the lot. It's little things that can get you caught. Another agent's cover was blown because of his vest. Don't worry, we're much better at it now; we even employ an artist to make the clothes look worn.'

Robert was feeling like a pincushion by the time the last pair of trousers had been fitted.

She turned over the Maltese cross Diana had given him. 'No name on the back, that will be fine.'

'What about this?' Robert pulled Davide's talisman from the pocket of his jacket. 'It's made from Italian wood,' he said with a grin.

'Well then, I think we can allow it.' Lieutenant Swan separated the clothes to be altered and smiled at Robert. She handed him a cardboard portfolio. 'These are your prints, just in case you are asked. They are valuable, so look after them. You will find a list of their dates, etcetera. Please learn them.' She hesitated before handing Robert the last item on her list, four small packages in a brown envelope. 'I hope you will never need the last one.'

Robert took them out of the envelope and looked at each of them in turn. He stared at the last one, a small white pill marked with the letter 'L'.

'It's your lethal pill, dear. If you find yourself in an irreversible situation and you want a way out, swallow this and you will be dead in six seconds.'

Robert shook his head. 'No thank you, I'd rather not.'

'I'm afraid it's part of the kit.'

Robert was about to reply when a man in a white coat entered. 'You're with me now,' he said. 'It will only take a few minutes.'

Robert followed him into a small studio where a series of alphabetical charts hung on the wall.

'The eye test is authentic,' he confirmed, seeing Robert's puzzled face. 'It wouldn't do to give you glasses that didn't work.'

He took an ophthalmoscope from the pocket of his coat and asked Robert to sit down.

'I'll have the glasses ready in the morning,' the optician said when he had finished. He held the door for him and Robert walked towards the lift. He left via the back entrance, and went to a phone box.

'Can we have supper, Douglas, after I've seen my grandfather?' he asked, waiting for the pips.

He heard the warmth in Douglas's voice. 'Of course. No meat, I'm afraid, but the best my ration book can provide.'

'I'm leaving the country for a while.' Robert put down his fork. 'Not sure how long, actually, but if anything goes wrong, will you keep an eye on Mama and Diana, and my grandfather? I saw him earlier and he seems very frail.'

'You know I will.' Douglas picked up his glass of claret. 'I'm not at liberty to ask where you're going, I suppose?'

'Sorry.'

'Quite understood. I'm involved in something rather interesting myself.' Douglas helped Robert to another glass of claret. 'The study of trauma on the central nervous system as a whole. Fascinating really.'

'Sounds it,' Robert replied, casting his eye around the large living room. He'd never really noticed before, but there were no photographs of Douglas's late wife; in fact there was nothing to suggest that anyone lived there at all.

'I know what you're thinking,' Douglas said. 'The flat could do with a woman's touch.' He pulled out his pipe and knocked it on the table. 'I've been single for too long and I'm rather set in my ways.'

They were standing at the front door when Douglas shook his hand. 'Come home to us safely, Robert,' he said. Then he blinked rapidly, and added, 'I've not been entirely honest with you old boy, done a bit for SOE myself. Put in a good word for you, actually.'

'I should have known.' Robert smiled at his godfather. 'I am so relieved to be doing something useful again.'

'That's what I thought, but your mother would probably kill me if she knew. Just remember, if you're ever in trouble, I'll come and find you.'

'Your kindness has meant everything.'

'Likewise, Robert, you mean everything to me.'

Chapter Thirty-three

Davide was milking Rosa when the barn door opened. He sensed it was Diana by the soft swish of her skirt, the hint of her scent. He squeezed the last drop of milk into the bucket. Diana was walking through the hay towards him, her eyes fixed on him. His heart lurched as it always did when he saw her. 'It's you.'

She took the bucket away from him and put her hands on his shoulders. 'Is that a good thing or bad?'

'Good.'

'Will you kiss me?' She leant down and brushed her lips against his, then she pulled him towards her. Finally he dragged himself away. 'I have a list to complete and you are distracting me,' he grinned.

'Come on, I have something to show you. Can you spare a few minutes?' She took hold of his hand and they went outside. 'Look, up there in the tree house.'

Above them on the ledge, three pairs of eyes peered at them. 'A second clutch of kestrels,' he breathed. 'And their Mama?'

'She's never far away. I've watched her feeding them. If you wait, she'll come.' Diana looked up as one of the fledglings flapped from the ridge and landed only feet away. It stared up at them, its small body covered in down.

'It is a female, you can see the barring on her back,' Davide said, pointing, and while the little fledgling hopped across the grass, he held Diana in his arms.

That night Davide sharpened his tools. In the morning he went back to the tree house to study the kestrels again. As the days passed the fledglings explored increasing distances from the nest, their flight feathers growing fast. By the end of two weeks Diana's carving was ready. He wrapped it in tissue paper and waited for her to come.

It was dusk when she arrived. Her skin glowed pink from her bath and her hair was wrapped in a towel.

'I made this for you,' he said, handing her the gift. 'I hope you like it.'

Diana opened the tissue paper. She was silent as she examined the carving.

'It is made with the wood from the olive tree we cut down at the end of last year. It's not much, I know, but—' He got no further.

'It is the most beautiful thing that I have ever seen.' She touched the delicate wings that were opened, ready for their first flight into an uncertain future. 'One day your talent will be known not just by me but the world.' She stroked the delicate feathers, then she put the bird down carefully and unwrapped the towel from her hair.

Dawn was breaking as Diana rose on her elbow and looked down at Davide. The tautness had gone from his face and his body was relaxed beneath the thin cotton sheets. She kissed his shoulder and rested her head against him, feeling the rise and fall of his chest against her cheek. She wanted to keep the moment, to love him for ever, but with the turmoil in Italy increasing daily, she was convinced he would leave.

*

Davide was on the way to his parents' house in Mengaccini when Pipo cycled past, applied the brakes and dragged his foot through the thick white dust. The two men clasped hands.

'Good to see you, Davide. It's been a while, but with no petrol, there is no bus.' Pipo grinned ruefully. 'Cigarette?'

'Why not?'

'You haven't heard the news?' Pipo passed the packet to Davide.

'What news?'

'Italy has surrendered.' When he saw Davide's face he was concerned. 'It's good, no? We will have the British and Americans as our allies. Democracy will return.'

Davide gave a hollow laugh. 'But at what cost, Pipo? We will now be overrun by the *Tedeschi*. It's all well and good to surrender, but every day without Allied forces arriving is another day for the Germans to occupy these lands, these villages. And if it's German soldiers patrolling our streets, they won't be so tolerant when they hear of the Jewish boy and his English girlfriend.'

'You are being a pessimist, Davide. Think of the bigger picture. In the end Hitler will surely fall and Italy will be free. Antonio, Signor Innocenti's nephew, wants me to join his band of partisans. I can't stick around here any longer. Why don't you come with me? Together we can fight for our country.'

'I need to be here to protect my family, and I can't leave Diana.'

'The partisans need you more.' Pipo ground out his cigarette. 'Remember what I have said, Davide, there is always a place for men like you.'

'I would be of more use in the north where I grew up. I know every cart track, every cave in Bolzano,' Davide stated.

'Well then, when the time comes, go north to Bolzano my friend, but first let us meet in the bar.'

Pipo climbed back on his bicycle and was gone in a cloud of dust.

Diana was in the church teaching the children when Signor Innocenti put his head round the heavy door. Nico trotted across the tiled floor towards him.

'Signorina, I have something to tell you.'

From his face Diana could tell it was important.

'Maria, you read to the class,' she told a little girl with pigtails.

'Is something wrong?' Diana had the usual moment of panic.

'No, not wrong, Signorina, good news. Italy has surrendered, the war will be over soon.'

In October 1943, a month after Italy's surrender to the Allies, Alessandra was in the study. She switched off the news and called to Signora Carducci.

'Are you quite well, Signora?' the older woman asked.

'I think so.' Alessandra indicated a chair. 'Italy has declared war on Germany. If the last months have been difficult, it is going to get very much worse.'

Signora Carducci crossed herself. 'God help us all,' she replied.

When the old woman had gone, Alessandra took out her diary.

So, my darling Anthony, from this day, 13 October, Italy is at war with Germany and I am very much afraid.

Last month Mussolini was dismissed by the king, imprisoned by the Italians and then rescued by Germans. On Hitler's orders, he was returned to Salo in the north as puppet head of a Fascist republic, but he will be of little influence. It is the Germans who will govern us now. The Allies have landed in the south and the fighting is fierce. Planes fly over us filled with bombs and they are allied bombs. So many beautiful towns and cities are being destroyed. For the past year

Milan, Turin and Genoa, Italy's industrial triangle, have suffered repeated attacks.

I haven't heard from Robert in months. I am convinced he no longer works at Group Operations Centre. I promised him that if danger came to these parts I would take Diana and leave, but there is the problem, Anthony, I fear we have left it too late; and even if we were to leave, where would we go?

With my love and devotion always, and until the next time.

Your loving wife, Alessandra

Chapter Thirty-four

When Robert returned to the flat in Baker Street, he found a note on his pillow.

'*Meet me in my office at 8 a.m. Please bring any items to be stored in a suitcase. Yours truly, Edna Swan.*'

As he packed away his belongings, he could hear his father's words in the hall before he died: '*Work hard and you will have a great future ahead of you.*' Robert brushed his fingers over his Wings and closed the suitcase, wondering what his father would think of his prospects now.

Lieutenant Swan was waiting for him. She took the suitcase, handed him the file and a wallet of money.

'These days everything has to be signed for, have you a pen?'

Robert produced his red Parker pen, a present from Douglas.

'Good, at the bottom please. The wallet contains the equivalent of one hundred pounds in lire. We'll send more via a courier, but please use sparingly. We'll need the pen too, I'm afraid.' Robert signed the receipt and gave her the pen and the key to the suitcase.

'I'll keep everything safe, don't worry. Outside the door you'll find your kit. Good luck, Robert,' she said, and her eyes softened. 'And God bless.'

Lieutenant Swan wanted to hug the boy, take away the

apprehension in his eyes, but from now on his life would hang in the balance. He might be shot immediately; he might be interrogated and tortured. She opened the door and he stepped through to an uncertain future.

Robert's train left Paddington in the early hours. When he arrived at Newquay, a chill breeze swept off the sea. He spotted a RAF officer hurrying down the platform to meet him.

'We'd better get going if you are to fly tonight.' The officer glanced up at the clouds. 'St Mawgan Coastal Command airfield is not far from here, ten minutes or so. The car is over there.'

At the airfield, the officer guided him up the steps of a Wellington Bomber.

'How old is she?' Robert asked, running his hands over the crazed paint.

'Don't worry, she may look a little rough at the edges, but she is a sturdy old girl and won't let you down.' The officer smiled reassuringly. 'Not as manoeuvrable as a fighter, of course, I assume you were in fighters? Let's find you a place ... oh, and don't forget to plug in your intercom lead, but keep it switched off unless you need to speak.'

He introduced Robert to the captain, a confident young Flying Officer called Beamish, and departed, waving at the door.

'We'll fly across the Bay of Biscay in darkness to avoid any marauding fighters,' Beamish assured him with a grin. 'Come to the cockpit if you like.'

Startled by the ear-splitting noise as each of the two Hercules engines were run up to test for full power, Robert wedged himself behind Beamish's seat. It was his first time as a passenger since his training days and he didn't like it at all. Now it was the pilot's job to get the lumbering tub off the ground and to keep them safe; he had no control. As the plane began to rumble down the runway, Robert shifted his gaze from the green fluorescent glow of the flight instrument panel and stared ahead as Beamish steered the gradually accelerating aircraft between the lines of bright runway flares. The rumbling lessened as the aircraft gathered speed, and Robert's stomach lurched as the end of the runway rapidly approached. Suddenly they were up and Robert relaxed. As he made his way down the fuselage he peered rearwards from the astrodome. The runway lights were already extinguished and there was not a glimmer from the blacked-out airfield or anywhere else.

The Wellington arrived at an RAF base near Cairo the following afternoon. As Robert stepped from the plane into the hot, white light, he shaded his eyes. At once his senses were assaulted by the smell of palm trees and fuel and the musky scent of a flower he couldn't identify. It was a world away from damp, bombed-out London.

'Enjoy Cairo,' Beamish winked at him. 'If I didn't have to get a ton of stuff from the embassy packed into this old girl, I'd love to show you around.' Robert thanked him and said farewell to the rest of the crew.

He could see a car shimmering on the tarmac near the airport building and a stout figure in a white suit and a cream Panama hat waving to him. Robert picked up his suitcase containing his new Italian belongings and walked into the heat.

The man shook his hand then escorted him to the car.

'I'm Major Adderley, in charge of you while you are here. I'm taking you to our place in Cairo. You must be boiling in those clothes. As soon as we arrive, I suggest you change.'

'It's good to see a bit of sun,' Robert replied.

Their journey was hindered by the traffic. Trams, buses, civilian cars and army vehicles hooted their way through the streets, competing with donkey carts laden with vegetables. Flocks of sheep were herded by old men and young boys. On the pavements, khaki-clad officers weaved between Egyptians wearing traditional robes. It was a riot of colour, smell and noise.

'Bit different, eh? You'll get used to it. You'll be staying at the house for the next few days while we tie up the arrangements for your journey to Malta and onwards. During that time you'll meet your radio operator and have a chance to rehearse your mutual cover stories.'

They finally passed into the quieter, more affluent area and stopped outside the gates of a large colonial villa, surrounded by a high wall, bedecked with flowers.

'Jacaranda,' Adderley pointed to the purple blooms that trailed down the walls. 'Pretty, ain't they? There's a good garden and a swimming pool. Now I suggest you get changed.'

'You haven't been here before,' Major Adderley stated, when Robert arrived on the veranda. 'I should tell you that, regardless of the reputation it enjoys among the three Services, it's a damned dangerous city. Now the Desert Campaign is over, it's a hotbed of political intrigue and rumour. Sorry, old chap, but you must avoid the well-known European hotspots, such as the Turf Club, the Gezira and especially the nightclubs; honeytraps all of them. I'm responsible for you until you leave for Malta and I'm sure I don't need to remind you that our security as a clandestine organisation can be easily compromised, even by our own people.' He paused to mop his brow on a handkerchief that he produced from his jacket pocket. 'So this is your base until further notice. It's comfortable enough; plenty of drink and with two or three other birds of passage passing through, like you.' He blew his nose with the same handkerchief. 'Is there anything you don't understand?'

'No sir.'

'I can see you are disappointed but it can't be helped.' He glanced at his watch. 'Time for a sundowner.'

'Can't argue with that,' Robert replied with a rueful grin.

Robert was lying by the pool on his first morning when he noticed a young man with a shock of red hair sitting in the shade. Though his arm was in a sling, he got up and ambled towards him.

'Drink?' he asked. 'I know it's not the Continental, more's the pity, but there's a good supply of booze in the cupboard. It's little consolation, but we can have whisky for breakfast if we wish.'

Robert chuckled. 'Well then, yes please, Gin and It, but I'll get it, if you tell me where.'

The young man glanced down at his sling. 'Leave it to me. I can do a lot single-handed.' He flashed a quick smile. 'Back in a moment. I'm Tom, by the way, Tomaso to my future Italian comrades.' He sauntered off and came back carrying a silver tray with two large cocktails wobbling on the top.

He put the tray down and handed one to Robert. 'Excuse me, I must head back to the shade.'

Robert followed him and as he looked into his smiling, freckled face, the sanctions imposed by Adderley were suddenly bearable. Robert learnt that Tom had been recruited into the SOE after the African Campaign.

'I was spotted speaking Italian to our prisoners of war during Operation Compass. It must have got back to the powers that be, because two and a half years later, I was recruited.'

'Where did you learn Italian?' Robert asked.

'Since we are both being posted to the same arena I can't see that a little information will do any harm. I lived in Italy as a child, Florence actually. Can't say any more, you know how it is.'

'I do,' Robert replied.

Tom finished his cocktail and waved to the white-jacketed servant boy who came from the house towards them. 'Two of the same, thank you.' The boy took their glasses and disappeared down the path. 'Of course, my father would say I drink too much. When the war is over I shall stop.'

'But it's not over yet,' Robert laughed, 'so it seems there is still a hell of a lot of drinking to be done.'

'What happened to your arm?' Robert asked when they were on the third cocktail.

Tom groaned. 'Nothing dramatic, I'm afraid. I was doing my training over here, and I fell off a makeshift wall. Very embarrassing, actually, so I'm grounded. But now you've arrived it might not be so dreadful after all.'

They chatted together through the day and into the evening and had just finished a substantial dinner in the dining room when they returned to the wicker chairs outside.

'That certainly makes a change from rationing,' Robert commented, sipping his coffee. 'Flambéed banana. I haven't seen one in years.'

'You can get anything over here,' Tom mused. 'Fillet steak every night of the week if you wish.'

'I'll drink to that.' Robert took a sip of port and leant back in his chair. They were silent for a moment, listening to the distant sounds of Cairo.

'Have you lost anyone close to you?' Robert finally asked Tom.

'My best friend,' he replied. 'We were at school together. He died at Dunkirk. He was only eighteen, blown to smithereens apparently, nothing left. Fucking Krauts, the boys were waiting on the beach to be rescued.'

'I'm so sorry.'

'Everyone has lost someone.'

'My best friend was shot over the Channel,' Robert said with a raw choke. 'He got back to base; crash-landed in a field. They wouldn't let me help him.' He felt his eyes fill and quickly blew his nose. 'This is stupid,' he muttered. 'I think it's the booze, sorry.'

'Not just booze, it's the fucking war! A year ago we heard that my brother was captured and sent to a Japanese prisoner-of-war camp, in Burma; we still don't know if he's dead or alive. Shouldn't have said that, bloody indiscreet, but it gets to you.' He jumped to his feet and undid his sling. 'Come on, Robert, enough, let's go for a swim.'

They stripped to their underpants and dived in. Tom turned over and floated on his back. 'That's Orion,' he said, pointing. 'When I was a child I wanted to be an astronomer. Man is in the process of destroying the earth, but from up there we are nothing. It puts all this into perspective, doesn't it?' The two young men floated on their backs, staring up at the million pinpricks of light that shifted and moved in the blackness.

On the second evening, they visited the bazaars in the unfashionable areas of Cairo. As Robert picked through the assortment of artefacts, he spotted a small terracotta panel.

'From the tomb chapel of Nebamun,' the stallholder assured him. 'Extraordinarily old and valuable.' Robert remembered his visit to the British Museum with his mother and sister. The panel was obviously a fake, but he would buy it for Diana. 'Really?' he asked. 'From Nebamun? I have seen the originals.' He winked at Tom.

'I swear by Allah, the genuine article,' the stallholder was gabbling in broken English.

'You realise you're being conned?' Tom whispered in Robert's ear.

'Don't worry, I'm an expert,' he grinned, and after several minutes of bargaining, the transaction was complete and the panel was wrapped in brightly coloured cloth.

'Let's get out of here,' Robert laughed, and together they strolled down the street.

*

The following morning, Robert received a note from Adderley.

'Your radio operator will meet you this afternoon in my office at Menashe Avenue. Three o'clock. I enclose directions.'

After a light lunch, Robert looked at his watch.

'Sorry Tom, better push along.'

'I wish you luck with Adderley,' Tom laughed, 'and don't get lost on the way.'

As Robert threaded his way through the noisy, crowded streets, he well understood why so many officers had applied to stay. Cairo was exotic and exciting, a heady combination. He was still reflecting when the narrow alleyways opened into wider, residential streets. He climbed the steps to the pillared building and knocked on the door. A girl opened it. Her back was turned as she talked to a servant, and for a brief second Robert studied her. She wore a simple floral dress that skimmed her slim body. Her eyes, when she finally turned towards him, were grey flecked with gold.

'You must be Roberto.'

'And you are?'

Adderley came down the corridor towards them. 'It seems you have already met Giulietta, your radio operator. Stop gawping, young man and come in, it's too bloody hot to be out in the sun.'

Robert followed them inside, his face burning with embarrassment. The beautiful girl with the Titian hair was his radio operator, his so-called wife. He had presumed she would be pleasant but ordinary, someone who would blend into the background. This description did not apply to Giulietta. He stumbled to a chair upholstered in bright yellow silk. After a cup of sweet tea, he had regained some of his composure.

'Of course, Robert, you know that El Alamein was the key to our success and to the subsequent collapse of the Axis forces in North Africa.' Adderley proffered Robert a tray filled with an assortment of cakes. 'It also ended the threat to Cairo, the Suez Canal and the oilfields of the Middle East.'

Biting into the sticky confection, Robert feared he was about to receive another sermon. As Major Adderley lectured his small audience, Robert glanced surreptitiously at the glorious girl on the stool opposite. She looked like something from a fashion magazine, her long legs elegantly crossed, her cup held between tapering fingers with finely rounded nails. She must have had the same training, he mused, tearing his eyes away, but he would still feel responsible for her safety. It was a daunting, disquieting and yet altogether exciting prospect.

'Are you listening, Robert? You seem to be miles away.' Robert's head jerked up.

'Yes, sir.'

'You look tired. I'm told we'll have to restock the bar at your digs. I suggest you take it easy. Tomorrow night is your last and you have a long journey ahead. Cairo to Malta, Malta via sub to the Italian mainland where our agent, Flyte, will pick you up as arranged.'

Giulietta could see the Englishman was uncomfortable and she had found it amusing. He was gauche and young, twenty-three at the most, but he was attractive. When he tripped on his way to the door, her amusement changed to frustration. She was meant to work with this man, to support him in the field.

He wouldn't last a week, Giulietta surmised, and that would put her in danger. She'd soon put a stop to any romantic fantasies.

'Are you married?' she asked.

'No.'

'Well I have a fiancé, so this arrangement is in name only.'

'Of course,' he had replied, his face flushing.

He was halfway down the street when Giulietta caught up with him.

'You see that building over there? Full of German spies, apparently.' She indicated a house at the end of the street. 'They sneak in and out wearing the most distinctive clothes. They should look a little elusive, don't you think? Are you elusive, Roberto?'

Before he had time to reply, she had kissed him on the cheek and peeled away. 'Goodnight, Roberto. See you in two days.'

When he got back to his room, Robert stripped off his clothes and lay on his back. The fan whirred overhead, the air fluttering over him, cooling his body. Giulietta was his radio operator, nothing more. He remembered her eyes mocking him but also her small white teeth and wide mouth laughing up at him. He had noticed the men watching her as they passed. He groaned. His first impression of her had been correct. There was nothing inconspicuous about Giulietta. He pulled the mosquito net around him and watched the flies gather on a brown patch on the ceiling. His life expectancy was limited and his prospects were nil. In any event she had a fiancé, probably some dashing, smooth-talking Italian diplomat.

At somewhere near dawn Robert dressed and slipped from the side door of the house. The streets were empty save for a beggar sitting cross-legged on the pavement, and a few stray dogs scavenging in the road. He waved at a servant boy who was watering a garden behind high metal gates and gave a few piastres to the beggar. There was a smell to Cairo, a pungent, sweet aroma. He would keep this memory, the mist shrouding the streets as the light emerged, the city quiet at last. One day in the future he would return.

He started to laugh. Giulietta was a hot-headed Italian, entirely unsuitable, and yet he couldn't get her out of his mind. He thought of the girls he'd met in the last three years. Sweet Nora of course, then Gillian Goodacre with the generous thighs, and a short fling with Serena Wainwright, daughter of one of the senior officers at Group Headquarters. He had liked them all, particularly Nora, but he had never felt the force of attraction that had hit him the moment he saw Giulietta. Was it her seductive voice, he wondered, or her slim figure? Perhaps it was the mane of Titian hair that she tossed provocatively, or her feline eyes. Perhaps it was Cairo itself.

On Robert's final night in Cairo, Adderley sanctioned a trip to Giza. 'When it's dark,' he added. 'It can't do any harm.'

As they stood in the shadow of the Great Sphinx, Tom spoke, his voice hardly above a whisper.

'I like to believe that we won't be forgotten if…'

'If we die, you mean,' Robert finished Tom's sentence.

Tom nodded. 'I say we forge a pact, right here in the desert. We'll make it through this bloody war and have lunch when it's over'

'It's a date.' Robert grinned. 'The Savoy.'

Chapter Thirty-five

Adderley was at the airport to see Robert and Giulietta off the following morning. His orderly took three suitcases out of the car and took them to the plane.

'Remember we are relying on you.' Adderley mopped his brow on the now filthy handkerchief. 'Good luck and Godspeed.'

The journey from Cairo to Malta continued uneventfully. While Giulietta read, Robert studied maps of the area around Arezzo.

They had just begun the descent to low-level when the plane shuddered violently. Robert was thrown backwards. He could hear the deafening rattle of machine-gun fire from the gun turret above his head. He scrambled to his feet, every nerve in his body alert. 'Lie on the floor and strap yourself down,' he instructed Giulietta, as he clambered towards the cockpit.

The pilot's eyes were fixed ahead and to his left as he struggled to weave the Beaufort bomber away from a Messerschmitt 109. Robert could see the enemy turning rapidly, lining up ahead of them.

'If we can shake him off we could still stand a chance.' The pilot's words were cut off as tiny streaks of light flashed towards them and a shower of bullets ripped through the fuselage. He slumped forward.

'See to him, I'll take over,' Robert immediately commanded the navigator as smoke poured from the port engine. The navigator unclipped the unconscious pilot and pulled him onto the floor while Robert manoeuvred himself into the pilot's seat. *It's only a control panel*, he thought, staring at the dizzying array of dials, but every switch, every knob, seemed in a different position. The white altimeter needles were spinning round in front of him. The aircraft was rapidly approaching a dive. He could hear the wings and fuselage creaking under the strain. He had to get the nose up. As he eased the control column towards him, the nose lifted obediently until they were once again flying straight and level. 'Jesus God,' he exhaled. He turned off the fuel supply to the port engine, pressed the red fire extinuisher button, and the flames died away, but they weren't through it yet. The 109 was out there somewhere.

He adjusted his straps, plugged in the RT lead and he again searched the sky. He checked the aircraft for damage; the flaps didn't work, but the undercarriage went down with a clunk. He lifted the wheels and set the correct course for RAF Luqa.

'Will he make it?' he asked the navigator, glancing at the inert man on the floor.

'It's a question of how quickly we can get him to a hospital.'

Robert twisted around to see Giulietta struggling to the front. 'Are you OK?' he mouthed.

'Don't worry about me, you fly the plane and I'll help the pilot.' She grabbed a dressing from the navigator and, applying a considerable amount of pressure, she pushed it into the wound in the pilot's shoulder.

Robert gripped the control column. He would be landing an unfamiliar plane with no flaps and no port engine, on a runway destroyed by the enemy.

Holding the plane steady, he approached the aerodrome and dumped all but a small amount of fuel. With the wind almost dead on the nose he put the undercarriage lever in down position as he lined up to land. The damage to the runway caused by the Luftwaffe and the Regia Aeronautica made an already difficult landing now seem impossible. He was coming in too fast. He held his breath and prayed. The aeroplane hit the ground with a bounce, bursting a tyre. It careered along the pitted runway and slewed towards a group of buildings. The dispersal hut came ever closer. At only twenty yards from the building it came to a stop.

At once a fire engine and an ambulance hurtled across the runway to stop beside the damaged plane. A doctor jumped out and scrambled on board, taking over from Giulietta.

'You might just have saved his life,' he congratulated her as the ambulance men lifted the pilot through the hatch and placed him on a stretcher.

'Amazing landing, sir,' the navigator said as he shook his hand.

'Very well done, Miss. A good show all round.'

'Welcome to Malta, or what's left of it,' pronounced a Royal Navy lieutenant in a crisp, white uniform, as he opened the door of a waiting jeep. 'Hop in and I'll take you to your billet for the night in St Pauls' Bay. If I may say so, sir, that was quite an entry.'

'It wasn't the most elegant.'

'In these conditions it was remarkable. The Jerry have made a pretty awful mess I'm afraid. Rommel and the Axis forces have reduced the island to rubble.'

He looked then at Giulietta and handed her a towel. 'I'm afraid, Miss, you could do with a bit of cleaning up.'

Giulietta smiled shakily and proceeded to rub the blood from her hands.

As they drove through the desecrated landscape Robert stared from the window.

'You didn't tell me you were a pilot,' Giulietta said at last.

'You didn't ask me,' Robert replied.

As Giulietta soaked in the bath at the Officers' Rest Camp, she pondered on Robert. She had never met anyone like him before. On the one hand he had seemed gauche, but on the other he was very much a man.

But he was a fellow agent and they had a job to do. In any event, she was three years older than Robert and she had said she was engaged. But she would never marry Fabio, no matter how suitable her parents deemed him to be.

She recollected her last conversation with her parents before she had left Cairo. 'How could you do this?' her father had implored. 'I know what you are planning – how could you take these risks, and what about Fabio?' Her mother had nodded in agreement.

'What risks? You were the journalist who wrote about the Fascisti that caused us to flee Italy in the first place. Don't talk to me about taking risks; you took risks with our lives. And forget about Fabio – he does not love me and I certainly don't love him. I am not going to marry him.' She hurtled up the stairs onto the flat roof where she fumed until her father came and found her.

'You are our only child, you are all we have.'

'I will not stand by and see Italy destroyed in this war. You are older now, but once upon a time you would have been fighting too.'

Her father was defeated. His hands dropped to his sides. 'What can I say? You have the fire in your belly, Giulietta.'

Chapter Thirty-six

Signor Angelini was waiting on the loggia when Alessandra came outside. He was wearing a rumpled suit and a panama hat. He took off the hat when he saw her.

'Signora.'

'Davide is not here, he is tending the vines on the far side of the estate.'

'It is you I came to see. We are leaving and I wanted to say goodbye.'

Alessandra's hand flew to her mouth. 'When?'

'First thing in the morning, I'm afraid. The priest came to our house to warn us. The Germans are rounding up the Jews. I had thought with a new name we might be safe ... I was foolish.' He shrugged his shoulders. 'It is time for us to go.' He blinked, and Alessandra put her hand on his arm. She could feel his fragile bones beneath his jacket.

'Is there anything I can do?'

'You have already been too kind.'

He pulled something from his pocket and handed it to Alessandra. 'I noticed that when you read, you always fold the corners of the page. A silver bookmark to prevent this, a token of our friendship.'

'Thank you,' she managed, turning her head, because he mustn't see the tears building.

'I have engraved the quotation by Leopardi on the front. *Death is not an evil because it frees us from all evils.* In case we do not meet again, this will remind you of the funny Jew who enjoyed so much talking to you.' He returned the hat to his head. 'I would be grateful if you could ask my son to come to the house in Mengaccini at six tomorrow morning. He has plans, Signora, that he will of course discuss with you.'

Alessandra took his hand. 'Of course. It is an honour to know you, and thank you for this beautiful and constant reminder of our friendship. See you here again very soon, when the world is a better place.' Alessandra closed the door on Signor Angelini, her heart heavy with sadness.

Davide got out of bed, pulled on his trousers and crept to the window. Outside, animal footprints broke the surface of the wet grass in an irregular trail. They must belong to the wolf he'd seen crossing the brook at the end of the summer.

Diana's dark curls were spread on the pillow. Her arm was thrown carelessly across the counterpane. How innocent she looked, and yet she gave herself to him with a lack of restraint that delighted him. He lay down beside her and he could hear her gentle breathing. The down on her skin was fair and she smelt of soap. He picked up her hand and kissed the soft flesh of her palm, inhaling deeply, trying to imprint everything about her into his memory. The girl he loved was courageous and yet he had seen the fear in her eyes. He looked at his watch; Signora Durante had told him his father wished to see him but she hadn't said why. He leant over the bed and Diana lifted her hand to his hair.

'Don't go, *amore.*'

He didn't want to leave. He wanted to move into her arms.

'I'll see you later.' He kissed her forehead. 'I'll be back before eight.'

Davide pushed Nico inside the house and shut the door behind him. Through the glass he could see the dog's face looking up at him. 'Sit,' he instructed, and the dog sat. He headed into the garden. Avoiding the spider's web that hung from the gate in a tracery of dew, he vaulted the wall and entered the woods. He scrambled down the hill, catching at the branches to stop himself falling. He was about to jump down the bank into the lane when he heard a voice calling his name. He looked around but the lane below was empty.

'Davide,' the call came again, more insistent. 'Here, in the tobacco barn.' Fear triggered in his brain. He slipped back into the cover of the trees, making for the barn. He went inside and as his eyes adjusted to the darkness, Sofia came towards him.

'What is it? What's wrong?'

'They have seized your family.'

'What are you talking about?'

'That Fascist from Umbertide, Guido Tremonti and two German soldiers. I passed your house and witnessed everything. I slipped in here in case you came.'

'You are making no sense, my father wanted to see me.'

'They have taken them all, dear little Lotti, Jaco as well. They pushed them into the back of a truck.' Sofia put her hand on his arm.

'I must go to the house,' he stammered.

'You cannot, they'll be waiting for you.'

'I will kill them for this.'

'They will kill you first.'

Davide wasn't listening. He was at the door when she grabbed his arm.

'No, not like this.'

Davide's mind was racing. He had to rescue his family but

Sofia was right, he couldn't do it alone. Signor Innocenti's nephew was a partisan. He had to find him now.

'My gun, I need that. It is hidden beneath the blankets in the chest at the top of the stairs. Is there any way you can get it for me?' he pleaded.

Sofia nodded. 'I'll say your mother does the laundry for the Villa Durante and I need to collect it. Meet me in the hut by the abandoned quarry in an hour.' She gripped his hand. 'And if there is any trouble, don't come after me.'

She loosened her hair and went outside. He could see her lightly crossing the road, and then he could hear her flirtatious laughter as she spoke to one of the soldiers. He crept round the side of the barn to get a better view of the house. He caught sight of her as she was walked through the front door.

Sofia was carrying a laundry basket when she returned downstairs.

'I need to search the contents.' The soldier lifted a sheet from the top of the basket.

Sofia drew back.

'It's the laundry.'

'I have orders,' he replied.

He was young, Sofia guessed, about her age with dark hair and bright blue eyes, the sort of boy she might have liked if times were different. 'I'll be in trouble if I'm late,' she smiled, pushing the hair from her face.

He stepped forward but she backed further away. He looked indecisive, then dived at the basket. It fell to the ground, the laundry scattered. They both stared at the gun on the terracotta tiles.

The soldier leant down and picked it up. He looked first at the gun and then Sofia. 'You'll be shot if I tell my superiors. I could shoot you myself.'

Sofia's heart was pounding in her chest. She straightened her shoulders and faced him. 'Well then, get on with it,' she taunted. 'Shoot me. Shoot an unarmed girl. It's what you do, isn't it?'

'It is not what I do. But I will not be made a fool of by a silly, flirtatious girl. My superiors can deal with you.'

'Your superiors? So you have no courage yourself. You Germans are all the same. Bullies.'

Sofia saw the anger flicker in his eyes.

'Enough.'

But it was not enough, Sofia was enraged. 'Why don't you tell your mother that you shot a girl for trying to help innocent people?'

'Jews.'

'So Jews are different, are they, they are not people?' Sofia paused for breath. He would shoot her himself, she was sure of it. She had gone too far. Then she saw a change come over the soldier. His eyes shifted away. 'I am only following orders.'

'Orders.' Sofia laughed sarcastically. 'Where is your humanity? You have done a terrible thing today.' She leant back against the wall and glared at the soldier. After a moment he picked up the basket and handed it back to her, keeping the gun.

'What is your name?'

'Sofia.'

'Go, Sofia. Get out of here before I change my mind.'

Sofia began to run.

'My name is Sergeant Hahn, Stefan Hahn, if you should need me,' he called after her.

When Sofia arrived at the quarry she was panting. She put down the basket and went to Davide.

'I was searched. The soldier kept the gun, I'm sorry. You have to get away from here, now.' She pulled an envelope from the pocket of her skirt. 'I found this tucked inside the chest, it's addressed to you. The soldier let me go, but he may well change his mind. Find where they have taken your family, and good luck, Davide.' Sofia disappeared down a small path, the laundry basket balanced on her hip.

Chapter Thirty-seven

Davide remained in the quarry after Sofia had gone. What had his family done to anyone? His creative and gentle father? His sweet mother and his innocent brother and sister?

He leant against the rock face, remembering his father's words. 'The Jews, our people, are being exterminated while the world sits by.'

Diana had advised him to get them away, but he had been convinced he could protect them. If only he had listened. Now he would fight to free them.

He took the letter from his pocket, opening the seal on the ink-stained envelope.

My darling son,
The Germans have been stampeding through Italy as your
father predicted and, though we have been praying for a
miracle, it hasn't come.

Tonight the priest came to our house and we are in danger.
If we do not see you, Signor Innocenti will give you this letter
and tell you our plans. Do not come after us, but be on your
guard always. We will survive, we are a strong and proud
people. Be cautious, my darling. Knowing you are safe gives
me hope.

As I write this, I know the time has come to tell you the truth. All these years I have harboured a secret and I am afraid you will be unable to forgive me. I will begin where it started so many years ago.

Your grandfather, as you know, was a musician, and a fine one. My first memories of our house in Bolzano are rich with the sound of music. For a month each winter, my father, Uncle Peter, Mama and I travelled to Kitzbuhel for the skiing season. There he played the violin at the Grand Hotel. How I used to long for December. I would disappear to the slopes at every possible moment. Imagine, your mother an accomplished skier! One day after a small accident on the piste a young man came to my aid. He was German but charming and courteous. For four weeks we were inseparable. I invented a myriad of excuses to my parents for my absences. I was a young woman in love and everything seemed possible. But, Davide, unmarried, I fell pregnant. I never told the young man, the shame was too great. The reality was in front of me. There was a world between Friedrich and me. We could never have married.

What I did next you may think unforgiveable. When we came home the following week, I agreed to marry your father. He was diffident, naïve and had always been in love with me. The match was approved, both families delighted. When eight months later you were born with blond hair and blue eyes, he never questioned your legitimacy. He accepted you and loved you with his whole heart. He was too honourable to raise any suspicions if he had them.

I know you will be shocked and angered. You will question me and your identity, but you should know this: you are the son of Signor Levi, your true father and his love for you has never faltered. I can also promise you that I have loved him faithfully for the entirety of our marriage, he is truly the best of men.

Davide, with the world in turmoil, your paternity may save you. His name, should you ever need it, is Friedrich von Albrecht.

I hold you in my heart always,
Your Mama.

Davide put the down the letter in disbelief. He knew only too well the strength of love's passion, but his mother had lied to them all. It seemed that the man he had called Papa for the last twenty-five years of his life was not his father. The man he had loved with every fibre of his being was not his flesh and blood. It explained everything; the strange looks in the synagogue, snatches of conversation overheard but not understood. He was an imposter, a bastard, someone else's son. He remembered his father's explanations to everyone: 'My boy is a throwback, my grandmother, she had blonde hair just like Davide.' He must know, the poor man.

He took a pencil stub from his pocket and scribbled the name on the envelope over and over again. *Friedrich von Albrecht*. How sinister it looked. How German. Everything he had believed in was a lie. His real father was from an affluent German family. He was probably a Nazi involved in the persecution of his race and he would have to live with that. But the truth was he couldn't live with it. The Nazis had taken his family and they would pay for it.

Sofia dropped the basket on the loggia floor. The laundry spilled around her.

'Signora,' she cried.

Alessandra hurried from her study.

'Something terrible has happened. They have taken them.

274

The Angelinis, Lotti, and Jaco. They have all gone,' the words tumbled out in a rush. 'I was able to warn Davide.'

'But they were due to leave this morning.'

'*Si*, Signora but Guido Tremonti got to them first.'

Alessandra held on to the table.

'Signora Carducci,' she called, and the older woman came running. 'I'll explain in a minute, but please will you fetch Davide's clothes from the barn. Hide them in the chapel. Sofia, you go to the school, tell Diana to send the children home. She must go to the top meadow and stay there until it is safe. I will remain here, I have no doubt that Guido Tremonti will turn up soon.'

Sofia had returned and was upstairs when Guido Tremonti appeared on the doorstep, a *squadrista* on either side.

'Signor Tremonti.' Alessandra held out her hand. 'I haven't seen you since that wonderful Christmas party some five years past. How is your family?'

'I'm not here to talk about my family. We are looking for Davide Angelini.'

'He has gone to Calabria.'

'I am told he was here only yesterday.'

'Yes, but he left this morning, Sofia can confirm this.' Alessandra's voice was calm as Sofia appeared down the stairs. 'Sofia, please explain to the Captain that Davide is no longer here.'

Sofia deposited her bag of cleaning materials on the floor and smiled at Guido. 'Sadly he has left us for Calabria. Can I assist you in anything else? Coffee? Only acorn, I'm afraid.'

Guido smoothed his hair. 'And your position in this house?'

'I'm the cook.'

'Well, Sofia the cook, if you see this Angelini, you will tell us?'

'*Ovviamente*, Signor.'

'No coffee, thank you.' He turned back to Alessandra. 'I will talk to your other staff, and where is your daughter?'

'Diana has gone to the market, but I will fetch Signora Carducci and her niece.'

Signora Carducci came in first. 'So, why is a good Italian boy throwing in his lot with the Germans?'

'Watch what you say, old woman.'

She sniffed. 'Davide has left, more is the pity. There is too much work for an old woman like me. All our young men have gone, and for what? Look around you; the workers are women and old men. My sister's great-nephew Luca, one of our elite Alpine troops, went off to the Russian front in forty-two. He hasn't been heard of since.'

'Shut up, old woman, enough. And what have you to say, Beatrice?' Guido barked.

Alessandra turned sharply. Guido had known the girl's name.

'I haven't seen him for a while,' Beatrice mumbled.

'You told me you had, so you are lying to me?'

'No sir, I mean, I don't know sir.'

'I will be watching you, Beatrice, and you Signora.' Guido was at the end of the loggia when he gave instructions to his men.

'The hens, kill them all,' he said.

Signora Carducci tried to shield Alessandra as the men approached the henhouse. 'Don't look, Signora,' she pleaded, but Alessandra couldn't help herself. She couldn't block the panic and chaos as her precious hens tried to get away, she couldn't avoid the sound of flapping wings as their necks were broken, one by one.

The men threw the carcasses into the boot and as the car disappeared down the driveway, Alessandra slumped to the ground.

Later Alessandra voiced her suspicions to Signora Carducci.

'Ah, *Dio*, I will kill her myself, the ungrateful girl. I have watched over Beatrice and that simple brother of hers since their mother's death and this is what I get for it. Why didn't you tell me before?'

'I didn't want to concern you.'

'Forgive me, Signora. I must leave this house at once.'

'No you will not,' Alessandra said, taking hold of her arm. 'We are only responsible for our own actions.'

'But I brought her here. Agh, poor Lotti, Jaco, the Signor and Signora; they are good and honest people. You can't punish a man for worshipping the wrong God.'

'I believe it is the same God,' Alessandra reminded her.

When the coast was clear, Diana returned to the house. 'We must help the Angelinis,' she exclaimed, running to her mother.

'Of course,' Alessandra soothed. 'We will do all we can.'

When she saw Beatrice being forcibly held by her aunt, her anxiety increased. 'What is going on, what has she done?'

'My niece deserves to be shot, she betrayed the Angelinis to that pig Tremonti. Perhaps I will shoot her myself.' Signora Carducci twisted Beatrice's ear so that she yelped with pain.

'What did you tell him?' Alessandra asked Beatrice, her voice measured.

'Nothing, Signora, I promise you.'

Diana stepped forward until she was directly in front of Beatrice.

'I didn't mean to say anything,' the girl whimpered, 'but Captain Tremonti forced me.'

'How did he force you, Beatrice?' Diana probed, her voice like steel.

'I needed to buy medicine for my brother. He is not well, and I have to look after him.'

She turned to Alessandra, pleading. 'We are on our own, Signora... I have to do everything.'

'You haven't answered my daughter's question. How did he force you?'

'I stole from you. Only small things at first, a little sugar, some butter, but then I took a gold bangle. The Captain saw me trying to sell it in the jewellers in the square. He confronted me and said I couldn't own a pretty bangle like that and he was right, Signora. He said if I didn't give him information about the Angelinis my brother would be shot.'

'So that was why you were sneaking below my bedroom. Nico heard you,' Diana affirmed.

'The Captain promised no harm would come to anyone.'

'And you believed him? You are a coward and a thief. And what about Davide? Would you have him taken too?' Diana looked at her with loathing.

'No, Signorina, I like him, not that he notices me of course. It is always about you. You are pretty, and he loves you. You have everything,' she glanced around her, 'and I have nothing.'

Diana drew in her breath. 'Are you in love with Davide?'

The girl shook her head, staring at the floor.

'Do you realise what you have done?'

'I didn't know this would happen. If I could change it...' she cried.

'It is too late for that. Go from here and don't ever come back,' Diana shouted, her eyes filled with angry tears.

Chapter Thirty-eight

Davide took one of the many tracks to the *fattoria* and slipped into a stable to wait for Signor Innocenti.

'It's me,' he called softly, when the estate manager entered the yard.

'Come inside, quickly.' Signor Innocenti checked it was safe before ushering him into the kitchen.

'Davide, I'm so sorry. They were packed and ready to go. Doctor Biochetti was finding them a safe house. If only ...' his words trailed off.

'I have to find them,' Davide exclaimed, his face stricken with grief.

'Of course, but if you go to Umbertide, Guido will arrest you on sight. I'll go instead. Conserve your energy today,' Signor Innocenti advised.

'I have to see Diana.'

'But not at the Villa Durante, they'll be watching.' He put some soup on the stove. 'No, Davide, stay here, I'll get word to Diana. She will bring your things to the barn above the lake at dusk. Come back here afterwards when I should have some news. Then we can make a plan.'

*

Carrying a rucksack, Diana skirted the lower meadow and took the shortcut to the lake. When she arrived at the barn, Davide was waiting for her.

She threw herself into his arms. 'They can't keep them, surely? Not Lotti and Jaco, they are children. I am sure they will let them go.'

Davide kissed her forehead and held her tight, knowing the pain he was going to inflict. Even if his family were to be released, he would still have to leave.

Diana drew back. 'You are going, aren't you?'

'I'm sorry, I must.'

'Where? What will you do?'

'I'm going north, to help the fight to bring freedom to our country. I can't stand by any longer. And you wouldn't love me if I turned my back on this madness.'

He lifted her chin and looked into her eyes. 'You have made me happier than I could have believed possible. So no more sadness; I want to remember your beautiful smile.'

She gave him the rucksack, her mouth trembling. 'I've packed some clothes, food, and a little money.'

'Thank you, I will pay you back.'

Diana shook her head. 'At least let me do this for you.'

'Keep away from the *Fascisti*, from Guido Tremonti,' Davide warned. 'One day he will pay for what he has done, but for now I must know you are safe. And if you are ever in doubt, you will leave, promise me?' He took her face in his hands, kissing her tears away.

'I promise.'

'I have to go,' he said, releasing her arms. 'I will come back to you, God will lead me back to you.'

It was dark when Davide returned to the *fattoria*. The wind was whistling through the trees and Davide could feel the chill in the air. He knocked on the door. Signor Innocenti pulled him inside and led him towards a chair by the kitchen fire. He fetched a bottle of grappa and squatted down so that their faces were level.

'Now you will drink.'

'Tell me, quickly, what did you find.'

'It is not good news, my son. I cycled to Umbertide. I thought I could plead with the Mayor; he is a well-known Fascist, but we were at school together, childhood friends. I believed it might count for something. I was too late. I spoke to my nephew Antonio, asked the partisans to help us, but your family had been taken from the prison, directly to the station. Of course I went after them; I saw everything, Davide. It was being used as an assembly point and there were Jewish families being herded into the cattle cars. I will not spare you: the trains were heading straight to Germany.'

'I should have known.' Davide put his head in his hands. He wasn't seeing Signor Innocenti, only his family on the platform, his mother crying.

'Jaco, he didn't struggle?'

Signor Innocenti paused, recalling how Jaco had fought, kicking and screaming, and only his mother's pleas had saved him.

'No,' he said, putting his hand on Davide's arm. 'He was quiet, a great support to your mother. They allowed your sister to take her violin, small consolation, I know.'

'What do you think will happen to them?' Davide asked.

'We have both heard of the camps. Let us hope it is just for internment.'

'Then I can do nothing,' he responded, his voice flat.

'What could you possibly do against their guns?' Signor Innocenti commiserated. 'Now you must try to sleep. At dawn you should leave for Arezzo.'

'Arezzo?'

'Among other things, the doctor plays a vital role in the

growing resistance movement. He will be able to link you with the partisans in the north.'

'I had no idea.'

'In these times it is dangerous to know anything, my friend.'

At sunrise, Signor Innocenti bade him goodbye.

'Go. Help set our country free. And I will pray that one day your family will come back to you. If only I were younger...' he sighed.

'Your place is here, old man.'

Davide pulled on his hat and put the red scarf knitted by Signora Carducci around his neck. He stood beneath the porch. 'Look after her, Signor.'

Signor Innocenti clasped his hand. 'I will protect Diana and her mother.'

Chapter Thirty-nine

It was dark and the van driven by Agent Flyte was speeding through the Italian countryside somewhere between Livorno and the isolated farmhouse to the south of Sienna, where Robert and Giulietta would stay the night. In the morning he would take them to their final destination in Arezzo.

As the wooded hillsides gave way to the *Crete Senesi*, the strange lunar landscape of undulating hills that loomed in the darkness, Giulietta slept on, her face pressed against the glass. Occasionally Robert glanced down at her, longing to reach out and touch the freckles on her nose. She opened her eyes and looked up at him. 'We must be there?'

'Not far,' he replied, looking away, but still she was on his mind. For the next few months Giulietta would be at his side. He would live with her, work with her – and despite his best intentions, he would probably fall in love with her.

He remembered drinks in the Officers' Rest Camp bar, Giulietta's eyelids drooping.

'You look exhausted, you should go to bed,' he had suggested.

'I will go when I wish, Roberto.' She had lifted her chin, her eyes flashing.

'Well, I'm tired,' he had said at last.

'You saved my life, but you have little stamina,' she had taunted him.

'Goodnight, Giulietta.'

The following evening they had been sitting on a low wall overlooking the sea, when Giulietta spoke. 'You have a reason for being here, Roberto?'

'I am sure it is the same as yours. Freedom and democracy.'

Giulietta nodded. 'Italy is my country and I will fight for it until my last breath. Do you want to know why I am your radio operator, Roberto?' she had asked, jumping down to paddle in the sea, pulling up her skirts and flashing her long legs.

'Two years ago I presented myself to the British Intelligence in Cairo and asked if I could become a courier. They dismissed this out of hand. Apparently, I was too pretty, not inconspicuous enough. Pah, I was angry of course, but at least they were aware of me. A few months later I realised I was being observed. They were stupid to think I wouldn't notice them. I turned and gave them a piece of my mind. They laughed and said I had better come back to headquarters and meet the Major. I started as a translator and the rest you know.'

It was late when they finally turned in. This time Robert walked her to her bedroom door.

'Tomorrow we are on a submarine, no? And will you attempt to save that too?' She had leant on the doorjamb, teasing him, and somehow he had walked away.

Robert remembered the ride from the submarine in the small dinghy, and Giulietta gazing towards the Italian shore.

After ten minutes rowing they beached and Giulietta was carried ashore by one of the ratings.

'Welcome to Tuscany,' a voice said softly, and after identifying code names were exchanged, Giulietta picked up a pebble and rubbed away the sand. 'Take this,' she had said to Robert. 'It is a stone of Italy, my Italy, and you will know why I'm here.'

Chapter Forty

Diana left Nico outside the gate of the Angelini family home and walked up the short path to the door. Now the German soldiers had gone and, as Davide had requested, she was collecting his mother's candlesticks and the donkey.

She stood in the narrow hallway. Boots lined the wall, and a case lay open at the bottom of the stairs. Items of clothing were discarded nearby. A small green coat hung on a peg; Lotti's coat. She'll get cold, Diana thought, her throat tightening. She could hear music coming from the end of the corridor, a violin. She ran towards it, opened the door but the room was empty. Tears sprang to her eyes. The family had gone.

She found the candlesticks where they had obviously been abandoned in haste on the dining-room floor. Signor Angelini's designs for his commissions were scattered close by. Diana gathered them together and put them into the sack she had brought and went outside.

The donkey that had pulled the cart all the way from Bolzano looked over his stable door.

'I've come to fetch you,' Diana said stroking his head. 'I'll look after you until your family returns.'

*

Diana was leading the donkey when Pipo drew his bicycle up beside her.

'*Buongiorno*, beautiful Diana, first it was a goat, then a dog, now you have a donkey too. Soon your Ark will be filled to capacity. But you are crying, what is wrong?'

'Davide's family have been taken and now he has gone to join the partisans in the north. It's terrible. I feel so helpless.'

Pipo flung the bicycle to the ground and put his arms around the sobbing girl.

She looked up at him. 'You are good to me, Pipo.'

He laughed softly. 'You didn't always think that. I remember the first time we met, you were angry with me.'

'Of course I was.' Diana managed a wan smile. 'We had just arrived in Italy, the bus was late to pick us up and you drove so badly. You told my mother you were twenty-one when you were only sixteen!'

'You didn't know that at the time, and I got you to Mercatale.'

'The first day I went to school, what was it you said to cheer me up?'

'*The first day is always the worst day*.' Pipo smiled.

'And that other time when Davide didn't come?'

'I don't remember, but I would look after you until my dying breath. Now wipe your eyes, for I have a thought.' Pipo raised Diana's chin. 'I was going to join the partisans here. Would it make you happier if I went north with your boyfriend? Kept an eye on him for you?'

'You'd do that for me?'

Davide limped into Arezzo twelve hours after leaving Signor Innocenti. When the coast was clear he crossed the piazza and headed towards the Corso Italia.

At number 39 he pulled the bell.

'*Si*?' A middle-aged woman opened the door. 'Who shall I say is calling?'

'Davide Angelini.'

The woman looked at him closely. 'You look exhausted, you had better come in.' She drew him inside, shutting the door behind him. 'Wait here.' She disappeared into the back of the house and Davide could hear doors opening and closing, the sound of voices. He was standing by the fireplace when Doctor Biochetti entered the hall. He pulled off his hat.

'Davide, how good to see you.' The doctor wrung his hand. 'I was expecting to hear from your family, but you have come instead.'

'They've been taken,' Davide blurted. 'All of them.'

Doctor Biochetti gasped. '*Dio*, not Lotti and Jaco?'

'My brother and sister, my parents. Gone.'

'My poor boy. When did this happen?'

'Yesterday morning. They are on a train heading for Germany.'

The doctor shook his head. 'Why didn't they come to me sooner? They knew about our network.'

'They were already packed, but it was too late. I wanted to go after them but Signor Innocenti stopped me. He said another dead Jew means nothing to the Nazis. I can no longer help my family, but I can fight back. Will you put me in touch with a leader in the north?'

'Why not here in Arezzo? Signor Innocenti's nephew, Antonio, needs good men like you.'

'I'll be more use in Bolzano, I know it so well.'

'Then I'll give you a letter of introduction, but first food, a glass of brandy and a good night's rest. You have a long journey ahead.'

When Davide rose early next morning, Doctor Biochetti was waiting for him. 'There is someone to see you, Davide, he says he is a friend, but I have to be sure.'

'Who?' Davide asked, immediately on edge.

'His name is Pipo.'

The doctor took both men into the dining room. 'No one can see us in here,' he assured them. 'But as a precaution, I will pull the curtains.'

They were sitting at the table when the same middle-aged woman brought them some freshly baked bread, a large piece of cheese and a jug of milk.

'I was going to join Antonio's resistance fighters,' Pipo explained to the doctor, while wolfing down a large piece of cheese. 'But with all this, I couldn't let Davide go north on his own.'

'That is good of you, Pipo, but I will be fine.' Davide interjected.

Pipo looked at the doctor and shrugged his shoulders. 'For one year I drove him to work in my bus, we lived near to each other, drank beer together. Now when I say I will go north with him, he doesn't need me.'

'That is not what I meant.' Davide managed a weak smile.

'Well then, the Jew and the bus driver, a good combination is it not? I am sure God would have something to say about that.'

Chapter Forty-one

Friedrich von Albrecht sat at his desk in the vast library of the Palazzo della Mostra. Comfortable armchairs covered in dark green velvet were scattered around the room, and books lined the walls. Some of the titles were in German, some in Italian; Bolzano and the Alpine foothills had been fought over for centuries. He stared at the photo in front of him. His wife smiled from the frame, her glossy hair caught in a slide, her arms around their two children. He missed Rudi and Axel dreadfully; they were delightful little boys, full of love and laughter. He pictured them running across the grass towards him, jumping into his arms. They had come to him later in life; perhaps that was why he treasured them so much.

Why was he in Northern Italy anyway? It was certainly not out of choice. At the end of the last war, when the German army was disbanded, he believed his fighting days were over. He had gladly returned to his peacetime occupation as a lawyer but in 1938, when it was clear that war was inevitable, the Wehrmacht mobilised the resource of officers and he was once again a soldier. 'At fifty I am too old for a command in the field,' he had reassured his wife, but Ursula had looked at him knowingly.

'They will have something else planned for you. You will not remain unnoticed.' She had been right of course.

He had proved his ability as a staff officer and now five years later here he was in Bolzano as Colonel Commandant of a vast military region. His task was a large one and more than he wanted: to enforce total control of the Italian civil authorities and to safeguard the security of the logistic infrastructure supporting the German forces. He felt too old for such things.

He walked across the thick Persian carpet to the drinks table, unscrewed the whisky bottle and poured a liberal amount into a crystal glass, followed by two cubes of ice from a silver bucket. Replacing the tongs, he returned to his desk. The war had reached a critical turning point. Germany would lose; it now seemed inevitable. The desert war was over, their hero Rommel defeated; the battle of Stalingrad lost. Sicily had been invaded and now the British and Americans had a firm foothold on the Italian mainland. He ran his hand through his thick silver hair. How had his countrymen allowed Hitler to dupe them? He thought back to the early days. Initially he had disliked Hitler as a common upstart, a demagogue with powerful rabble-rousing talents, but later his opinion, as with most of the German aristocracy, had changed in Hitler's favour. The answer was not difficult to find. The crash of '29 had been yet another blow and, with the German economy at its lowest ebb after the Great War, and the punitive sanctions imposed by the Treaty of Versailles, Germany was in turmoil; his own family holdings had halved.

'Perhaps Hitler is not so bad,' his father had said. 'He promises economic growth and stability. He believes he is the man to rebuild Germany into a major world power. If this is the case I will support him, and I believe you should too.'

Freidrich paced the room, stopping at the window to stare into the piazza below. It was eight thirty and after the curfew. The square was empty. How desolate it seemed.

He remembered the evening before he had left for Bolzano, in October '43, having dinner with Ursula. 'My new position,' he had said, while carefully filleting his sole, 'is to keep the supply lines open, so that the weaponry and equipment, and the oil to keep the engines running, can get through. With the Italians changing sides, they are also under my jurisdiction.'

'Really,' she had said vaguely, and he had felt the usual disappointment. For once he had hoped she would be interested in the measure of his duties; he was, after all, leaving in the morning.

'Dearest Freidrich,' she continued, 'it is hardly time for a history lesson. Do what you have to do and come home.'

He had stared at her, amazed. As he ate the rest of his dinner in silence, he wondered why she had married him. Of course he was rich in comparison to many of his fellow Germans, and aristocratic. In the eyes of her family he was a good catch, but they had nothing in common. Had he ever loved her, he wondered. Probably not, but he had bowed to pressure from his father.

How he would have appreciated someone sympathetic to talk to, someone who possessed compassion as well as beauty, but that would never be his wife. He grimaced, thinking about his new orders. Finding and eliminating the partisans was one thing, but the recent edict by Feldmarschall Kesselring guaranteeing immunity to any commander who exceeded normal restraint in dealing with them was quite another. He was a soldier, not a murderer.

There was yet another aspect to his new posting that he found entirely contemptible. A new concentration camp was being built in Bolzano and a transit camp for prisoners heading for the concentration camps in the north. He hadn't fought, spent his youth in the trenches knee-deep in filth and been decorated for his bravery, only to be responsible for the incarceration and probable death of Jews and gypsies. This was abhorrent to him, and his orders for that evening weighed heavily on his mind. His first consignment of Jews would be stopping at Bolzano on their way to Germany. In the small station the train would refuel, and the Jews incarcerated in his temporary blocks would be taken from their cells and herded onto the train. He was expected to supervise the delivery of this wretched human cargo.

He couldn't forget he had once been in love with a Jewish girl, her eyes, more green than brown, her white arms and flawless skin. He was young and idealistic back then and the fact that she was Jewish was of no importance. But she had disappeared, without saying goodbye, and for that he was angry. Now all these years later he was in Bolzano, the town of her birth. He hoped she was safe.

Chapter Forty-two

'Doctor Biochetti is a true patriot, he knows everyone and is trusted in the community,' Agent Flyte said to Robert, stopping the van in the Via Mazzini. 'He will be your first link with the partisans, and your point of contact outside the SOE if any trouble occurs.' He shook hands with both Robert and Giulietta and restarted the engine.

'Good luck, my friends.'

'Welcome.' Doctor Biochetti took them through to the dining room.

He pushed aside a pile of papers and dumped them on the floor. Taking a red woollen scarf from the back of a chair, he swore softly. 'My last visitor has forgotten this, he'll have need of it, I'm sure. Come, sit, have something to eat. This afternoon, I will drive you to your *pensione* at Palazzo del Perro. I have taken the liberty of buying you two bicycles.'

The doctor studied the young couple as they ate the breakfast his indefatigable housekeeper had provided. The girl was eating the sugared bread with an appetite that amused him. The man was more reserved. He looked young, but they all did. Were they really married, he wondered, pouring the last of the black-market coffee into the girl's cup. And was Roberto really Italian, though he did speak the language fluently? It was probably a cover story, but for reasons of their safety with the partisans and the Germans it was better not to know.

'You have come at an opportune moment,' he said, leaning back in his chair. 'The Germans have seized control of this region, and we need your help. The village of Palazzo del Perro is a good base for your operations.'

For the next half hour they discussed the overall situation in Tuscany, and then more locally. Robert's first contact would be Antonio, the leader of a local group of partisans. He would meet him the following morning at ten o'clock at a farmhouse, two kilometres from the village heading east. 'You can't miss it,' the doctor said. 'There's a small shrine to Our Lady at the end of the lane. Antonio is honest and with no communist affiliations. He comes from the Niccone Valley not far from Cortona. Remember, Roberto, there are still many Fascist sympathisers in our midst.' He looked then at Giulietta. 'And I must warn you, radio detecting vans have recently started to patrol the area. Be cautious.'

It was late afternoon when Doctor Biochetti and his two passengers left Arezzo for the short journey to Palazzo del Pero. As the sun dipped behind the city walls, Robert gazed from the window of the van. It was difficult to imagine the turmoil and unrest that was fermenting in the woods and hills outside. Bathed in the late autumn sunshine everything looked tranquil, untouched by human disturbance. Not far away his mother and sister lived at the Villa Durante. It would be hard not to see them, nor contact them, but at least he would know if they were safe.

'As a doctor, I am able to obtain a limited quantity of petrol. It has some benefits.' The doctor's cheerful voice broke into his thoughts. There was something reassuring about him that reminded Robert of his father. The thought would give him comfort in the uncertain days ahead.

When they reached the top of the hill behind Arezzo, the road dropped away down a gradual incline. Here, at the point where several valleys met, and streams and rivers converged, was Palazzo del Pero.

Doctor Biochetti stopped the van in the middle of the village and Robert climbed out, untying the bicycles in the back. A memorial to the Second Italian War of Independence stood in the centre of a small square, where a group of elderly men were playing cards.

'Do you play cards, Giulietta?' the doctor asked her.

'They are playing Scopa, my father's favourite. I will challenge them sometime.' She looked up at him. 'I am rather good.'

'I have no doubt,' Doctor Biochetti chuckled. 'But this lot have a great deal of practice. They would probably continue to play while the guns shoot around them. They are a lazy bunch, they would rather their wives do the work. It's always the same.'

He pointed to a large villa on the other side of the road. 'Your *pensione*. I suggest that you remain here.' He lowered his voice, 'Bruno, your host, despises the *Tedeschi*; he lost three brothers to the Germans in the last war. He has scores to settle. You'll be as safe as you can be here.'

Robert went first, carrying the suitcases. He set them down on the path and looked up at his new accommodation. The house was square with stone quoins at each corner. Jasmine grew up the pale apricot walls. Weeds pushed their way through the gravel, and four Ilex trees cast shadows over an unkempt parterre. He smiled as an elderly gentleman walked down the path towards him.

'*Buona sera*, Signor. You must be Bruno.'

'I am that man.' Bruno put out his hand. 'I can see you like my house. It once served as a hostel for pilgrims on their way

296

to Assisi, but for the last hundred years it has been run by my family as a *pensione*.' He shrugged his shoulders. 'But of course you need money to run a house like this. And where is the money and where are the visitors? Ah, Dottore.' He smiled as the doctor came towards him pushing the bicycles.

'So, my friend, you will stay for a drink?'

'I'm afraid not,' Doctor Biochetti apologised. 'I need to get back.'

'Always in a hurry, always rushing this way and that. You'll get an ulcer.'

'Ah, you are pretty,' Bruno exclaimed, when Giulietta finally arrived. She set the last suitcase on the path.'

'And you are a handsome man,' she laughed.

The doctor patted him on the back. 'I have to go, Bruno, but I am glad to see you haven't lost your touch. I'll drop by one of these days for a quiet chat, I promise.'

He set off down the path, turning to wave at the gate. 'Good luck to you all.'

'A glass of grappa, don't forget.' The old man lifted his hand, then turned back to his guests. 'Now my charming young people, I will show you the house.' When Giulietta went to pick up her suitcase, he admonished her. 'I may look weak, but Signorina, let me do the honour.'

As they followed the old man into the hall and towards an elegant staircase that swept upwards to the first floor, he cautioned them. 'Be careful, the stone post is broken, up there, see?'

'We will,' they both replied, though Giulietta wasn't looking at the newel post, but instead at a large chandelier that hung from the ceiling. 'It's Venetian, isn't it?'

'*Si*, it arrived when I was a small boy. My father had it shipped from Murano, first by sea, then by land, and it arrived in an enormous wooden crate.' He chuckled. 'It's a little dirty, but it's lovely, I agree.'

'Oh yes …' She paused, gazing up at the chandelier. 'It certainly is.'

Guilietta was full of contradictions, Robert thought, watching her. At one moment she was a fearless warrior taking on a man's world, the next she was a captivated child. He laughed to himself and continued up the stairs.

Bruno turned the key in the lock. 'This is your room.' He opened the door to a spacious but sparsely furnished room looking on to a south-facing balcony. 'Down the passage there is a bathroom and toilet. There is hot water between six and seven.'

Accepting the first week's rent, he pushed the money into the pocket of his jacket and gave them the key. 'If you want to make use of my cellar, for anything other than drinking my wine, it is yours.'

When the old man had gone, Giulietta exclaimed in delight. 'Proper plumbing,' she said, 'and hot water.'

Robert looked at the sleeping arrangements. Two wooden beds were side by side with only a small table between them. He would be in the same room with Giulietta. If he stretched out his arm he could touch her face, he would hear her soft breathing.

He looked up to see Giulietta dragging a large fabric screen across the floor. She put it between the two beds and wiped the dust from her hands. 'This is my bed, and this is yours, Roberto,' she said with a triumphant smile.

After an excellent supper cooked by Bruno, Giulietta left the men and returned upstairs. She unpacked the wireless from her suitcase, lifted a small table into the middle of the room and put the set upon it. When she was sure the lane outside was empty and the coast clear, she hung the aerial wire from the balcony railings, disguising it among the jasmine. She would make one quick transmission to SOE headquarters to confirm they were in location and were maintaining a listening watch at the prescribed times, then she would turn off the set and pull in the wire. She had always known the dangers, but as she tapped in the code in her own unique way her heart was beating fast. This was no longer an exercise in the safety of the training camp, it was out in the field for the very first time.

The following morning Robert took his bicycle from the porch at the side of the house and set off for his first meeting with Antonio, the leader of the Aquile, at the farmhouse near the shrine. As he cycled up the dusty track he was fizzing with adrenaline at being back in the field. He was finally going to put his training to use. Yes, he was nervous, who wouldn't be? Not only would he be putting his new identity to the test, but he had to make the partisans respect him. He pondered on their pseudonym. Every band chose a name, but theirs interested him – he would soon find out if they lived up to it.

When Antonio ambled towards him, a cigarette in his mouth, his dark eyes filled with humour, Robert knew they would get on.

'So, Roberto,' the other man said, shaking his hand. 'You have come to help the Aquile. We lack arms and experience, but like our namesake the eagle with whom we share this inhospitable terrain, we have strong hearts. Will you help us to get our claws?'

'That is why I am here,' Robert smiled.

For the next hour, Antonio described the men in his band. He outlined their strengths and weaknesses. 'Each man has a different motivation. There are the patriots, but there are also those avoiding conscription. Lepre, my second in command, joined because of his intense hatred of the Germans; Dario to avoid their munitions factories. We are lucky, he also hunts for our food. Against my will, there is Francesco, the baby of the group. He ran away from home to join us. Others are here just for the excitement.'

'And what's your reason, Antonio?' Robert asked.

'If I am correct, you and I have the same reason, the freedom of our country.'

While he smoked another cigarette, he told Robert of their training to date and he detailed their limited supply of arms. When they finally went their separate ways, they shook hands once again.

'We have an enormous task ahead of us,' Robert affirmed, 'but trust me, Antonio, I shall do all that I can.'

When Robert entered their room Giulietta's back was turned from him as she folded her clothes and put them into the bottom drawer of the chest. Her soft, cotton dress clung to her body, caressing each contour. Robert felt a frisson of delight watching her as she pushed the drawer shut and turned round.

'So you like this Antonio?' she asked.

'You'll meet him. We're seeing him at a bar later.'

She raised her eyebrows. 'You may be seeing him, Roberto, but unless you ask me properly you will be going on your own.'

Robert laughed. 'Forgive me, that was rude. My dear Giulietta, would you do me the honour of accompanying me to see your cousin Antonio.'

'So he is now my cousin, is he?'

'Please, Giulietta?' Robert looked at her winningly and Giulietta started to laugh. She picked up her cardigan and threw it at him and soon they were both laughing.

Robert and Giulietta parked their bicycles outside the village and ambled through the narrow alleyways towards the centre.

'It is so good to be back in my country,' Giulietta said, moving close to Robert, her voice low. 'I was a child when we left, but

I have always longed to return. Look, this village is beautiful, even the name, Civitella. In Italy we do it so well, the houses, the church, and the school all grouped around the piazza.'

'Italians certainly know about architecture,' Robert agreed.

'They know about a lot of things, Roberto.' She looked at him with laughter in her eyes.

Robert held her gaze, but he could feel his cheeks burning.

'When this is all over,' he said, recovering his equilibrium, 'I'd like to be involved in the rebuilding of cities destroyed in the devastation. My best friend wanted me to join him in his father's aeroplane factory, but since his death I realise that's not for me. I want to do something for the future. Something that will last. Do you know what I mean?'

'I do.' She put her arm through his and they strolled into the centre.

They passed the cistern in the square and sat down at a metal table inside a small bar. They ordered two beers and a bowl of olives from a waiter in a striped jersey. At the table next to them a young girl and her father were playing chess.

For a moment the girl looked up at them. She had a blue bow in her hair, which matched the colour of her eyes. '*Buona sera*,' she said, and then she bent her head and the game resumed. Robert watched as she deftly moved her knight one left and two forward and checked the king. Her father realised he was unable to move and he laughed. The game was over. 'Checkmate,' she said, deadpan, and the father threw up his hands.

'She is good, no?' He turned to Robert. 'I teach her too well.'

'She certainly is,' he replied.

When Antonio arrived, he pulled Giulietta to her feet and kissed her on both cheeks.

'I'm late, apologies little cousin. But you are still the most beautiful girl in Italy apart from my Rosalie. Roberto, you are a lucky man. You are coming to my wedding?'

'*Ovviamente*,' Giulietta said, warming to the charade. 'I have bought the dress already. How is the family? And the bambini? And Uncle Pietro is he still as fat? He promised Mama to go on a diet.'

'Ah, promises, promises.'

Antonio went to the next-door table and picked up the little girl, swinging her round. 'So Teresa, you win against your father again, huh? Next time you have a better opponent with me.'

The child grinned. 'I don't think so. I could still beat you.'

'Next week then! It is a match.' Antonio tickled her under the chin. 'Now go and play with your brother Basilio and act like a normal child your age.'

Robert, Antonio and Ulisse, the child's father, pulled the tables together.

While Teresa played tag around the cistern with her brother, a young boy with long, unruly hair, the adults drank beer. They had finished their glasses and were about to leave when three German soldiers sauntered across the square and entered the bar. The two children stopped running. Everyone was silent. Giulietta glanced at Robert.

The soldiers made their way over to the table. The tallest of the three spoke in heavily accented Italian. 'I haven't seen you before and your pretty friend. You are not from this area?'

'Wife,' Giulietta interjected.

'Of course, if I had a woman like you on my arm I would make her my wife immediately.' He winked at Robert.

'We are from around here, actually.' Robert smiled at the soldier. 'But I work in Florence. I'm a print dealer; let me know if you wish to buy anything to send home.'

'Thank you.' The German nodded. 'For now I need a beer.'

They moved towards the wooden counter and Antonio stood up.

'So,' he said speaking loud enough for anyone to hear. 'Mama says if I am late for supper again, she will kill me. Forgive me, Roberto, but I value my hide more than another drink.' There was general forced laughter and by the time the soldiers had ordered their beer, Antonio had gone.

It was getting dark when Robert and Giulietta arrived back at Palazzo del Perro. They had been silent all the way home and as they parked their bicycles, Giulietta turned to Robert.

'We didn't give anything away?'

'No, Giulietta, we did not.'

'We probably shouldn't have been there.'

'We need to blend in to our surroundings, so it is right to be there, but you are hardly inconspicuous.'

'So it's my fault.'

'I didn't say that.'

'Well, you thought it.' Giulietta didn't say goodnight as she headed for the stairs.

Chapter Forty-three

A month after their arrival in Palazzo del Pero, Robert entered the *pensione*. 'Good evening, Signor,' he called.

The old man looked up from his newspaper. 'A good day, Roberto?'

'Fair.'

'That is not altogether good.'

Robert smiled wryly, for Bruno was right. While his work with the partisans was progressing, it was not fast enough. His job was to train these men, make them successful saboteurs. But at this moment they were unprofessional and undisciplined. It would take several weeks before they were fit enough, strong enough, but, more importantly, capable of taking on the Germans.

Lepre, Antonio's second in command, a tall man of few words and even fewer teeth, was conscientious, but there was so much work to be done. He thought back to his own relentless training at Arisaig. Tomorrow he would push the men harder and harder still. They would do exercise after exercise until they were able to accept orders without hesitation. Until they understood the mantra he had learnt at Arisaig: *kill or be killed*.

When he voiced his concerns to Giulietta she went to her suitcase and took out a knife.

'I can help you, Roberto.'

He looked at the knife in amazement: 'That's a vicious-looking weapon for a slip of a girl.'

'Don't make fun of me,' she retorted angrily. 'I am offering to help. It wasn't just the men who did combat training in Egypt. Women were taught not only to defend themselves but how to kill. Stand and I'll show you.'

A second later Robert found himself on the ground with a knife at his throat. He started to laugh.

'I think you have proved your point, but the men would never take orders from you. As far as your countrymen are concerned, the woman's place is in the home. But I could certainly do with your help. While I train the men you could observe, tell me who I can trust, who is capable of undertaking operations and who I should let go. We can only have the best.'

From that day Robert and Antonio pushed the partisans to their physical and mental limits. Every trick Robert had learnt at Arisaig, he passed on to the men. With Giulietta watching critically from the sidelines, the discipline improved. Slowly their hand-to-hand combat skills became stealthier, more deadly and their aim with a gun more accurate. Even the laying of charges was acceptable. There was one problem, however: the promised drop of arms still hadn't come. There was always a reason, and as Giulietta turned off her set each night she became more despondent. Without arms there could be no operations, without ammunition they might as well not be here.

The weather had been raw on the hillside, but it had been a good day. Robert took the stairs two at a time and opened the bedroom door. Giulietta wasn't there but items of clothing were strewn across her bed; a silk slip, a brassiere, the skirt she had worn. He could hear the water pipes choking and gurgling from the bathroom down the hall. In a few minutes she would emerge, wrapped only in a towel and she would look at him, one delicate eyebrow raised. Then she would disappear behind the screen and hum tunelessly. He was sure she had moved the screen a little, only an inch, so that through the small gap he could view the soft flesh of her thighs, her firm breasts. Several times he had caught her looking at him, appraising him with that half-smile on her face that he had come to know so well. He was tempted to stay, but he would prove that he was stronger than Giulietta, that he could resist her charms.

He changed his shirt, putting the stone Giulietta had given him on the beach at Livorno back into the breast pocket. Then he headed downstairs.

Giulietta came from the bathroom and started to dress. She could hear the gramophone playing in the drawing room below. Roberto would be relaxing, his eyes half-closed, his foot tapping to the sound of the music. The top two buttons of his shirt would be undone, showing a glimpse of his bronzed chest. Her body was alive with passion, but the charade must continue. She laughed at her own conceit, believing she had Roberto on a string, but she was the one who watched through the screen, longing to go to him. Wanting him was distraction enough; having him would make things impossible.

She looked at her watch; it was transmission time. She smiled grimly: nothing like a little fear to focus the mind.

Heaving the chest of drawers to the side, she levered up the floorboards to reveal the cavity below. The space was large enough to for her to hide in if she curled up tightly, and her transmitter.

She opened the doors to the balcony and draped the antenna over the side. Tonight as she turned on her set, a fleeting thought came to her. She was living on the edge, flirting with capture, torture and death. But she didn't want to die. She plugged in the crystal and her earphones, then the aerial and earth rod and finally the batteries and set the wireless to 'transmit'. As she adjusted the tuning dial to pick up the crystal's frequency and the tuning bulbs burst into life, she remembered her father's vision of democracy. While Hitler and Mussolini lived, Italy would never be free. It was also her vision. At once her fear of the radio-detecting vans evaporated and she was caught up in the excitement of tapping out the dots and dashes of her encrypted call sign and message, the bulbs flashing as the Morse code was relayed. Once sent, the set was switched to 'receive'. She didn't have to wait long. Over the crackle and static, a coded message was coming back.

It would be another week before Giulietta would receive the instructions she had been waiting for. As she deciphered the code, she was jubilant. At last she had something positive to say. The equipment they so badly needed was coming. Once Robert was satisfied the men were ready, their operations could begin.

Robert saw Giulietta arriving before everyone else did. The double doors of the crumbling stone barn were open as she approached, pedalling furiously up the track to the top of the hill. He could see a flash of white knickers and her long legs as her skirt lifted in the sharp breeze. He glared at his men who were now staring at her with open appreciation. 'Get on with your work, and stop looking at my wife,' he growled.

As she drew nearer she threw down the bike and started to run. 'The shipment is due next week,' she panted, her cheeks glowing a soft pink. 'At last we have something to fight with.' She kissed him on the mouth and he was lost for words. The men cheered but many of them were wary of Giulietta. She was the woman who watched them, took notes, and reported back to Roberto. But today they could feel her excitement, and as she drew Robert aside, they began to whisper among themselves.

As Robert squeezed her hand, she grinned. 'That kiss was for appearances only.'

Robert laughed and was turning to go when she stopped him. 'There is something else. Two new agents are coming. You are to instruct them on our training programme, involve them in operations and then send them on to Florence.'

'It's perfect timing.'

Giulietta paused. 'One of them is a woman.' She watched his reaction.

'That's good news, Giulietta; when you need a break, she can take over from you.'

'I won't need a break,' she muttered, but he had gone, striding to the front of the barn.

'Gentlemen, listen carefully. Soon we will get our explosives, and enough guns to create real trouble. You may think the training I have already given you is sufficient, and though I can see a great improvement, I will teach you again.' He cast his eyes around the barn. 'You now realise that to be effective in our task, discipline is vital. Discipline depends on our trust and respect for each other. We are engaged in a life or death struggle in a common cause.' He let the silence build until he was sure of the impact of his words. 'Our success depends on it, our survival depends on tight security. The two go together hand in hand. Anyone who is not prepared to commit himself totally to these two principles should leave now.'

Giulietta's heart lurched. Roberto commanded the attention of this ragged bunch of men. As she cycled back to the *pensione* she realised that with so little time left to finish the training, the two new agents would be useful. Any personal feelings were absurd.

After a few more days of training in the technique of laying explosive charges, the use of hand grenades and the sten machine carbine, Robert judged the group was ready to begin operations. With Antonio and two others, they searched the area for a suitable drop zone. 'It needs to be tucked away in a valley, shielded by rising ground and accessible by road with clear navigational features that can be seen from the air,' he told Antonio. Two days later they found the perfect spot just north of a fork in the River Tiber, about twenty kilometres east of Arezzo. 'The moonlit river will offer a perfect lead-in to the drop zone,' he said.

That night he drafted a message for Giulietta to code and transmit, requesting his specific needs, and providing the drop-zone map coordinates. The response from SOE headquarters was prompt. A date was set for a night when the moon would be almost full, leaving a couple of nights in reserve, if low cloud prevented the drop.

Giulietta had completed her transmission and had received instructions. She decoded them quickly, her heart beating fast. This was more than mere conformation of the drop, much more. She ran to the bathroom and banged on the door.

'Roberto, you must come out and quickly.'

Robert entered the passage, a towel wrapped around his waist, his hair tousled. She pulled him into their bedroom. 'We have our first operation,' she said, her eyes bright with excitement. 'Headquarters have called it Operation Vampire. They want you to blow up a railway bridge crossing a main road over a canal, five kilometres west of Arezzo. If you are successful, the road, rail and river communications systems will be disrupted, hampering the German reinforcement in the north.' Her words came out in a rush, most of them unintelligible.

'I think I'd better see the transcript.' Robert took it from her and read it quickly.

'At last we are in business.' He hugged her. 'Now the real work can begin.'

Chapter Forty-four

It was the beginning of December and as Alessandra looked at her accounts book, she sighed. The war was four years old, money was running out and the badly needed repairs to the roof remained undone. But if the Allies' campaign of aerial bombardment continued, it would be a miracle if the house survived the coming months, let alone the roof. The raids were indiscriminate now, day or night it made no difference. She shivered, remembering her close encounter in Foligno, the industrial area of Perugia. She had left Signor Innocenti at the timber yard to go to the market, wandering into the Piazza della Repubblica. Young boys were playing football, their mothers chatting nearby; a girl was pushing her doll's pram. Then the bombs fell, Allied bombs meant for the railway station and maintenance yard. A stray shell landed on the café at the corner of the square. Alessandra had been thrown backwards by the blast, hitting her head on the cobbles. For many moments she had lain there in shock until a young woman had helped her to her feet. Blood trickled down her cheek; she wiped it away. Although dazed and covered with dust, the only damage seemed to be a few cuts from flying glass. Two little boys were not so lucky. One of them, with long skinny legs, was lying face upwards staring at the sky; the other, a small child with curly hair, lay with the football beside him. Women were wailing. She was trying to help when Signor Innocenti found her.

'Come, Signora, there is nothing you can do here,' he had said, taking her by the arm, supporting her. As she had reluctantly stumbled away, she heard one mother's bitter words: 'Now our children are killed by the Allies. The so-called liberators have become our enemies.'

Alessandra closed the accounts book and returned inside, but the memory of the woman's accusations at Foligno refused to go away. She took a piece of dried mint from the cupboard to brew herself a cup of tea and, as a diversion, she made an inventory of the stores. It didn't take long. The larder shelves were emptying fast and all signs indicated a big freeze ahead. She realised, as she sealed the lid on the polenta jar, that they were fortunate in comparison to the cities where many of the occupants were starving to death. Above the Niccone Valley, they were blessed with heavily wooded hillsides, concealing curious hidden pastures surrounded by scrub. Due to this unique topography and the fractured nature of the landscape, it was almost impossible to come upon these grasslands unless by chance. The rough terrains also provided the farmers with a means of moving their livestock and keeping them safe.

Despite their ingenuity, life was still hard. The Germans confiscated flour, wine, cheese, anything they could lay their hands on, anything the locals had been unable to hide. Though everyone shared as much as they could, it would be a lean year ahead and the small bands of partisans emerging from the woods would go hungry along with the rest of them. Even Dario's contribution from the dwindling population of wild boar, wouldn't last. To Alessandra's relief, the olive crop, though late, was plentiful. There would be oil for the lamps and for cooking, and they would have soap for another year. Signor Innocenti and Diana were picking the olives now.

She pulled on her boots and went outside.

Leaving the stream behind her she continued through the small coppice and into the top meadow. She saw Diana high up in the branches of an olive tree.

'Your daughter is like a cat, no?' Signor Innocenti grinned. Alessandra nodded as Diana moved through the trees, running her hand through the branches, sliding the last olives into the waiting nets.

'This is just the distraction she needs, Signor Innocenti, thank you.'

'It is I that should thank Diana,' he replied. 'I know with her school closed for the holidays, she has more time to worry about Davide, but it is a greater help to me.'

Signor Innocenti moved to the next tree and with the long rake he swept the branches.

'Have you noticed my fine new net?' He indicated the large sheet on the ground where the olives were dropping. 'It is a gift from the sky. Antonio my nephew gave it to me.'

'A parachute?'

'I'm not at liberty to say, Signora.' The old man tapped the side of his nose conspiratorially and Alessandra smiled. His nephew Antonio had the same charm. It was rumoured that he had formed a successful group of partisans near Arezzo.

'Will you thank your nephew, and if he should come across any other gifts from the sky I am sure we would make good use of them.'

Alessandra was cutting the last scrap of ham from the bone when she raised the subject that had been on her mind.

'Diana, I have been really concerned about our situation since the armistice.'

'We're fine.'

'Let me finish, this is important. We are English and have

always been the enemy. As we know only too well from our experience with Guido Tremonti, the Fascists still in league with the Germans are the worst kind. Rome is expected to be liberated in a few months' time. When that happens, the Contessa di Sorbello has insisted we go to Rome and stay in their family apartment. It is a kind and generous offer.'

'What about my school, the people who work here? The Germans will take our house and what will happen to the animals?' Diana demanded.

Alessandra put down the knife. 'If we remain here the Germans would take us, Diana! We would endanger the people who work here; they are much safer without us. You can close the school temporarily and, God willing, the animals will be safe in the upper meadow. Signor Innocenti will keep them well hidden. I'll not risk our lives.'

On her way back to pick the olives, Diana stopped by the lake. It was here that Davide first made love to her, first held her in his arms. It was on the top of the hill overlooking the Castello di Sorbello that they had watched the sun set. Her happiness had been all-consuming but now he had gone. She had received one short note sent from Arezzo on his way north. *I will not be able to write to you, but you will be in my thoughts, my dreams.'*

She sat with her back against the trunk of the willow tree, Nico leaning on her shoulder. She kissed his soft head. She could feel the sadness building in her chest. She pulled Robert's last letter from her pocket. It was written months ago and the paper was crumpled and torn. *'I have a new job now, darling De, it means I will be out of touch for a while, nothing dangerous.'* They would both be out of touch for a while and of course it was dangerous. She was fearful for Robert, for Davide, for Lotti, Jaco, for everyone and everything. The nightmares that had plagued her in the years since her father's death had started again, but they were no longer about her father, they were about the Angelinis. She could imagine Jaco struggling as he was forced into the back of a truck, his face angry and defiant, and Lotti screaming.

Chapter Forty-five

On 5 December the recently inserted agents Patrizio and Eva arrived. To Robert's surprise and delight it was Tom who brought them. Robert clapped him on the back. 'What are you doing here?'

'We travelled together from Cairo,' Tom explained. 'I was asked to drop Eva and Patrizio on my way north.'

'And then?' Robert queried.

'I'm to coordinate the disparate partisan groups from Florence up to Bolzano. A sizeable area. We need them to work together or at least to work alongside each other if a large operation is planned. My job is to push that along and, of course, provide them with the necessary money and arms.'

Robert started to laugh. 'You didn't tell me any of this in Cairo.'

'I didn't actually know back then. Not sure why they picked me, I stick out like a sore thumb, but my colouring is not exclusive to the Brits. Giulietta's hair is not red exactly but...' Giulietta noticed him looking at her and came over.

'So Tomaso, the arm, is it healed?' she asked, smirking. 'Have you fallen off any more walls?'

'*Non e giusto,* that's not fair,' he exclaimed. 'Do not forget I saw your attempt at the tree. You didn't get halfway across.'

As Robert observed them, he realised Tom's mannerisms had changed, everything about him seemed more Italian.

'So you two trained together?' he asked, feeling a little left out.

'We certainly did.' Tom winked at Giulietta and looked at his watch. 'I'd better be off, I have a long drive ahead.'

As he was leaving he drew Robert aside. 'Cairo was fun.'

'You could say that,' Robert agreed.

'Make sure you take care of yourself, old chap.'

'And you.'

'I'll do my best to bugger up the Jerry,' Tom quipped.

When Tom had started the engine he called through the window to Robert.

'I hope you haven't forgotten our plan?'

'Would I ever?' Robert replied.

Bruno was delighted at the arrival of the two new agents and the prospect of the increased rent. To mark the occasion, he fetched a good bottle of wine from the cellar. Giulietta was not happy at all.

The house in Palazzo del Perro had become her temporary home, Bruno was her friend and now blue-eyed Eva had pushed her way in. 'Can I help you, Bruno?' she had asked, and Bruno had let her pour his precious wine. She remembered their first meeting with the newcomers a few hours before.

'I have heard so much about you,' Eva had said, smiling at Robert. And as an afterthought. 'You must be Giulietta.'

'Another attractive agent,' Robert teased Giulietta later, but she wasn't amused.

When she lay in bed that night she was ashamed. Her attitude was unprofessional and irrational. Patrizio was a skilled engineer experienced at handling explosives, and Eva spoke fluent Italian. They would make an excellent team.

*

On the morning of the drop, enough wood and brush was collected for three small bonfires to guide the plane to the drop zone. Expectations were high; each metallic cylinder would contain two hundred and twenty pounds in weight of supplies, enough to keep them in action for weeks. The day came, the drop was confirmed by the BBC in coded messages. That evening everything was in order. The sky was clear, but a few worrying clouds scudded across the moon. At the required time the fires were laid, and torches placed in a pattern of lights across the field, but as Robert and the partisans waited anxiously, the weather changed.

Very quickly clouds blocked out the moon. 'That's ten-ten cloud coverage,' Robert lamented. 'They'll not be able to see a thing; the drop is impossible.' With huge disappointment Robert gave the order to abort. 'Clear the bonfires,' he instructed. 'Hopefully we can have another crack at it tomorrow.'

The following evening was clear with bright moonlight, and despite Robert's concerns it remained clear. The fires were lit and torches placed once more. The partisans were split into groups, some at the drop zone to gather up the cylinders as quickly as possible, others posted along the lanes as lookouts. The men again waited anxiously, but there was no sound of a plane. Robert had nearly given up hope when he heard a noise he knew so well: the familiar drone that always made his heart beat faster.

Giulietta flashed the identifying code letters in Morse to signal to the pilot that all was well.

At five hundred feet above ground level the Halifax released the canisters. The parachutes opened and the canisters floated to the ground, landing with a thud. Suddenly the field was full of men running to retrieve them. They were quickly stashed in the lorry, the fires were extinguished and covered with brush and leaves. When they left, to the casual eye on the ground the field was just a field.

Later, in their bedroom, Giulietta opened a bottle of wine.

'A small glass to celebrate,' she grinned.

Robert toasted her, his face serious. 'I was concerned about you at first, Giulietta. You didn't fit my idea of a radio operator, too glamorous, too...' He paused, knowing all the things he would like to have said. 'I was wrong. You are diligent, brave and extremely good at your job. Your fiancé is a very lucky man.'

Guilietta blushed. Though she liked the compliment, she was too proud to tell him there was no longer a boyfriend, let alone a fiancée. She was reluctant to admit she had lied.

It wasn't until the following morning Robert learnt from a local farmer that within an hour of their leaving it, four German armoured cars with mounted machine guns had roared down the road to the drop zone.

It seemed that despite all their precautions, nothing was secure.

Chapter Forty-six

One evening Diana was returning from the meadow when Nico started to growl. She grabbed him by the collar and let herself in at the back door. Collecting the shotgun from the hall cupboard, she peered through the window. A man was collapsed on the loggia floor. From the look of him, he was both sick and emaciated. He was no threat.

When the man opened his eyes, there was a gun pointing at his head, and a great white dog standing over him.

'Who are you?' Diana demanded. 'Are you German?'

'Scottish.'

'Your name?'

'Fraser McNicoll,' he whispered. 'And please, would you take that gun from my head?'

Diana lowered the shotgun. 'What are you doing here, I could have shot you?'

'I'm an officer in the British Army, and an escaping prisoner of war.'

'How did you get here?'

'I'm sorry, I didn't mean to frighten you. I was heading south to rejoin my regiment when I became ill. And I'd be grateful if you could call off your dog.'

'Nico, enough.' Diana grinned. 'I'm sorry that was inhospitable, but we have to be sure. Are you on your own?'

'I got separated somewhere near Cortona. I told the lads to go on, I couldn't keep up with them.'

The girl ran her hand over his forehead. 'We had better get you inside.'

By the time Alessandra came downstairs, Captain Fraser McNicoll was propped up on the sofa in the drawing room.

'Diana, who is this man?' she exclaimed. 'What on earth is going on?'

'I found him on the floor of the loggia, Mama. It's OK, he is one of us, or rather, he is Scottish,' she laughed.

'Are you sure?'

'Say something, Fraser McNicoll,' Diana ordered.

'It's true ma'am, I'm Scottish.'

'I believe you.' Alessandra smiled. After she had taken the man's temperature she put a blanket over him. 'How did you find us?' she asked, holding a glass of water for him to drink.

He pulled a silk handkerchief from the pocket of his trousers. On one side was a map of central Italy.

'It's our duty to escape.' He took a button from his pocket and grinned sheepishly. 'Anything to hamper the Jerry. It's not a button, see?' He handed it to Alessandra and she realised it was a tiny compass. When she put it in the palm of her hand, the needle swung to point north.

'A lad in the POW camp told me about the Contessa; he said she would take me in. He showed me where it was on the map, but it seems this isn't the castle!' Diana and her mother glanced at each other.

'No,' Alessandra confirmed. 'This isn't the castle.'

*

When Signor Innocenti arrived, he showed little surprise at their new visitor.

'So it has started,' he said.

'The Sorbello family were hiding escaping prisoners of war and you knew?' Alessandra queried.

'I did, but I couldn't say. They have been taking them in for many weeks now, it was only a matter of time before they came here. I'm sorry, Signora, I didn't mean to keep you in the dark.'

'I understand,' Alessandra said, putting the thermometer back in its case. 'But the captain is ill, he needs medical attention. Is our local doctor trustworthy?'

Signor Inoccenti shrugged. 'I have my doubts, so I'll make a telephone call to Doctor Biochetti. We don't want the fascists or the *Tedeschi* sniffing around.'

An hour later Doctor Biochetti was leaning over the patient. 'He is suffering from malnutrition and hypothermia, keep him warm but if the fever increases bathe him in tepid water.' He put his stethoscope back in his bag and turned to Alessandra. 'He needs simple food, and somewhere to recuperate. He's been living rough, and probably hasn't eaten for days. He is weak, but he's young and should recover relatively quickly. Now if you will forgive me, Signora, I have several more patients.'

Alessandra hadn't seen the doctor properly for months but could tell from his manner that he was still disappointed with her, and rightly so. He had given her flowers on her birthday and she had repaid his kindness with a stupid letter sent shortly afterwards. *'I couldn't consider a relationship, it is too soon after the death of my husband.'* How presumptuous he must have found it. He hadn't offered a relationship, it wasn't a proposal of marriage. He had simply bought her flowers!

She, of course, knew why she had sent the letter. Her growing feelings for the doctor felt like a betrayal of Anthony. When it was too late, she had realised that was foolish. Anthony would not have wanted her to grieve for ever. He would have wanted to set her free.

She had tried to apologise but when she had bumped into him in Cortona, she had been too embarrassed.

Now, face to face with him, she realised how much she had missed him.

'We have a barn in the upper meadow where the animals winter. It's a bit rough, but it will be much safer for everyone if we move the captain there.'

The doctor nodded his head in agreement. 'Good day, Signora, I will return to check on the patient tomorrow.'

It was dark when Doctor Biochetti closed the door on the Avorios' isolated farmhouse. The Signora wasn't the only one to have *visitors*. There were others beginning to open their doors, despite the danger to themselves.

On this occasion the young British soldier with a gunshot wound to his abdomen wouldn't last the night, but at least he'd made him comfortable. He shook his head at Signor Avorio, who waited patiently in the small kitchen below. 'If your mother-in-law could remain with the patient tonight it would be a kindness. The *sergente* will die a long way from home.'

The doctor wound his scarf tightly around his neck. So many wounded, shot and suffering from malnutrition, but the partisans and the escaping POWs weren't the only ones. He thought of the little girl whose eyes he had closed the previous night. A simple virus, but her fragile little body had no way of fighting it. He wouldn't be paid, of course, but he wouldn't have charged anyway; a cabbage here, a box of eggs, that was how they all survived.

As he started the van he thought of his pregnant wife Anna whom he had loved and lost.

He had been on the other side of the mountains tending to a sick patient when she went into labour prematurely. She was rushed to the hospital, but the baby had not survived. He would never forget the doctor's face when he arrived too late, knowing instantly that he would lose Anna as well. He held her hand as she quietly slipped away, unaware their little girl had died.

His mind unwittingly returned to the English Signora. He thought he had seen a flicker of interest in her eyes, but he had to protect himself; there had been too much pain before.

It was eleven o'clock in the morning when Signor Innocenti put his tools away and stretched his aching back. He had been working since dawn. Now a partition separated the sleeping quarters from the animals and a fire burnt in the grate. Two cots were set up with fresh linen. To the captain who had been sleeping rough for the last three weeks, the barn would be a palazzo in comparison.

He put some hay down for Rosa and went outside. He would help the women bring the patient to his new quarters.

When Doctor Biochetti returned two days later, the fever had broken and Captain McNicoll was sitting propped against the pillows in his new wooden cot.

He read the thermometer and put it back in his bag. 'Another week and you'll be ready to leave.'

Captain McNicoll grinned. 'Not sure if I want to,' he said.

'You wouldn't know this was here,' the doctor observed a short while later as he walked down the meadow with Alessandra.

'No you wouldn't,' she agreed.

'So,' he said casually, scrambling down the narrow path and negotiating the stones over the stream, 'if more escaping prisoners happened to pass this way, would you be able to help them?'

'I am sure,' Alessandra, replied in the same even tones, 'if these prisoners were in need of assistance we would never turn them away.

Doctor Biochetti thanked her.

He would have liked to stay for a drink; indeed he thought the Signora was about to ask him but it was better this way. She had said in her letter she wouldn't consider a relationship, and he certainly wouldn't try and change her mind.

When the doctor had gone, Alessandra remained in the meadow. A cold wind blew from the east. She shivered, pulling her cardigan around her. Though Doctor Biochetti didn't look like her husband, there were similarities between them. They were both tall, but the doctor's dark hair was streaked with grey. His mouth was wider than Anthony's and the way he smiled was different. And as for his clothes... She smiled, thinking of Anthony's impeccable wardrobe and the doctor's darned jumpers and frayed shirts.

She had wanted to ask him for a drink but had lost her nerve. She was on her way down the hill when Diana came up behind her.

'Come on,' she teased. 'Stop thinking about the doctor.'

Chapter Forty-seven

Robert and Antonio were lying in the undergrowth, surveying the subject of their first operation, when Robert spoke in a whisper. 'We have been instructed to bring down as much of the bridge as possible, then rail, road and canal routes will be out of action for weeks.'

'You're the expert, Roberto.'

'Actually, the new man Patrizio is the expert. As an engineer, he knows exactly where to place the charges. I can't see the Germans rebuilding it in a hurry.'

'What about the guards?' Antonio asked. 'I've counted four so far. They have changed ends twice since we have been here, so that's every ten minutes. We need to come up with a way of distracting them.'

When they had seen enough they crawled away on their bellies until they reached their bicycles.

Later in the barn Robert picked their saboteurs. 'Patrizio and I will lay explosive charges under the central span of the bridge. Antonio, if you and Lepre could stage an accident below the railway bridge to distract the guards? Pietro, Francesco, you will be our backup should anything go wrong. The purpose of this operation is to disable the main line running north/south from Florence. It will be a risky operation. If we are successful this will be a massive blow to the Germans, hampering their transportation of ammunition and men.'

After several days of planning, observing and positioning, the evening of the operation came. The accident staged between a donkey cart and a motorcycle went according to plan. The donkey bolted on cue when the full headlights shone in his eyes and the entire load of fruit and vegetables tipped into the road. Amid much cursing and swearing, the contents of the cart were loaded again, to the amusement of the guards. This gave Patrizio and Robert enough time to strap the explosive charges to the central part of the bridge and to make a hasty exit.

The operation would have been faultless if Francesco hadn't mistakenly believed a guard was raising his gun. Suddenly a barrage of shooting followed. The situation would have been critical if the charges hadn't blown at that moment, allowing the partisans and their leaders to get away safely. The guards weren't so lucky. One was killed when the bridge collapsed. Another was injured by gunfire.

The success of the operation and the loss of their men provoked a furious reaction by the German authorities. Word went out that the SS were on the rampage, but nothing had prepared Robert for their revenge.

The saboteurs were in the barn for a debriefing when Francesco, the youngest member of the partisans, came in. He ran straight to Giulietta.

'They have killed them, ten innocent villagers, my fourteen-year-old cousin among them. They picked them at random, forced them to stand in front of a ditch. They put a pistol to their heads. Shot them one by one. Can you imagine their fear? My cousin didn't die immediately, she begged for her life but they shot her again. Do you know who saw it all, who witnessed the massacre? Her sister, who is ten. She had been playing in the woods and was hiding behind a tree. They would have shot her too if they had found her.'

Giulietta held Francesco in her arms. He was seventeen, a boy, and he should never have been here at all. When she spoke, her voice faltered. 'This has happened because of us. How can we live with that?'

'Roberto was sent here to train us,' Antonio consoled her. 'And he is doing it well. Too well for the Germans. It must continue. The reprisals will happen again, as surely as night is day, but unless we stand up to their tyranny, we will never be free.'

Robert's face was grim. 'We are engaged in warfare, but the Germans are engaged in murder. There is the difference.'

Chapter Forty-eight

Beatrice was waiting in the loggia.

'What are you doing? Diana said, advancing towards her. 'I told you never to come back.'

'I want to help you, Signorina. I have done wicked things and though I can never put them right, if I do some good, perhaps God will forgive me.'

Diana put the laundry basket on the table. 'Why should I believe you? You have betrayed us. The Angelinis were taken. They could be dead now! No. My mother will never have you back.'

'I beg of you give me a chance. I have prayed for absolution. A voice in my head told me to return here, to be of service to you, and to spend the rest of my life helping your family.'

'You have taken advantage of my mother's generosity. You are a thief!'

The girl didn't move. 'I swear on my brother's life, you can trust me,' she pleaded. 'I have sinned and I will be punished. Let me serve you while I can.'

'No. Get out,' Diana stormed.

The following day Signora Carducci approached Alessandra.

'Signora, please listen to what I have to say. I have learnt that my niece has been helping both the partisans and escaping prisoners of war. Although I wanted to kill Beatrice myself when Davide's family was taken, I am now convinced that she was used by Guido Tremonti for his own purpose. It doesn't excuse what she did, but I believe she was naïve. She is desperate to make amends. Would you allow her to return? On my honour as an Italian, I will make sure she serves you well.'

That afternoon, Beatrice presented herself to Alessandra.

'I'm ashamed, Signora, at the part that I have played. But you have to believe me I didn't mean them any harm. Captain Tremonti lied to me. He is a bad man.'

Alessandra thought of the British officer in their barn, and of Beatrice's damaged brother. Perhaps it was time to forgive?

'My daughter has agreed that we should give you another chance,' Alessandra said, her eyes cold as she appraised Beatrice. 'If you let us down again, I shall inform the partisans, and believe me, they will not be merciful.'

From that day Beatrice, Sofia and Alessandra became responsible for Captain McNicoll's care. They cooked for the patient, washed for him and tended to his needs. They learnt that as a member of the 2nd battalion, Black Watch, he had fought and been captured at Tug Argan in British Somaliland in August 1940. After being shipped back to Italy, despite repeated escape attempts, he had remained incarcerated until the doors were thrown open by the Italian prison guards following the armistice.

'It's a bit like a dream,' he said looking up at the two girls who were making his bed. 'For months I longed to see a pretty girl, and now I'm surrounded by them.' Sofia laughed, chiding him, but Beatrice was confused. That night she rummaged through the trunk in her dead mother's room and found her English dictionary. While her brother ate his supper she pored over the pages.

'He says that I am pretty,' she smiled. Her brother laughed and picked up his sausage with his fingers.

'And I think that you are pretty too.'

The following day Fraser McNicoll caught hold of her hand.

'Such a bonnie lassie,' he said. 'Has anyone ever told you that your eyes are beautiful, dark one moment and filled with light the next?'

Again she rushed home. Taking the stairs two at a time she studied herself in the mirror. She had never considered herself attractive. Her hair was nothing special, brown like most Italians, but her eyes, yes they were nice eyes, large and surrounded with dark lashes. She untied her hair and tried on her best skirt with the white cotton blouse that showed off her small waist. She would wear it tomorrow for Captain McNicoll.

'Good morning,' she said in English, which made Captain McNicoll smile.

'Where I come from they would say your voice is like music.'

'Where's do you come from?' she asked.

In a mixture of faltering Italian and English, aided with sign language they continued their conversation.

'The northwest of Scotland, a long way off,' he said.

'What do you do in usual times?'

'I'm a fisherman. I have three boats.'

'Tell me about the sea.'

'Have you never been to the sea?'

Beatrice shook her head, her eyes shining as she looked at him.

'Och, it's a fine thing, some days it is gentle and smooth as silk, and when I sleep at night I hear it lapping on the shore. Sometimes it is angry and it hurls onto the beach roaring like a lion.' He laughed, throwing back his head, opening his mouth wide so that she could see his teeth. Beatrice thought he looked like a lion with his mane of red hair and his big frame that every day grew stronger.

'One day, wee girl, I'll take you there,' he said. 'You'll love the smell of it, salty and fresh and the feel of the spray as it dries on your skin.'

That night Beatrice closed her eyes tight shut so that in her mind she could hear the murmur of the sea as it lapped on the shore.

Just before Christmas, when Fraser was well enough, he was anxious to get on his way.

'Though it's hard to leave,' he said solemnly, 'I must get back to one of the Black Watch battalions still in the European theatre. I should go before the weather really sets in.'

He left them dressed in a thick jersey knitted by Signora Carducci, and trousers they found in the attic. His underclothes were requisitioned from Signor Innocenti's wedding chest. Diana handed him matches, a small amount of provisions and money with two well-worn maps that would guide him further south.

Alessandra took his hand. 'Happy Christmas and God bless,' she said. 'I hope that one day soon you will return as our guest in happier times.'

Signor Innocenti showed him a track behind the barn that led into the hills. 'Keep away from the towns,' he instructed, 'but if necessary, I have a contact here.' On the map he pointed to the small hill town of Narni. 'Number seven. Via del Campanile.' Then, taking Fraser's hand, he shook it hard. 'I could do this the Italian way,' he teased. 'But we'll spare your blushes.'

Captain McNicoll turned last to Beatrice.

'Never forget what a beautiful lassie you are.'

'Thank you, Captain,' she said in halting English. 'And I think you are also beautiful.' Fraser McNicoll laughed and kissed her on the cheek. He held her for the briefest moment, slung his rucksack over his shoulder and walked into the hills. Beatrice returned to the barn. She lay down on the small bed and buried her face in his pillow, breathing the last scent of him.

Chapter Forty-nine

After Christmas, following the success of Operation Vampire, the Aquile were given another act of sabotage to undertake. As an added precaution, Robert instructed Giulietta to contact headquarters and make a request to change her call sign. He decided on *Built to stay free*, an anagram for the Statue of Liberty, coded into numbers. It was a tribute to Harvey.

'Patrizio, I need your advice,' Robert said, coming into the barn. They talked quietly in the corner, Robert revealing his new orders. 'London has asked us to knock out the Electrical Transformer Station at Castiglion Fiorentino. Apparently the RAF has tried but without success. If it's all right with you, I'd like you on the team. You are not due in Florence for a while.'

'If the transformers are smashed, then the power to the whole town will be affected, making it easier to target the Jerry,' Patrizio mused, the idea taking hold. 'I reckon it'll take about six months to rebuild. Yes I'd say, a good plan all round. Of course, we will have to get past the guards.' He looked up at Robert. 'We'll need a layout drawing of the transformer station.'

'That might be difficult.' Robert thought for a moment, then his eyes lit up. 'But I believe I know the perfect person to get hold of it.'

A week later Robert grinned at Patrizio, holding up a plan.

'Where did you get that?' Patrizio exclaimed.

'Giulietta has advantages over a man,' he smiled. 'I gave her the task of finding the original electrical engineer; she loves a challenge. She found the man, went for a drink – and bingo, she had the drawings! Don't worry, she kept her distance.'

As Robert and Patrizio hunched over them, they worked out a strategy for the following Thursday, when, if Robert's calculations were correct, there would be no moon.

With their appropriated German truck loaded with charges, incendiary bombs and some plastic explosives, together with a rope ladder and wire cutters, Antonio, Robert, Patrizio and Lepre drove to the transformer station. They parked in a dark lane. Robert put on a pair of rubber gloves to protect him against the electric wire at the top, and threw over the rope ladder. He climbed the wall, then jumped down the other side and opened the entrance gates to let the other three in. It took an hour to place the explosives on each of the transformers and five minutes to be out through the gates again. The guards were inside playing cards by the brazier and hadn't noticed a thing. This time the operation was faultless. The transformer station went up in a blaze of light and explosions.

The next evening the partisans met once again in the barn and Robert and Antonio were able to report a complete success. At the end of the night Robert once again addressed the men.

'I know some of you have not yet had a chance to show your talents. Trust me, you will soon. The Germans will not take this lying down and I fear there will be more reprisals against innocent civilians. Now you must disperse, go to ground for a few weeks. Be careful if you are returning to your homes. I will remain here, but please keep your heads down and cause no trouble. I will get instructions to you all before our next call for action.

Chapter Fifty

The New Year passed with little to celebrate. Soon another visitor arrived at the Villa Durante and then another, passed on by the Sorbello family at the Castello and by Doctor Biochetti. For weeks it went on like this in the coldest winter for years.

Towards the end of January the lake iced over and Signora Carducci struggled through the snow to reach the barn.

'As if the war is not enough,' she grumbled, blowing on her frozen fingers. 'It is too much for old bones like mine.'

'Our new visitor is suffering from hypothermia,' Doctor Biochetti said to Alessandra one evening as he came in to the loggia, stamping the snow from his boots. 'I have asked Signor Innocenti to keep the chimney going. His core temperature is low and he is much confused. We don't want his heart stopping. Beatrice has offered to spend the night, just in case.'

'I expect you need a drink,' Alessandra offered.

'Sadly not this evening,' he shrugged. 'I have more patients to see.'

'Of course.' Alessandra swallowed her disappointment. 'Perhaps next time.'

The following week the doctor was walking up the meadow to the barn when Alessandra ran after him.

'I'm sorry,' she said, catching hold of his arm.

'For what?' He continued walking.

'Stop.'

He dropped his medical bag onto the ground.

'For my letter. It was presumptuous.'

'I admit it was a little confusing.'

'Am I forgiven?'

'I am thinking very hard.'

When Alessandra looked into the doctor's face, he was smiling. A warm feeling went through her.

'I think, Signora, we can be friends. Now if you will excuse me, I have a British soldier and a wounded partisan who wait in the barn.'

'Yes of course. Thank you, Dottore.'

It was now the end of February and as Alessandra stood on the terrace watching the winter sun disappear behind the hills she was concerned. Despite the work they were doing with the injured men and the importance of Diana's school, the danger came ever closer. But with the occupation in the north, and the battle still raging at Monte Cassino in the south, there was nowhere else they could go.

It was another two weeks before the doctor would accept a drink from Alessandra. Perhaps he had been making excuses, he wondered as he walked through the frosted grass towards the house, but tonight, if she asked, there would be no more excuses.

As one drink turned into two he watched her sitting on the chair opposite, her elegant fingers playing with a row of jade beads, her face animated as she recounted a story. How he longed to lift the strand of hair that had fallen over her cheek, kiss her slim, white neck. When she laughed, he laughed, because she was intoxicating, and vibrant. When her eyes shadowed he felt her distress.

'I worry about my son,' she confided, 'every single day, and I have absolutely no idea where he is. How I wish he was doing a desk job; he has certainly earned it.'

'I do not know your son,' the doctor replied, 'but I imagine he is resourceful like his mother, someone who does not shy away from risk if it will help other people. So my dear Signora, I would suggest you live in the belief that he is safe and one day soon he will come home to you.'

Alessandra looked into his kind face and she felt reassured.

'Do you know,' she said some time later, 'this has been a most enjoyable evening.' She fixed her green eyes on him.

'I am glad if I help to put some happiness there.' He stood up. 'You will have to forgive me, I am forced to go.'

'I'm not sure that I shall.' Alessandra held out her hand. He took it and Alessandra felt a frisson of pleasure. Then she started to laugh. 'Oh Dottore, I have never seen you with two matching socks. I will have to ask Signora Carducci to knit you a pair.'

After the doctor had gone Alessandra picked up the diary from the table beside her. Pages were filled with her neat writing, entries describing her growing love of the land, of the people who had welcomed her into their lives. She had written of her struggle to keep the estate afloat in times of hardship and un-certainty, and she had described the bravery and the courage she had witnessed every single day. Here were her trials, tribulations and triumphs, all dedicated to Anthony. She unscrewed the lid of her pen and stared at the page. Why did her mind keep straying to Doctor Biochetti?

Eventually she put down the pen. She couldn't write an entry tonight, she would write it tomorrow.

*

By the end of the winter many more fugitives found shelter in the outlying farms. The farmers hid them and fed them, asking for nothing in return.

'He has a Nonna too,' an old grandmother said to her. 'How could we turn him away?' Alessandra nodded, giving her a basket of eggs from her new hens. The old woman was right, they would never turn them away.

Chapter Fifty-one

At the beginning of March 1944, Davide lay on his bunk in the mountain hideout. Outside, the men from the Bolzano Brigade congregated around the fire. He could hear the faint murmur of voices, their occasional laughter, but he wanted silence, time to reflect on the past.

So much had happened since his family had been taken. The journey with Pipo had been arduous, a long slog north from Arezzo. They had walked, stolen bicycles, even hopped on trains. On the last night they had scrambled onto a German munitions wagon going right into the centre of Bolzano. Pipo had been a great companion, remaining cheerful and positive, helping Davide through his darkest hours. He remembered their search for the partisans in the mountains north of Bolzano, trudging through the deep snow. They had finally encountered the dark-eyed, wild-looking men in a wooden hut in the forest. There, they had been held while the partisans circled around them.

'Do you think we are fooled by your accents?' Giuseppe the leader had mocked, pulling off Davide's hat to reveal his blond hair. 'No, you are German spies. Men, take them outside.'

It was Pipo's intervention that had saved them.

'Before you exclude two able-bodied men from your band, please see the letter of introduction.'

Davide had handed over Doctor Biochetti's letter and Giuseppe had grudgingly read it.

'You, a Jew?' He scrutinised Davide then started to laugh. 'Have you ever seen a Jew that looks like this?'

Some of the men sniggered.

'Do I look like a German? Pipo protested. 'I am a bus driver, but one that is willing to risk his life for you. That is, of course, if you don't shoot me first, and my friend here is a Jew. Pull down his pants and you can see for yourself.'

Then Marco had stepped forward, the boy Davide had known a lifetime before at school in Bolzano.

'It is the blond Jew,' he had laughed, clapping Davide on the back. 'Giuseppe, trust me, this man has more reason than anyone to hate the *Tedeschi*.'

Giuseppe looked at him suspiciously but called off the men.

That night they remained under guard, but the following day Davide had been given a test.

'You can show us your commitment,' Giuseppe had challenged, handing him a gun. 'There are no prisoners in the mountains, prove that you're not a spy.' He had led him to a patch of ground on the frozen hillside, where a captured German soldier was kneeling in the snow. Davide's hands were shaking. How could he do this, he wondered, tying the scarf around the soldier's eyes. How could he take another man's life? But as he held the pistol in his hands, felt the cold steel of the trigger, he thought of his parents on the train to the camps, his brother and sister.

Giuseppe soon came to depend on him. Without any material support from the Allies, his sabotage ideas were both necessary and ingenious. He was also fearless; it was only his love for Diana, and his desire for revenge, that made him want to stay alive.

He remembered his next encounter with the Germans. It was Christmas Day and they had ambushed a truck. After removing the soldier's uniforms, and relieving them of their arms and ammunition, they had left the men in their underpants in the freezing cold. On this occasion Guiseppe had been merciful and the soldiers were spared.

Pipo had a comment in German for the shivering soldiers.

'On Christmas Day, it is the Good Lord's will thou shalt not kill.'

Then it was Davide's turn to come up with a proposal. After studying detailed maps, and spending days with Pipo and a local mountain guide doing a recce of the area just south of Brennero, his plan was formulated. The perfect location was found, a hanging valley with very steep sides. His aim was to hamper the major road and railway line from Munich via Innsbruck to the Brenner pass, and on to the south. It was a highly important route for the Germans to carry troops and supplies. The objective was to trigger an avalanche way above the hanging valley, on the big open snowfields beneath the rock crags at the top. This would gather sufficient snow and momentum to sweep aside the trees on the forested slopes below. By the time it reached the road, the hurtling mass of trees, boulders, rocks and snow would demolish everything in its path. It would take weeks, if not months, to clear. The operation would require their entire team of partisans. It needed to coincide with a large convoy of German troops and ammunition going south.

With weeks of preparation behind them, they were finally ready. At dawn on the morning on the operation, the partisans had gathered together at the foot of the mountain. They were dressed in camouflage white with crampons strapped to their boots. Each man carried an ice axe. They divided into teams with a rope tied between them. Their rucksacks were filled with weapons and explosives, their shovels were strapped on the back. Davide looked up the mountain, and pointed the way forward.

They ploughed through the deep-lying snow and began the gruelling climb to the top. Eventually they had reached the spot where the dynamite was to be placed, just below the mountain crest along the ridgeline. He gathered the men together. 'The longer we are here the more chance of being spotted. *Allora cominciamo*, let us begin.'

The partisans dug three deep holes and planted six sticks of dynamite in each, with a length of waterproof fuse wire attached. This slow burning wire was stretched ten metres away from the holes and connected to a pencil timer. Once the safety pin had been pulled, they estimated they had about three minutes before the dynamite would go up.

Far below them, another team had set a charge on a rocky outcrop overhanging the road, planned to go off five minutes before the main explosions.

When the warning came from Guiseppe on his stolen radio set, the fuse on the smaller charge was ignited. The rocks crashed down. The road was blocked. There was no chance for the German convoy to escape. The three fuses along the ridgeline were set off simultaneously, causing three separate explosions. By this time the partisans had retreated over the ridge and were on their way down the other side. At first the ground rose and fell, then the snow began to move. The resulting avalanche was merciless, the huge barrage of rocks and snow gathering momentum as it hurtled towards the trees.

The Germans were totally unprepared and were cut down before they knew what had hit them.

Just over a mile away in the heavily guarded railway tunnel, the noise was overwhelming. The final team of partisans took advantage of the ensuing chaos and panic. They slipped down the bank into the tunnel, hidden by the swirling clouds of vapour caused by the avalanche. They easily and quickly disposed of the shocked and terrified guards. Plastic explosives were set, and in another mighty explosion, the tunnel collapsed before reinforcements arrived.

Chapter Fifty-two

Spring had come and Robert, Antonio and the Aquile partisans were together once more. Many had come back from their farms, while some had returned from the hills above Arezzzo where they had been fed by the local farmers. Francesco returned from helping his mother. Before long Robert's group of partisans were creating trouble again. Some of the operations were successful, other were not. They stole vehicles from under SS noses and ambushed armoured cars. They blew up railway lines and bridges. Anything to hamper the Germans.

By way of Giulietta's transmissions, Robert received their instructions, and made his requests for arms. When the RAF were planning to bomb the railway station in Arezzo, it was suggested by Group Headquarters that a smaller raid be carried out by the partisans on a fuel depot close by. The Germans would be distracted by the bombing, and in terms of reprisals, it would be difficult to lay the blame at the partisans' door. It seemed too good an opportunity to miss.

The Allied bombing went according to plan; both the station and the railway lines were put out of action. The raid by the partisans was doomed from the beginning. The guards were waiting and they opened fire. The more experienced partisans managed to engage the guards, giving a brief window for the men to get away. Young Francesco was not so lucky. At the final moment while running for the lorry, he was shot in the back as Antonio held out his hand to grab him. He managed to haul him into the back of the lorry but the boy died in his arms.

Giulietta was cycling towards the barn with Eva when Robert hurried down the track towards them. He waited until Giulietta had got off her bike.

'Bad news, I'm afraid. It's Francesco. He was killed in the raid. I'm so sorry, Giulietta, I know you were fond of him.'

Giulietta looked at him, her eyes round with shock. She spoke at last. 'He was so young, too young for all of this.' She drew in her breath to stop herself crying. 'I must tell his mother.'

'I am sure she would appreciate it from you.'

'Shall I come with you?' Eva asked.

'No, thank you. I would rather go alone.'

As Giulietta cycled down the hill she remembered the first time she had met Francesco in the barn. He had come up to her with a cheeky grin.

'This is for the Signora,' he had said, producing a square of chocolate. 'When I marry it will be to someone like you.'

She had comforted Francesco on the death of his cousin. Now she would tell his mother that her son was dead.

Chapter Fifty-three

It was late May and Beatrice was changing the bandage on a wounded partisan when the soldier came. It was Sunday, her day off and she was spending it at home. Her house on the other side of the valley was secluded and unprepossessing, not the sort of house that would garner attention, but on this particular morning it did so. Her brother was singing in the garden as he dug up the carrots. Occasionally he would rub his muddy hands across his face, and he would laugh a little and look up at the sky. After a relentless winter, the sun was shining at last and the birds were singing in the trees. He was pulling a handkerchief from his pocket when he noticed a man staring at him, a big man with a gun slung across his shoulder. Beatrice's brother waved as the man approached.

'Good morning, are you alone?' the man asked, with a strange accent that he found hard to understand.

He cupped his hand to his ear, trying to explain his difficulty, but in this he failed. Getting agitated he pointed towards the house. '*Sorella dentro,*' he said. 'Sister inside.'

The man hesitated then he walked to the door and knocked. There was no answer; he knocked again. Beatrice remained motionless in the attic bedroom. The partisan pointed to his gun. Beatrice crept past the window, where she could see a German soldier below. She retrieved the gun from the table and returned to the bed.

'You must leave,' she pleaded. 'Climb the bank at the end of the garden and drop down into the railway cutting. When you reach the tunnel, you'll find a track to the hills.' She tied the ends of the bandage and gave him his shirt. 'Your shoulder's healing well. Go, please leave us.'

The man ran down the stairs and into the garden. He had reached the gate when the shouting began. A shot rang out behind him. He scrambled up the bank and slipped down the other side.

Beatrice and her brother were taken into the small kitchen. Her brother was confused. He didn't like noise; it hurt his ears, and the man with the gun was slapping his hand on the kitchen counter. They were told to sit and wait; they didn't have to wait long. A black car stopped outside the door and two officers got out.

'You will come with us,' they barked and Beatrice's brother, who had never been in a car, began to cry.

'It's all right, we are going to the *dottore*. Nothing is wrong, I promise,' Beatrice crooned, but he didn't believe her and the crying increased. When the officer shouted at him, a stain spread across his trousers. Beatrice took his hand. She wasn't frightened for herself. Since the day she had returned to the Villa Durante, she had known her fate. Looking into the eyes of the Madonna in the small family chapel, she had seen it written there, and she accepted it, but she didn't want this for her brother. She had vowed to her mother to protect him and now she had failed.

When they reached Umbertide they were taken from the car to the *Posto di Polizia* and pushed into a damp cell.

'Smells bad,' her brother said, clutching her arm.

'Not that bad.' She arranged a blanket around his shoulders

and told him a story. Later she had to pee in a bucket in the corner, something she had never had to do before.

'That's private,' he said.

'Try not to look,' and Beatrice turned away while he did the same.

The following morning she was taken to a room where Captain Tremonti was waiting for her. She was told to sit on a wooden chair.

'So,' he said. 'We meet again.'

She dropped her eyes.

'You work for Signora Durante?'

'They sacked me after you left.'

'You are lying, Beatrice.'

She looked up. 'Do you believe they would keep me after their friends were sent to the camps? I think not, Signor.'

'So why do you harbour criminals and fugitives?'

'The man came to my door. He said he was a Fascist shot by the partisans. I believed him.' She could see hesitation in Guido Tremonti's eyes.

'If that is the case he would come to us.'

'Everyone is frightened of you, even the Fascists.'

He stood in front of her. 'You will be shot, but if you tell us the truth we will spare your brother.'

'Signor, I have always told you the truth and it has been my demise.'

As Beatrice was led from the room, his voice echoed down the passage towards her. 'You will be shot in the market place tomorrow, and as an example to others foolish enough to betray us, we will shoot your brother also.'

'Please, not my brother,' she pleaded, turning her head to look back at him.

'You should have thought of that before.'

*

That night, lying on the narrow stone bench, she thought of her life. Would anyone mourn her passing? Would Fraser McNicoll? During his convalescence, he had depended upon her in a sweet and charming way, and though she wasn't sure what it was to love a man, she believed she could have loved him. Perhaps if he learnt of her death he would shed a tear. Would her aunt forgive her? She had shamed her truly, but hopefully in death she would be forgiven. She thought of Signora Durante and her daughter and of the misconceptions between them. When she had first arrived she had been overwhelmed; who wouldn't be? It was a big house and she had never been in one before. Looking back, her words could have sounded rude, but they were not meant to be. And if she didn't smile when they greeted her, how could she when her stomach was a tangle of nerves? Yes, she admitted now, at first she was jealous. Diana was confident and beautiful and had the love of a man who looked more like a god than any man she had seen before, but she had never wished her harm. Would she forgive her? Nothing she had said would lead the enemy to the Villa Durante. She smiled. How strange it was that on the eve of her death, she had done something at last to be proud of. What would happen to her house? She was anxious suddenly: the beans would be coming and who would pick them? She realised the irony and laughed; tomorrow she would be dead and her beans would be of little importance to anyone.

She could hear her brother snoring. Her silence had signed his death warrant, but in truth she couldn't have left him behind. She stood up and walked over to him. She kissed his forehead and tidied his hair. She loved him completely and now she would be with him at the end. She looked up; there was a small window high in the wall. If she stepped onto the bench she could look out, see the stars glittering in the blackness. How strange that this should be her last glimpse of the night sky.

She got down from the bench and, kneeling on the cold floor, she started to pray.

'Dear God, protect the Angelinis; they are not of our faith, but please bring them home.' For the first time she was able to see it as it really was. She hadn't meant to betray them. She had stolen out of need in her desire to protect her brother. Captain Tremonti had used her in the most cruel way. But life was often cruel and it was not her job to question why.

There had been moments filled with brightness, and Fraser McNicoll had been part of them. 'Please let him hear the sea lapping outside his bedroom window, let him get home,' she prayed. As the light filtered through the iron bars she looked across at her brother. He didn't deserve this end. All she could do now was pray to the Virgin Mary that they would have a quick and painless death.

The following morning at nine o'clock Beatrice and her brother were taken into the square. In the distance, she could see the vendors selling their vegetables in front of the damaged buildings. Why their new allies were dropping bombs on a small market town was a mystery, but then war was a mystery. The tobacconist where she bought her matches was standing, but glass from the windows lay shattered outside. They should clear it up, she thought, irritated; children would cut themselves. She had always loved market day and now they were shooting her on market day. If she craned her head, she could glimpse the fabric shop on the corner. The tablecloth she had been saving up for had been put aside for her; she hoped someone would tell the shopkeeper that she would no longer need it.

A small group of onlookers had gathered round; they whispered together in shocked voices. Beatrice and her brother were tied to a post where they normally tethered the cattle. Her brother whimpered.

'I love you, my dearest,' she said gently, 'I will always love you.' She raised her head and scanned the crowd. At the back she saw Diana. When their eyes met, Diana's smile was filled with concern, and yes, forgiveness. Beatrice was no longer afraid. Diana made the sign of the cross, her eyes fixed on her, and Beatrice felt her courage and love envelop her. She looked at the soldiers who now raised their rifles. She reached for her brother's hand and said her final prayer. She shut her eyes tight, and the last thing she heard was the roar of the sea.

Chapter Fifty-four

Signora Carducci was waiting at the end of the drive when Signor Innocenti stopped the cart. He flicked away the flies with his whip and helped Diana down.

'It was a good thing that you did today, Signorina. You gave Beatrice the courage to meet her maker. You are a brave young woman.'

Tears stung Diana's eyes. 'It was Beatrice who was brave, Signor.'

She put her arms around Signora Carducci.

'*Dio mio*,' the old woman sobbed. 'May God bring her peace and her brother – such a gentle boy, he never hurt a fly. Thank you for being there, it would have given her strength and the hope that you had forgiven her.'

'I have forgiven her. Guido Tremonti was the sinner, not your niece.'

Diana turned and stumbled up the drive. At the fork by the cypress tree she sank to the ground. She had never witnessed life so violently taken, nor could she forget the look in Beatrice's eyes in her final moments. And her poor, simple brother, clutching hold of her hand until the bullets slammed into them and they slumped forward together, tied to the post.

She could still see the red stain blossom on Beatrice's floral blouse.

It was all over in a second: life then no life. The crowd had remained silent, a tableau frozen in time. Then like a reawakening they had moved, crossing themselves as they fled the market square.

Diana walked on, her steps quicker. High above the trees an eagle soared. She could hear branches bending in the breeze, animals rustling in the undergrowth. The seasons turned, the animals lived and died, just as her life was constantly changing.

When she arrived up at the house, she went first to the loggia. Alessandra opened her arms and Diana fell into them.

'It's all right,' Alessandra murmured, kissing her forehead. But nothing was right any more.

Chapter Fifty-five

Davide was sitting in a dry ditch beside the railway line from Innsbruck. He glanced at his watch; there was a least half an hour before the targeted train would arrive. He took out his knife and began to whittle at a small piece of wood. He was now known as *Il Scalpello*, the chisel, for the small carvings he gave to the men. 'I always wanted to be known for my sculpture,' he admitted to Pipo. 'In my wildest dreams, it was not in this way.'

It wasn't long before *Il Scalpello* came to the attention of the Germans and a price was put on his head.

As the carving began to take shape, he remembered his most ambitious idea. What an elaborate charade it had been. First there were background checks by their informant on the young and naïve Sergeant working at the munitions supply depot. Then they had to steal uniforms, find an expert to forge the papers and commandeer a suitable officer's car and lorry.

When these tasks were completed he had made the phone call to the depot. 'Sergeant, this is Major von Sydow,' he had said in fluent German from his childhood.

'I am in charge of the logistical supply depot at Bolzano. I wish you to prepare the following order to release to Hauptmann Adler. He will be arriving in forty minutes. Are you ready, Sergeant?'

'Yes sir.'

Davide could almost hear his heels clicking.

'Then take this down. I need four mortars, three dozen pistols, ideally Luger semi-automatic, forty K98 Mauser rifles and ten MP40 sub-machine guns with maximum ammunition. Herr Hauptmann will be carrying the relevant paperwork from group headquarters. Check it carefully.'

'Of course,' the Sergeant replied. 'We've been detailed to keep our eyes open. I'll check our supplies immediately.'

'Very helpful, Sergeant. What is your name?'

'Vorgimier, sir.'

'Ahh, do you come from Leipzig?' Davide enquired.

'Well actually, yes, sir,' the sergeant stuttered.

'I believe I know your family. I came to your house once. Do you remember me?'

'I am not sure that I do, sir.'

'No, probably not, you were a young boy at the time. Well, Sergeant Vorgrimier, it seems we both find ourselves in Italy working in logistics, and we are both kept busy by the partisans.' He had laughed at this and so had the Sergeant. 'One more thing, we need you to supply Herr Hauptmann with ten decent bottles of schnapps for the Commandant's birthday party and a cake. I am informed Black Forest gateau is his favourite. Can you get hold of one?'

'It shouldn't be a problem, sir.'

'Just to remind you this is totally confidential. We wouldn't want to ruin the surprise. No need for you to call the base. Pass my regards on to your mother.'

When he put down the telephone he had given the thumbs up to Giuseppe. Then came the second and more dangerous part.

Pipo, impersonating a corporal, had driven them to the base, with Marco dressed as a private. When Davide stepped from the car looking every inch a German officer, he saluted. '*Heil Hitler*,' he said, handing the sergeant the papers.

'I assume everything is ready. Get your men to load the weapons and ammunition, quickly now. We need to be on our way.'

'Yes Hauptmann Adler. I hope your commandant enjoys his party.'

There were tense moments as they waited for the gates to be opened, then they were through, rattling down the road and the gates were shut behind them.

'We've done it!' Davide was triumphant. 'We've actually done it.' Pipo clasped his hand, 'You are a genius, my friend.' As the tension lifted they had started to laugh. 'Did you see the sergeant's face? He was nearly genuflecting. *Dio mio*, it was funny.'

'I thought I would piss in my pants,' Marco had added.

'I need to stop the lorry or I will piss in mine,' Pipo declared.

That night at their hideout in the mountains above Bolzano, there was a party to end all parties. As they sat around a roaring fire the schnapps was drunk, the cake eaten.

'That is the best gag ever played on the *Tedeschi*.' Giuseppe was holding his sides as the tears rolled from his eyes. 'You are a brave man, Davide.'

'I couldn't have done it without Pipo and Marco.'

Marco lifted his glass. 'One day I'll return to my farm to breed horses and I'll never leave it again.'

Davide had smiled. Small, wiry Marco always talked of his horses.

'What is the future you dream of, Davide, when all this is over?' he had asked, a little maudlin from a surplus of schnapps.

'To be with the girl I love.'

'To women, horses and home.' Marco raised his glass.

Davide took a carving from his pocket and he gave it to Marco. It was a small wooden horse.

Davide put his knife away. It was time to stop reminiscing about the past and mentally prepare for the job in hand. He looked at his watch. According to their informant, the train was due to pass through Trento some time before midnight. As the minutes ticked by, he ran through the last details.

Pipo, now an expert in explosives, had laid the charges in the narrow cutting. If all went well the explosions would derail the steam engine, destroy the central wagons and, with luck, the rest of the train. This would disrupt one of the main supply routes and deal another serious blow to the German troops at the front. Giuseppe, who was crouched next to him, broke into his thoughts. 'Cigarette?' he offered.

Davide took one. 'Are you sure our informant is reliable?'

Guiseppe nodded. 'I've told you, the signalman is as honest as you or I.'

'That doesn't inspire me,' Davide grinned in reply.

He peered over the side of the ditch. He could hear the men murmuring, a muffled cough. He ground out the cigarette. Suddenly the signal they had been waiting for echoed down the line.

'It's coming,' the lookout called. The ground vibrated slightly and the clatter and puffing of a steam engine grew louder. But instead of travelling through at speed as expected, it was moving slowly. Pipo crept up the cutting towards them. His face was grim.

'The detonator timings will be incorrect. But it's too late, there's nothing I can do.'

'*Dio Santo*,' Giuseppe exclaimed 'We're done for.' He flipped the stub of his cigarette into the air.

Davide watched the red glow rise into the blackness and he watched it fall. The Germans would see it. The gesture would be their downfall.

The engine shuddered to a screeching halt, stopping a few

metres short of the first charge. Instantly, night turned to day as a white beam pierced the darkness. As the searchlight made sweeping arcs, the machine guns began to spray fire indiscriminately.

'They can't see us, stay where you are,' Davide shouted to the men down the line, but Giuseppe had already broken cover. Others followed. Giuseppe was halfway across an open field when he was cut down and fell on his face in the mud. Marco was shot, but he continued to run, dragging his leg, until the Germans were upon him, and he was hauled kicking and screaming away. Davide could hear the guns firing, he could see partisans butchered as they tried to escape, but there was no sign of Pipo.

He waited. While the soldiers concentrated their efforts on the field, he scrambled from the ditch and sprinted behind the getaway lorry. He would go the other way. If he could make it to the hills he had a chance. When the searchlight had moved around, Davide slipped from behind the lorry and ran for his life. He dived into a field of sunflowers. As he pushed aside the stems, his heart was pumping in his chest. He could hear the soldiers shouting behind him, their voices strident, but he kept on running. He reached the woods that climbed upwards into the hills and it was then that he heard the dogs. They were baying as they locked on to his scent, yelping in excitement. There was a stream on the other side of the woods, if he reached the stream he would throw the dogs off his trail. He scrambled up a bank and was halfway down the other side when his ankle caught in the undergrowth. He fell. The sound of the dogs grew louder. He scrambled to his feet and limped into the cover of the trees. He was sweating profusely. The dogs were nearing their prey.

They were upon him before he reached the stream.

Chapter Fifty-six

Alessandra was in the hall when the doctor put his head around the door. It was an early June morning and Alessandra had at last changed her winter skirts and jumpers for a summer dress.

'Signora, it is good to see you. You have discarded your clothes. How charming you look.'

Alessandra's mouth twitched but she did not correct the doctor. 'Thank you, Dottore,' she smiled.

'Forgive me, Signora, but you have heard the news? The Allies have liberated Rome.'

Alessandra clasped her hands together. 'Dottore, this is wonderful. At last we can see an end to this.'

'It is good news, but it is not over yet! *Alora*, it is time for you and your daughter to leave. While the Allies continue to force the Germans up the Italian peninsula, you are in grave danger. Not only from the troops. There will be deserters roaming these hills, disenchanted soldiers with nowhere to go. They will have no money, no food. I am worried for your safety.'

'We must leave as soon as we can,' Alessandra agreed, her mind going into overdrive. She would start packing immediately, organise the house, the animals, talk to Signor Innocenti and the Contessa.

The doctor broke into her thoughts.

'The Contessa is making the necessary arrangements at her apartment in Rome and I have managed to acquire a Red Cross van from the hospital. If it is agreeable, I will take you myself tomorrow afternoon.'

'So soon?'

'*Sì*, Signora. The journey will not be without danger. We will have to get through the German lines.'

When Diana arrived from her school later that day Alessandra was waiting for her. She steeled herself, knowing there would be resistance.

'Diana, Rome has been liberated, we will be leaving tomorrow afternoon.'

'That is impossible ... My school, I have to make arrangements. Mama, you can't just spring this on me, expect me to drop everything.'

Alessandra could see the familiar look of determination on her daughter's face.

'I'm sorry, Diana, but this is not negotiable. We are going to Rome.'

'Why should we go if the children have to stay?'

'Because we are English, Diana.'

'You are only half English.'

'Here, there is no difference. I have spoken to the Contessa. She will take the children up to the Castello if they are in danger. She is an influential Italian; they will not touch her.'

'But Mama!'

'I don't want to leave any more than you, but we promised your brother and I owe it to your father. Nico will be safe at the *fattoria*, Signor Innocenti will look after him.'

'If we are going, Nico comes too.'

'We can't travel with a large white dog.'

Diana glared at her.

'All right,' Alessandra said. 'Nico comes too, but before you even ask, the goat does not.'

Chapter Fifty-seven

Davide was pulled from his cell and dragged to a room at the end of the corridor. He was thrown inside.

'So, we have our prisoner.'

He looked up into the impassive face of a German officer. 'My name, which you will hear often, is Captain Bayer. I hope we have been treating you well.' The officer was of medium height and build with an ordinary appearance. Perhaps, Davide thought as he struggled to his feet, his job made him feel less ordinary.

'So,' Bayer said. 'Are you the man they call *Il Scalpello*?'

Davide said nothing.

'We have been hoping to catch up with you.' Bayer snapped closed an index file, and scrutinised Davide. 'You have been the cause of considerable inconvenience, but fortunately you are now in our custody. We need dates, the members of your organisation, the location of your hideout. Otherwise things will become unnecessarily difficult.'

Davide was looking beyond the captain. A pile of photographs was stacked on the surface of a wooden desk, and a dentist's chair was bolted to the floor in the centre of the room. Webbing straps were attached to the sides. A clock ticked on the wall; a camera hung from a hook nearby.

'You must realise that everyone talks in the end, so why don't you save yourself trouble and tell us the details? We can even attend to your ankle.'

Davide could feel sweat break on his forehead; his ankle was the least of his worries. He fixed his eyes on the clock and watched the seconds go by.

'I have to warn you, I have very little patience.' The captain picked up the photographs and leafed through them. When he came to the end, he dropped them back on the table.

'Call the photographer, then take him back to his cell. The SS keep meticulous records. Every inmate who passes through our door has a photograph taken before and afterwards.'

As a flashbulb popped in front of him, Davide speculated on the meaning of *afterwards*.

The following morning the guard unlocked his cell and took him to the same room at the end of the corridor.

'You are an obstinate man,' Captain Bayer said by way of a greeting. 'Your men have been captured, so you might as well answer our questions. Everyone breaks in the end.'

'They will never talk,' Davide responded.

'Ahh, I have been told you speak fluent German. Major von Sydow, wasn't it?'

'You misjudge us if you believe your crude methods will make us give in.'

'Give in! Your people have already betrayed their former allies.'

'Then why was it so important to find me?' Davide challenged.

'Strap him in the chair and call Herr Kohler,' Captain Bayer ordered the guards.

They had just finished tightening the straps when a short, thickset man in a stained overall entered the room. He carried a bundle of tools. But they weren't tools, Davide observed, as he laid them out on the desk. They were medical instruments.

'*Klappe Auf*!' Herr Kohler was standing above him with the largest of the instruments. Davide clenched his jaw.

'You will open your mouth.' Kohler nodded at the guards and they tilted the chair backwards so that he was lying horizontally.

'We will remove one back molar at a time, a long and painful procedure. You are currently fit, and you are young, so the teeth will not pull easily.' Kohler's voice came from far away.

'This,' he said, 'is a mouth gag. It will keep your jaw open and depress your tongue.'

The guards held him down, as Kohler levered open his jaw and forced the gag inside. Davide choked as with each turn of the screw the gag expanded. When his mouth was wide apart, Kohler produced a pair of forceps from the pocket of his overall. Blood thundered in Davide's ears as Kohler fixed the forceps around the lower left molar and pulled.

'This is going to be difficult,' he pronounced, as he rocked it from side to side. Blood seeped down Davide's throat. He wanted to swallow but his tongue was tied down. He could feel his flesh tearing, the bone jarring. He could hear the roots breaking as the man bore down on his tooth, until at last it loosened and gave way. Kohler held up the tooth, a triumphant grin on his face. 'It seems you have thirty-one left to pull.'

A guard unstrapped him and tipped him forward. Blood gushed from his lips. Davide gasped as the pain and shock invaded his body.

'Take him away,' Captain Bayer ordered. 'Perhaps by tomorrow our guest will have changed his mind.'

Davide staggered unaided to the door, but when he reached the corridor, his legs gave way. The two guards heaved him back to his cell. He could hear the key close in the iron lock, then silence as he sank to the floor. He closed his eyes. He wanted to sleep, but the thought of further torture tormented him. There would be more days like this, more hours of unendurable pain. He prayed he would have the strength to remain silent.

At six o'clock the following morning Davide opened his eyes. A moan escaped his lips. Where the tooth had been his gums were a mess of bleeding flesh and there was a pounding ache in the centre of his head. He was applying pressure to his temples when the door clanged open, reverberating in his ears like a bell. A guard prodded him,

'Still with us, then?' He slammed a tray on the floor beside him. Davide picked up the beaker and let the water trickle down his throat.

Davide was left a day and night before he was taken again to the room at the end of the passage.

'So,' Captain Bayer enquired. 'Do you wish for more of the same punishment?'

'I have nothing to say.'

'It has always interested me how a small change can alter one's appearance; the mere loss of a tooth. Before our session you could have passed for a German.' Bayer took a mirror from the desk. 'You may care to take a look?' When Davide averted his face, Bayer grasped him by the hair.

'Now you can see how changed you are.'

Davide's bloodshot eyes had shrunk to the back of his swollen face.

'I can see only improvement,' he whispered defiantly. 'Perhaps you should try it.'

Captain Bayer wanted to ram his fist into the prisoner's face: instead, he called for the guards.

Davide was dragged across the floor. He could see on the desk a small carved horse – the one he had given to Marco.

'Ah, the horse.' Bayer's grey eyes fixed on him. 'Unfortunately, your friend died while trying to escape; do you wish to see the photograph?'

Marco was dead. Tears pricked at Davide's eyes. He looked at the captain. 'How frustrating for you.'

Captain Bayer flexed his fingers. The prisoner was insufferable, but he would teach him a lesson. He would break him in the end. 'I'll leave you to Herr Kohler.' He walked out, leaving the prisoner strapped to the chair.

Davide tensed in anticipation of further pain. He ran his tongue over his cracked lips, explored the hole, the exposed gum. At any moment Kohler would return.

It was not long before his tormentor's chilling voice invaded his consciousness. 'So, we meet again.'

For the next hour, Davide endured the agony of torture. This time it was the lower right molar; then, when he was near to breaking point, he was returned to his cell.

Davide judged the time by the small patch of light that waxed and waned on the stone floor. Hunger gnawed at his belly, but he couldn't eat; fear plagued him. On the third day, when the guard put the key in the lock and the door opened, he was unexpectedly taken outside.

As he limped around the camp yard, he lifted his face to the sun. Far above the perimeter walls, a solitary kestrel was soaring; he could hear the strange, mewing cry. He remembered the fledglings he had seen with Diana, and for a brief moment she was in his arms again. He could smell the scent of her hair and feel the touch of her fingers on his skin. Hear her words, 'I love you, Davide. I have always loved you.'

Then the daydream slipped away. Beyond the circle of dust, prisoners in flimsy, striped uniforms shuffled into domed work-shops. But, he realised, they were the lucky ones. It was the Jews and partisans like himself whose fate was sealed. For the partisans it was execution, for the Jews it was transit to Germany. He thought of his family. There was no justice and no way out.

On the eighth day, Captain Bayer came to his cell. 'You are no longer of use to me. Today you will be shot. Have you anything to say?'

'Nothing that will change the outcome,' he replied.

As the door closed on the captain, Davide sank to the floor and thought of his end.

They would take him into the sunshine once more, past the huts and the guardhouse, past the gates that had once signified freedom. At the wall beyond the workshops, they would shoot him. Would they take a photograph for their records, he wondered, to cover their tracks? Would he become another prisoner trying to escape?

He could see Diana swimming in the lake. 'One day these laws will be swept aside and you will marry me,' she had whispered, her beautiful face inches from his own. But there would be no wedding. They would never have the glorious future they had dreamt of. He recalled a night shortly before he had left, walking with her through the meadow, making love in the hay barn with the moon, a sliver of silver, shining through the open door. A barn owl, wraithlike and mysterious, flying into the rafters, and Diana's childish wonder. He had wanted to capture the moment, hold it for ever. Now all his memories would be gone. He would never hold her again, nor would he hear his sister playing the violin or his father's dear voice. 'My talented, wonderful son.' Except that he wasn't his son. '*Your father is the man who brought you up, loved you. It is not who you are, Davide, it is what is inside you,*' his mother would have said.

At six o'clock a guard came. He was carrying the jacket they had confiscated on his arrival.

'Get up. The Captain wants to see you.' He grabbed Davide.

Once again, he stood before Captain Bayer who was tapping the letter from his mother on the desk.

'The guards found this.'

'So?'

A pulse beat in the captain's cheek. 'They should have checked your clothes on your arrival. It was an oversight. They have been reprimanded.'

'It is a private letter, what is it to you?'

'It has our colonel's name on the envelope. Explain yourself.'

Davide remembered the aftermath of his mother's revelation, scoring the name in fury on the envelope over and over again. His mother's belief that one day the name might save him.

'If you wish me to explain, I will do so, but only to the colonel whose name is on the envelope. I suggest you show it to him immediately.'

Chapter Fifty-eight

Colonel Commandant Friedrich von Albrecht was sitting at his desk at Palazzo della Mostra when the call came. He pushed his papers aside and ran his hand through his thick silver hair. He had no wish to go to the camp. It sickened him, made him ashamed to be German. He had demanded the dismissal of 'Butcher Kohler', but it had been met with raised eyebrows from his superiors in Germany. He felt a growing distance between himself and his compatriots.

He took the car to the camp and was shown into Captain Bayer's office. The room was obsessively tidy, but totally lacking in character, like the man himself. Friedrich shuddered. Bayer was a despicable man; in fact they all were and, shamefully, he was part of it. A prisoner was brought to the room. He stood in the doorway until the guard pushed him forward. A young man with blond hair and a battered face.

'You may stand outside,' he instructed the guard.

When the door had closed behind him, he studied the young man.

'The Captain tells me the guards found a letter in your clothing,' he said. 'My name was written there. For what purpose?'

'Do you recognise me, sir?'

'I do not. But I hardly think that is relevant.'

'I am the son of a woman you once knew. A Jew.'

'Why should that interest me?'

'It will, sir.'

Freidrich was disconcerted by the prisoner. There was something familiar about him, something he couldn't understand. He wanted to leave the room, breathe the cold mountain air. As he looked at the dignified man in front of him an image came into his mind. A young woman was skiing towards him, her eyes wide in excitement. Then she had fallen in the snow.

'Haben Sie sich verletzt, are you hurt?' he had asked, leaning towards her, holding out his hand.

'I don't think so.' The girl's gaze was steady.

'What is your name?'

'Rachel.'

'Tell me then,' he demanded. 'Who is this woman you speak of?'

'The woman's name is Rachel, and I am your son.'

Chapter Fifty-nine

It was early morning and Guido Tremonti was at his desk in the National Republican Guard Headquarters in Umbertide when Major Richter entered.

He stood up and saluted. Guido liked working with the Nazis. He was ambitious to rise through the ranks. The Axis powers might be temporarily weakened, but they would make a comeback and rout the enemy.

'What can I do for you, Major?' he asked.

'Three soldiers are missing, suspected deserters. Your men know the terrain, we need to find and detain them immediately.'

'Yes sir.' He would deliver them to the Major; it would hasten his promotion.

'Report back to us at once, is that understood? Lieutenant Weber from my staff will assist you.'

Guido clenched his jaw; he didn't need assistance. This was Italy, his country, after all.

Sergeant Hahn was in the hall when he overheard the Captain giving orders to his men. He listened carefully. His chance encounter with Sofia, the beautiful and defiant girl at the house of the Jew, had made him question his ideals, his allegiance, everything.

'We've been detailed by our German comrades to apprehend three deserters,' Captain Tremonti ordered. 'Tano, pick five of your best men. Later this morning we will arrest the English women at the Villa Durante. They have been at liberty for long enough. There will be no mistakes.'

The Sergeant grimaced. Captain Tremonti was well known for his brutality. Sofia worked for the English women. Should he warn them? Should he risk his own life?

Alessandra was in the loggia telling the household her plans when she started suddenly. A motorcycle was speeding up the drive.

A German soldier jumped down and came towards them. Everyone froze.

'*Entschuldigen Sie.*' The soldier stopped in front of Alessandra. 'I have to warn you. The Fascist captain is coming for you. You must take your daughter and leave.' He nodded at Sofia. 'Assure your employers I speak the truth.'

'They should go now?' Sofia queried.

'For their safety they must leave right now.' The sergeant turned on his heels and went back to his motorcycle.

'Thank you, Stefan,' Sofia called after him.

'Diana, go to the *fattoria* at once,' Alessandra said, trying to keep her voice level. 'I will follow as soon as I've gathered some things. Signor Innocenti, please ask the doctor to come now, this afternoon is too late.'

Stefan had reached the end of the drive.

In his native Germany he was used to tracking animals with his father. He could approach them noiselessly, unseen. He could follow trails with only the smallest trace of a passing stag or wolf. He could recognise their footprints, their droppings, flattened vegetation, and he could wait. He noticed the broken twig. It was snapped in two and the break was recent. One of the deserters was in the vicinity, he was sure of it. The man would be desperate, a threat to the women at the Villa Durante. He would catch him and eliminate that danger.

Stefan dragged his motorcycle into the bushes, lit a cigarette and sat with his back against a tree. He waited like a hunter to sense the presence of his prey. He ground out the cigarette and crept forward through the woods until he reached a clearing. A bank rose on one side and a stand of young trees on the other. He climbed the bank. The deserter was near him now, he could almost smell him, but then there was something else: a scream. Dread built in his stomach.

He could see two figures outlined against a small lake. A woman was grappling with the deserter. The man was ripping at her blouse, pulling at her skirt. As she clawed at his face a sharp blade glinted between them.

In a flash of white fur, a great dog launched through the air, bringing the man to the ground. As the dog sank sharp teeth into his neck, shaking him, tearing at his flesh, the man cried out and plunged the blade deep into the dog's chest. There was a loud yelp as the animal fell. Stefan flew across the ground. Coming up from behind he yanked the deserter by his hair, drawing his head backwards, and with a clean sweep he slit the man's throat.

'Nico!' The girl stumbled towards the dog and collapsed onto the ground beside him. She buried her head in the thick, white coat. She looked up at Stefan, her face covered with the dog's blood. Her eyes were pleading. 'You have to help me, please. We need to save him.'

He knelt on the ground beside her and felt in the dog's neck for a sign of life. He could feel a small flutter beneath his fingertips. 'He's alive, but his pulse is weak.'

'We must get him to the *fattoria*. The Doctor, he's our only hope,' the girl was sobbing now.

'No Fraulein. I'm sorry for you, but I must go.'

'Help me, please; you have to help Nico.' The girl was grabbing his legs, holding on to him.

'I'm sorry.'

'He is my dog.'

Stefan wanted to disentangle her hands, get out of this place, but there was something that made him turn back.

'If I'm caught giving assistance to the enemy, I will be shot.' He glanced down at the girl, at her distraught and bloodied face, her torn blouse, and he knew he would take that chance.

'I will return to pick up the body of the deserter after you and your mother have left. Hopefully I will have come up with a story my superiors will believe.'

Stefan staggered down the hill with the dog in his arms. 'What am I doing,' he asked himself. '*Ich muss verruckt sein*, I must be mad.'

The old man he had seen earlier ran across the square towards him, scattering the children who were grouped around the pump. 'Quick, bring him inside,' he said, pointing towards an open door.

Stefan lowered the dog onto the kitchen table. It was probably dead, and his superiors would be on their way. They would see him helping the English girl. The situation was beyond hope.

'Thank you for what you have done for us,' the old man said and Diana looked up at him. 'Thank you,' she whispered. Then Stefan was gone, running through the door towards his motorcycle.

As he roared off in the direction of Umbertide, he questioned himself. What made him put his life in danger? He had prevented the capture of the girl and her mother. If discovered, the punishment would be severe.

But he knew why. He had been drawn to the tight-knit community because it reminded him of home. He remembered the day he first saw Sofia; he had understood her bravery, and despite his allegiance to the Führer, he couldn't walk away.

*

Doctor Biochetti glanced around the room. The dog lay inert on the table, his tongue lolling from his mouth. He threw open the curtains to let the light flood in, then he opened his bag.

'The chest wall has been punctured,' he explained to Diana. 'I suspect it's full of blood, my only hope is to drain it.' He yanked the disc-shaped resonator from the end of the stethoscope and took a scalpel from his bag. Parting the dog's fur, he made an incision between the ribs and forced the tube into the chest cavity.

'Water,' he instructed, pulling the earpieces from the other end. Signor Innocenti returned with water and Doctor Biochetti plunged the two ends into the jar. There was silence. The doctor's shoulders sagged. It was too damn late. He would go through the motions, listen for a pulse, but the dog was dead.

He was cleaning the wound when a pink tinge began to infuse the water. '*Grazie Dio*,' he exclaimed. 'Look Diana, blood is coming from the chest cavity. The lungs can expand, and the heart can pump more strongly. Nico has a chance.'

The water turned from pink to crimson and Diana held onto a large white paw and cried.

'I've done what I can for him.' Doctor Biochetti tied a knot in the final stitch and cut the thread. 'I can do no more. The next few days are critical but your being here won't change anything. We must leave immediately for Rome.'

'I can't, he saved my life.'

'I'll take you and your mother as far as Viterbo; my contact will meet us there. I'll return for the dog… Can you hear me,

Diana? He'll come to my house; he'll be my patient. I promise you. It seems that Guido Tremonti is after you and your mother, there is no time to lose.'

Diana leant over Nico and kissed his soft muzzle. 'I'm coming back for you, Nico. Please be here when I return.'

'I will look after him, I give you my word.'

Chapter Sixty

Colonel Friedrich von Albrecht sat in the library. His revolver was on the desk in front of him. He picked it up and studied it. Would it be easy, he wondered? He had seen death so many times, but his own was another matter.

He had known immediately the young man was his son.

'I need proof,' he had muttered, knowing the proof was in front of him.

'Read the letter, I imagine you speak Italian,' the young man had challenged, staring at him with clear blue eyes so like his own. Friedrich had wanted to weep. He had called the guard who was waiting outside the door.

'I will take this man with me, he has information.'

'Do you need an officer to come with you, sir?'

'No, I am armed, the prisoner is not.'

Ignoring the guard, he walked down the corridor with the prisoner in front of him.

'Take me back to the Palazzo della Mostra. Now.'

The driver had taken them back to the palace, and while the young man looked from the window, Friedrich had watched him. Behind the ugly bruises, he saw his own face, and yet there was something else, some indefinable quality.

'So you feel guilty?' the young man enquired.

379

Friedrich said nothing. He was ashamed and appalled.

They arrived at the Palazzo and, despite curious glances, he had taken the young man upstairs to the library.

'Your butcher has been at work,' Davide said, when the door was closed behind them. He opened his mouth, exposing the raw flesh.

Friedrich had looked away.

'Please read my mother's last letter before she was put on a train to Germany. I am sure you remember her.'

Freidrich had never forgotten her. He knew with sickening clarity that everything the young man said was true. He looked at the crumpled paper and walked to the window.

Then he started to read: *My Darling son...*

As he came to the end of the letter he read her final words.

Davide, with the world in turmoil, your paternity may save you. His name, should you ever need it, is Friedrich von Albrecht.
   I hold you in my heart always,
   Your Mama

With Rachel, Friedrich had felt the intense passion of first love, but when she had left without saying goodbye, he had taken her flight as a betrayal. No other woman had ever lived up to her. By now she may well be dead.

Only a week after his arrival he had been required to supervise a desperate human cargo, a consignment of Jews from the temporary holding camp in Bolzano. When he had entered the station, the train was already packed. Jews from other parts of Italy were crammed together without food, water or sanitation. Shocked by their plight, he had demanded they be given water and air. Despite his show of mercy, he had no option but to let them go on their way. He remembered the faces – men, women, children needing his help. Rachel may have been among them.

He turned back to Davide. 'You must get away from here. I can give you money, clothes, but only a limited amount of time. Captain Bayer will come after you. Rejoin your men, do whatever you can to survive. The war will soon be over. You will have your country returned to you, the atrocities will be over, and the Nazis will get what they deserve.'

He emptied the wall safe. 'My spare gun.' He passed it to Davide. 'This money should keep you and your comrades going for a while. After you have gone, my fellow officers will find out the truth, they always do. There is nothing I can do for your family, for your mother, but I am glad I can be of help to you.' He went to his bedroom next door and returned with a bandage and some clothes. 'These will fit you, but first let me dress your leg.'

He had cut the prison trousers and run his fingers over the swelling.

'It is not broken and this will give you support. You must be able to run.' His touch was gentle as he wound the bandage round the swollen leg.

'You have been giving my men quite a run around,' he said with a wry smile.

'I've tried,' Davide agreed.

'There is so much I would like to know about the man they call *Il Scalpello*. Sadly there isn't the time.' Friedrich raised his head and their eyes met, and as he looked into the young man's face he knew he would hold this image in his heart, he would take it with him to the end.

'You must go,' he said, when Davide had pulled the trousers over the uniform. 'There is a passage in the Palazzo della Mostra, once used for Renaissance intrigues. It has amused me in the past. Now it will save your life.'

He had taken a book from one of the shelves and pulled a lever. The bookcase opened to reveal a passage. 'This will take you beyond the wall at the back of the palace. From there you can get to the hills.' Davide nodded and took the proffered money. 'And what of you? How will you explain my escape?'

Von Albrecht's expression faltered. 'Don't worry about me,' he replied quietly. 'Go,' he urged again.

Slipping into the passage, Davide had turned towards his father. 'Thank you,' he smiled. Then he started to run. He didn't look back.

Friedrich had helped himself to a large glass of whisky which he drained and returned to his desk. He picked up the photograph of his wife and children; how glossy they looked, how well fed. The irony was, of course, they looked like their mother; it was Davide, his Jewish son, who looked exactly like him.

And Rachel had gone to the camps. The only woman he had truly loved and he had sent her on her way. He now understood Davide's indefinable quality: it was sensitivity, Rachel's sensitivity. He put the photo of his wife and children face down on the desk and tears welled in his eyes. Ursula would marry again without a second glance, but Rudi and Axel were his life, his joy. He would never see them again.

He took the revolver and put it in his mouth. A single shot sounded in the Palazzo della Mostra.

Chapter Sixty-one

Doctor Biochetti parked the Red Cross van in the piazza by the *fattoria*. He hurried to collect their luggage.

'The Allies are strafing the roads so I'm hoping this van will caution any trigger-happy airmen, he explained to Alessandra. 'Signora, you sit by me in the front; Diana, if you don't mind getting in the back. First you need to take this pill, it is entirely natural and it will help with the trauma.' He handed her the pill and a small round tin.

'Please rub this tincture on your face as we need to make you look ill. *Mi dispiace*, it smells foul but it will cause temporary swelling. If they stop us you must say you have diphtheria. The *Tedeschi* hate any form of illness. I'll tell them we are on our way to the hospital in Rome. Can you do this?'

Diana nodded, but it was as if she didn't care.

Guido told the driver to go faster. The English girl had always frustrated him. He had dispatched the Jew's family but not the Jew himself. Everything had conspired against him, but today he would pick up the girl and her mother, and she would beg for him.

'Guido, be careful,' his mother had warned. 'Don't you see we are losing the war? You will be called a traitor and you will be held to account.' But he didn't listen, she was a stupid old woman.

A Red Cross van swerved in front of him. A girl with a white face stared at him through the window. She looked sick. *Bloody peasant*, he thought. She probably had some vile disease.

*

They were nearing Orvieto when Doctor Biochetti slowed the van. 'There's a roadblock ahead.' He looked over his shoulder into the back. 'Are you ready?'

Diana lay down on the mattress. It wasn't difficult to look sick because her face was burning and her stomach was knotted into a tight ball. Images of Davide and her brother came into her mind. Were they dead or alive? She screwed up her eyes, trying to block the other images, – but it was futile. Once again, she was walking through the woods on her way to the *fattoria*. Nico was diving in and out of the bushes. She had turned to call him when she had seen the man lurking in the shadows. For a brief second she had stopped, rooted to the spot, but when he advanced towards her, she had started to run, her legs pounding over the rutted ground. But he was gaining on her and she was petrified. They had reached the lake when he caught up with her, she could see his matted hair and bloodshot eyes. His smell, alcohol and sweat. When she saw the knife, she had known she was not just fighting for her honour, she was fighting for her life. Then in a flash there was Nico.

Sister Maria had once said *put your fears into a box and let God take the key*, but at that moment it didn't seem to help because she couldn't visualise the box in her mind.

She was trembling when the doctor wound down his window. 'Papers, please.'

Doctor Biochetti smiled at the soldier and handed him the papers.

384

'And what is your purpose?'

'The girl has diphtheria, we need to get her to the sanatorium.'

'But you have come from Arezzo.'

'The Americans, they bomb everything, even my hospital.'

The soldier walked round the van and peered through the back window where Diana was lying on the mattress. He could see her pale face, hear the rasp of her lungs. His hand was on the door when the doctor cautioned him.

'Diphtheria is contagious.'

The soldier drew back his hand. 'How contagious?'

'Very.'

He nodded at the guard and the barrier was raised.

They joined the main road five kilometres north of Viterbo. 'You can relax,' the doctor sighed. 'We have done it, we've passed through enemy lines.'

The road ahead was choked with jeeps, trucks pulling field guns, lorries stacked high with ammunition and transporters loaded with Sherman tanks, the long convoy making the air a heavy mixture of dust, petrol and diesel fumes. Soldiers waved and cheered as they passed on their way to the front, but Alessandra did not. She would give her life for Diana but she'd failed her. The deserter was dead, but Diana could have been raped, even killed. Her chest was tight, she could hardly breathe.

They finally arrived in Viterbo and Alessandra climbed from the van. She looked across the square to the ruins of the bombed-out cathedral. A single window remained; a tracery of lead, gaunt and empty. The lectern was thrown into the corner, the pews scattered. The smell was there, dust, animal and human remains.

'The Porta Romana station was used as a German supply depot,' Doctor Biochetti explained. 'It's always the same, the Allies need to bomb the station; the rest of the town suffers.'

'But they were our bombs,' Alessandra whispered. 'Allied bombs!'

A car clattered over the cobbles towards them. A woman with short hair peppered grey climbed out and gripped her hand.

'I'm Manuela, your lift to Rome,' she said. 'Ah, Signora, it is sad is it not, everything destroyed. Further south, Montecassino, our famous monastery, flattened.'

'It is beyond comprehension,' Alessandra replied, her face gaunt in the evening light. 'I am ashamed.'

She looked up at the doctor and he put his arm around her. 'You are an exceptional woman, as I have told you before. I also believe that after many years of acquaintance we should be less formal with each other. My name, if you are agreeable, is Vittorio.'

Chapter Sixty-two

Giuseppe's death in the field by the railway cutting left morale among the partisans at an all-time low. Factions had developed and cracks were beginning to show.

After yet another squabble between them, Pipo realised something had to be done. As they sat around the camp fire, he got to his feet.

'I didn't come all this way to fight my comrades,' he said. 'I came to fight the enemy. Tonight, I raise my glass to Giuseppe and our lost friends, but also to the future. He would not want us to mourn, he would want us to finish the job. *Miei amici*, let us make his sacrifice worthwhile. Let us pull together to rout the enemy.'

The effect of his speech was unanimous. 'You will be our new leader,' the partisans declared.

'If a vote is taken and that is the outcome, then I will lead you,' Pipo agreed. 'But I have to tell you the good news first. I have heard from an Italian cook at the camp, our friend and comrade in arms, *Il Scalpello* has escaped. He will be on his way back to us. Are you sure he would not be your choice?'

There was a murmuring among the partisans.

'We will take a vote,' Gino said.

To Pipo's amazement the vote was unanimous. He was their new leader.

As he shook the men's hands afterwards, there was a lump in his throat. Something extraordinary had happened to him since joining the partisans. He had discovered traits he never knew existed and for the first time in his life he was respected.

'*Grazie molto*,' he said, standing by the fire, watching the men's faces. 'I am truly honoured and I will not let you down. I wish to continue the job Giuseppe did so well, but we need to find new operations, new targets. The railways are too well defended, we have seen to that. But there are other ways to annoy the *Tedeschi*, other targets. I've decided we should go for an airfield. Any ideas?'

For the next hour they discussed possible targets, deciding on an airfield five kilometres outside of Bolzano.

'So,' he said beginning to enjoy his new role. 'Tomorrow we will plan the first operation. With God on our side, *tutto e possibile*.'

That night he thought of his life. It now seemed that after a childhood of abuse and neglect, anything was possible. His mother had died in childbirth; his father blamed him.

'How did I beget such an idiot?' he had yelled, returning home from a drunken evening with a stick in his hand. 'You killed your mother and now you are killing me.'

At fourteen he had tried to run away, only to be dragged back home. Finally, his grandfather had stepped in, and he had lived above the stable in Mercatale, driving his donkey cart to and from the market. When he had wanted to drive something bigger, he had lied his way into driving buses. He was appreciated by the local community and there were no more beatings from his father. Then Diana had come into his life.

He would never forget picking her up from the station in

Camucia with her mother all those years before. She had been fourteen then, a bedraggled child, wearing a blue coat with mud around the hem and dark curls that were wet from the rain. But when she had looked at him with large, defiant eyes, she had touched something inside him that made him want to protect her.

For the next two years he had driven her to school every week and it had become his goal to make her happy. He would think of new ways to make her smile.

He remembered the moment when his friendship changed to love. It was the day Davide had failed to arrive at the bus stop. Diana had looked so sad and vulnerable, her beautiful eyes filled with distress. No one would ever love him like that. With a jolt he had realised it was Diana's love he wanted. And now he had come to Bolzano because of Diana.

The following morning Davide limped back into the camp. He looked gaunt and thin, but at least he was alive.

When the partisans asked about his escape he was reticent, telling them only of Marco.

'He didn't break,' he said, his voice gruff. 'He kept our secrets to the end.' Then he drew Pipo aside. 'I will tell you everything, Pipo,' he said quietly. 'But later.'

They had gone for a walk and as they looked out over the mountains and valleys, now filled with summer flowers, Davide unburdened his soul. When he had finished he had looked at Pipo, his blue eyes anguished.

'Guiseppe was right, I am German. Do you know how that makes me feel?'

'In your heart you are more Italian than the rest of us,' Pipo had replied, passing him a cigarette.

'I heard my father shot himself, do you know if it is true?'

389

'*Da vero*. One of the Italian cooks at the camp told me. He obviously died to protect you. He wasn't all bad, Davide.'

'In the short time I was with him, I came to like him. It may sound extraordinary, but I am sad not to have known him better.'

As the two men walked back to the camp, Pipo had tears in his eyes. 'I feel privileged that you have told me. In all my life I have never had such a friend.'

'It is a relief to share this with someone I can trust completely,' Davide paused for a moment and cleared his throat. 'If anything happens to me, will you please look after Diana? She is so fond of you.'

Pipo smiled wryly. 'Nothing is going to happen to you, Davide.'

Chapter Sixty-three

That evening Pipo and Davide hid behind a refuse dump which had a clear view of the airfield. It was grass with no paved runway. There were five hangars with fuel and ammunition bunkers.

'By the look of it,' Pipo said, peering through his binoculars, 'the base only services aircraft and carries out repairs and maintenance. Not the real thing.' His voice was disappointed.

'Let's see what are they repairing.' Davide winked at Pipo. 'I bet you there will be something interesting in those hangars.'

They didn't have to wait long to find out. Two guards approached one of the hangars. They slid open the door. Inside were five Messerschmitt 109s.

Pipo punched his fist in the air. 'With limpet mines, they shouldn't be difficult to blow,' he whispered.

'We have to get past the guards first.'

'There is that small problem, my friend,' Pipo chuckled softly.

They waited until it was dark, long enough to discover that several of the floodlights above the barbed wire fence were broken.

Pipo pointed at the shadows below. 'This will be good cover for the men. You and I should hit this larger hangar, what do you think?' Pipo was drawing a plan of the layout as he spoke.

Davide agreed. 'We can place the charges on the planes and prime the explosives.'

'Gino will act as our lookout.' Pipo was thinking aloud. 'Luca, the new man, can lead another team to hit the fuel and ammunition dumps.'

Filled with enthusiasm, Davide gave the thumbs up. Pipo finished the plan and put it in his pocket. They collected their bicycles and cycled back down the road.

On the night of the mission, Pipo parked their recently acquired builder's truck at a wooded spot about a hundred metres from the perimeter fence. Hidden beneath the building materials and tools were the explosives and machine guns. The other partisans arrived separately, quickly hiding their bicycles in the woods.

Once the six men were together, Pipo took out his sketch of the buildings. He pointed to an illuminated hangar on the right. 'Luca, that hangar is yours. It contains the fuel and ammunition bunkers. Once we are through the fence we separate. Gino, keep with us and good luck to you all.'

Pipo and Davide carried the explosives, limpet mines, timers and bolt cutters, and each had a pistol jammed in their trouser belt. Gino had a machine gun and a grenade belt strapped around his chest.

'It looks clear,' Pipo whispered. 'Keep in the shadows.'

They sped across the grass to the perimeter fence, Davide quickly cutting through the wire. Pipo was about to climb through when he felt Davide's hand on his shoulder. He froze, hearing the sound of whistling. They dropped to the ground, just in time to see a guard appear around the corner of the hangar.

Davide drew his pistol but the man ambled past. When all was quiet, Pipo signalled for them to go on.

He found the side door to the hangar and they slid silently

through, to be hit with the familiar smell of fuel, engine oil and grease. High in the roof, dimmed lighting filtered down and illuminated the area. All types of machinery and aircraft parts filled one end. At the other end were the planes. They were about to move forward when Pipo put up his hand. Above the hum of idle machinery, the faint sound of conversation drifted towards them through an open door. Pipo felt a jolt of alarm. He glanced at Davide who nodded his head, and pointed towards the planes.

When all five Messerschmitts had a limpet mine under each wing, they rejoined Gino.

'With the timers set for ten minutes, we need to get moving,' Pipo whispered, pointing to the door at the back.

They were halfway across the hangar when a shout made them spin round. A guard was silhouetted in the doorway. Before he could fire, Gino sprayed him with his machine gun. Davide and Pipo dived behind a workbench. They pulled out their pistols and waited for the mayhem to begin. Within seconds the place was alive with guards armed with automatic weapons, firing wildly in the direction of the three partisans.

Bullets ricocheted off the wall and machines. Gino wrenched a grenade from his belt, pulled the pin and lobbed it towards the door. A loud bang echoed around the hangar as the grenade went off. Then silence. Pipo looked at his watch. 'We have three minutes before the timers go off,' he yelled. 'We need to get out of here fast.'

Davide went first, followed by Gino. Pipo ran backwards bringing up the rear. He was nearly at the door when another shot was fired. He lurched forward and slumped to his knees. Blood began to soak through his shirt.

'We need to get you out of here!' Davide urged, running back, trying to help him. 'Come on, Pipo, put your arm around my shoulder. Gino, cover us.'

'Davide, we'll never make it. I'll slow you down. You must go,' he urged. 'Get out of here.'

Davide hesitated.

'Gino, give me the machine gun, I can cover you,' Pipo ordered. 'There'll be others.' He was gasping, now trying to get his breath. 'Leave me while there's still time.'

'No, I'll stay with you. Gino can make it on his own,' yelled Davide.

'And Diana? What will she do when you're gone? You have to go. I gave her my word.'

He looked down at his wound. 'I'm done for anyway, my friend. I can hold them off.'

Davide wavered.

'If you don't go I'll shoot you myself.' Pipo grinned weakly. 'Now get out of here.'

As Davide and Gino ran from the hangar, Pipo leant back against the wall, the gun in his lap. He would protect his friend to the end. He grimaced; the pain was so strong it took his breath away. His vision was coming and going, but he must remain focused. Today he would do something truly worthwhile for Davide and the girl they both loved. For Pipo this war was never really about Italy. He wasn't fighting for his country, he'd been fighting for his friends, his little patch of home, for the people and places he'd known, not the governments and leaders he'd never voted for nor listened to. There were many paths to being a fighter and this was his path, no grand philosophies, no grand ideas, just love. As his strength ebbed away, he balanced the machine gun on his arm. He could hear the guards running across the tarmac, entering the hangar. He opened fire. Bullets rained into him.

*

Gino and Davide hurtled towards the gap in the wire fence and squeezed through. Both stopped at the sound of automatic fire. Then there was nothing. Davide knew his friend had gone.

'Come on, Davide. Head for the truck. Let's hope it's still there.'

The other team of partisans were waiting nervously with the engine running.

'Pipo?' asked Luca. Davide couldn't reply. Just as they dived into the back with the others, the limpet mines in the aircraft hangar exploded. The van rocked with the force of the shock-wave.

'Right, let's go.' Luca put the van into gear. They were racing down the road when the fuel and ammunition dumps went up. They were showered with debris and peppered with bullets fizzing through the air.

As Davide looked back, he knew that another man had given his life for him.

Chapter Sixty-four

Robert and Antonio were preparing for the largest and most daring sabotage operation the Aquile had carried out thus far. They planned to cut the power supply and destroy the transmitter masts to the German radio networks in Arezzo and Perugia. If successful, they would disrupt the High Command communications and coincide with a major Allied ground thrust to pierce the Germans' defensive Trasimene Line. Timing was critical. The operation needed the participation of at least twenty partisans and significant material support. Patrizio had just finished assembling an explosive device in the barn when Robert came in.

'Your chemical factory might give us away,' Robert grinned.

'I'm hoping the Jerry won't come here, but don't worry, I can pack this lot up in a jiffy. When I'm done let's go for a drink.'

They were sitting in the small bar in Palazzo del Perro rarely frequented by the Germans when Patrizio laughed softly. 'We're somewhere in the depths of Italy and my mother thinks I'm designing bombs in an underground bunker in Wales.'

'My mother will be frantic because I haven't written, but I believe she would prefer this to Spitfires,' Robert mused.

'I wanted to fly but I failed to get in,' Patrizio confessed.

'Don't worry, old chap, I got in by slightly nefarious means.'

Robert drained his glass of beer. 'Anyway, what's wrong with designing bombs, it would have been fascinating and an amazing contribution.'

'But not the one I wanted. Look at me, Robert, I'm a short, thirty-year-old bachelor who couldn't get into the Air Force because of appalling eyesight and I'm not particularly attractive to the opposite sex. I wanted a bit of adventure, to use my skills in explosives. I didn't ask for Italy but I love it here. I feel truly alive for the very first time.'

'Well, I'm delighted that you came. This op wouldn't have worked without you.' Robert lowered his voice when a stranger entered the bar. 'I'm afraid as soon as the preparations are complete, you and Eva will move on to Florence. Giulietta is being extracted back to Cairo.'

'At least I can help while I'm here.'

Robert grinned. 'Truly, you couldn't have come at a better time.'

Robert smiled at Patrizio. In normal circumstances their paths would never have crossed. Friendship was one of the few compensations of war.

In preparation for the operation, Giulietta transmitted Robert's instructions to the new Special Operations Executive headquarters in Bari.

The resulting air drops went without mishap, but Robert was acutely aware each transmission brought the Germans closer. He had watched Giulietta as she sat hunched over her transmitter, carefully carrying out her routine of coding and decoding the messages. His stomach churned as he silently urged her to finish and though he didn't want her to leave, he knew that it was time.

He was cycling home when a white Lancia van nearly knocked him over. To the untrained eye it was merely a van but not to Robert. Inside it would be fitted out with a wireless direction finder with an aerial to locate a Morse code signal within an arc of three hundred and sixty degrees. He imagined the soldiers adjusting their apparatus, trying to pick up a contact. With the two directional finding stations outside Arezzo and a series of triangulation measurements the Germans could fix on a wireless operator within a one mile radius. Robert feared the van was now on its way to fix on Giulietta.

He reached the village. He had to get to the *pensione* before the Germans. He turned right and raced into a side street. She may be broadcasting – the wireless antenna would be hanging from the window. He was panting, the sweat running in his eyes. He reached the *pensione*, threw down the bike and flew up the stairs. Giulietta was heaving the chest of drawers across the floor when he burst into the bedroom.

'The antenna, is it out?'

'No,' she said, her expression changing.

'We have to clear the room, I think they are on to you. We'll take everything up to the barn, the radio, the codebooks, your messages. The lot. If they find anything suspicious Bruno will be dragged down to the Gestapo HQ.'

Giulietta quickly recovered the radio and put it in the small suitcase, along with the antenna. She collected all her codebooks and papers, stuffing them haphazardly into a bag.

'We haven't any more time.' He caught her hand and they ran along the landing and down the back stairs.

Robert peered from the side door; he could hear a van come up the lane.

'Come on,' he urged, 'follow me. I've found another way to the barn, we have to warn Eva and Patrizio.'

Robert and Giulietta arrived at the barn as the last rays of sun set behind the hills. Patrizio and Eva were waiting for them.

'It's time you were both gone,' Robert informed them. 'The

Germans are determined to find us. We've been lucky so far, but they will not stop looking.'

They were joined by Antonio and Lepre a short while later.

Antonio ground out his cigarette, his face grim.

'The *Tedeschi* went through every house in the street. Fortunately I glimpsed Bruno in the garden. If they had a fix on the *pensione*, they would have taken him.'

Robert's face relaxed. 'I'm going back to check on him.'

Patrizio, who was hiding his equipment and Giulietta's transmitter beneath the barn floor, heaved the last slab into place and spread some straw over it.

'Are you sure they won't be waiting for you?'

'The Hun won't expect me to return after they've turned the house over. Lepre, would you mind sending two men to cover the street, just to be sure.'

'If you are going, we'll all come together,' Giulietta declared.

The small band arrived at the pensione to find Bruno sitting on the bench outside the front door with a drink in his hand.

Giulietta ran towards him and hugged him. 'Are you all right? I was so worried.'

'What is the fuss? You can see that I'm alive.' The old man smiled, but his face was strained.

'I am sorry we had to make a hasty exit.' Robert grasped his hand in a firm grip. 'It's been quite a day.'

'Forgive me, you can see that I am shaking,' Bruno replied. 'The excitement this afternoon. The *Tedeschi* asked questions: where were my visitors? Did I operate a radio? I told them that I'm a crazy old man, and as if I'd know how to operate a radio. As for my visitors, they were probably in a field making love. After checking your rooms, they seemed to believe me, but they'll be back.'

'I hate to put you in danger,' Robert apologised.

'I knew the risk when I offered to put you up. But I don't wish to know any secrets. It's not good for an old man's heart.'

With all the equipment now in place, Giulietta's part in the operation was complete.

Tomorrow Agent Flyte would take her to Bari, where she would be extracted for debriefing in Cairo.

As she packed her clothes into a suitcase, her emotions were in turmoil. On the one hand, she recognised it was time to leave for other duties in Cairo. On the other hand, she couldn't bear the thought of being apart from Roberto. She would never forget the courage and endurance of her countrymen, but also their suffering. She vowed she would return.

Robert came to stand at her side. 'I'll miss you,' he said lifting a strand of hair that had fallen over her forehead.

'I'll miss you too,' she replied. She put her hands around his face, forcing him to look at her. 'You won't get killed,' she said. 'You had better not get killed.'

Chapter Sixty-five

Dinner that night was held in the old family dining room, a room reserved for special occasions, because to Bruno it was a special occasion. His guests had brought excitement into his life that he hadn't expected to see again, with a little intrigue and glamour. As he unlocked the cupboard and brought out his mother's Venetian glass, he thought of his guests. Giulietta was passionate and spirited and had carved a place in his heart, whereas voluptuous Eva was a woman you could dream of making love to. He would miss them both. Roberto was a dear boy madly in love with Giulietta and she was in love with Roberto. He chuckled to himself.

Giulietta's departure was timely. The tactics of the Germans were changing. He remembered his lost brothers. It was a different war but the slaughter was happening again.

Tonight they wouldn't think of war, they would have a feast, and he hoped when Eva looked back, she would remember the old Italian who had given her supper on the finest porcelain, using his family silver. It would be his final celebration.

After a first course of ravioli filled with porcini mushrooms, gathered by Giulietta, and a casserole of wild boar, the small shoulder joint kindly donated by Dario, Bruno made a toast.

'To Giulietta, we wish you a safe journey home. There are

those among us who will be sad at your departure.' He grinned at Robert, and raised his glass. 'I salute you all. Eva, Patrizio, may you have every success in routing the *Tedeschi* further north, and may you keep safe while doing it.'

He sat down and Eva stood up. Her hair was hanging loose to her shoulders and she was wearing a silk dress that accentuated her curves.

'Thank you, Bruno.' She raised her own glass. 'One thing I have learnt from you, Roberto, it is important to know when it is time to leave. Every day we hear of cells compromised, partisans and agents shot. The roundups are an everyday occurrence.' She looked now at Giulietta. 'You have shown exceptional courage, and though I can see you do not want to leave, it is the right decision. You have done more than your remit. It's time to go home.'

Giulietta's face was flushed and her eyes were glinting. She picked up her glass and drained it.

'What gives you the right to tell me when I should leave?' she snapped. 'You have no right, no right at all.'

There was silence in the room while everyone stared at her.

Bruno looked at her in surprise.

'I'm sorry, that was uncalled for,' she stammered. She got up, her chair scraping against the floorboards and ran towards the door.

Robert got up to follow. 'Good night Bruno, and thank you,' he said. 'That was a wonderful evening but I need to go after her.'

Giulietta was locking her suitcase when Robert came in. She pushed it beneath the bed.

'I think it's a good job you are leaving tomorrow, the pressure is obviously getting to you. You are an agent, Giulietta, what were you thinking of?'

'You allowed her to tell me what to do,' she replied.

'What?' he said. 'Eva was just being kind.'

She went to push past him, but Robert caught her hand.

'What on earth is wrong with you?'

'It's the way she looks at you... *Roberto, help me with this strap; Roberto, how do I clean my gun?* It makes me sick.'

'What are you talking about?'

Giulietta put her hand on her hip and did a poor imitation of Eva.

'Roberto, I am so feeble. Help me.'

'Are you jealous?' He started to laugh.

'Stop laughing at me.'

'I'm not laughing at you I'm just...'

Soon Giulietta was laughing too.

'Sshhh.' Robert pulled her towards him. 'You must know I'm in love with you.'

'I have a fiancé,' she said primly.

'Tell him he can't marry you, because I want you.' Robert pulled her into his arms. She looked up at him, her eyes dark with longing as he lowered his head towards her.

As they lay in bed afterwards he rejoiced that this extraordinary woman had given herself so completely to him. He kissed her again, running his hands over her body.

'What about your fiancé? I hope you will tell him it is over,' he teased.

'I'll think about it,' she grinned in reply. Then she was serious. 'I love you Roberto, truly love you and I'm not sure if that is a good or bad feeling because I've never felt it before.'

Robert was aware in that moment that he wanted to marry her. He couldn't ask her, not yet, not until the operation was complete. Then he would go to Cairo to find her.

*

Next morning, Robert was shaving in the bathroom when Giulietta marched in and slammed the door behind her.

'If you get killed, don't expect me to mourn you,' she ranted. 'I have done so much for you and now I'm being sent home like a child before the operation is completed.' He turned around, his face still covered in foam. Giulietta laughed. She wound her arms around his neck and kissed his soapy face. 'Make love to me, Roberto,' she said at last. 'Make love to me here in the bathroom, now.'

'Ask me nicely.'

'Please, Roberto,' she smiled, and for the first time in his life Robert knew he could do anything, be anyone, because Giulietta loved him. He pushed her back against the wall, raised her skirt and pulled off her pants.

The small group gathered at the gate of the *pensione*.

Giulietta took Eva aside. 'I'm sorry,' she said. 'That was rude of me last night, I hope you will forgive me.'

'Of course. We've all been under pressure. Now, have a safe journey back to Cairo.'

Eva kissed Robert on the cheek. 'Goodbye,' she said, blushing a deep pink. 'I hate parting, but I'd like to think that when this beastly war is over we can meet in London.' Robert took both of her hands. 'I'd like that very much, Eva.'

'Thank you, Patrizio.' Robert shook his hand. 'Your help has been invaluable.'

'I have learnt from a very good man.'

Eva hugged Bruno. 'Goodbye, dearest Bruno,' she said, tears filling her eyes. 'I'll come back to Palazzo del Pero, I promise.'

'Of course you will. In Italy we say *Arrivederci*, until we meet again.' Eva pulled away. 'Must go.' She ran towards the van, and slammed the door behind her.

'Goodbye, dear friends,' she called, winding down the window. 'Goodbye, my dear new friends.'

Agent Flyte started the engine. 'I'll be back later, Giulietta, then it's Bari for you, and home to Cairo.'

*

Robert was returning to the village, when he saw a van outside the *pensione*. He propped his bicycle against the wall and slipped through the side entrance, alarm building in his chest. Giulietta would be inside and Bruno. Voices were coming from the drawing room. He headed towards them and peered through a crack in the door. Tom was standing in front of the fireplace.

'Tom, it seems you can't keep away,' he grinned. 'It must be my charm.' He was halfway across the floor when he stopped in his tracks. Giulietta was coming towards him and there were tears in her eyes. Bruno was drinking a glass of grappa, his normally jovial face anguished. Tom spoke first.

'I'm so sorry, Eva and Patrizio were stopped at a checkpoint on their way to Florence. They tried to make a run for it. They're both dead, Flyte too, I'm afraid. There are Krauts everywhere – but don't worry, I wasn't followed.'

Robert sat down, his face drained of colour. 'They only left this morning. It doesn't seem possible.'

'I'm taking their place in Florence until we can train up new people. It means I will be based there for the next two or three months. The situation is pretty dire.'

Giulietta sank onto the sofa beside Robert and leant against him.

'We need to get Giulietta out now,' Robert urged. 'She mustn't stay a moment longer.'

'You're right,' Tom agreed. 'As soon as possible. Unfortunately, I can't help you with that. If you don't mind, old man, I'd better get going. I had hoped to see you in happier times.'

Robert went outside with him to say goodbye. 'When we were in Cairo, I was longing to get back into action, now I long for it to be over. If we get through this, I'll be amazed.'

Tom shrugged his shoulders. 'There is a large SS headquarters in the centre of Florence and they are really gunning for the partisans. Rumour has it they will blow all the bridges over the Arno to delay the Allied advance. It's not only people, Robert, it is history that is being destroyed.'

'Any news on your brother?'

Tom's eyes filled with tears and Robert looked away while he composed himself. His friend was twenty-two, for God's sake, yet he looked forty.

'He died working on the construction of a railway bridge over a river. Kwai, I think its name was, between Thailand and Burma. He was dehydrated, we heard, then beaten where he fell. No shade, red-haired like me; if the work didn't kill him, the sun would have.'

'I'm so sorry, Tom.' Robert wanted to hug him, but for a moment the two young men stood awkwardly.

'Oh God,' Tom said at last, 'it's all so bloody, isn't it? In Cairo everything seemed so far away. Anyway, I had to tell you myself, about Patrizio and Eva, I mean.'

Robert grasped his friend firmly by the hand. 'I appreciate you coming.'

'Wouldn't not have, old man.'

Robert coughed. 'You had better make that lunch.'

'Try and stop me,' Tom replied.

'I can't go. I won't leave. Not now, not after this,' Giulietta begged Robert later.

'You have to, its more crucial than ever. It's not just for your safety, Giulietta, it is also for ours.'

'So, you will give up this attack? I need to know, will you carry it through?'

'We have gone this far. We have to continue.'

Dario was waiting in the lane while Giulietta said goodbye. She kissed Robert then she felt in his breast pocket for the stone. 'My stone of Italy has kept you safe. Stay safe for me.'

She went next to Bruno. 'Look after him,' she whispered. She ran to the car and slammed the door.

Robert and Bruno remained by the gate until the car was only a flicker of light winding up the tree-lined avenue.

Chapter Sixty-six

The explosives were in place to sever the power, and to topple the relay masts on the first two sites in Perugia. At the third site, in Arezzo, the explosives would be strapped to the masts once they had bypassed the heavily guarded gates. Robert and Antonio went through the last details of the planning and when they received the code word for the start of the attacks on a Cairo-based BBC frequency, they summoned the teams.

'Are you sure you want to go through with this?' Antonio said to Robert as they waited for the men beside the lorry. 'I have a bad feeling in my gut.'

'It's your call, Antonio. Everything is organised. It could just be a run of bad luck,' Robert pondered. 'But I don't think so. I agree with you there have been too many mishaps. Tomorrow we should call every man into the hut and question them.'

Antonio lit a cigarette. 'I have been through every member of the team, even you. But we'll get to the bottom of this. We must discover the traitor before it is too late. Let's call this our last operation for now.'

Robert nodded. 'For now.'

The men arrived and they climbed onto the lorry. Antonio started the ignition.

'Don't worry, we'll find him,' Robert said softly, sitting on the front seat beside him.

'Or her.' Antonio looked at his friend.

At first the operation went according to plan. Two out of the three groups attacked at midnight at the precise moment the artillery barrage opened up to launch the Allied advance. The stations were silenced for a critical twenty-four hours. The third operation started smoothly. Robert, Antonio, and the eight partisans parked the getaway lorry in a wood outside Arezzo and hid the keys. Under cover of darkness they made their way up the wooded hillside. It was hard going, slipping and sliding on the wet ground, made more difficult with the weight of their rucksacks full of explosives and cutting gear. They could see the transmitter masts at the top, outlined against the sky. They'd practised for it, rehearsed every detail, but from this angle, as Robert looked up at the huge masts, the task was formidable.

He raised his hand and they moved forward again, each man knowing the next minutes were crucial. They'd come out of the wood and were now vulnerable. They waited at the bottom of the bank, hugging the grass while the searchlight swept over them. When the searchlight had passed, Antonio crept up the bank and cut the wire on the perimeter fence: they had three minutes to get in. He slipped through the fence and the others followed suit. Now to set and detonate the explosive charges. They were making their way to the masts when the Germans opened fire.

Lepre had reached the other side of the fence when Robert and Antonio were caught in the gunfire.

'I've been shot,' Robert hissed, biting back the pain.

'Me too,' Antonio yelled. 'I think it's only a flesh wound but we can't do anything until we get to the lorry. Here, let me help you.' He grabbed Robert around the waist and together they slid and stumbled down the bank and into the cover of the woods. Lepre was waiting for them. 'There is no lorry,' he said. 'It's gone.'

'Then we must separate. I'll stick with Roberto but you'll have a better chance without us. Go, Lepre.'

As Lepre disappeared at a run Antonio leant against a tree, inspecting the wound in his side. He pulled his belt from the top of his trousers and tightened it around his ribcage. 'To stem the blood,' he winced, panting heavily. 'And you?'

'It's my chest,' Robert gasped, 'but we need to get out of here now. They're coming.'

'There's an old tobacco barn on the other side of the woods. It's our only chance. If we can make it till then.'

They staggered through the woods, supporting each other, stopping occasionally to catch their breath. Finally, they reached the tobacco barn. They slipped inside and Robert collapsed on the floor. Blood was seeping through his shirt. 'Doesn't look good,' he panted.

'Let's push this into the wound, Roberto. Grit your teeth, this will hurt,' Antonio warned, making a dense ball of leaves. He plugged the injury with the tobacco dressing and placed Robert's hand over it. His friend's eyes were closing and Antonio lay down beside him, pulling a covering of tobacco leaves over them. 'We'll be hidden here,' he murmured, his voice slurring. 'But for now, I need to rest. We'll get out of here in the morning.'

Chapter Sixty-seven

'He's not dead, come quickly.' A blurred voice entered Robert's consciousness, then another. 'Quickly, take his legs.' He tried to lift his head, but it was too much effort. Hands lifted him; *sweet Jesus, the pain*. He was lowered into a cart and, as he closed his eyes, he drifted into oblivion.

Robert woke to find a pair of gleaming eyes hovering above him. An old woman's face came into focus.

'So you're alive; we thought we'd lost you. Two days you sleep. Now you live. Food, do you want something to eat?' She spoke rapidly, high and bright, like a small bird.

'Just water, please.'

She held a glass of water to his cracked lips, then she hobbled out of the room. A few minutes later she returned with a tray.

'You won't survive without food.' She spooned some broth from a wooden bowl and held it towards him. He opened his mouth like a child.

'You are lucky that this year we have an early harvest, otherwise we wouldn't have found you.' She shrugged her shoulders. 'We hid you both in the crop cart and brought you here. God tells us to help our neighbours. If the *Tedeschi* have forgotten his words, we have not. Now rest, then I shall tend to your injuries.'

She came back an hour later with a bowl of warm water, a

sponge and various ointments, and pulled back the blanket. 'First we will have the nightshirt. Tut,' she scolded when Robert held on to it. 'I have two sons and nothing you have is going to shock me. Besides, I've washed you before.'

Robert reluctantly lifted his arms and let her remove the flannel nightshirt. He looked down. His skin was tinged a bluish grey. His body was lacerated from the barbed wire fence. An assortment of dressings had been taped to him. The old woman pointed to one of them just below his heart. 'German bullet.' She puffed out her chest. 'I've dug it out, cleaned the wound and used my remedies. So now we clean it again.' Robert winced as she pulled at the dressing. She delved into her pocket and held up a spent and distorted bullet, and the fragments of a stone. 'This stone saved your life. The bullet's strength was weakened, otherwise you'd be dead.' She dropped it into his hand. Robert stared at the small shard, the surface smooth and speckled like an egg. It was the stone he kept in the top pocket of his shirt, the one Giulietta had given it to him on the beach at Livorno. For the first time since the ill-fated raid, he smiled.

With deft fingers, she removed the roots and herbs that were packed over the wound to reveal the jagged hole beneath. The edges were swollen and angry and while the old woman cleaned, probing into his flesh, Robert bit his lip to prevent himself from screaming. All the while he held onto the thought that Giulietta's stone had saved him.

When she had re-dressed the wound he watched her set to work on the rest. Though her hands were worn, her touch was as delicate and light as a butterfly. She applied her unguents and strange poultices and when she had finished, he collapsed back onto the pillow. 'Thank you,' he said.' I owe you my life. Is my friend here too?'

The old woman cleared her throat. 'The man we found with you is dead, I'm afraid. He died yesterday morning. He had lost too much blood, there was nothing more we could do. We buried your friend last night. If you like, we will show you the place.'

Robert turned his face to the wall. Antonio was dead, and these kind people were risking their lives for him. Only the week before he had shared a bottle of wine with Antonio. He could see him now, his gun discarded on the ground beside him, his dark eyes shining as he produced a photo from the pocket of his coat.

'I brought this to show you,' he had said. 'My beautiful Rosalie. We have named the day, a real day.' He had winked at Robert, remembering the night at the bar with Giulietta. 'I want to have a family with her, Roberto, and I fight for our future to be free.' Antonio had loved life, he had loved his people and he had sacrificed everything for the freedom of his country.

'The others?' he asked the old woman.

'I'm told three partisans and two *Tedeschi* were killed.' Somewhere in Robert's brain he could hear Antonio's recent words. 'Someone has betrayed us. It is no coincidence, my friend.'

For two days and nights the old lady nursed him, but on the third day she came to him. 'I have been told by the village elder that you must leave for your safety and ours. You will be collected tonight by one of your people.'

Robert took her hand. 'I owe you everything, thank you.' The old woman nodded and hurried from the room. When Robert was dressed he went downstairs. Her husband sat in front of the fire.

'Take my coat. It has kept me warm for fifty winters. It will serve you well. And when this is over, you can bring it back to me.' Robert shook the old man's hand and went outside into the night, the coat wrapped around him.

*

Lepre arrived at the appointed time to take Robert to Palazzo del Perro. As he climbed on to the back of his motorcycle, he bit his lip to stop himself crying out. His wounds were healing but the pain was excruciating. For the next hour as the bike twisted and turned on the winding road, each bump and rut sent a ricochet through his body.

'You have to let me rest,' he gasped, tapping Lepre on the shoulder. Lepre stopped the bike and helped him down.

'*Mi dispiace.* I am sorry, I should have gone slower.'

Robert grimaced. 'I'm not quite as strong as I thought.'

Eventually they arrived, to be met by an anxious Bruno who led him inside. 'Sit,' he instructed. 'I will build up the fire in the kitchen.'

Robert obeyed and Bruno came to sit down beside him.

'I feel old, Roberto,' he mused. 'With all this – Patrizio, Eva. I didn't even know if you were alive.' He shrugged his shoulders. 'I'm no longer a praying man,' he said, placing the last of the kindling beneath the smouldering log. 'But I thank God for your safety. Drink this cognac, I've been saving it.'

They sat with their hands wrapped around the glasses.

'We have ignited them,' Bruno said. 'Three *Tedeschi* shot in Civitella...' He glanced at Robert. 'The Aquile has temporarily scattered, but the SS will hunt them. They will have their revenge. Then they will come for Civitella and for this village.'

'You must leave,' Robert pleaded.

Bruno held up his hand, silencing him. 'I have spoken with Lepre and in your absence, we have made a plan. First you will go to a safe house to recuperate. When the dust has settled you must return to your men. They are in disarray without Antonio. They need you to direct them so they can fight again.'

'But I need to get back to them now.'

'Look at you, weak like a child. You must be strong.' Bruno put down his glass and his voice was firm. 'It is all arranged.'

'What about you?'

'I am not worth shooting,' the old man smiled.

Robert jumped at the sound of knocking.

'That will be the doctor. It's time to go. In case we don't meet again...' He took Robert's hand. '...God bless you.'

Chapter Sixty-eight

The circuitous route Doctor Biochetti chose from Palazzo del Pero took them through dense woodland. They had reached the escarpment behind Arezzo when a man ran out in front of the car. Doctor Biochetti recognised him immediately as Silvio the mechanic, by the livid scar on his forehead. He'd stitched it only the month before. The doctor slammed on the brakes.

Silvio pulled open the door. 'Help me please, I need to get to my family in Civitella. I'm told the *Tedeschi* are coming.'

As they neared the hilltop village, it was obvious they had come too late. The medieval walls rose like a mirage from the darkness below. While the doctor grabbed his medical bag, Silvio jumped from the car and ran into the dusk.

Robert followed. As he entered the village, smoke billowed through the trees and sheets of paper fluttered over the hot embers. Charred beams lay among blackened stone. The flame-throwers had destroyed every house in their path. He limped through the lanes and alleyways where he had walked with Giulietta, coughing as his lungs filled with acrid smoke. He reached the piazza. Some women were howling, holding on to each other; others were quietly weeping over their loved ones who lay motionless as if asleep. They had been fathers, brothers, sons. The church, where only hours earlier they had been celebrating their feast day, was reduced to rubble. The air reeked with the cloying smell of death.

Robert stopped beside a young woman. Blood stained the front of her shirt and in her arms she cradled a child. She looked up at him.

'My son,' she sobbed, 'my baby.' She wiped the soot from his forehead and rocked to and fro.

An old woman, dry-eyed, shuffled across the square towards her and sat in the dirt. 'They dragged him from church and shot him with his father, seven years old and they shot him.' She threw up her arms. '*Bastardi*,' she yelled. 'Our men returned from the hills. The *Tedeschi* said there would be no reprisals. So many dead, yet there is no one to pray for them. Don Alcide our priest was the first to be shot.

'Look,' she thrust the charred and blackened paper into Robert's hand. 'The service sheet for our feast day.'

Beyond the village cistern, Robert saw a girl in a white cotton blouse and a patterned skirt. She had a blue bow in her hair. It was Teresa, the young chess player he had met in the bar with Giulietta, and the dead man who lay at her feet was her father. He knelt down beside her.

'I couldn't make him better.' Teresa held out a handkerchief red with blood. 'I tied it around his head, but I couldn't make Papa better.' Robert knelt on the ground and gathered her into his arms.

Doctor Biochetti found them together.

He spoke gently to the young girl. 'Please tell your Mama the doctor is here to help you. Roberto, may we speak?' Robert set the young girl back on her feet and moved out of earshot.

'I must stay here to treat the wounded and to help bury their dead,' the doctor said softly. 'Will you be able to drive?'

Robert nodded, 'But surely I can be of some assistance. At least let me be useful.'

'No, Roberto. You must concentrate on the future, on getting well, so that you can avenge us. I was taking you to the house of an Englishwoman and her daughter at Sant'Andrea di Sorbello. They have provided shelter for many of our sick and injured soldiers, but they have finally left for Rome. Their estate manager remains, he'll look after you.'

Robert paused for a moment, stunned. The night had taken on the quality of a surreal dream. If he revealed that the two Englishwomen were his mother and sister, he would break every code of secrecy, but in these chaotic days, surrounded by death and destruction, surely these rules did not apply. 'I need to tell you something, but it must go no further.'

The doctor waited.

'Signora Durante is my mother and Diana my sister,' he revealed.

The doctor drew in his breath. 'I had no idea. Your mother believes you are working in intelligence, somewhere secret in England. That's why I never made a connection. Now, of course it doesn't surprise me.'

'Tell me they are well, I have been so worried about them.'

'I took them to Rome myself. They are extraordinary women, both of them.'

For a second the doctor faltered and his hands began to shake. 'You will have to give me a moment,' he said, glancing back at the square. 'I'm a doctor, but this is beyond comprehension. Our men killed, women raped, and the children, dear God, they were innocent children. Three German soldiers killed by reckless partisans, the result a massacre.'

'When I met first this little girl, Teresa,' Robert spoke in a hushed voice, 'she was playing chess with her father and now this. You will look after her?'

'Of course.'

Robert's voice was filled with emotion. 'She had a brother. The last time I saw them they were running around the cistern.' He looked at the rows of hastily covered bodies lining the square. 'I imagine the boy is…' He could say no more.

Before he left, he returned to Teresa. She hadn't moved.

'I will take you to your mother.'

She shook her head. 'Mama is with Basilio… Someone must stay with Papa,' she whispered.

He pulled a clean handkerchief from his pocket and gave it to her. 'I have to go now,' he said, 'but I will return, I promise.'

As he walked from the square, he turned back to see her staring after him, holding the doctor's hand.

He had left Val di Chiana and Cortona behind him when he pulled in to the verge. He banged his hand against the steering wheel. Where was man's humanity? He wanted to scream and rant against a world where such cruelty existed. Instead, he started the engine and drove on through the night. His mind was in turmoil. He had believed his mother and sister to be safe, little knowing they had thrown themselves into danger.

As he passed the Castello di Sorbello and turned into the drive, he remembered the doctor telling him an anecdote about the Contessa.

'There is a Castello near Mercatale,' Doctor Biochetti had said, 'Owned by an ancient Italian dynasty, the Ranieri di Sorbello. It was requisitioned by the Germans months ago. The *Tedeschi* think they know what's going on, but while the officers sleep in their beds, the Contessa hides Allied servicemen in the tower above them.'

But, Robert thought, as he climbed from the car, the elegant Contessa wasn't the only woman in the valley willing to risk her life in order to provide a refuge for others.

Signor Innocenti was standing in the doorway of the *fattoria* when Robert arrived.

'So you have come back to us.' He gripped Robert's hand. 'Thank God for that mercy. Tonight, you will sleep in the house, but in the morning, I will take you to the barn.'

He helped Robert to the bedroom and was about to leave when Robert stopped him.

'I want to talk to you about your nephew, Antonio, Signor.'

'How is he? He is clever, no? Leader of the partisans. You wouldn't believe it, he was so naughty as a child,' Signor Innocenti chuckled.

'It's not good news.'

Signor Innocenti looked at him, his face bewildered. 'He is injured? I must tell my sister.'

'I'm afraid he is dead, Signor.'

The old man sank on the bed, and Robert sat down beside him, his strength gone. 'He was a brave man, Signor, and loyal. He was my dear friend and I owe my life to him.'

'How shall I tell his Mama and Rosalie? The wedding was planned. How shall I tell them?' he pleaded.

'It is the most difficult thing to do,' Robert said. 'But you will find the courage. We all do. I am so sorry, Signor.'

The following morning he moved to the barn.

'I never expected to nurse you,' Signora Carducci said, arranging the covers over his makeshift bed. 'But with God's blessing you are alive.' Robert's eyes closed and the old woman took a small book of folk stories from the pocket of her apron and began to read to him. When he was asleep she uncurled his fingers and put the small wooden sculpture Davide had made for him on the table beside him. Then she thanked God for small mercies: it was the talisman that had brought him home.

Robert woke to find Rosa gazing at him from the other side of the partition. The cow twisted her neck to pull a strand of hay from the rack. How simple to be Rosa, to have a life measured in milking times and food. Outside, the birds were singing and the war seemed miles away. Today he could sleep if he wished, or walk to the lake where he had gone with his sister. He remembered asking Diana about the two fishing rods side by side on the jetty, and the moment he realised that he was no longer the only man in her life. Instead there was Davide – if he was still alive.

He now knew about Davide's family and it all made sense. '*Il Scapello*' was well known among the bands of partisans scattered through Italy. His acts of reckless courage were legendary. But he wouldn't think of that today. He recalled fragments of Signora Carducci's story. It had been filled with hope and had reignited his will to survive. One day the war would be over and if God was on his side he would marry Giulietta. He could see her walking in the meadow filled with wild orchids, taking his hand in her own. 'I won't ask you to tell me how you got this,' she had said, turning it over, tracing her fingers over the burns, but he had wanted to tell her.

'I was shot down,' he had revealed. 'Over the Channel. I couldn't open the hatch, the plane was on fire. I had seen men burn to death, Giulietta. I thought I would be one of them.' As the old panic threatened to overwhelm him, Giulietta had lifted his hand to her lips.

He went out through the barn door. The birds were still singing and the distant hills shimmered in the morning sun, but against the backdrop of beauty, he could hear rumbling in the sky. The noise grew louder as a formation of Allied bombers flew slowly and lazily towards him and the meadow reverberated with the noise of their engines. When the meadow was silent once more he sank to his knees. The war had never gone away, it was surrounding him.

On the morning he was due to leave, Robert went up to the Villa. Signor Innocenti unlocked the door.

'It is dark, I'm afraid, but we have boarded the windows.'

'Signor, I just want to be here for a while so that I can take something with me.'

'But we have hidden many of your mother's possessions,' the old man apologised.

'I don't mean possessions, just memories.' Robert walked into the study and put his mother's favourite record on the gramophone. He would leave not knowing if they would all make it through the war, if they would be reunited at the end. 'You must never tell my mother I've been here. She can't know anything. Will you give me your word, and that of Signora Carducci?'

The old man nodded. 'Of course,' he vowed, but as Robert wandered through the rooms, 'The Lark Ascending' floating up the stairs, he was tempted to leave a clue; something, anything to tell his mother that he was safe.

'Roberto,' Doctor Biochetti said, when he arrived to collect him. 'Bruno has been taken.'

'He's an old man, it's senseless,' Robert despaired.

'It is all senseless, but the Aquile need you now more than ever. Give them back their discipline so they can fight again. Civitella must never happen again, and you, my friend can help us to prevent it.'

'Do you think one man can make a difference in all of this?' Robert turned his back on the doctor. 'Do you really believe I can make a difference?'

'Yes, Roberto. Please, for the memory of Antonio and for the innocent farmers caught in a war they neither want or understand. Come with me.'

Chapter Sixty-nine

Robert returned to the Aquile and his race to retrain the men began. Their new quarters, an abandoned monastery in the rugged and inhospitable terrain above Palazzo del Pero provided the perfect environment. A safe place where Robert could plan his strategy, but also examine the past operations.

As he lay alone in the monk's cell each man came under his scrutiny. He thought of Giulietta looking up at him from the transmitter where she worked.

'We must change your call sign,' he had said to her. 'We are no longer secure.'

'Now?' she had said, alarm registering on her features.

'Now,' he had replied.

Every man suspected another. There was an atmosphere of mistrust in the mountain hideout. When his men failed to look him in the eye, he realised he did not escape suspicion.

'Someone has betrayed us,' he said, facing the men as they dined in the refectory. 'There will be no radio contact, no airdrops and no backup. We will be working independently; it is to be the toughest challenge yet. Some of us will not return. We know the terrain, we can be silent and, God willing, luck may be on our side. *Dobbiamo essere vigili.* Vigilance is key. Don't trust even your closest neighbour. From now on there must be no contact with your families until our work is done and we have pushed the *Tedeschi* into the sea. Is that understood? Let's get on with it. Long live freedom!'

They were once again a disciplined, fighting force, with Lepre a strong and determined leader. After a successful sabotage operation on a German ammunition supply depot, they were ready for another raid. This one was personal to Robert. If Bruno was alive, his rescue from the clutches of the retreating German army was imperative.

On the night of 14 July, Lepre, Robert and ten chosen partisans stormed the prison in Arezzo. To their astonishment the fascist police surrendered quickly and no shots were fired. After confiscating their weapons, Robert pushed them into a cell and locked the door behind them. He passed the keys to Lepre. 'Release the prisoners,' he said.

Running through the walkways he called Bruno's name. There was no reply. He was giving up hope when he heard a faint cry from the end of a corridor. There was a small door, but he had no key.

They shot the lock and broke through the door. Bruno was cowering in the darkness.

'Why did they put you in a broom cupboard?' Robert grinned, as they helped him down the corridor.

'They thought they could sweep me away,' Bruno replied.

'At least your humour is intact. They didn't hurt you?'

Bruno shook his head. 'Stupid fools kept me alive because they thought I might lead them to you.'

Robert supported him through the alleyways and back streets, skirting fallen masonry and debris from the shattered buildings. The City of Arezzo was another victim of the war. When they reached the Corso Italia, the doctor opened the door and Robert pushed him gently through. 'You are safe now, Bruno,' he uttered. 'It's over.' Doctor Biochetti put an arm around the old man's shoulders and guided him along the passage. After a few shuffling steps Bruno turned. 'Thank you,' he said, his eyes watering. 'I will await your return.'

Robert nodded, too choked to speak, and he broke into a run.

4

End Game

Chapter Seventy

It had been six weeks since Alessandra and Diana arrived in Rome and they had been waiting desperately for news of home, of Robert and of Davide.

On 7 July Diana sprinted up the wide stone staircase and into the drawing room of the apartment. She held a newspaper in her hand. 'Mama, it's true.' she panted. 'Umbertide has been liberated. We can go home.'

'Is it really possible?' Alessandra switched off the wireless and looked up at her daughter. For the first time Diana noticed the lines at the corner of her eyes, and strands of silver threading through her dark hair. Her shoulders were sagging and Diana knew it was her turn to take care of her mother.

'The Doctor was right. The Germans are being pushed further and further back up the Italian peninsula. It will be over soon, Davide will be safe and Robert will come home.' She knelt at her feet. 'Come on, Mama, don't cry. You've been so strong for everyone, you can't give up, not now.'

Alessandra went into the bathroom and Diana followed. She took a cloth and began to wipe the basin. Diana put her hand on her mother's arm.

'Stop, Mama, it is already clean. Let's go out. I want to rejoice in the fact that this is nearly over and they will return to us.'

Alessandra twisted her wedding band. 'I wish we knew where they both were; then we could really celebrate.'

'Let us enjoy this moment, Mama. I truly believe that when the war does end, they will come home.'

That night Alessandra dreamt of the doctor. His lips were on her face, in her hair, and she was breathing in the scent of him, but the image blurred and changed and the man making love to her was Anthony.

All day she thought of her dream and all day she battled wth her guilt. She had shared vows with her husband and he was slipping away. She was healing, though part of her didn't want to. His voice was distant in her memory and even the way he had looked was fading.

She thought of going to confession, talking to a priest. She tried to write in her diary and failed. Once again it was Diana who came to her rescue.

'Mama,' she said, coming into the bedroom they shared and taking the diary from her hands. 'You don't have to be lonely or feel guilty. I have seen how it is with you and the doctor. It is more than all right with me, I promise you. And I know Papa would approve.' She looked at her mother sternly. 'I also think it is time you stopped wearing his pyjamas.'

Alessandra smiled. Her daughter had become a remarkably wise young woman.

Much later she took the pyjamas, folded them carefully and packed them in the bottom of her suitcase. Diana was right, it was time to put the past behind her. The seven years without her husband had left their mark, just as life had taken its toll. 'What would you want me to do?' she whispered. 'What shall I do, my love?' In her mind she could see Anthony's face smiling at her, his eyebrows lifting in gentle amusement.

The following week they began the journey home. Their lift,

a jeep driven by a young officer from the Indian 10th Infantry, weaved slowly through the traffic. As the towns and villages passed and the landmarks became familiar, Alessandra wondered what would await them on their return.

*

Diana's head was resting against her mother's shoulder when she opened her eyes.

'Are we nearly there?' she asked, biting her lip.

'Very nearly,' Alessandra replied.

As Diana felt her mother's closeness she was comforted. The deserter was dead, the past was over and the future beckoned. Davide was alive, she was sure of it, and Robert too. They would both come home.

Her mouth began to move in prayer. Soon they would be at the *fattoria*, she would see Signor Innocenti and Nico. 'Please let them both be safe,' she whispered. 'Let Nico be alive.'

She climbed out of the car. Her legs were heavy as she walked towards the piazza. A magpie flew over, then another; it was a good omen. She was halfway across the square when the old man opened the door. She ran towards him.

'Signor Innocenti,' she cried, hugging him.

'Thank God you are home,' he said, his face wreathed in smiles. 'We have been waiting for your return.'

She drew back. 'Tell me about Nico,' she stammered.

He turned around and there in the doorway the white dog stood. He limped towards them, his tail swishing. Diana knelt in the dust beside him and tangled her arms around him.

He licked her hand.

'Nico,' she vowed. 'I will never leave you again.'

She looked up at the sound of a small bleat to find Griselda trotting across the square.

*

As Alessandra had predicted, the Germans had retreated through the Niccone Valley and looting stragglers had come to their door. But her small household was safe. So were the animals, hidden in the meadow above the lake. When Alessandra stood in the garden among her wrecked flower beds in a sea of broken glass, the small cherub shattered nearby, she drew everyone around her.

'All is well,' she said, laughing and crying at the same moment. 'The house is still standing and though a little damaged, it can be mended.' She looked at a puzzled Signor Innocenti. 'I have not lost my mind, Signor, I assure you. I am laughing because most of the important people are here with me again. The rest are just things. Do you remember your words when we first arrived? *There is nothing that cannot be fixed.* So Signor, we will fix them again. Of course,' she mused, picking a rose that had survived the onslaught, 'I would be overjoyed if I knew that my son was safe.' She turned to Signora Carducci who looked rather red in the face. 'Are you quite well, Signora?'

'Yes. No.' The old woman glanced at Signor Innocenti imploringly.

'She is quite all right Signora,' the old man said.

The one time Alessandra cried bitter tears of rage was when she opened the door to her bedroom and recognised a small pile of soiled chiffon in the centre of the floor. It was her dress by Schiaparelli. Anthony had chosen it for her at the salon in Paris. 'It would look better on you,' he had whispered, as a model floated past. Afterwards he had paid a ridiculous amount for the tiny slip of fabric. Now she would have to throw it away.

She had finished sweeping the glass from the drawing-room floor when Signora Carducci came in, struggling beneath the weight of a large sack. She tipped the contents carefully onto the sofa.

'The picture you like,' she said holding it up. 'Joseph the

Carpenter, your ornaments and the little silver jug. Also, your favourite photographs.'

Alessandra kissed the surprised old woman. 'Where did you hide them? You are resourceful, thank you.'

'It was Signor Innocenti. He carried the sack to the tree house before Ro... Before the *Tedeschi* came and they were too stupid to look. In truth, I believe *all* your precious treasures are safe.' At this the old woman started to chuckle and departed the room, leaving a confused Alessandra staring after her.

That night Alessandra wrote a letter to her son.

My Darling,
I am not sure if you will get this, but I will send it to your old address and hope it will find its way to your door. I think about you always.
We have returned to the Villa Durante, and though the house is a little worse for wear, it is still standing. More importantly all the people who work here are safe, except Davide who is risking his life somewhere in the north of Italy with the partisans. I am told it is the most dangerous occupation of all.
Wherever you are, please take care and come back to us.
I love you always
Your Mama

Alessandra was waiting at the top of the steps when Doctor Biochetti arrived.

She took a deep breath. 'You risked your life for us; you saved Nico.'

'I have come to check on the white dog now.' He smiled down at her. 'And to see you.'

Alessandra could feel herself blushing. 'Thank you, I ...'

'Now, let us relax together and enjoy a glass of wine.' He produced a bottle of Brunello from behind his back. 'I take the impudence of bringing some Tuscan red, though not as good as yours.' He smiled again and Alessandra noticed the laughter lines at the corner of his eyes. She took him into the small sitting room where she uncorked the bottle and put the 'Lark Ascending' onto the gramophone. She turned the volume low and sat down next to him. When she spoke, he had to lean towards her in order to hear. 'My husband loved music and taught me to appreciate it. Before we married I only listened to jazz.'

Vittorio took her hands. 'It is correct that you still remember your husband with such affection, I too remember my wife every day. It is good to love him, Alessandra, but it is possible to have another love. I have grown so fond of you and I have hopes you might feel the same about me.'

He took the glass away from her and put it on the table beside her.

'You are a beautiful woman and I cannot help my feelings. I am in admiration of everything you have done, but now I think is time for me to stop talking.'

As Alessandra felt his arms surround her, a feeling of utter relief coursed through her. Then his lips found hers and his hands were in her hair, on her body, and she was winding her arms around his neck, pulling him towards her. She wouldn't fight these feelings any longer.

They lay together, his body leaning into her, his arm curved around her waist. She could hear his quiet breathing, feel it soft against her skin. She wouldn't have believed it was possible for her body to have responded as it had after such a long time, how his caresses had caused sensations she had never experienced before. She was amazed that Vittorio had the energy to immediately take her again, less urgently admittedly, but it was so natural it felt as though her limbs were no longer hers; their hands touching, holding each other, were indistinguishable. Later as she watched him sleeping she thought of the words of Kahlil Gibran, Anthony's favourite poet. *It takes an hour to like someone, and a day to love someone, but it takes a lifetime to forget someone.*

She was able now to let go of Anthony, but she would never forget him.

Chapter Seventy-one

On 16 July, as Allied troops were advancing towards Arezzo, teams of partisans came down from the hills. The Aquile were among them. At seven o'clock in the morning the Italian tricolour was unfurled on the Town Hall's bell tower by triumphant partisans, and the bells were rung in celebration. Three hours later the first Sherman tank, driven by a member of B Squadron 16th/5th Lancers, and adorned with the Union Jack, rolled into Arezzo, and made its way to the square. As Robert walked the newly liberated streets with Doctor Biochetti, they were deserted. Thirty percent of the beautiful city had gone, destroyed by both the Allies and the Germans. Later he would be horrified to learn that more than twelve thousand civilians from Arezzo and surrounding areas had been killed during the Nazi retreat.

As they returned to the doctor's house, both men were silent, reflecting on the horror of war.

Before they had supper, Robert made a transmission to Bari, using the transmitter Giulietta had left behind.

'It's extraordinary,' Doctor Biochetti mused as they sat with a glass of wine in the dining room of the house in the Corso Italia. 'It is not only the British who have liberated our little city. The New Zealanders, the Nepalese Gurkhas, so many different nationalities have been involved. It's difficult for many Italians to see beyond the bombing and destruction – hard to recognise how much we owe. But without the Allies help, we would not be free. I want you to know, on behalf of my countrymen, that we are truly grateful, Roberto.'

'It has been an honour to know you, Dottore, and a great relief that we are nearing the end. Next week I am to be relieved from further operations and returned to Bari for debriefing. Would you mind if I was picked up from here?'

As Robert said goodbye to the men of the Aquile at the old monastery he felt a sharp sense of loss. He had seen these men through adversity and suffering; he knew their frailties and their strengths. It would be their final parting. But the time was right. Despite his training and commitment, he was near to breaking point. The massacre at Civitella had brought him to the edge. He couldn't sleep, and when he did, he dreamt of burnt houses, charred flesh. He could hear Teresa's voice, 'I couldn't make my Papa better.' Her sweet face haunted him. One day he would return to find her, he would fulfil his promise, but for now he would return to the Corso Italia to await further orders.

The following morning at eleven o'clock, a Sergeant Pennyfold and a Corporal Smith from the King's Dragoon Guards arrived in a jeep to collect him.

'Would you like some refreshment before your journey?' the doctor offered.

'I'm afraid we haven't the time.' Sergeant Pennyfold picked up Robert's suitcase and threw it in the back.

'Sit in the middle would you, sir,' he instructed Robert.

'If you don't mind I'll stay by the window.'

'Sorry sir, orders.'

Robert glanced at the doctor. Something was wrong; he wasn't being taken for debriefing, of that he was sure.

'The transmitter is upstairs, I'll run and fetch it.'

The two soldiers glanced at each other. 'Don't be long, sir.'

Robert went inside the house, the doctor following. The Corporal hovered in the doorway.

'Something's not right,' Robert pronounced quietly.

'I know,' the doctor agreed. 'One moment.' He disappeared into his surgery, reappearing seconds later with a prayer book. 'We have a saying in Italy: *Qui gatta ci cova*, there is something fishy going on. When you need help, look at the marker, my friend.'

Robert tried with little success to engage the soldiers in conversation. They were approaching Umbertide when he took a pack of cigarettes from his trouser pocket.

'Would you like one?' he offered. 'Nazionale, they're strong, but you get used to them.'

'No thanks,' they muttered, averting their eyes.

By the time the jeep had left Umbertide, Robert knew with certainty there would be no Bari and no extraction.

Chapter Seventy-two

The runway was melting when the plane touched down in Cairo. Douglas Gordon took off his tweed jacket and stepped outside.

'Can I take your bag, sir?' the driver greeted him and ushered him towards a car. 'Sorry, it's as hot inside as it is out, but it will cool down once we get going.'

Douglas gazed from the window at the hubbub outside. He felt a stirring of excitement. There was something about the city that enthralled him; it was a city of extremes.

He remembered the first time he had come here, leaving Magdelene behind. He winced, thinking of her soft, pleading voice as he had left her.

'Do you have to go?' she had begged. 'I don't want to be in London alone.'

But he had gone anyway, kissing her tenderly before he left. '*Meine Leibling*, I will be back before you know it,' he had said as he caressed her hair, but this was a lie. Everything was on offer in Cairo, things that could dull his misery, things he would never ask Magdelene for. He had known how much she wanted children but the shrapnel deep in his groin had made that impossible.

'Why did you marry me?' he had cried after a clumsy attempt to satisfy her early in their marriage. 'I am useless to you.'

'Because I love you,' she had said, looking up at him, her eyes filled with tears.

He had said it then, the words that had changed her feelings towards him for ever.

'You could take a lover, he would give you a child. It's all right with me.'

'All right with you!' Magdelene had drawn back, her eyes filled with horror. 'You wish to make me a whore with another man's child? How dare you.'

'I thought that's what you wanted.'

'That shows how little you know me.'

How he had misjudged the situation. Magdelene would never consider being with another man, he knew that now.

From that moment, the fabric of their marriage disintegrated. Douglas had slept on the sofa night after night as Magdelene withdrew from him. Whenever he tried to hold her he could see her bewilderment and pity.

He pushed the memories aside and looked past the children begging for piastres, to the narrow alleyways teeming with brothels beyond.

First, he would meet Major Adderley and discuss the latest security problem. Afterwards he would have a couple of gins at the Gezira Sporting Club and then he would visit the houseboat on the Nile.

Douglas had a spring in his step as he walked from the Cairo terminal building to the waiting plane. He was going to Rome, the city of the ancients where he and Anthony had spent an idyllic summer in their university vacation so many years before. They had danced in the fountains, felt the vibrancy of the streets and bars at night. It was here he had discovered that art and passion were at the very core of the historic city.

Everything had gone according to plan, but it was more

than that: fate had stepped in. After a couple of drinks in the Gezira Sporting Club, he had been in good time for the allotted appointment with Major Adderley. Having demolished several sweet pastries and two cups of tea, he was stifling a yawn when Adderley's monologue on the latest Allied victories finally came to a close.

'A bit of a problem, old chap,' he had said, flicking his fly swat against his boot. 'There is a good chance that young Marston has been passing information to the enemy. We thought him thoroughly reliable.' Douglas had registered surprise and indeed shock. Robert had come on his recommendation; it was impossible. Robert was one of the best.

'That's where you come in,' Adderley had said, popping a stray crumb into his mouth. 'We need to make sure he gets a fair trial. There is enough evidence against him; the Germans know everything he's been up to.'

Douglas leant forward, his sandy eyebrows drawn together in concern. 'I'll leave for Rome in the morning.' He accepted one last pastry, satisfied he could save his godson. He would never want Robert hurt, but in war you had to decide where your priorities lay. Private lives took second place to serving your country.

After finalising the details, he had left the residential area for a bar in one of the densely populated alleys. He'd been given his new instructions and in return he had handed over an envelope updating his superiors on his recent activities. The dark-suited contact had disappeared into the throng outside, leaving Douglas to unwind. It was the moment he had been waiting for. He had removed his jacket and, loosening his tie, he had lain down on a velvet sofa and lost himself to the hookah. Enveloped in the exotic blend of tobacco he was able to see things more clearly. His masters were confident of his loyalty and satisfied with his progress. The truth drug he had been working on was now in the development stage and if it reached its full potential he would be indispensable.

Much later he had risen to his feet and summoned a horse-drawn garry to take him to the houseboat on the Nile.

As he pulled himself up the steps towards the open door of the plane, the searing metal handrail burnt his hand and he gasped involuntarily. *They should have a sign to warn you*, he thought. *Bloody Egyptians*.

Chapter Seventy-three

Robert stood in front of Major Templeton in the same penitentiary that had housed the German army headquarters until six weeks before.

'Sit down, Mister Marston.'

'Flight Lieutenant Marston, Sir.'

'Yes, I can see that. Do please sit down.'

The Major looked up from his file. 'So what have you got to say?' he closed the file with a snap.

Robert exhaled. He had been rehearsed for every situation but this.

'I have done my duty to the best of my ability, and I'm not sure what I'm doing here.'

'I don't need to tell you that espionage is a capital offence.'

'I have worked with the Aquile, trained them and nearly died for them. I fought in the Battle of Britain, worked in intelligence, why on earth would I betray my men?'

'Why would anyone? It appears you visited Berlin several times before the war.'

'I was a schoolboy, I went with my godfather.'

'And the two agents, Eva and Patrizio, you are the only person to have known their movements.'

'With each transmission, the Germans came nearer to

pinpointing our position. But you already know this. It is the reason my radio operator was extracted.'

'The Germans knew her call sign.'

Robert exploded. 'So that is why you have me here. It's ridiculous, we both know the Germans have had great success in breaking codes.'

'I don't need to remind you, Mr Marston, we wouldn't have you here if we did not have good reason.'

'Well, it is the wrong reason,' Robert declared.

Douglas settled down on the parachute packs in the rear fuselage. He leant against them, relaxing as the aeroplane gathered speed. He had always liked the surge of power as the aircraft lifted into the air, the feeling that you were free. But the feeling was temporary. He seethed with anger that boiled inside him, against the people he loved. His mother had died in childbirth and his father, Archibald Gordon, a major in the Black Watch, had been killed in the first months of the Boer War. From there he'd been foisted upon Great-Aunt Agatha, a spinster who disliked the inconvenience of having a child in her care. When Douglas turned eighteen he had enrolled at medical school with his friend Anthony Marston. For the first time in his life he had experienced the exuberance of youth. It was in Rome, after a particularly drunken evening, that he had made an amorous advance on his friend. Anthony had been quick to brush it away and make a joke of it. Nothing more was said, but all these years later Douglas could still feel the sting of shame and confusion.

When war came in 1914, Douglas persuaded Anthony to enlist with him into his father's old regiment. Following a few months intensive training they had been sent to join their comrades fighting in the cold, muddy trenches in northern France. For a year they fought together, lived together and supported each other. After a particularly brutal barrage of German shelling, it was Douglas who had comforted the exhausted and bewildered Anthony.

In September 1915 their war had come to an end after the initially successful but horrifically costly attacks at Loos. The 9th battalion suffered over 700 casualties. Anthony and Douglas had both been caught in the same burst of machine-gun fire. Anthony was severely wounded, and the English stretcher-bearer took him to the field hospital, while Douglas, presumed dead, was left in no man's land. When he showed signs of life he had been dragged to a German field hospital by an officer hoping for information, but after a cursory examination a sign was posted on his blanket: '*Water only, beyond medical help*'. It was the vigilance of a young German nurse that had saved him. '*Er Lebt noch*,' she had yelled, seeing a flicker of movement. 'We need a drip and an orderly now. Take him to theatre.'

Douglas was moved from the lines of the dead and, despite the fact that he was English and the enemy, he had been treated with respect. Magdelene had saved his life and his sanity. Throughout his recovery he watched for her, making excuses to call her to his side. During his subsequent incarceration as a prisoner of war in Germany, he kept in touch with her, writing long and devoted letters. To his amazement his affections were reciprocated despite his terrible injuries. Soon Magdelene was more than an acquaintance, she became his best friend and the mother he never had.

While Anthony had survived the war as a decorated hero, Douglas would for ever remain the prisoner of his nightmares.

'I was told you were dead, you cannot imagine my sense of loss,' Anthony had said to him when they were reunited. Douglas didn't care about his loss; Anthony had been saved while he was left to die. People like Anthony were always saved.

When the war was over the two young men had returned to medical school to finish their studies. Anthony specialised in general medicine but Douglas chose neurology. On his graduation, he had returned to Germany to find Magdelene. Accepting the position as house assistant at Universitätsmedizin Berlin, he continued his studies on the brain and all its complexities. It was here, under the great German neurologist, Carl Bergermann, that his political views had begun to change.

'Read this,' the professor had said, handing him a book with a red cover. 'You will find *Mein Kampf* particularly illuminating.'

Douglas had found it more than illuminating. As Europe struggled through the depression, Nazi ideology seemed fresh and new; a solution.

Reunited with Magdelene, he had returned with her to England. They married in church and Anthony gave her away. When Anthony's first child was born he had asked Douglas to be godfather.

'I can't think of anyone I like and trust more,' he'd said. 'It will be just like old times.' But it hadn't been like old times. While Anthony's private medical practice grew as he was drawn into the circle of his rich patients, Douglas struggled to find the funding for his research projects.

Magdelene, now a naturalised British citizen, had secured a job as science lecturer at London University. Her salary supplemented their income and for a while they were content, but when her mother died she had felt isolated and alone.

'Don't you see, Douglas, I should have gone back to Germany to be with her, I let her down,' she said, her eyes puffy with tears.

As Britain's relationship with Germany deteriorated, so did Magdelene's confidence. Her new intake of students were aggressive in their anti-German sentiments, and they clearly had no respect for her. The situation spiralled out of control when one evening she came home early with a bruise on her forehead.

'Do you know what happened today?' she cried, pulling back her hair to reveal the blue swelling. 'A student threw a stone at me as I left the building! I can't live like this, Douglas. I can't go to work, not any more.'

'It won't happen again, it's disgraceful. I'll talk to the faculty. It's all right, my darling.'

'No, it's not all right. I have no friends in this cruel country. I have tried, don't you see how I have tried? I am going mad with it all, Douglas, mad.'

'But I'm here.'

'You are always working, and there's the other thing.'

'You mean my... my impotence,' Douglas shouted.

'I'm so sorry.'

'You finally realise I'm not enough for you?'

'You are a considerate husband, but...' She had turned her back on him and walked to the window. 'I shall be interned in a camp if I remain here. '

'Are you going to leave me?' Douglas's face crumpled.

Weeks later Magdelene had left him but not in the way he had imagined. All his medical training had not prepared him for the shock of seeing his wife with her wrists slashed, in a pool of blood, dying on the bathroom floor.

Chapter Seventy-four

Robert returned to his cell. He had watched his friends blown out of the sky, he had seen Harvey trapped in the burning wreckage of his plane, he had risked his life for his country and this was how he was repaid for the sacrifice. It was a travesty. Someone had betrayed them, someone knew his every move.

He was nearly asleep when he remembered Doctor Biochetti thrusting the prayer book into his hand. He retrieved it from the table and opened the cover. The bookmark fell to the floor. He rubbed it between his fingers and peeled away the coating to reveal a tiny metal pick. He had used one before at Beaulieu in Hampshire, the finishing school for spies. 'If you have one of these and a hairpin or something similar you can pick almost any lock at all,' his teacher, Blacker, a reformed criminal, had cheerfully informed him.

Douglas awoke when the plane hit a patch of turbulence. He'd been dreaming about Anthony's accident. In his dream, his friend's eyes had mocked him as he hit the windscreen. He unscrewed the top of his flask and tipped his head back, letting the whisky burn the back of his throat. Why did Anthony continue to plague him? He was successful now, in control. He no longer had to suffer his old friend's charm, his easy-going nature; he no longer had to watch the adoration of his children, his wife! And yet he had needed to be with Anthony and Alessandra, wanted to be near them, punishing himself by seeing them together, seeing their beautiful children and wanting the life they had. When the German military intelligence organisation, the Abwehr, had approached him, he was ripe for the picking. The country of his birth had betrayed him and it was only right that someone else benefitted from his genius. The decision that had initially seemed so difficult was easy in the end. Their flattery had poured salve onto his battered confidence and he had agreed. As time went on he had become more and more entrenched.

Douglas frowned, remembering the lunch with Anthony. They had been on their second round at the King's Head, the pub around the corner from Douglas's laboratory, when Anthony put down his pint.

'I'm not going to beat about the bush, I can't, not any more.'

'What are you talking about?' Douglas felt the heat rise in his face.

'Since Magdelene's death you've changed. I've been concerned for months. You have seemed ill at ease, nervous in my company. Last week I was on a house call when I saw you getting off a tram. I am afraid to say I followed you, not out of suspicion, you understand, but out of concern. You can imagine my surprise when you met a man on Ealing Common and he slipped an envelope into your coat pocket. It was the day we were meeting for a late lunch at my club.'

'One of my students,' Douglas bluffed.

'I looked at the envelope while you went to the gents.'

Douglas's heart was pounding. He had to find an explanation that would satisfy Anthony.

'It seems you have forced my hand. You must never repeat

what I am about to tell you, but I'm working on a secret project for the British government.

'Since when does the British government code in German?'

Douglas clenched his fist. He couldn't mistake the disappointment in Anthony's eyes as their lunch came to an abrupt end.

'Why, Douglas, old boy, why?'

There were a million reasons why, but he would never have told him.

'You know I won't be able to keep this to myself,' were the last words Anthony said to him.

The plane lurched again and Douglas hit his head on the fuselage. He cursed and felt the spot. He must concentrate on the present. His new job for the Reich Main Security Office under direct control of the SS was more challenging than his work for the Abwehr, but he was lucky, the truth of his treachery to his country had died with Anthony. The SS were rewarding him handsomely and the partisans in the Italian peninsula had been seriously challenged. Of course, with the German position becoming more precarious daily, he might have to change sides once again.

It had been easy to break the call signs. Just a few minutes with a piece of paper – the boy should have been more original. *Brown Ale 8*, an anagram for Lowenbrau! One letter missing indicated by the eight. It was an irony that the anagrams they had so enjoyed had given him the key. The subsequent call sign was just as easy.

With access to Robert's transmissions, Douglas knew his movements and plans. But he didn't sabotage every operation, he selected carefully so as not to alert the partisans. It was a shame about the two agents shot on their way to Florence, their information would have been useful; but that was the fault of over-zealous soldiers. Unknowingly Alessandra had been useful too. 'My letters to Robert take weeks,' she had complained shortly after the war began. Douglas had offered a solution, enabling her to send letters via their agent in Spain where they were intercepted, read and sent on their way. How Anthony would have despised him; but then love and hate were so intertwined.

He glanced at his watch. His plane would arrive at Ciampino Airport at 1400 hours.

Chapter Seventy-five

Robert looked up from the bed as the key turned in the lock.

'There's a visitor for you,' the young private said.

'For me?' he queried.

'Yes sir, Professor Gordon has flown in from Cairo.'

Robert was elated. The man he trusted with his life had come to his rescue. 'When can I see him?'

'After he has finished with Major Templeton, sir.'

Robert clasped Douglas's hand. 'When did you find out?'

'Yesterday. A stroke of luck, I was at a meeting with Major Adderley. He told me you were in a spot of bother, and here I am.'

'You have come all this way for me?'

'Of course.'

'What I would do without you?'

Douglas smiled. 'I'm always here for you, Robert, you know that. I've persuaded Major Templeton that there must be some mistake. He assured me you'll get a fair hearing.' He sat down on the only chair and tapped his pipe on his trousers.

'Now you can tell me everything. Start from the very beginning.' But though he coaxed Robert, willing him to let down his guard, he found him wary, different from the young man he had last seen in London.

'Forgive me, Douglas,' Robert said at last. 'I don't want to talk about the war, I want to forget, just for a while ... Do you remember France in thirty-eight, lunch in that café in the Champs Elysees?'

'The prostitute who tried to solicit you, and you thought she was asking the way!'

'How naïve I must have seemed.'

'Just young.'

'And Berlin, the beer cellar. How I loved those long glasses. I got a little drunk. '

'Ahh, Lowenbrau! Don't tell your mother, she'll never forgive me.'

'And now the world is upside down.'

'What's an anagram for *I run to escape*?' Douglas asked.

'Don't know.' Robert managed a grin.

'*A persecution*. Thought it was relevant at the moment. Now, cheer up, old man, we'll get you out of here, I promise.'

'You know how grateful I am,' Robert said as Douglas was leaving. 'But there is something else I must ask. Please can you help me find who betrayed us? I owe it to my men. It has to be someone I have trusted completely. Even if I end up being shot, I'll find out, Douglas, I must.'

'I have no doubt that you will,' Douglas stuttered in reply.

During the drive through the city back to his hotel, Douglas was agitated. As a fighter pilot Robert had been to hell and back but he had still believed the best of his friends. Now he was a leader of men, used to plotting, planning entire operations, being in charge. Robert was no longer malleable; there was a new defiance, and something more, his innocence had gone. Douglas had underestimated his godson, he was more of a threat.

Douglas found the restaurant in the Campo de Fiori easily. Despite the ravages of war, it was still open, still packed with people.

He sat down at one of the small tables overlooking the square and clicked his fingers at the tired-looking waiter.

'A half bottle of house wine please,' he said.

'*Si*, Signor.'

The waiter returned with the wine and as Douglas sipped it he remembered coming here with Anthony, stopping in front of the statue that towered above the square depicting Giordano Bruno, the philosopher and Dominican friar tried for heresy and burnt at the stake.

'He died in the name of freedom. Nothing really changes does it?' Anthony had mused. Douglas had agreed then, but not now.

The waiter arrived with his plate of pasta and put it in front of him. Douglas picked up his fork but this too had lost its appeal.

In the morning he would return to see Robert, continue the double game. The British army allowed him unlimited access, believing he might be able to coax some sort of confession out him, while the SS wanted more information on the movements of the partisans. As he helped himself to another glass of wine a thought occurred to him. If Robert was shot, his own future was secure. Robert was the only person who could possibly guess his secret. But he wasn't sure though that he could let him die. The young man adored him and if something went wrong with the Reich, Robert might yet be a useful bargaining tool. There was more than one reason to keep his godson alive.

Chapter Seventy-six

Robert's court martial was set for the following week. As he idled his time in the hot, airless cell, he wondered where his future lay, or if he had a future at all. He toyed with the idea of escaping and examined the tiny window, the steel door. His only chance was the small metal pick, but it was no use without a tension tool. He would secrete a fork from his supper tray, hide it beneath the mattress and hope it would do the trick.

Though his godfather would do everything in his power to help, it was quite possible that he couldn't change the outcome. It was curious, though, how much Douglas knew about his operations in Italy. He had obviously underplayed his own position within the SOE. But would he have access to such classified information? He paced the cell, a million questions whirling in his mind.

Douglas visited Robert again the following afternoon. 'Not sure how you survive in these conditions,' he panted.

'I don't have much option.' Robert observed dryly. 'It's not the Ritz, I'm afraid.'

'Thoughtless of me, you know I'm not good in the heat.'

'You might try removing your jacket,' Robert smiled.

'I have just had news that might affect you personally,' Douglas put his hand on Robert's arm. 'Not about your mother or Diana, but a friend of yours. Tom, I believe his name was.'

'Was?' Robert pulled away. He leant against the wall to steady himself. 'Was? What do you mean?'

'The SS have been on the rampage in Florence. Two days ago they rounded up at least thirty partisans; they were all shot. I am informed your friend may have been among them.'

Robert didn't know if he could take any more. 'Are you certain?' he asked.

'No, not certain, Robert, but it is quite probable.'

Douglas drew his chair closer. 'I know this isn't a good time, but we need to get to the bottom of your predicament to come up with a strategy for your defence.'

For half an hour Douglas probed, but Robert remained reluctant to go into details.

'You've had a terrible run of bad luck,' Douglas said at last. 'It can only get better.'

'I'm not sure that I would call being shot as a traitor better,' Robert replied.

'Don't think like that. Let's be p-positive, young man.' Douglas's face was perspiring as he struggled with the words.

He was at the door when he turned back to Robert. 'Is there anything else you would like me to do?'

Robert handed him a letter. 'I have written to my mother; would you send it for me? I want her to know what has happened.'

'Of course. Poor Robert. I don't suppose they'd give you a beer in this godforsaken place?'

'Unlikely,' Robert grimaced.

'On my way out, I'll see the sergeant in charge, they may bend the rules, but I doubt they'll have your father's favourite brew.'

*

Robert was on his bed, his eyes closed, when Sergeant Pennyfold came into his cell with a jug of water.

'You've got a good one on your side, sir,' he said, setting it down on the table. 'Professor Gordon's persuaded Major Templeton to lend him a car and a driver to take that letter to your mother himself.'

Robert sat up. 'That's odd, he didn't tell me his plans.'

'Are you all right, sir? You look a bit peaky,' the Sergeant commented.

'I'm fine; thank you.'

'Not that it will be much consolation to you, sir, but we're all rooting for you.'

'I've just learnt that a good friend and colleague may be dead. Any chance you could ask Major Templeton about the execution of partisans in Florence? It would mean a lot.'

'I'll see what I can do, sir. Not that I hold out any hope.'

'Even if I were a traitor, my hands are tied in here. I just need to know.'

'I'll do my best, sir.'

As the door shut behind him, Robert dragged the chair to the window and climbed up. Douglas didn't say Tom was dead; just that he might be. He wouldn't believe it until he had proof. He could see a vehicle coming to a halt at the yard gates. An officer jumped out, undid the padlock, parked the jeep and took out the keys. He was whistling as he ambled into a shed at the back of the yard. Seconds later he came out of the shed with no keys. He was still whistling as he let himself out of the yard.

Then the streets were quiet again.

As the shadows moved across the walls, Robert paced the cell. Nothing made sense any more. Why hadn't Douglas told him he was intending to see his mother? Something was wrong and he couldn't put his finger on it. There was something strange about Douglas today, something that bothered him. He kicked the wall. He was going mad. Douglas had come all this way for him. He was like a father. But then again, why had he told him about Tom? Wasn't it bad enough to be incarcerated here without adding to his misery? He hoped to God that Tom had survived.

He pulled the pillow beneath his head and stared at the ceiling. He couldn't allow emotion to get the better of him. He had to work out who had betrayed him. There must be a clue: no one was infallible. He had to use his intellect, think incisively, to pick up every possible indication.

He wondered about Giulietta clinging on to his arm before her departure. 'So will you give up this attack? I need to know, will you carry it through?' She said she loved him, but perhaps she was playing him along. He remembered his conversation standing by the lorry with Antonio on the night of the operation in Arezzo. 'Don't worry, we'll find the traitor,' he had said. 'Or her,' Antonio had replied.

Surely not Giulietta. He couldn't bear to think that everything had been a lie.

Then there was Davide, was he a German spy after all? Or was Doctor Biochetti a traitor? It was ridiculous, but not impossible. Or Bruno? No, he had been imprisoned for days.

He drank some water. Douglas's suggestion was extraordinary. They would hardly offer him beer. For a brief moment he recalled the cellar in Berlin. Douglas giving him Lowenbrau, telling him it was his father's favourite.

Robert started to sweat. Had he been programmed by Douglas? He had fed him anagrams for years. His favorite as a child had been *The Morse Code*, he remembered his excitement when he had worked it out. 'Here come dots.' He had been rewarded with a bar of chocolate. Douglas specialised in neurological research. Was he part of one of his projects?

The call sign, an anagram for Lowenbrau, was a salute to

Douglas. He had been stupid to think it was infallible. Douglas knew him so well. He was the one person who could break it.

He remembered General Struthers' words. 'Is this anything that could lead the enemy to us?' At the time the answer had been emphatically no; now he wasn't sure. But what reason did Douglas have to betray his country? Was it Magdelene? He rarely spoke of his wife. Could the awful circumstances of her death have turned him? He remembered his father whispering to his mother, handing her a newspaper. Later he had found the article. '*Wife of celebrated neurologist Douglas Gordon commits suicide after an anti-German campaign.*' For a young boy the words were strange and difficult to read. Then there was that incident on the way back from the airport, and Douglas's reaction to the banners. '*Nazis go home*'. Could he have a motive? The more Robert probed, the more credible it became. The trips to Berlin for numerous unspecified meetings, and Cairo, a breeding ground for spies. But this was still circumstantial. He needed more.

He tried to pinpoint something about Douglas that had been bothering him during the two visits to his cell. Yes of course – his stutter. It had seemed more pronounced. The more Robert thought it through, the more he recognised the signs. Douglas taking measured breaths before each word, slowing his sentences down as he tried to control it. Then he pictured Douglas's expression. 'Tell me everything,' he had said the day before and that flash of irritation quickly masked when Robert didn't comply. What was that all about? And why was he actually here?

Robert made himself recall every detail of their recent conversations, then he went further back, looking for hints, anything to make sense of this foreboding. Anagrams were a clue to his personality. Everything was hidden away. With this information, Robert realised, all his messages could be decrypted by the Germans and the contents passed on for

459

Douglas to read. And there would be money. Douglas would be well paid for his betrayal. And what about this business with Tom? How did he know of his friendship? He hadn't told anyone outside his small nucleus of fellow agents. The only radio contact he had with Tom had been a coded message from him on his arrival in Florence. Just one word: *Savoy*. But of course this would be a footprint in the sand to Douglas. While his heart needed some convincing, logic told him there was no other explanation.

If Douglas was the double agent, he had caused the death of Antonio, Eva, Patrizio, Agent Flyte and undoubtedly many more. Tomorrow he would be on his way to his mother at the Villa Durante. Robert was sure he wouldn't hurt her; he'd been in love with her for years. But he couldn't ignore the evidence. He had to get to his mother before Douglas; he must get out of this place.

It was two o'clock in the morning when Robert retrieved the tiny metal pick from his prayer book and took out the fork. He could hear Blacker's voice ringing in his ears. 'Easy, boy, listen to the lock, love the lock, then it's yours.' He bent the end prong of the fork to a ninety-degree angle, and pushed it all the way to the back of the lock. Applying tension in a clockwise direction, he inserted the pick above it, raking it towards him until he could feel the tumblers clicking down. When all the pins were aligned he held his breath and the lock opened.

He tiptoed past the guardroom where two men were chatting quietly. One of them coughed and he heard a chair scrape back, then footsteps.

'Going to point Percy.' It was Pennyfold's voice, followed by a low laugh from the other man. 'What?'

'My new expression from the Aussies.'

'That's the third time you've been in an hour; something wrong with your bladder, mate?'

'Yeah, yeah.'

Robert flattened against the wall, his heart pounding. The footsteps went in the other direction and Robert waited, not daring to breathe. A few minutes later Pennyfold returned and the talking resumed. Robert tiptoed to the door, drew back the bolts and sneaked outside.

Peering through the locked gates into the yard, he counted three motorcycles and two jeeps. This time he'd be breaking back in. After several attempts, the gate grated across the cobbles. Robert ran to the shed he had seen from his cell and pushed the door open. In front of him was a wooden board filled with keys. He started to panic. There was no time for mistakes. He grabbed three sets of keys and ran to the nearest bike. He pushed the first into the ignition, but it didn't fit. 'Fucking hell! Bastard,' he swore, pushing in the second set. He bit his lip, beads of sweat breaking on his forehead. He grunted in relief when the key turned. He was in business. He wheeled the heavy motorbike towards the gates, panting with the effort. He cursed as it scraped against his leg, ripping his trousers. A dog barked nearby and a light snapped on in a room above him. A man in a vest flicked a cigarette through a window and banged it closed. Quiet returned. Robert heaved the bike through the gates into the street outside. When he reached a small back alley he threw the spare sets of keys down the drain, and propped the bike against the wall.

At Beaulieu he had been taught how to start and ride a motorbike in adverse conditions, but to kick-start the machine in a dark alley with the British Army headquarters right around the corner had not come into his studies. At least the warm air would help. With the bike in neutral he turned the fuel tap on, opened the choke, pushed down the float button on the carburettor once, and then turned on the ignition. He brought his foot down hard on the starter pedal and urged it to start – it didn't. He muttered to himself, 'Wait, don't panic, don't flood it with petrol.' With his heart in his mouth he tried again, and to his relief the engine turned over and roared into life. Robert climbed on the bike and skittered across the cobbles and into the streets of Rome.

He was in open countryside when he let the throttle out. He had gone about ten kilometres when he stopped to check the fuel tank; thanks to the British logistics team it was over half-full. Behind and in front of him, the empty road stretched to the distance. On either side were the wooded hillsides and rolling meadows of the Lazio region. It would double, triple the journey time if he went cross-country but he could take no chances. If Douglas left first thing in the morning he might still beat him. He drove up a bank and into a field and, with only the stars to guide him, he rode north. He had a long journey ahead.

It was six o'clock in the morning when the British headquarters in Rome realised their prisoner was missing.

Major Templeton was furious. 'I can't believe it,' he stormed. 'Now go and bloody well find him.'

Sergeant Pennyfold looked sheepish. 'It might not be so easy, sir, he's trained to evade captivity.'

'Get on to Major Adderley in Cairo, I need to know everything about this man. His contacts, his friends, where he would go, and I need to know it now. And when is Professor Gordon returning? Good God, man, I lent him my car! Show me on the map where he is going.'

'I don't think the prisoner would go to his mother's house, sir, he knows his godfather would have to turn him in. It is more likely he would head to the mountains.'

'It's not your job to think, Sergeant!' Major Templeton said.

*

The hills were shimmering in the heat when Robert arrived at the outskirts of Perugia. From here, as the terrain was familiar, he could save valuable time. He had reached Umbertide when the engine began to splutter and surge. He was running out of fuel. He cut the engine and pushed the bike along a small track. Each second that passed, the danger to his family increased. Douglas was either entirely ruthless or mad; probably both. He stopped at a rundown farmhouse and knocked on the door. He flattened against the wall as an old man peered outside.

'Who's there?

Robert stepped in front of him. '*Mi scusi*, I need some petrol, a matter of life and death.'

'There's no petrol here, not since the war came, but if you are brave they may have some in the farmhouse down the hill. '*Brigata Nera*.' He spat on the floor, showing his disgust. 'Though of course they deny it now.'

'I'll need something to siphon it with.'

The old man shuffled to a drawer in the kitchen. 'You're in luck.' He handed a piece of rubber hose to Robert. '*Buona fortuna*, young man.'

Robert pushed the bike down the hill towards the farmhouse. In the courtyard a motorbike was propped against a pigsty. The yard was silent, the pigsty empty. Robert fed the tube into the fuel tank and sucked. Spitting out the fuel he put his thumb over the top of the tube and lowered it into his own tank. The fuel flowed from one to the other.

He was on the bike and halfway down the drive when he heard shouting behind him. A rifle shot whistled past him. He opened up the throttle and roared away in a cloud of dust.

Chapter Seventy-seven

Sofia and Alessandra saw him at the same moment, a man advancing through the meadow towards them.

It was not Vittorio. Alessandra would have known him anywhere; this man was shorter and thicker set. She shaded her eyes and her heart started to race. It was Douglas Gordon. Something had happened to Robert. Douglas was going to give her bad news. She held onto Sofia.

Clasping her books to her chest, Diana hurried from the school-room and continued up the drive. By the time she had climbed the stairs to the loggia she was panting. 'One of my pupils has learnt the entire alphabet, Mama, it is so encouraging.' She stopped, her hand flying to her mouth. 'Douglas, what are you doing here? What's wrong? Robert. Is he—?'

'No, Diana, Robert is not dead, he is alive and well, I assure you.' Douglas walked across the loggia towards her.

Her mother was hunched on the sofa opposite. 'It's all right, Diana,' Alessandra confirmed. 'Listen to Douglas.'

'Something urgent has brought you. What is it?' Diana's voice had risen. She clutched the back of a chair.

'Sit down, Diana,' Douglas said, 'and I'll explain.'

This was not going as he had planned. Alessandra should

have been pleased to see him, but she had been distraught, and now Diana was overreacting and he would have to explain all over again.

'There has been a misunderstanding,' he began.

'But my brother would never betray anyone,' Diana declared when Douglas had finished. 'He is loyal and honourable. Who has done this terrible thing?'

'I don't know, but we shall get to the bottom of it.'

'Bottom of it? Rest assured, Douglas, my brother is not involved.'

Douglas patted her on the shoulder. 'Poor Diana, I have brought you something that might cheer you up.' He produced a bottle of Dom Perignon champagne from the briefcase at his feet. 'I have nurtured it all the way from Cairo.'

The two women looked at him aghast.

'We couldn't drink champagne, not at a time like this,' Diana exclaimed.

'Diana's right. Thank you, Douglas, but not now.'

Douglas felt humiliated. He'd come all this way; they might show some appreciation. 'I have arranged for you to see Major Templeton. May I suggest that I take you to Rome in the morning?'

'I can't wait till tomorrow. I want to see my brother now,' Diana declared.

'You won't be able to see him tonight.' Douglas forced himself to remain calm. 'The driver says there's a storm coming.'

'Douglas is right, Diana. We'll wait until tomorrow. Forgive me; I have forgotten my manners. I think we can manage some tea.'

It was late afternoon when Robert arrived at the bottom of the Niccone Valley. There were only another four miles to go. Despite taking back routes and tracks to avoid the British troops, he had made very good time. He stopped at a village pump to gulp some water. He splashed his face and continued along the track.

The teapot was on the table beside Alessandra when the doctor arrived. He ran up the steps towards her.

'My dear Alessandra. I am sorry…' His voice trailed off when he saw Douglas.

'Vittorio, this is Robert's godfather, Douglas Gordon,' Alessandra said, introducing them.

'*Buona sera*. You are about to see the worst of our weather, I'm afraid.' Doctor Biochetti smiled at the Englishman. 'I can see I'm intruding. Alessandra, forgive me, but I have some news; not good, I'm afraid.'

'I already know. I had no idea that my son was in Italy, and now I find he's in prison in Rome.' She stood up and walked towards him.

The doctor took her hands. 'Ahh,' he sighed. 'I am so sorry, Alessandra. I found out myself only recently. Your son charged me not to tell you. It was for your safety alone. You must understand it was extremely difficult to keep it from you, but I had to, we all had to.'

'So Signor Carducci and Signor Innocenti, they knew?'

'They did,' he admitted. 'Robert came here to recuperate after he was injured – don't worry, he is well, I assure you. I tended to him myself. He was with me when he was taken by the English soldiers.'

'Did you know he trained the partisans in Arezzo?'

'Yes, but again I had no idea he was your son.'

Alessandra's voice had an edge to it. 'It seems everyone knew except the people closest to him. And now he is accused of betraying his country and of being a spy.'

'Forgive me, my dear, I could not break my word to your son! He said you would try to find him, put yourself in danger.'

Alessandra sighed, her anger ebbing away. 'He was right, Vittorio. I couldn't have stopped myself. Of all the people in the world, I'm glad it was you.'

Douglas watched the proceedings with mounting frustration. This Doctor Biochetti seemed to have a special relationship with Alessandra. Were they lovers, he wondered? There would be men in her life of course, all that nonsense about remaining faithful to Anthony. But he couldn't stand it if they were lovers.

'I'm pulling a few strings in the right quarters.' Douglas drained his cup. 'I can assure you, all will be well.' He stood up. He was much shorter than the doctor and it made him feel inferior.

Doctor Biochetti looked from Douglas to Alessandra.

'It's true. Douglas has come to the rescue,' Alessandra assured him.

'Well then, I take my leave. I had hoped to give a final check to my canine patient. But with all of this, I can see you are occupied. I will come another day.'

'Thank you, Vittorio.'

'I have no doubt your son's innocence will be quickly proven.' He was about to leave when Nico limped over to him. He ruffled the dog's coat. 'You great brute of a dog,' he said.

He smiled at Diana. 'You must be glad that he has made such a good recovery.'

'It's a miracle.' Diana's face was animated; once again Douglas felt excluded. And now Alessandra had chosen to stand beside the doctor. They looked far too at ease with each other for Douglas's liking.

'What happened to the dog?' Douglas asked.

'He was run over.' Alessandra glanced at the Doctor. For some reason she wanted to keep the truth from Douglas.

'He was shot,' Diana said at the same moment.

'So he was shot and run over. Poor dog,' Douglas uttered.

He tried to make light of their lies but he was furious. Did they think him a fool? 'Quite a hero, aren't you, Doctor.' It wasn't a question.

'I just did what anyone would do,' the doctor confirmed. 'I know how much Nico means to Diana.'

So he had won over the mother and the daughter. Douglas's anger was mounting. 'You seem to know Robert well?'

The doctor studied him before answering. 'Well enough to know that he's a very good man, but then of course you know that; he is your godson. Please keep me informed, Alessandra.'

'We mustn't keep you, Doctor,' Douglas challenged.

'Of course, I can see this is not a good moment. *Buona sera*, Alessandra, and good luck; your son risked his life for us. He is not a spy.'

Chapter Seventy-eight

Robert reached the edge of the estate and pushed his bike into the bushes. The sky had darkened and the air was close and still. Keeping away from the drive he forced his way through the undergrowth, scrambling over the walls until he came to the clearing below the house.

By the time he reached the terrace, thunder was reverberating around the hills with increasing ferocity. Tiny flickers of light on the horizon had become blinding flashes that streaked across the sky. On the other side of the valley a tree caught fire in a spectacular display of pyrotechnics. Then the rain came, sluicing down the hillside and the fire was extinguished. Robert lowered his head and ran towards the loggia. Water dripped from his clothes, making a pool on the brick floor. He edged slowly, stealthily to the door, his footsteps deadened by the thunder. He could see Douglas through the hall window. At this moment he had no gun and no plan.

'This is our Vin Santo,' Alessandra announced, passing a glass to Douglas. 'I'm afraid it's the only wine the Germans didn't either drink or break.'

Douglas wasn't surprised. He had never liked sweet wine. He put down the glass and looked at Alessandra. She had lost the sophisticated London sheen, but she was still beautiful, though a little grey and a line here and there. He remembered the humiliating evening in Paris when she had rejected him, and the dance when she had chosen Anthony, but that was in a different lifetime. Now of course there was the doctor. Douglas needed to claim her, take her as his own. The evening was progressing nicely; he had dismissed his driver to the *fattoria*, and his bag was in the spare bedroom. Alessandra was relaxing. He leant towards her, putting his hand on her arm.

She took a sip of wine and shivered. 'Excuse me, Douglas... I need to fetch a shawl.' As Alessandra climbed the stairs she was confused. Why was Douglas acting so strangely? He seemed wound up like a coil. She could tell Diana sensed it too.

Diana glanced at Douglas. His sandy eyebrows were drawn together in a frown and his face was closed and unreadable. He had done so much for their family but she hardly knew him. Perhaps she hadn't wanted to, she realised. She had accepted him because he was her mother's friend and Robert's godfather but there was something about him that she had never liked.

For a split second, Diana caught his eye. His reaction was unguarded and she was afraid.

'Don't you like storms?' He was looking at her intently.

The girl didn't like him, Douglas was sure of it. His anger was bubbling beneath the surface, threatening to explode. It was over, all of it. Alessandra still wasn't interested in him; he could see that now. After all these years waiting for her and being nice to her family, she had fallen for some bloody dago. He glimpsed a white face flash past the window. He cursed inwardly. Was the doctor still lurking outside? He could feel the weight of the gun against his thigh.

His eyes met Robert's as he crashed through the door.

'It was you, Douglas. You all the time!'

Douglas moved in an instant, pinning Diana's arm behind her back until she yelped with pain.

'Let go of me,' she hissed, trying to twist away, but his grip became tighter.

'Douglas, I've been thinking, perhaps Robert...' Alessandra was halfway down the stairs when she saw her son in the doorway. She stopped in surprise. 'Robert?'

She was about to run to him, but the warning in his eyes prevented her. She turned to Douglas and froze.

'Douglas, let go of Diana at once. Robert, I thought you were in prison? What's going on?'

'Ask Douglas what's wrong,' Diana gasped.

'Be quiet, all of you.' With his other hand Douglas drew the gun from his pocket and pointed it at her temple.

'Douglas, what are you doing? Alessandra demanded. 'Put the gun down.'

Diana sank her teeth into Douglas's arm. She could taste his blood, and she could feel his flesh give as she sank her teeth deeper. He screamed and the gun dropped with a clatter. Before he could reach for it, Diana kicked it away with her foot and it skittered across the floor.

Douglas hit her hard and she reeled sideways. At that moment Robert launched himself at Douglas and Alessandra dived for the gun.

Alessandra stared at the two men wrestling on the floor. 'Robert, Douglas, get up both of you,' she ordered.

'Mother, give me the gun.' Robert got to his feet. 'I'll deal with this.'

'No, Robert you will not,' she said calmly. 'It seems I have been wrong about you, Douglas, but I'll ask you again, what the hell is going on?'

'He is working for the Germans, he is the traitor and has made sure I take the blame.'

Alessandra felt the cold steel butt of the gun in her hand. Douglas, the man she had trusted with her son's life, had betrayed them all.

'Why, Douglas? Was everything a lie?'

Douglas looked at her and sneered. His self-control had gone, all of it. 'You were easily duped, Alessandra.'

'And my husband, your best friend, was he easily duped too?'

'Best friend! I never had any friends. Anthony made me Robert's godfather because he felt sorry for me. It was always the same at school. He was a sucker for the underdog. But then he was on to me. It was all most unfortunate.'

Alessandra felt sick. 'On to you?'

'He had a feeling that I might be working for the other side, and the fool tried to counsel me.'

Alessandra leant against the newel post and gathered herself. She had to be strong for Anthony, for her children.

'Tell me, Douglas, what did you do? Did you kill my husband?'

'No, but if the delivery van hadn't done the job for us, we would have, I'm afraid. I didn't want to, but he would have broken my cover.'

Fury built inside her. 'You also tried to take my son as your own,' she said, the realisation dawning on her. 'All those trips with you when he could have come home.'

'Give me the gun, Alessandra.' Douglas held out his hand.

'No, I will not.'

She was aware of Diana and Robert glancing at each other, and Robert moving towards the umbrella stand in the hallway. Now she could see Douglas as he really was. The façade had dropped and in front of her was a weak man filled with jealousy and hatred. 'I thought you were a dear and loyal friend to us Douglas; why?' she asked, trying to reason with him, trying to buy some time.

'I did like you, Alessandra.'

'Were we pawns in your little game? And Robert, what of your godson?'

'I wouldn't want him to face a firing squad, but in life a man should only have one master. Your husband and son both chose the King, I chose the Reich.'

Alessandra raised the gun.

'Alessandra, put down the gun, think of all I have done for you.'

She would kill him. She had to kill him. Her finger was on the trigger; she fumbled with the safety catch. Her hand wavered Douglas could sense her indecision.

'Give me the gun, Alessandra,' he said slowly, his pale eyes staring at her, his words rendering her powerless. 'You will drop the gun.'

Alessandra started to tremble. *I can do this*, she thought, but as Douglas advanced towards her, she could feel her heart racing and sweat beading her forehead. She brought her other hand up to steady her aim.

In a blur behind Douglas, she could see Robert coming towards them, holding the walking stick Davide had made. She could see him raise the stick and bring it rapidly down. She heard the thud as the ram's horn handle met Douglas's skull. The blow felled him in an instant and he lay there, his eyes wide open. Blood trickled from his ear onto the white stone floor.

There was silence in the room. Diana put her hand to her mouth and started to scream. Robert moved towards her and took her in his arms. Alessandra grasped the banister rail. Then the door flew open and the doctor entered, glancing momentarily at the man on the floor.

'I had to come back,' he said, striding towards Alessandra, taking the gun from her hands. 'I knew something was wrong. I was halfway to Cortona when I turned the car around. I should never have left you.' He put the gun on the hall table and crossed the floor to the prone figure. He looked at Robert with a question in his eyes.

Robert nodded and the doctor knelt down, feeling for a pulse in Douglas's neck.

'Is he dead?' Diana stammered.

'Robert, take your mother and sister into the drawing room, and if you have any brandy, give it to them,' Doctor Biochetti instructed.

Robert did as he was told and returned to the hall.

'There is a faint pulse.' The doctor paused for a moment. 'I could of course try to resuscitate him, if that is your wish?' He glanced at Robert's strained face and back to the body on the floor. 'On second thoughts…'

Robert raised his eyebrows. 'How long will he last?' he enquired.

'Without any medical intervention, less than an hour. In the meantime, can you find a sheet to cover him? We wouldn't want your mother or Diana to see.'

Robert returned with a tablecloth. 'This will do.' He placed the cloth over his godfather, averting his face.

'Come along now,' the doctor advised, taking him by the arm. 'It is over, Robert, your work is done. I think we could both do with a brandy.'

5

Aftermath

Chapter Seventy-nine

Alessandra was standing on the terrace looking out across the dry landscape. In the distance Signor Innocenti was guiding the plough, the two oxen trudging before him. It was a biblical scene, one that would soon be obsolete. The old world was dying fast, the war had seen to that. The war had seen to everything.

So much had happened since Douglas's death over a year before. Hitler had committed suicide. Allied troops had breached the Gothic line, leading to the surrender of the German forces in Italy. There were celebrations and flags flying in every village. The Contessa held a large party in her garden at the Castello. Everyone was invited. This coincided with the German defeat in their own country and, not long afterwards, Churchill made his memorable Victory in Europe speech. It was the best birthday present Alessandra could have had. But the news was shocking in August when the atomic bombs were dropped on Hiroshima and Nagasaki. Although they ended the war with Japan, Alessandra would always wonder whether such devastation and death could ever be justified. She stopped listening to the wireless after that broadcast, she had heard enough news.

*

It would be several months before Davide returned.

Diana had been milking Rosa when Nico started to growl. In slow motion, she set the pail on the cobbles and opened the barn door. The dog charged into the distance. A figure was walking towards them out of the autumn sun. As the shimmering outline approached, she could see a man in a dark coat and a hat. There was something familiar about his walk, the slow, easy gait, the long legs. Then the figure bent down and the dog jumped in the air barking, and Diana was running. Alessandra remembered her daughter's cry as she threw herself into his arms.

'You've come back to me, oh my God, you are here.'

'I promised I would,' he replied.

Alessandra would often think of those who had gone, the twelve shot in Niccone, including the Avorio boys, dark-haired and dark-eyed. She had been to their confirmations and their *festas*. Her dear friend Signor Angelini had died with Rachel, his wife, along with millions in the concentration camps. He had foreseen the atrocities and everything had happened as he predicted. Jaco and Lotti had survived, but she could only imagine the horrors they had witnessed and suffered. She prayed that, with time, they would emerge from the shadows.

'They were at Dachau. It has taken me all this time to trace them, I am going to bring them home,' Davide had told them, his voice brittle. 'Jaco survived because of his will, and Lotti because of her violin. She was in the camp orchestra; apparently the commandant had an ear for music. It is strange, is it not, that a man who loves Schumann is capable of mass murder?'

She remembered picking them all up from the station, her shock at seeing Jaco's bones protruding through his thin rags, Lotti shorn and tattered, clutching her violin, and Davide's face. She feared for anyone who stood in his way.

Davide, the youth who had worked in their fields, had gone. He was now a man hardened by war and suffering. He had risen through the ranks of the partisans until he was a leader of a large group in the north. The communists had asked him to join their party at the end of the war, but he had declined.

'No more politics for me, just peace,' he had said. Alessandra knew there would be no peace. His soul was restless, and though he loved Diana fiercely, she would have to accept that she would never have all of him.

Davide had found Guido Tremonti hiding in a tobacco barn in the same field his family had supposedly found their Etruscan hoard.

'This is your man,' he called as he dragged him through the streets of Umbertide. 'Guido Tremonti, the man who murdered your children, and your children's children.' The crowds parted to let him through. Stopping at the market square, he tied Guido's hands to a post, the same post that had secured Beatrice and others.

'Have mercy on me, please, I beg of you,' Guido cried.

'Just as you had mercy on my family.'

'It wasn't me, I swear it was my father.'

'So you would blame your father?'

'Please, I beg of you.'

Davide walked away through the crowd. He did not look back.

Diana would never be the same again. She was tougher: the innocent girl had vanished. Perhaps when her own child was born the grief that she had so tightly locked away would dissipate.

They were married, and it was a fine affair.

'Would you walk me down the aisle?' Diana had asked the doctor when they were together in the garden celebrating her engagement.

'It will give me honour,' he had said, and Alessandra smiled to see the joy on his face.

'She asked me,' he said to her later. 'She actually asked me, it makes me so happy.'

'It makes me happy too, *mio amore*,' she had replied.

Robert came from London for the wedding and Giulietta, from Cairo. She was not the girl Alessandra would once have wanted for her son, but the more she knew her, the more she approved. She was strong and feisty and whatever path he took it would be easier with Giulietta at his side. For now, he was studying economics at Oxford.

'Harvey suggested I should become an engineer so that one day, we could take over his father's factory,' he said to his mother, 'but that dream is over. Instead of aeroplanes, I shall learn to rebuild the cities destroyed in this war.' Alessandra had smiled in relief.

'I will not marry your son until he has graduated,' Giulietta had teased her. 'I'll not be married to a student.' Alessandra shrugged her shoulders, because Robert loved her completely and it was his life.

Davide and Diana were married beneath a canopy in the garden with a view to the distant hills. A priest blessed them and a glass was smashed in the Jewish tradition. Sofia sang an aria, while Lotti played the violin.

Grandpa Peter, escorted by a nurse, had made the long journey from London. Nico bounded through the guests with a bow around his neck. His blanket was not allowed.

As they said their vows, Diana's hand smoothed the discreet curve of her stomach where the next generation was preparing to make its entrance into the world.

'I am not parting with my beloved sister, I am gaining a brother,' Robert had said in his speech, 'and I know you will cherish her and I couldn't think of a better man.' Davide thanked him, but his eyes were filled with tears.

'I will try to be worthy of you all,' he had said as he drew back the veil that fell like a cloud around Diana's face, his mother's veil that had come with her from Bolzano. He kissed Diana on the lips.

Throughout the ceremony Alessandra was conscious of Vittorio at her side, handsome in his new suit and crisp white shirt, and as Lotti played 'The Lark Ascending', she thought of Anthony. How proud he would be of the woman Diana had become, and he would have approved of Davide. '*You see my influence is still with you,*' he would have smiled. '*God in the open air and a mixture of faiths, I couldn't have asked for more.*'

Alessandra's thoughts now encompassed the four generations of the Durante women. She recognised a thread of courage, determination and strength linking them all; qualities she had not known she possessed until her beloved husband had died. She could see it in her grandmother, running the estate with an iron will; in her mother, bringing her up in a foreign country alone and with so little money; and of course in Diana, who had spurred her on when her own courage was failing.

When she had looked at her daughter on her wedding day, she little knew it would be her turn next. At Christmas that same year she had walked down the aisle of the church of Gesu in Cortona to meet Vittorio. She was not consumed with the same breathless excitement of her first wedding day all those years before, but with a different kind of happiness. In her middle years, she was blessed to have found someone to love.

With money from the sale of Vittorio's house in Arezzo, they had bought a flat in Cortona in one of the ancient buildings overlooking the square.

'For now it will be my surgery, but when we are old,' Vittorio had joked, 'and you are bored with your husband, you can sit on the balcony and watch the people go by.'

'I will never be bored with you, Vittorio,' she had said, looking into his eyes.

Chapter Eighty

Alessandra smoothed the crumpled letter that Robert had written from Bari in 1944 immediately after Douglas was killed. After reading it again, her mind returned to that dreadful day when Douglas had arrived unexpectedly at the Villa Durante.

She could still feel the gun in her hand and see Douglas's pale, hypnotic eyes. She could remember being led into the drawing room with Diana, gulping the brandy, sitting with Robert and Vittorio until the cars had arrived.

'I did it,' she had admitted to the major in charge. 'Douglas Gordon was a German spy. He threatened my daughter with a gun, it's there on the table.'

'How did you kill Professor Gordon?' the major asked, looking first at Robert, and then at Alessandra.

'I used the walking stick,' Alessandra had confirmed.

Robert stepped forward. 'My mother is trying to protect me. I hit the professor. I had to stop him, it was the only way.'

'Frankly,' Alessandra had focused her green eyes on the major, 'we wouldn't have had to do your job for you, if you hadn't been chasing around the country for the wrong man. I am sure that you will find sufficient proof that he is the traitor, not my son. I suggest you start with his briefcase.'

Though the major had looked abashed, he had not apologised.

'I am afraid, Marston, you will have to accompany us back to headquarters, and you will remain in custody until this matter is cleared up.'

'*My Dearest Mama*, Robert had written:

The past weeks have been shocking and almost unendurable. Douglas was a friend to us all and indeed a father figure to me. If I were to judge him unworthy of redemption, my faith in humanity would shrivel to dust. I choose to think that he was a tortured soul who cared for us in his own tormented way. I am convinced the hours we spent together did mean something. I believe this for my own sanity and, if possible, you should too. Though I have been officially cleared of all charges, tomorrow I will return to London for my final debriefing. If only I could see you.

Your loving son,
Robert.

Alessandra had not known what to believe about Douglas, but at that moment she hadn't cared. She had only been concerned about seeing her son. It had taken every ounce of her persuasion for the British government to agree to send her to England. 'We are still at war, madam,' she had been told, but after a campaign of pressure at their headquarters in Rome, she had arrived on British soil six weeks later. She put Robert's letter back in the diary, remembering the day in October when she had met him in Upper Brook Street outside the wreckage of their former home. The stairs led to the sky, and in the hall only the fireplace remained. Alessandra remembered the house as it once was, the portrait hanging there, her portrait. It had gone, along with the remnants of her old life.

'He was acquitted, you know,' she had said to Robert as they gazed upwards into the empty space. 'The van driver, Wilfred Archer. I pleaded for him. He had a sick wife and baby.'

'Of course you did,' Robert had replied, 'I wouldn't expect any less.' And as a light rain fell on the pavement they had considered another wet day when their lives had changed for ever.

In her mind Alessandra could see the table in the hall, where her husband kept his keys. She could see the small cellophane packet that remained there after the accident with the red stamp inside.

'A Penny Red for our fine young man,' Anthony had said, showing her the stamp on the night before his death. Anthony was right. Robert was the finest of young men.

'Your father would have been proud of you,' she had said.

'He would have been proud of you too,' he had replied, putting up his umbrella. Linking arms, they had walked together down the pavement away from the house and away from the past.

As they approached the Savoy, a young man limped towards them. He had red hair and even from a distance Alessandra had noticed the warmth of his smile. He had raised his hand in acknowledgement. For a moment Robert had hesitated, then he quickened his pace and started to run. 'Tom. Oh my God, Tom, you are alive!' They had hugged each other, cavorting around the street like young boys. When at last they broke away, Robert spoke coherently. 'I didn't think my letter had found you. I had begun to fear the worst, but I had to come here just in case.'

'Didn't you get my reply?' Tom's face looked momentarily concerned. 'I wrote from hospital after I was repatriated, confirming the date. I was shot in the leg this time.' He grinned sheepishly.

'We've made it to the Savoy!' Robert had clapped him on the back again, and the rejoicing continued.

'It will be a job at the Ministry for the rest of the war!' Tom laughed.

'How I long for a desk,' Robert said in reply.

Finally they walked back to where Alessandra was waiting.

'Mama,' Robert announced. 'May I introduce you? This is Tom, my very good friend.'

Author's Note

In November 2013 I visited Civitella. The dusk was gathering when I climbed the steps into the village, and entered the church.

I was standing in front of a small stone memorial when an old woman shuffled through the church towards me. In her hands she held rosemary for remembrance. She stared at me and I knew she wanted to speak.

'Tell me about it?' I asked. Tears filled her eyes and she beckoned me outside. She led me to the old cistern in the middle of the square, and I knew that in this peaceful spot some seventy years before, her life had been marked for ever. Drawing me through a gap in the buildings, she stopped at another memorial filled with the names of those who had died. 'They are all here,' she said. And I nodded, expressing my understanding.

When I left, she watched me go. I could only imagine the young girl faced with the death of her loved ones, and who now, all these years later, was still grieving.

Civitella is twinned with Kampfelbach in Germany; the desire among the inhabitants, and the many Germans who visit Civitella, is for reconciliation and peace.